MAY 2011

BY THE SAME AUTHOR

The Fox Boy

PETER WALKER

BLOOMSBURY
LONDON · BERLIN · NEW YORK

First published in Great Britain 2010

Copyright © 2010 by Peter Walker

The right of Peter Walker to be identified as the author of this work has been asserted by him in accordance with the Copyright, Designs and Patents Act 1988

No part of this book may be used or reproduced in any manner whatsoever without written permission from the Publisher except in the case of brief quotations embodied in critical articles or reviews

Bloomsbury Publishing Plc
36 Soho Square
London W1D 3QY

www.bloomsbury.com

Bloomsbury Publishing, London, New York and Berlin

A CIP catalogue record for this book is available from the British Library

ISBN 978 1 4088 1042 2

10 9 8 7 6 5 4 3 2 1

Typeset by Hewer Text UK Ltd, Edinburgh
Printed in Great Britain by Clays Ltd, St Ives plc

For Marie and Don

He, Michelangelo, is never less alone than when alone . . . yet he willingly keeps the friendship of those in whom rays of excellence shine forth – for instance, the illustrious Monsignor Pole, with his rare talents and singular goodness . . .

– Ascanio Condivi, *Life of Michelangelo*, 1553

Main Characters

Reginald or Pole, or Poole, born 1500, cousin of Henry VIII

Michael Throckmorton, Pole's courier

Pietro Bembo, Italian writer, poet, connoisseur

Michelangelo

Vittoria Colonna, poet and patroness

Henry VIII, King of England

Charles V, Holy Roman Emperor, ruler of Spain,
the Netherlands, Sicily, Peru, etc.

Francis I, King of France

Thomas Cromwell, Henry VIII's chief minister

Mary, Henry's daughter by Katherine of Aragon,
later known as 'Bloody Mary', born 1516

Philip of Spain, the Emperor's son, Mary's husband

Margaret Plantagenet, the 'Lady of Sarum', Reginald Pole's mother

Judith Tracie, Throckmorton's cousin and first love

Agnes Hide

Sir George Throckmorton, Michael's elder brother

Marc'Antonio Flaminio, Italian writer and poet

Lord Montagu, Pole's brother

Marquis of Exeter, Pole's cousin

Edward Courtenay, Exeter's son

Gian'pietro Carafa, Pope Paul IV 1555–1560

Ercole Gonzaga, Regent of Mantua

Stephen Gardiner, Chancellor of England

Prologue

ONE NIGHT SOME TIME ago three men broke into a room which is now famous all over the world and which even then, while under construction and shrouded in secrecy, was the subject of intense curiosity in Italy and beyond.

The term 'broke into' perhaps conveys the wrong impression. Using a key illicitly obtained, they made their way through the dark in almost complete stealth.

Right at the entrance, however, two of them stumbled, one after the other. This was because the door, which is framed in marble, has an unusual high threshold or 'saddle', to use the technical term. You walk into the room as if stepping through a window frame. Even today, in our own perilous but well-lit age, this can trip the unwary.

The first man cursed in Italian: he knew the obstacle was there but had forgotten. The second cursed, in English, because he stubbed his toe.

It would do no good to tell you what they said. Nothing dates with such finality as an oath. The '*fuck you*'s of the 1960s and the '*sink me*'s of the 1690s share the same doom. But two of those shadows slipping into the Medici chapel in Florence that night were young men in their twenties, for whom even the idea of their own death is hard to believe, much less the fact that one day they will have died so long ago they will seem no more than stick-figures from an antique age.

The Italian who led the way in was a workman on the site. Following him were two Englishmen. One was a scholar named Tom Lupset. The other was considered the most brilliant and accomplished young man in Italy. His name was Reynold or Reginald Pole. In Italy he was known as *Il Signor d'Inghilterra*, the English lord, or even the lord of England, although he was in fact an ordinary 'Mr'.

But he was a cousin of Henry the Eighth, and a much cherished cousin at that, which was itself unusual, for Henry preferred attention to be directed to his own accomplishments. As King of England, however, he was not in a position to shine in person in the Italian universities. And his cousin's reputation there reflected well on his own genius. Henry paid Pole one hundred pounds a year to maintain a magnificent household among the students.

The Italians for their part were very pleased with Pole. His lineage alone made him a figure of romance. He seemed to have arrived among them straight out of the beautifully named, if confusing, War of the Roses, *la rosa bianca e la vermiglia.* His mother was the last person to bear the surname Plantagenet. It was his grandfather who drowned in the famous butt of Malmsey.

As well as all that, young Pole was noted for scholarship and virtue. Not only the Doge of Venice and the political establishment of the Republic paid him compliments; he was befriended and praised by the leading scholars and intellectuals of the day – Erasmus, Bembo, Giberti, Sadoleto . . .

What amazed people about him most, however, was this: *he put himself to bed.*

We have a contemporary description of Pole: 'Of medium height, in complexion white and red, as commonly are the English, his face a little broad, with merry and benignant eyes, and in youth his beard was rather fair. Robust of body, seldom sick . . . he did not care for much personal service and often went to bed without assistance.'

And furthermore: 'He rose before daylight and dressed himself without any man's help.'

Pole had been a student in Padua since 1521. In 1525 he made his first visit to Rome. It was on the way back from Rome that we see him slipping into the construction site in Florence.

Entry into the Medici chapel was strictly controlled. Michelangelo, the architect and sculptor of the work, kept the keys; he was the last to leave at night and first back in the morning. A few months before, at the end of 1524, there had been a series of nocturnal break-ins. Nothing was stolen; the sole purpose seems to have been to look around the chapel, where, it was reported, a marvellous group of figures was coming into existence – gathering, as it were, at the tombs of two young Medici dukes, Giuliano and Lorenzo.

Michelangelo was furious at the incursions. To his mind, making a work of art was like making a child – something best done in private. For a week or two he made his foremen stay on site and keep watch all night. But it was midwinter, it was bitterly cold, they missed their lovely wives, and in any case nothing ever happened. After a while he had to let them go home again.

Cautiously, the midnight visits were resumed. This, after all, was Italy. In other countries, aristocratic pastimes were different – hunting, tournaments, mock battles where only the blows given to the peasants were real. But in Italy there was a great passion for art. Dukes and cardinals spied through keyholes, lured away painters, sculptors and medallists, swooped on commissions made by others. The Pope himself slipped into the Sistine one day to inspect the ceiling frescos before they were finished, only to be met by a rain of curses, and, so it is said, planks, thrown down by the painter, working alone high above him.

In the Medici chapel, however, any such seclusion was out of the question. Dozens of stone masons, carpenters, bricklayers and labourers were employed there. We have their names, we even know their nicknames – Chicken, Liar, Gloomy, Babyface, the Goose, Horse, Nero, Antichrist, Woodpecker . . . And when Antichrist and Babyface are on the payroll, even the best security arrangements tend to go awry. Which particular workman let in Lupset and Pole that night is uncertain. Let's say it was Woodpecker, if only because his name brings him closer to us than the others: across the centuries, you can still hear the very light, rapid action of his chisel . . .

So there they are – Woodpecker leads the way in, Lupset and Pole follow. Woodpecker stumbles, Lupset stumbles, then all three are inside the 'chapel of the princes'. High above them the cupola is unfinished; only a little starlight shines in. But then Woodpecker brings out the little lantern he has kept until now under his cloak, and suddenly, here and there among the builders' gear, they begin to see human forms, strange, splendid, some alone, some in groups, some carved in white marble and others, their direct forebears as it were, full-sized models made of dark tow, pitch and rags.

For five hundred years people have been trying to describe the peculiar melancholy conveyed by the statues in the Medici chapel. The figures are sublime, august, yet the atmosphere is muted, full of doubts and speculation, modest; it suggests something remote but commonplace, domestic almost, and inevitable. In short, the subject is the hour of death itself.

Pole and Lupset have no opportunity to consider their impression of the chamber. Woodpecker is in a hurry to leave. Temporary custodian of the Medici tombs, Woodpecker is a tyrant. His modern equivalents, glaring over their morning paper at American tourists, are not much better. Suddenly Woodpecker puts his finger to his lips. Then he blows out the lantern. He has heard a noise. They must not be caught there, especially not by Michelangelo, the terrible *maestro* with his 'eyes the colour of horn' (according to his contemporary, Vasari) 'flecked with bluish and yellowish sparks', of whom even the Holy Father in Rome is afraid. The three men stand there stock-still in the dark. But nothing happens. There was no noise. There never had been one. Michelangelo is still fast asleep in his house around the corner. Nevertheless the tour is finished. In a few moments Pole and Lupset are hustled out of the chapel, down the aisle of the outer church and then out into the street and away, through the city under the stars.

By that time, in 1525, among the nine or ten models made of pitch and tow, two or three of their marble descendants were almost complete – the figures of Duke Lorenzo, and his two companions, the *Dawn*, a beautiful young woman, reluctantly waking, and *Dusk*, a middle-aged man, looking back sadly at the end of the day.

It was this trio which stayed in Pole's mind when the lantern went out, and the next day, and indeed, for the rest of his life – the naked girl, the middle-aged man and the figure of Lorenzo, eyes shadowed by a helmet, the pupils un-engraved, the whole figure somewhat inert, withdrawn, elegant, sunk in thought . . .

BOOK I

I

I WAS JUST A BOY when my father died and left me his second-best ambling mare – grey, milky in colour and with black eyes, a sure sign of good disposition in a light-coloured horse.

My father was on his way to the Holy Land at the time, but his journey ended in Italy. In fact, it was on the road between Florence and Rome that he closed his eyes and ended all his journeys. Even as a young child, I knew that Florence was a long way off – further than Alcester, further than Bredon Hill, which I sometimes saw on the horizon, and away over the sea, which I had never seen but envisaged quite clearly. I knew exactly where Florence was, as my father had always promised that one day, when I had finished my studies, I could go there with my brother Anthony. Anthony, who was already in Italy, inherited my father's best horse, but I did not mind that. My eldest brother, George, inherited much more than both of us, which is say almost everything, and I did not care about that either. Every day I hurried out to watch for my grey mare. I must have spent hours sitting on the gatepost at Coughton looking down the road. This was partly to avoid the gloom in the house – my mother and aunts and sisters all wept a great deal on hearing of the death of my father, which made me feel sad, but I don't think I understood that he was in fact *never* to come back. So I stayed well out of the way, watching for the road to give up my inheritance.

The lads in the stables gave me a switch so that when she saw me she would know her master. In fact, we knew each other quite well already. Once at the Alcester fair I ran out across her path and she knocked me down: I can still remember being struck by her breast, which was surprisingly soft and silken, and then she ran on sure-footedly over me. Someone screamed. A woman I had never seen before swooped and picked me up and held me to her breast, also surprisingly soft and silken.

My father, who had been riding the mare, came back and leapt off, in a rage with everyone – with me, with himself, with the horse, perhaps with the woman holding me to her bosom. I was, however, quite unharmed.

After that, I felt we knew each other, the grey and I; when I used to go out to the stables and look up at her in the stall, there was a kind of severe understanding between us. A few years later she was ridden away to Italy.

She never came back. I forget the reason. Perhaps she was sold and the money was sent home, which would have been the sensible arrangement, but one which I didn't grasp. In any event, for a whole summer I sat on one of the gateposts, a globe of stone roughly pricked with yellow lichen, watching the road for my inheritance. One night I even dreamt that I was on her back and riding towards her owner, that is to say, towards me, asleep in bed at the time, at Coughton. This did not unduly trouble the dream. And now when I look back at my life, I think that perhaps its whole course was laid down right there, on that gatepost at Coughton in Warwickshire, looking down the road towards the wide world. Most people, thinking back to their childhood, can see signposts which long ago were pointing to their future. My intimation, however, was simpler than most: for me, the road *was* the road – and specifically, the road to Italy. For I doubt if anyone alive has ridden back and forth between England and Italy as often as I, Michael Throckmorton, Esq. of Warwickshire and London and now of Mantua. In short, it has been my whole career.

Of course I have performed a good many other feats as well – married twice, fathered six children, been twice to prison, become rich, and bred some excellent horses – but chiefly in my life that is what I have done: ridden back and forth between England and Padua or Verona or Venice or Rome, almost always in service to the most illustrious Mr Pole.

On his account I have met one emperor, two kings, a queen, two popes, and any number of lords, ladies, fools, thieves, liars and, I think, more than one murderer. On Pole's behalf I once made a long address before a king and queen and the greatest gathering of nobles and prelates ever seen in England. My voice did not shake at all: I had become an accomplished professional – a courier.

It was not an occupation I ever sought, although it is not entirely without honour, being carried out in the service of Mercury, who reveals to men the decisions of destiny, which are not necessarily pleasant. For this reason his servants are sometimes disliked and even hated; being in his service is not a safe occupation. This is something we couriers and envoys have to put up with, but we take due precautions: the god of the highway, the crossroads and the city gate, is also the patron of thieves, reporters and pickpockets. In short, we learn a few tricks to survive, but that in turn earns us even deeper suspicion.

On my very first mission, I noticed the mistrustful expression that greets you even if you have just crossed Europe in record time.

That was on the journey I undertook to deliver Mr Pole's great book or letter to the King. By that time, you must know, King Henry had divorced his wife, married Dame Boleyn and, refusing any longer to recognise the authority of the Pope, declared himself Head of the Church. One day, a year or two after these events, he remembered his beloved cousin, Reynald Pole, immersed in his studies far away in Italy and, recalling also his great reputation for wisdom and goodness, he sent a message requiring him to state his opinion of the changes in England. In reply Pole wrote a long, long letter – I think more than two hundred pages – and gave it to me to take to Henry.

So there I was, in front of the King, on one knee as required, holding out the leather satchel which contained the book.

The King stood looking at me for a minute as if I was an apparition from the underworld.

'You came on your own?' he said.

I nodded my head.

'That seems very strange,' said the King. 'Suppose this packet had fallen into the wrong hands.'

'The *wrong* hands!' I said. I felt my face burn. As if I would permit some stranger to disburden me on the road. I suppose I had rather a hot temper in those days.

'Ah, well,' said the King, pacifically, 'perhaps it's all right. After all – here you are. And they say that good writing is like a good man: it needs no protection as it makes its way through a wicked world.'

Then he unbent a little more and asked me one or two other questions – what I thought of the ladies in Venice, for instance.

I said that some were beautiful, but they were haughty and that I was thinking more of an English wife.

To this he said nothing.

He wore a gold dagger slung on a silk girdle from his hip. It was a magnificent object, with the face of a lion on the pommel, or was it a man or a woman turning into a lion?

He had made no move to take the satchel, and was still looking thoughtfully at me.

'Why you?' he said.

I was puzzled and said nothing.

'There are many gentlemen in Mr Pole's household,' he said. 'Why were *you* chosen as courier?'

'Oh,' I said, 'I'm the fastest.'

And at that His Majesty suddenly beamed and opened his hands, as at some charming new economy.

At the same moment Dr Starkey, the King's chaplain, came up and plucked the satchel from my hands as if it was his own trophy.

In a way, I suppose it was – Starkey was Pole's great friend, it was Starkey who had reminded the King of Pole's genius. If the King was pleased with Pole's book, that would be a great triumph for Starkey. All the same, I was enraged. I had been strictly ordered by Pole to hand the book to the King and to no one else. But what could I do? I didn't know how things were done at court; perhaps kings don't unwrap parcels. The satchel was of very fine leather. It was my own – I never saw it again, by the way. After that, I don't remember what was said, or how I left the room or the palace, or, for that matter, London. And this is my defect: not to be far-sighted and see what one day will be of importance. What I do remember are many things of little or no value to others and often enough of little or none to me.

Yet now that I have passed the age of forty – at which point, says Portaleone, who is my doctor here in Mantua, a man may without blame recount the story of his life and describe the splendid deeds he has done and the terrible things he has suffered – I must make do with the currency I have. And so there we were – the King's golden dagger was in front of my eyes, Starkey took the book out of my hands as if it was his own first-born child – and the next thing I remember is the following day, riding through Warwickshire, where as far as the eye could see the elms were casting noontide shadows as dark as inkblots in the middle of the fields. It was almost midsummer's day. Then a little later I rode through the six-furlong wood, where there is always feeding for fifty hogs, and I came in sight of Coughton, the house where I was born.

There I stopped short and rubbed my eyes. I don't suppose I actually rubbed them, it's only an expression for astonishment and not very apt: rubbing your eyes or any other member is not going to restore the world to its proper state. And at that moment it was in a most improper one. For the house was gone. In its place rose a pompous castle, or rather the commencement of one, fifty-feet high and adorned with oriels, battlements, turrets and pinnacles.

Above the arch of the gate were the family crest and the royal arms carved in stone, and an inscription, HA, both above and below: HA HA.

I forgot to say that when I got back to England on that first journey, these initials HA, of King Henry and his second wife, Dame Anne, could still be seen carved, painted, inscribed or sewn above archways, door-yards, the entrances to tunnels, stables and mews, on pelmets, cushions and the backs of chairs. By then, however, Anne had been dead for months, executed for treason, and the device was rapidly disappearing. But some people, such as my brother Sir George, for instance, were strangely languid when it came to removing it. On her coronation day, it was said, she wore a gown embroidered with tongues pierced by nails, just to show anyone who spoke against the marriage – HA – what they might expect. Now I suppose the joke was on her.

But for my part I felt a joke had been played on me. Everything was utterly different from what I expected. How often had I imagined this moment, my first sight of home, in the years I was away! Yet there above me stood strange bran-coloured battlements of newly dressed stone, and even the gateposts of my childhood with their old globes of stone were gone. In their place were two of those nasty sharpened pillars called obelisks. Nothing, in short, had kept faith with my imagination.

At that moment, on the threshold of my birthplace, I felt a pang of homelessness as sharp as any I had known on foreign shores.

Portaleone laughed very merrily when I described this.

'Everyone knows the memory plays tricks,' he said. 'Why should you expect your foresight to be any better? The mind looks both ways, like a man crossing the road who can be knocked down by a cart from either direction. Even so, you should have known your brother better. Of course he spent the family fortune on turrets and battlements! What – a man who sent you abroad to live on a pittance for five years! A brother? A fiend in human form, more like! And here is your other great defect: you are no judge of your fellow man.'

In point of fact, my brother George had given me the usual allowance. But I let Portaleone carry on lecturing me. He does not approve of our English inheritance laws. In any case, he has an upbraiding streak – he likes to stroke fur the wrong way. But as he is my physician, and now my literary advisor here in Mantua, I listen to him peaceably enough.

He then began to laugh and to shake his head. 'You are altogether too innocent, too trusting.' (This is not true.) 'Your memory plays tricks on you. Your foresight is faulty. What a start to this project! Still, it is a good idea to write your life story. I, as your physician, advise it. It will help with your insomnia. And it will send your readers to sleep as well. No, no – I'm only joking. But what do you intend to call your book?'

I said that I had thought of calling it: *My Life by Michael Throckmorton.*

'No, no, no,' he said irritably. 'A book should have a beautiful title. It is often the only part of it that will be read. But even the best books thereby gain a mysterious lustre. For example:

The Book of the Honeycomb's Flow

The Mirror of Gold for the Sinful Soul

or

The Banquet of Sapience

You see? Something of that kind would do. But in your case, as there will be but little sapience, or honey, what can I advise?'

Portaleone knows all about many high and difficult things – astronomy, the Talmud, the writing of comedies, the bloodlines of hunting dogs and so on – so I listen carefully to his advice. Even Cardinal Gonzaga, the Regent of Mantua, often calls him to the palace to 'drive forth the time' for no one is more eloquent, amusing and impromptu than my physician.

On this occasion, however, he tapped the end of his nose, meaning he would confer with his wisdom in private, and so we parted.

A few days later we met again in the street.

'I have a title for your book,' he said,

I could see he was laughing to himself, so I understood some asperity was coming.

'I suppose I must steel myself,' I said.

'Now, now,' he said, 'you are far too untrusting. It is a very good title. It came to me while thinking about your brother's gatehouse. *HA HA*, indeed! I propose you name your book after that very moment, when you found everything changed as if by sorcery. Even the little stone seats of your childhood had gone. In their place stood two obelisks. And what better title could there be for your book than an *obelisk*?'

'But why an obelisk?' I asked.

'Why?' he said. 'Why, the obelisk is the symbol of time itself. It is, after all, nothing more than the needle of a sundial, although in Egypt the needles grew to such a size that even the Romans, the most thievish of races, stole them from the banks of the Nile in order to adorn Rome, knowing they could do no better for themselves. And thus, being a symbol of time, which changes all things and is therefore the subject of all books, it would do very well on the title page of yours.'

'Yes?' I said, suspiciously. 'And there's something more?'

'Well, yes, perhaps there is an additional meaning – almost the opposite in fact, but instructive all the same. An obelisk, you must know,' said Portaleone, 'is the name of the printers' mark beside a passage of writing which is spurious or doubtful, error-ridden, false and not to be trusted. And as you yourself admit – your memory plays tricks, your foresight is poor, you are no judge of your fellow man. Why not declare all your faults at the outset, like an honest man crossing the border?'

'I see,' I cried. 'That's not a title you have given me – it's a confession or a curse or something just as bad which I can't think of at the moment. Well, I won't have it,' I said, and went off down the street in a rage. Our meetings often end that way. *As iron sharpeneth iron so does a friend sharpen the countenance of the other.* Those words might have been written for Portaleone and me. And it is not necessarily pleasant, to have your countenance sharpened.

But then, a few hours, or days, later . . . you may find you have come to agree with your enemy. This honing often takes place while you are asleep. In this instance a day or two went past and then I woke up and thought, 'Well, why not? Perhaps it has a certain ring to it. And I've nothing better in mind. Anyway, he's right – those obelisks I saw as I came out of the wood proved that nothing ever stays still or turns out as you might think.'

And in that same hour, still in my nightclothes, I came to my desk and sat down and with some reluctance wrote here (there was no room at the top of page one)

The Book of Obelisks

And thus, properly entitled, we may proceed, just as I did long ago, into the shadow of the new gatehouse arch, where my horse's hooves clattered very strangely to my ears, and on to the rest of this history.

I came out into the courtyard beyond.

And then I stopped, as if to rub my eyes again. For there in front of me was our old house, after all – or half of it – still crouching under its crooked roofline. And at the end of the yard were the same ancient apple trees, still crooking their fingers towards me like old widows, as I used to think of them as a child. I stopped and gazed all around, thinking of my poor dead parents with tears in my eyes, and then a door was flung open and out came one, and then another, and then half a dozen servants, most of whom I recognised though they had all changed in different ways, some being stouter and redder, others thinner and greyer or bent a little nearer to the earth – none of which amendments they seemed in the least aware of, crying out instead that it was I, young Michael, who had appeared in a new form – a bearded giant in a red cloak, a German, a Venetian, a perfect Turk . . .

Then the door on the other side flew open, and my sisters came out and began to cry – not solely I suppose at the sight of me, but over the years that had gone by and which would not be back again, and then I was surrounded by my many nieces and nephews, some of them very little children whom I had never seen before, who looked at me with shining eyes as if I had blown down from a hilltop or the clouds. Although my brother had been banished from court, he proved himself the King's most loyal subject by fathering more new ones than any other man in England.

Among the crowd, but standing back, I saw a pretty girl of seventeen or so, with dark hair and clear high colouring, looking most composed, although quite aware that, in this instance, she was an outsider. This was the first sight I had of my Gloucester cousin, Judith. In fact it was the first intimation that I had a Gloucester cousin at all.

Then my brother and his poor wife appeared. Sir George, alone of all the gathering, did not seem very pleased to see me. It was true I had sent no word of my arrival – yet how could I do that, since I myself was travelling as fast as any messenger? It also turned out that I had forgotten to write from Italy for half a year or so. But my real offence was more serious than that. I had arrived at the worst moment possible, just as the roast dinner was being served.

In a way I was glad of this. Arriving back home after so long, I almost felt that my head was among the stars. George, however, made it plain that home is also the place where, no matter how far you have wandered, you will be held strictly to account if the gravy is burnt.

2

THAT NIGHT, MY FIRST at home in so many years, I rode over to Weethley Wood just before the sun set with two of my nephews and four or five of the servants. For a long time the hunting rights in this wood had been under dispute between our family and the diocese; now we had it from a good source that the bishop's men were coming that very night to take four young goshawks from a nest high in the middle of the wood.

Our party split into two. Some went in among the trees, Tom Rutter and I hid on the outskirts of the wood. We stayed there and watched the moon come up. A little while later, four or five figures came past and went on into the trees. Rutter whistled softly into his fist. After a while an owl answered deep in the wood.

Then we came up behind the bishop's men, and we all fought in the dark with sticks and swords until they ran away. One of the bishop's men was Rutter's brother. He was the source of our information. All the same, both brothers fought manfully and gave each other some good blows with their staves.

The following morning I had a long talk with my brother George. When I told him that I recently had seen the King, he went very red.

'Did he mention me?' he asked, scanning my face earnestly.

'It was not that kind of conversation,' I said. 'I can't be sure what was discussed – the fall of Tunis, the state of the Venetian navy . . . There was no occasion to turn to personal matters.'

It had been four years since George was sent away from court. Every hour he dreamt of returning, but no word of forgiveness had come. While we talked, he seemed to look at me in a new light, his eyes darting up and down and taking in the worn jerkin and breeches and seven-day beard.

'Well, I hope you did not disgrace your family, that's all I can say,' he said. 'Heaven alone knows if you did not commit some solecism that will never be forgotten. For me, of course, it is different – I was brought up with the idea of the court. From the cradle, I thought of nothing but the services our father did there, and his before that, and his before that. I know at once, for instance, without even thinking, to whom one should bow, to whom bend the knee, to whom smile and whom to ignore, which ladies one might dance with and which to kiss. It was all mother's milk to me, I could do it blindfold, whereas, of course, for you, with different prospects . . .'

The reason George had been banished was this: one day, he approached the King and his secretary Cromwell, and announced that he desired to state his opinion about the plan to divorce the old queen and marry Anne Boleyn.

They both gazed at him in astonishment. Though at the time it was the sole subject on everyone's mind, in front of the King everyone was infinitely discreet and in fact behaved exactly like mice on the floor of a lion's cave.

'Well, what is it that you have to say?' said Cromwell.

'Your Highness must not marry this girl,' said George.

The King stared at him.

'And why not?' he said.

'Because,' said my brother, 'Your Highness's conscience will never lie easy. You have already meddled with the sister, and also the mother—'

'Never with the mother,' said the King in a low voice.

'Nor never with the sister either, so put that from your mind!' cried

Cromwell, and he turned to glare over his shoulder as he hurried after the King, who was walking rapidly away.

The next day George was summoned to see Cromwell and told to leave court at once, take himself off to the country and hold his tongue and mind his own business. For years he waited for forgiveness. During this time he diverted himself with building the gatehouse, impoverishing the estate and teaching the servants some of the manners of court.

As we spoke that morning, for instance, there in the dining room, Tom Rutter dressed in livery was standing behind my brother, glaring at the back of his head. During my childhood Tom was the chief captain of the stable lads, hapless victor in the village brawls and lord of the chaff-house where, to my wonder, he used to stretch out his hand like lightning and catch a mouse and squeeze it to death in his bare hand. Now he was being taught to lean forward and fill my brother's wine cup from time to time without being asked, and without getting drunk himself, in the process.

'You cannot imagine the difficulties that present themselves at court every minute of the day,' Sir George went on. 'Suppose you meet an ambassador coming round the corner. In the twinkling of an eye, you must recall his rank, the power of his country, and whether or not they are friendly to us at that moment. If, for instance, you were to run into this Duke of Muscovy who is supposed to be on his way here, then you should greet him *thus,*' and he rose and turned and advanced on Rutter, smiling delightfully and twirling his hand towards him.

'You see?' he said, standing back to study the effect. 'He is of exalted rank, but on the other hand he is from a very distant and barbarous land. In short, he is a kind of natural wonder, like the hippopotamus sent to the King of France, to which you may be as pleasant as you like without incurring any blame. If, on the other hand, it is the imperial envoy you bump into – a man of no rank, yet representing a great power – then you accost him thus', he bowed low to Rutter, 'unless, of course, the trouble over the excise has flared up, in which case you must do *this*—' and, looking coldly at Rutter, he gave him a curt nod and turned on his heel.

'You see how difficult it all is,' he said, resuming his seat with a sigh. 'It is exactly like the labyrinth described by the ancients, where the bull ate up the maidens. One must be cunning as a serpent and as watchful as a hawk. Above all, be discreet. There is your password: *discretion*.'

I left Coughton after a week, promising that I would return very soon, though how this was to be achieved I was not sure. But the fact was I had fallen passionately in love with Judith, my second cousin, my Gloucester cousin. I blessed Gloucester first for having bred her and then for being so generous or careless as to give her up. This was my first love. Until then my love affairs had, it now seemed to me, been nothing but aping and mimicry. For several days Judith and I had ridden around Coughton together, over the meadows and into the woods, always with the nieces and nephews in tow, and never a word of love was spoken, but one day I thought: 'Well, what more is needed? It is time I got married and there will never be anyone better.'

Still I said nothing, being naturally sly and suspicious, as younger sons have to be. Judith was free to marry, or rather she soon would be. She was an orphan, and not even a penniless one. In the meantime, my brother was her guardian. I knew he would stand in my way – it was in his nature, he couldn't help himself – but I also saw that Judith had a temper, and could stamp her foot at him and make him quail, for I had seen her do it.

I was almost certain that she returned my feelings. The gleam of merriment in her eyes was not just amusement. She was happy to be in my company for another reason. One night, sitting up late by the fire, she taught me a game of cat's cradle – the most complicated cat's cradle ever known, she said, in the world, or at least in Gloucester – in which, after many bewildering manoeuvres with a loop of silk ribbon, two lesser loops chase each other over the knuckles of the hand, and then, on the verge of parting for ever, they meet and embrace.

One of the loops, she said, was a woman, and the other was a man. For an hour that night we sat side by side, with our fingers like so many troopers, engaged in marches and counter-marches. Several times Judith burst out laughing at my clumsiness and several times she gave up the tuition completely, saying I was beyond all hope. I for my part was somewhat distracted by her lowered eyelids, the nimbleness of her fingers and a certain aspect of her upper lip. In fact, just as I was about to give up the tuition and lean forward and kiss her, Sir George came stamping in with his candlestick, and began raking out the fire and banging the shutters open and closed again and saying, 'Time to shut up shop!' As usual, this made Judith go pink with amusement, and thus we parted and went to our beds. But before we did, she gave me the loop of silk thread to keep and practise with.

The next day, the time came for me to leave. I had promised Dr Starkey and Cromwell that I would be back in London after three days, to see what message I might take back to Mr Pole in Italy. Now a whole week had passed. I suddenly became alarmed. Perhaps I had let this show of carelessness go too far. It is hard to make these calculations. In any event, I left the next day, as I say. Just before I mounted my horse, I had a word alone with Judith.

'I will be back,' I said. 'There is some information which I need, and only you possess.'

I looked straight into her eyes as I spoke. Naturally, just at that moment, she became inscrutable and gave no sign that she knew what I meant or what her answer might be.

I rode away just before dusk. A few miles down the road, Rutter came out of the hedgerow and we went together to Weethley Wood. There we dismounted. Rutter whistled softly into his fist. After a pause, an owl hooted. Soon his brother appeared. They cuffed each other about the head for a little while and then the younger one led us into the depths of the wood, to the foot of the tree where the goshawks nested. He was slighter in build than Tom and he went up that tree as easily as a man goes up his own stairs in the dark, and then he came down with two fledglings in his shirt. I slipped a hood on each and put them in a wicker cage and we went back to the horses.

Then I rode on to Inkberrow where we had a farm and I slept there the night. I left the next day and rode away for London feeling strangely solitary and sad. Of course I had no idea then that I would not see Coughton for many years.

3

CROMWELL, ALTHOUGH THEN NOT yet an earl or even baron of Wimbledon, was, after the King, the most powerful man in the country and nobody cared to cross or disappoint him. Yet when I, five days in arrears, presented myself at his house, for some reason I was quite calm and unafraid. I was led in to see him at once – leapfrogging over, as it were, many ladies and gentlemen waiting outside who, to judge from their very long faces, had been there the same amount of time. I felt conscious only of my distinction: I was more important than they. Even on the step of the gallows I suppose men take pleasure in precedence. Cromwell was indeed angry with me. I could tell that at once from a glint in his eye. Yet it was the glint of restraint. Think of a big sleek house cat that will not pounce until the mouse comes forward another inch. No, that's not right either: Cromwell had no intention of pouncing. He did not want to kill me or even alarm me. On the contrary, I was necessary to him alive, and at liberty and in good spirits. I suppose I knew that as well as he did. All the same, the dignity of his high office made remonstrance necessary. A frown deepened on his brow.

'Young Throckmorton!' he said. 'You have given me several sleepless nights. I was about to send the officers to beat the bushes and hedges to find you. "Has he fallen into harm's way?" I asked myself. "Or is it some young man's business he has run off on, which we older men have forgotten?"'

'O my lord,' I said, 'forgive me. Five years I have been away from home, and I had forgotten – I don't know how – how excellent the hunting and the hawking is in that corner of the country, much better than anywhere else in England or in Italy, for that matter. I could not bring myself to leave. As well as that, there was my family to see, and I had to go and stand at my mother's grave . . .'

Cromwell was watching me closely, thinking, no doubt, 'How great a fool *is* he?' But I could also see that he was interested in what I was saying. Remember: the father made his living fulling cloth in Putney, and now here was the son, Lord Privy Seal, soon to be ennobled, already amassing great estates and ruling over the peers of the realm, and, above all, wishing to be one of them. In short, hunting was now his passion. There is, after all, no accomplishment more necessary for a nobleman than to hold a hawk well on his fist.

At this point I opened the wicker cage.

'I have brought you a gift,' I said, 'from our own place. They are high-mettled birds, I can assure you: we know their parents, which are wild birds, pretty well.'

Cromwell thanked me abruptly – the frown deepened still more – and yet I knew he was pleased.

'You can see they are very young,' I went on, 'which is the very best thing possible. At this age they will completely forget their mothers and instead grow fond of and come to love the man who fosters them and brings them up. Master Secretary, if you want a loving bird that hears your voice and comes back to you from no matter what distance, there is no better way than to feed and handle and hood her yourself and caress her and cure her. I beg you to delegate none of these offices but keep them for yourself.'

'Yes, yes, very well,' said Master Secretary, and then he stacked some papers sharply to show the time had come for business. Yet as we then spoke I noticed that several times he threw a glance at the young goshawks which had just arrived in that room at the centre of power from the top of the highest tree in the middle of Weethley Wood. And they were indeed a fine sight – a princely gift, in fact, little princes of the air, fierce and erect.

At the sound of each of our voices, they turned their hooded heads together first in one direction, then in the other.

The business in question was Mr Pole's book.

'Do you know, Michael,' said Cromwell, 'what is in this book?'

At that I became angry. The book was sealed, I cried, when I left Italy and sealed when I reached England. Did he think I had stopped by the side of the road to meddle with it or read it by candle in some French inn?

'No, no,' he said soothingly, holding up his hand. 'No one accuses you of any misdemeanour. I ask merely if you know, roughly, the matter, the argument, of this writing?'

'As to that,' I said, 'I was supposed to tell you – but perhaps I forgot – that never did a man put pen to paper so unwillingly as Mr Pole, but none the less he obeyed the King's command to write and state his opinion truly and plain, without colour or cloak of dissimulation, which the King most princely abhors, and that if what he has written is displeasing—'

'Displeasing?' said Cromwell. 'Oh no – it is far from displeasing. It is very clerkly written, some of the matter could not have been handled better. We – the King, that is – perhaps does not agree with everything he has written. In fact, we disagree with all of it. That is what makes it so desirable now to confer in person. Letters are dead things. The living man is, as it were, heaven-sent. In short, the book has marvellously whetted the King's appetite to see the author stand in front of him again. How long is Mr Pole to remain lost to his native land, living *in umbra* – in the shadows – drowned in his studies? The King desires you therefore to repair to Italy at once and to tell him to return. Indeed, we want you to do more than that. You must persuade him to come. Put him up on a horse yourself if necessary and seize the bridle. Will you do that, Michael? You are to leave at once.'

Thus I returned to Italy and completed the first of my round journeys. I left London the next day. It was the height of summer. The heat was unexampled. Even on the sea, the air breathed hot on us. Halfway over the Channel, late in the afternoon, I saw a shooting star that trickled down the sky as if it were melting. The great heat did not abate all the way to the city of Verona, where I found Pole waiting for me.

I conveyed the King's command that he return home at once, adding that letters are dead things, that a living man is heaven-sent, etc., and that no one understood how long he meant to live in the shadows and drown in his studies.

Before leaving London I had, on Cromwell's order, gone to see Pole's mother, the Lady of Sarum, in her house at Dowgate. She was an old woman, tall and thin, with eyelids like acorn caps – one of those elderly ladies who look as if a puff of wind could carry them off and yet who have a will of iron.

She told me she had known my father, and that she knew why I had now come to see her. 'You are going back to Italy to see my son.'

'Yes, madam.'

'He has written a wondrous great book for His Grace, and now you are to bring him home.'

I bent my head.

'Do you see this?' she said, pointing to words picked out on the wall: *Spes mea in Deo est.* Her hand was trembling a little. ' "In God Is My Hope." Tell him that by this token his mother greets him, and begs him now to come home again and be a comfort to her in her old age.'

I repeated all this to Pole.

'And what do you think I should do?' he said.

'You must obey your sovereign lord, and your mother, and go home,' I said.

'And what will happen when I get there?'

'Well,' I said, 'I expect you will be dead within a week.'

'What?' he cried.

'The King will put you to death on the spot.'

'Good God,' he said, 'then why tell me to go?'

'I promised Cromwell that I would.'

There was a pause.

'I see,' he said.

After a while he asked, 'How are you so certain of this?'

'Starkey let me know,' I said, 'although he didn't mean to. He is not very discreet. I do not think he is suited to life at court.'

And then I described how, just as I was leaving the palace after seeing Cromwell, I had bumped into our old friend.

'Doctor Starkey!' I said, 'how are you?'

He was as white as a sheet, and seemed to have aged ten years.

'I think I must be in a nightmare,' he said.

Then he stopped himself and gave me a peculiar look, as if we had never met before, and he turned and went away.

So all the way from England to Italy, from Calais to Montreuil, to Abbeville, to Fontainebleau in the forest full of wolves, past Sancerre on the right, on to Nevers and down to St Jean and the river which has no fish in it and makes men deaf with its noise, and then over the mountains and across the plain, all that way in the great heat, I was thinking 'And as soon as I get there, I'm going to have to turn round and come straight back'.

For I had promised Cromwell that, if Pole refused to return, I myself would immediately go back to England.

But I had also lied to Cromwell: I had a very good idea of what was in the book which Pole wrote for the King, and I knew that he could never go back, not if he wanted to keep a head on his shoulders.

4

HOW I, OF ALL people, came to be in possession of this information, then known to only a handful of people in the world – Pole himself, and the King, Cromwell and Starkey – was one of those strokes of chance, or, if you prefer it, the tricks played by the god of the crossroads by which the course of your life is changed, although you may not realise it at the time. Everyone can think of an instance in their own story.

In my case, I was not even awake as I came riding up to the crossroads of my life, but fast asleep in my bed in Pole's house in Venice, where I lived along with several other Englishmen. It was late in the morning, but then I was in my twenties; the young consider the night is their natural field of operations and forgo many hours of day without disquiet. In any event, there I was, still asleep, nearly at noon, when I heard a distant voice crying out '*Maggiore! Maggiore!*' ('Greater! Greater!')

This rather puzzled me – which is possible in sleep – since, being the youngest and least distinguished member of the household, I was in the smallest and highest room of the house, in fact an attic where sounds rarely penetrated. And what did it mean, this '*Maggiore! Maggiore!?*' In my half sleep, I thought it was a signal to me. But who could be calling so loudly? I got up and stumbled down the stairs. My head was bad. The night before, Morison had been teaching me to drink Friulian reds. It was already very hot, one of those stifling days which Venice sets like a trap for her citizens. I remember the dry odour of marigolds – Italians believe that marigolds keep a house cool at night – and of the salt sea, with hints of dead cat: in short, the aroma of Venice. And down there at the front door, with the sea rocking on the marble step, I found a great altercation in progress.

Although violent, it was of a simple nature. A messenger had arrived with a bundle of letters for Pole, sent on from one of the embassies. Now Pole – '*il Signor*' as we called him – was away at the time, and while the messenger was prepared to leave the letters, or to take them away and bring them back later, he utterly refused to go in search of Pole, who was at the time on the nearby island of S. Giorgio Maggiore.

This seemed reasonable enough, but our Sandro, who served as butler in the household, would not hear of it. The messenger must go to the island at once. Who could doubt the letters were of the greatest importance? Was not Pole a friend of the ambassador, not to mention the Doge?

The courier was unmoved. It was not his job to chase all over Italy for vagrant foreigners, no matter how exalted.

The two stood on the wide stair, battling it out at the top of their voices.

'My God,' cried Sandro, 'what are things coming to when a common messenger no longer performs his basic tasks?'

'I'll take them back, or I'll leave them with you, but I'll do no more – take it or leave it,' cried the messenger.

At this point I intervened. I said that I would take the packet over to *il Signor*.

Now this greatly disappointed both combatants – what's that phrase about anger as sweet as honey in the veins? Sandro turned on his heel haughtily, saying 'Oh, I give up', and he went off downstairs. He had a difficult life, our Sandro: he saw himself as a scholar, and indeed he *was* a scholar and was busy translating St Basil, yet

Pole also put him to work as butler, and when the cook fell ill he sent Sandro down to the kitchen to oversee the pantry and even, on occasion, to cook.

The messenger, whose face I can no longer bring to mind, slapped the packet into my hand and turned and also went away muttering. The local boatmen, rocking on their little skiffs, had been highly pleased with the entertainment and were also sorry to see it concluded. But I myself was very pleased to be out of that hot attic and within half an hour crossing the strait, on which the sun, at every instant, carelessly lit a thousand sparkles while the noontide clouds carelessly put them out.

I had never been to the island before. I knew that Pole had once stayed there with Pace, the last English ambassador, and on landing I went first to that house, but was directed instead to the monastery. I was then led this way and that around many long Benedictine corridors until we came to a narrow door. I went through this and found myself in a little wood. This astonished me: living in Venice you almost forget that fields and trees exist. Even the richest citizens hardly bother to bring horses over on the ferry, for the streets are no wider than windowsills and you have no more chance of a gallop on a live horse than on those bronze steeds above the porch of the cathedral, which always look as if they mean to leap downward and scatter sparks over the square one night but which never will. In short, you live in a world of water and walls and occasionally glimpse a garden the size of a handkerchief. Yet here were trees arching overhead, and a green field beyond, and there were even some birds singing nearby, exactly as if they were in a wood in England.

I went down a path towards the open garden, where I saw '*il Signor*' Pole, with two or three other men talking under the shade of a tree.

In those days, Abbot Cortese and all the clever young men who gathered around him, such as Pole, were reading Luther and the new thinkers. I paused for a moment, somewhat embarrassed at the thought of interrupting such a high discourse, but Pole caught sight of me and came over and took the bundle of letters. I should have left then, but instead I remained looking all around in delight. Pole was amused at my reaction to a bit of green grass and leafy shadow. As their discussion was coming to an end, he said, he would show me the whole garden. Then Abbot Cortese, who always loved to honour *il Signor*, declared that he would come along as well and show me the rest of the island, and so we set out on this great perambulation.

Now this intimidated me a bit. I would have been happy to roam about the place on my own, but to be led off by these great personages . . . After all, I was not only the youngest of Pole's household, but also the most ignorant. I should say now that I had not been sent to the University of Padua because I was a great scholar. In fact, I went abroad under something of a cloud. I was completely innocent in the case: the mercer was stabbed on account of a certain want of courtesy on his part, and although I was present I did not draw my dagger. I think I can safely say I have never shed innocent blood. But we were mad young fighting fellows in those days and there was a good deal of trouble about the mercer. So it was judged best for me to go and see the world and then to continue my studies. My brother paid my way. That was how I came to be under Pole's roof in Padua and in Venice. Even then, I often did not see him for months on end, and when we did meet I used to think he looked puzzled at the sight of me, wondering what I was doing on his stairs. Yet in point of fact, these two grandees, Pole and the abbot, could not have been easier company. Pole explained to Cortese that his family and mine had had a long alliance, and then Cortese entertained himself by repeating my name – '*Trock-mor-ton-e*' – and inquiring as to its origin. I explained it meant the moor with the rock on it, and that led to the question of the words 'moor' and 'rock' and in the end he laughed and said it was no wonder that no other people in the world had ever learnt English or ever would, it being so strange and abrupt a tongue, with the syllables hanging in mid-air.

During this discourse, we had gone round the whole field and through the kitchen gardens, and then Cortese led us up the stairs of the old bell tower to show us the island at our feet, and I looked out and saw the city just across the water, and the great lagoon stretching blue and green in all directions. Pole, meanwhile, had been turning over the letters in his hand, glancing at the dates and datelines and, as Cortese was pointing out the sights, he began to open one or two of them.

So it was there on the tower of S. Giorgio Maggiore that the news first reached us of a great and fearful shift in direction of events in England.

This came in the form of a report sent by the imperial ambassador in London, which had then been copied on to the embassy in Venice.

> Yesterday were dragged through the length of the city three Carthusians and a Brigettine, all men of good character and learning, who were put to death in the place of execution, for maintaining that the Pope was the Head of the Church universal . . . The King's son, Richmond, was there, the Duke of Norfolk and other lords and courtiers were present, quite near the sufferers.

And there was a second letter, which came from Paris, and which was more terrible still:

> These men the King caused to be ripped apart in each other's presence, their arms torn off, and their hearts cut out and rubbed upon their mouths and faces.

On reading this, Pole looked staggered. He went pale, and Cortese asked him sharply what the matter was. He answered, in Italian and, for some reason, while speaking to the abbot he handed the letters to me – though I suppose there was no reason why not, for the information was not secret. These were, I think, the first death sentences carried out under the new laws devised by Cromwell. They came as a bitter shock to Pole, who above all had always loved the King, his cousin, so much so that he now had the look of a man transfixed by a sword who at first does not credit what has happened to him.

There was another letter in the bundle, in the handwriting of Tom Starkey, Pole's closest friend, and it was to this that Pole now turned, eagerly, as if hoping it would disprove the power of the sword. This is what Starkey wrote:

> At the last parliament, an act was passed that all the King's subjects should, under pain of treason, renounce the Pope's superiority; to which the rest of the nation agreed, and so did these monks, three priors and Reynolds of Sion, though they afterwards returned to their old obedience . . . Reynolds, whom I have often heard praised by you, would admit no reason to the contrary . . . They were so blind and sturdy they could neither see the truth in the cause nor give obedience to those who could. Therefore they have suffered death according to the course of the law . . . This is the truth for . . . I was admitted to hear Reynolds' reason and confer with him . . . I conferred with him gladly for I was sorry to see a man of such virtue and learning die in such a blind and superstitious opinion. But nothing would avail . . . It seemed they sought their own deaths, of which no one can be justly accused.

'*Reynolds*?' said Pole. 'Not Reynolds!' He gazed at us for a moment as if he could not make us out.

'But who is Reynolds?' said Cortese.

'Reynolds . . . Reynolds,' said Pole almost to himself. 'He was my teacher. He taught me the ancient languages. What! "The king caused his heart to be cut out and rubbed on his lips". I do not believe what I am reading. I cannot. Reynolds! A man with the spirit and countenance of an angel. "It seemed they sought their own deaths"? Oh, Tom. Tom Starkey! For Shame!'

Below us a flotilla was sprinting towards the open sea – the Turkish threat had increased that month and the Jewish corsair with his thirty foists was prowling near Corfu – and from the city amid its smoke and hum came a strange sound every five seconds or so, a regular thud like a crack of a whip. I think it came from the Arsenal where they were building ships, but all the time, as the news sank in, I kept wondering what it was, as if hearing for the first time the great clockwork of mankind. Pole, meanwhile, had taken his letters and shuffled through them all again, and began to read the first one again, aloud, and to the end:

> People say the King himself would have liked to see the butchery, which is very probable, seeing that all the Court and the Privy Council were there . . . and indeed it was thought he was one of five who came there . . .

'*He*? Who? Does he mean the King?' said Pole, muttering to himself, but then went on:

> It was thought he was one of five who came there accoutred and mounted like Borderers, and armed for secrecy, with visors before their faces . . . and when they spoke all dislodged . . .

'What does it mean? What is he saying?' said Pole. 'The *King* was there? Ah, you wretch! You went to watch the fun! But you kept your face hidden . . .'

I was astounded to hear the King spoken of in this way, but that was how his new image first came to me. In fact, I could never think of him again without seeing a man in a Borderers' helmet – a very good helmet it is, too, with the moveable cheek-pieces, and a keel hammered into the central ridge for strength – watching behind a closed visor as four of his most learned subjects were tortured to death.

How long we stayed on the bell tower I am not sure. When we first went up, the Alps were shining with snow to the north, but then a wind sprang up – you could hear the squeak of a weathercock shifting this way and that above our heads – and the mountains faded like the daytime moon and soon the plains on the mainland were lost in a haze. I could still see some domes far away, perhaps those on the big church in Padua, which the licentious students liken to a woman's breasts. In the other direction, many leagues out to sea, a ship under full sail was coming towards us with all diligence and yet it was so far away it seemed motionless. I began to wonder how to make my departure, but then Cortese and Pole, who had been talking earnestly all this time, ended their discussion. They came down with me and I said my farewell and went to the jetty.

But before I sailed off, Pole sent a man after me, and then he himself came down to meet me as I returned to the monastery. He spoke with great earnestness and asked me to forget everything that I had heard.

'I spoke out of turn,' he said. 'My thoughts were disordered. I need time to think. Say nothing, Michael – especially in our own house, where letters fly out the door to England every hour of the day.'

I promised to keep my counsel. I knew that by then Pole had already been ordered by the King to write his opinion on the Divorce and the new laws in England. I knew also that he hadn't started yet. Everyone said he was 'collecting his thoughts'. Now it seemed he would have to start a new collection.

He made me repeat my promise; I did so; we shook hands and then I left and crossed back to the city.

5

AFTER THAT I DID not see Pole for several weeks. In the meantime, I said nothing to my friends about my journey to S. Giorgio Maggiore. There was a sort of rivalry in the household for *il Signor*'s favour, and some of them – Lily and Friar and so on – might consider that I had stolen a march on them, hopping out of bed and over the sea to take letters to Pole when no one else was looking. So I said nothing, even to my bosom companion of the time, Richard Morison. He, in fact, was more anxious than anyone to secure Pole's love and approval. He was not then one of our household, but was eager to be taken in, and he rattled on day and night about the excellent Polonus, as he called Pole, and the great Aristotle, whom they had in common.

'If only I was living with you all,' he said to me. 'Polonus and I could read Aristotle together and we would certainly become close friends. Does he realise how learned I am in Greek, Michael? Does he know how short of money I am? You must let him know; I depend on you.'

The problem for Morison was that he was always poor. A day after his allowance arrived he was penniless again. It was amazing to see his money disappear. Have you ever seen a fox pluck a chicken? Feathers fly in all directions. And yet Morison was a very bad candidate for poverty. He had a portly frame, his eyes gleamed with joy as he entered a room looking for pleasure. In his case, Venice was more dangerous than Padua: 'There is more liberty to sin in nine hours in Venice than in nine years in London' is the saying today, but it was just as true then.

Earlier that year Morison had fallen ill, and, alone in his poor lodgings, cold and hungry, he became frightened for his life. That was why he was desperate to join our 'family'; he needed to get a roof over his head.

I myself, his junior by several years, used to give him clothes and lend him money. Off we would go down the street at sunset, Morison in my old green velvet breeches and cap.

'I must be your man, for I wear your livery,' he would say with a shout of laughter. 'I therefore request an advance of wages.'

And so I would lend him a golden crown.

In Venice it was possible to go for days without even catching sight of Pole. When he went out, he, like everyone else in that watery city, needed only one boatman to accompany him. But on the mainland, on *terra firma*, it was a different matter. There, great lords and patrons always went about accompanied by a number of horsemen, and later that same summer, when the heat of the city drove Pole first to Padua and then into the Eugenean hills, I often accompanied him, visiting his friends – the noble Priuli, for instance, the very reverend Giberti, the famous Bembo, who was then his closest friend.

All of these lords received my master with the greatest affection. Bembo especially held him in high regard, not only on his own account, I used to think, but because he was kinsman of a great king, and he always begged him to stay, or sought to lure him away to his country villa called Noniano. The first time Pole went to visit Bembo in Padua that summer, we were there only half an hour when suddenly the order came to get ready to depart: Bembo had decided that we must all set out at once for Noniano, a few miles away across the plain. The reason? To listen to a nightingale.

It seemed that over the previous weeks a particularly melodious bird had been heard there, pouring out its song at night, and the more enthusiastically the nearer Bembo came to listen. Of course, Bembo was one of those men who always had the best of everything. His library, his beautiful mistress, La Morosina, their handsome and witty infants, his garden, his roses, his strawberries . . . It was now clear that no one in history had ever been sung to so sweetly as he by *his* nightingale.

For my part, however, I was very pleased to be off. Even in Padua I felt the constraints of city life and I was always longing to get out on the plains under the open sky. In fact, on that occasion I could not restrain myself. No sooner were we through the city gates than I rode up to Pole and asked him if I might gallop ahead to exercise my horse. He gave his permission and away I went. I raced ahead for a mile or two, then came back just as fast and much exhilarated. Pole laughed. '*Temere juvene et furioso*', he said – 'rash and furious youth' – and Bembo gave me an approving look. Until then he had not noticed my existence.

I knew him, of course. He was famous for many reasons: his mistresses, his love sonnets, his influence in high places. Above all, Bembo was a climber. In his youth, it was up ladders into bedrooms. At twenty-two he went to Sicily and climbed Mt Etna, just for pleasure, and then wrote a book about it – the first book ever printed in the modern script, in round letters, that is, derived from the inscriptions on Roman monuments which have survived the dark ages.

In his book he describes the terrible fields of stones on the ascent, the views as far as Naples, and the prodigious winds that beat about the summit.

Twenty years later, he was standing at a high window in Rome beside Pope Leo and looking down at the pilgrims streaming towards the Vatican. 'Whatever else Christianity may be,' he is said to have remarked, 'it is a most *lucrative* fable.'

Now he was more famous than ever, not for his own deeds or words, but as a character in a book which everyone in the world was then reading, *The Courtier*, written by a friend of his named Castiglione. This book tells the story of a group of friends who four nights in a row stay up late in the palace at Urbino, discussing a single subject – the qualities of the perfect courtier. He should, for instance:

- be well born and of a good stock
- be portly and amiable in countenance
- not use any fond sauciness or presumption
- dance well without over-nimble footings
- ride well
- hunt and hawk
- sing well
- play the lute
- be nimble at tennis
- swim well
- leap well
- run well
- vault well
- wrestle well
- cast the stone well

Most of the qualifications I was pleased to think I possessed, but of course a truly valuable courtier must be able to do more than dance and sing well and vault over a horse, and *The Courier* goes on to address much weightier matters. Now I was young at the time, and bold, and curious, but riding out to Noniano that day I did not imagine I would have the chance to ask Bembo about this book, in which a character named 'Bembo' makes many speeches on liberty and on love which had greatly moved me. But that afternoon Bembo insisted that I, as one of Pole's familiars and a fellow countryman, dine with them both. To my surprise I found at dinner that I was not at all in awe of him, unlike many others. In fact, he reminded me for some reason of the knave of hearts, whom you see on the playing cards and who is not, after all, a formidable figure. In any case, I found I could talk to Bembo quite easily and began to ask him about the book, *The Courtier*, and whether it truthfully described what had happened in the palace at Urbino, reminding him of how the story ends, when 'Bembo' makes a great speech on love – first the human passions, then the affections, then intellectual love and then spiritual, until, mounting higher and higher on the stair, as it were, he comes in sight of that high summit where 'the soul wakes from sleep, and opens the eyes, which all men have, but which few use' and sees the fire of divine love burning in all things.

There the book ends. The conversation is broken off. One of the friends says:

> 'We'll meet again tomorrow.'
>
> 'Not tomorrow, but tonight,' said Lord Cesar.
>
> 'How can it be tonight?' quoth the Duchesse
>
> 'Because it is day already,' said Lord Cesar, and he showed her the light that began to enter the clefts of the windows.
>
> Then everyone stood up in wonder. When the windows were opened on the other side of the palace that looks towards the high top of Mt Catri, they saw already in the east morning like the colour of roses, and all the stars voided except Venus . . . from which appeared to blow a wind that filled the air with biting cold and began to quicken the birdsong from the hushed wood on the hill.

'Of course, it didn't really happen like that,' said Bembo, laughing. 'We certainly stayed up all night and saw the dawn appear at the shutters more than once, but I'm sure we never discussed one subject four nights in a row. Nor was I capable of making such an edifying speech. Yet the tale is not to be dismissed. A writer must be permitted some falsehood – just sufficient in order to tell the truth. Remember the story of the marble doors in Rome which learnt to speak, and thus many deplorable cases of adultery were revealed.'

'Well,' I said, 'I have never met anyone before who is also a character in a book. Did you feel pleased to meet M. Pietro Bembo on the printed page, or did he seem like a wretched usurper?'

Bembo burst out laughing again.

'I see your familiar is not afraid of asking difficult questions,' he said to Pole. 'In fact,' he turned back to me, 'it is rather odd to come across a man of your own name, age, manner and opinions, making some speeches which have never crossed your lips. But this too must be forgiven, if the object is a good one. *The Courtier* presents itself as a book of laughter and pleasantries, but its aim is deadly serious: to teach a prince how to govern well. Is there anything more important? After all, if an ordinary man lives badly he harms only himself and perhaps a few around him. But if a ruler governs badly so many evils arise – injustice, cruelty, corruption, war – that it may truly be said to be the deadliest plague on earth. Here in Venice, perhaps we are in less danger than elsewhere—'

'Why is that?' I asked.

'Here we have a republic and are governed by many rather than one,' he said.

'Why does that matter?' I pressed.

'The evils of scorn or pride or greed enter the mind of a single ruler more easily than that of the multitude, which is like a large body of water, and less liable to pollution than a small one,' said Bembo. 'For example, God has given man liberty as a sovereign gift, and it is against all reason that it should be taken away from him, yet this often happens under the rule of princes. So what is to be done? What safeguards can be imposed? Above all, a prince must have good advisors. This is the real question posed by this book. Who is the most valuable courtier of all? *Someone who tells his prince the truth*. That is what a prince, more than anyone else, stands most in need of, and yet most often lacks. His enemies will not do it – they are happy to see him remain in ignorance, knowing it will ruin him. Nor will his friends, who are afraid that if they rebuke him on some matter, then they will lose favour and be shut off from access. So instead they become his worst flatterers. And thus a prince, his mind corrupted by seeing himself always obeyed and praised, wades on to such self-love he will admit no good counsel and takes the view that true happiness is to do whatever he desires. And then he comes to hate justice and reason as a bridle on his happiness. In the end he resembles one of those *colossi* you see being led through Rome on holidays, which look like great men in triumph but are in fact filled with rubbish and rags and tow.'

During this speech, Bembo had forgotten me and turned all his attention to Pole.

'This pertains to you more than to anyone,' he said. 'Not only is your country ruled by a single prince, but he is one who has loved you, lavished expense on your education, and is therefore entitled to expect extraordinary gratitude. How are you to repay him? With lies? With flattery? With silence? Of course not! You know your duty. You know your debt!'

Pole listened to this exordium with grave attention and concern. I was reminded of a war horse which pricks up its ears and stirs uneasily at the sound of a bugle, and I realised that Bembo was at that moment encouraging Pole to take a drastic and dangerous step with regard to the King, to whom Pole must very soon send his book.

'I know it is easy for me here in my retirement and ease,' said Bembo, 'to urge action on someone else. But you are young and now you stand at the crossroad of your life. What, in short, are you going to say to your prince? Everything depends on that.'

'I have not yet decided,' said Pole. 'There are so many different considerations that my thoughts go round and round in circles and

I can see no way forward. How I can state my true opinion of the King's actions, when he has been so loving and generous, not only to me but to all my family, my mother and brothers? Who, by the way, are still in England, and in his power. What would happen to them if I were to offend him?'

There was a silence, and then Bembo rose from the table and ushered Pole out on to the portico, and thence led him down the steps into the garden. I followed behind discreetly, with my hands behind my back and a serious expression on my face, as befits a young secretary accompanying his master. In truth I was anxious to hear what would be the outcome of this discussion and hoped that I would not be sent away so that they could talk with greater candour. Bembo however seemed to forget the topic; he began to show off his garden, his salad herbs and strawberry beds, his roses, both red and white, which grew in abundance, his chestnut trees, soughing and bending in the hot wind that was blowing across the plain from the south that day, and a single rare tree, called a plane, which he said no one else has ever managed to grow outside its native Sicily as it needs the smoke of a volcano in which to flourish. Finally, standing on the bank of the river towards the end of the afternoon, Bembo began to talk again where he had left off.

'I have often thought,' he said, 'about that night a few years ago when you saw certain magnificent figures in marble, in the church of San Lorenzo in Florence. It has always stayed in my mind although I was never sure why. But now I see it. It is quite clear. That night you saw a sign of your destiny.'

At this Pole looked startled, as is only natural, but Bembo went on imperturbably.

'And who are those splendid figures gathered at the tomb of Lorenzo?' he said. 'There is *Dawn* and *Dusk*, of course, of whom all the world has heard, but who is the third? Don't imagine that it depicts young Lorenzo himself, whom I used to know, and who was, frankly, something of a fool. No, it is an image of the Thinker, of the

Contemplative Life; it is Contemplation itself that the artist meant to portray. That night in Florence, I believe, you saw an image of yourself and your own destiny. How many years have you spent in study of the ancient writers, the prophets, the philosophers? And what is the point of a contemplative life? Was it for your private pleasure? Of course not. Does a man sail around the world and come back and keep secret what he has seen? All your study, all your learning – all your travels, as it were, into the past – *wasted*, unless you put it to use in the hour of need. This the great paradox: it is not only your prince and your nation you serve by telling the truth, but you yourself. And remember Isaiah, who saw his people loaded with chains and injustice. The time has come for you, too, to be unsparing, and lift up your voice like a trumpet!'

I could see at once that this speech served its purpose. Pole's demeanour changed. He looked pale and resolute. And then Bembo, having got his way, changed as well and he began to talk in a more gentle way as we set off walking along the bank, where the sound of the running water seemed more pleasing as the dusk fell. The wind had dropped, as well, and the light of sunset began to colour the sky.

'It is a very beautiful conception, of course, the whole thing,' he said, 'that splendid figure, with *Dawn* and *Dusk* as his attendants. After all, those are the natural companions of thought. Look about us now, for instance. Here we are: the sun is about to set, those birds flying above the river are on their way home to their nests. Yet if you tell yourself a lie, and say that it is dawn, and the sun has just risen – see how everything changes! The birds seem to be setting off on great adventures, and those peasants crossing the field over there take on quite a new air, and even the river seems to roll towards the sea more gaily. So you see the power of a thought – even a wrong thought – over the mind! And more than any other creatures, men are misled by illusions. That is the real task of wisdom: to tell the difference between things that appear roughly the same. And all of this, he – I mean, Michelangelo – constructed for the tomb of poor young Lorenzo, who was a budding tyrant and committed folly upon folly, and then died an absurd death . . .'

At this thought, Bembo looked quite cheerful.

'I must tell you,' he said, tucking Pole's arm under his own and turning back to the house, 'what Michelangelo said when someone plucked up courage and told him that the statue of Lorenzo looked nothing like the real Lorenzo. "Him?" he said. "In five hundred years no one will give a damn what he looked like." '

6

WHEN SUMMER WAS OVER, Pole came back to the city and our household resumed its former rhythm. By that time we had moved to the big house on the Grand Canal belonging to M. Donato. Even with the constant threat of the Turks, every day was carnival day in Venice, the canal was crowded with boats day and night from St Thomas's ferry as far as Charity. And we were at the centre of it all, in the middle of the web. Ambassadors and other grandees came in and out the door every day. Pole held banquets twice a month. The French ambassador came to stay, and then the English agent, Edmond Harvel – Siggy, we called him – moved in as well, his own house being small, cold and foul and filling with water at the least provocation. We knew everything that was going on in the world. And the news that year was tremendous, every day brought prodigies. The Turk was defeated in the east: crossing the Euphrates he lost 150,000 men and all his treasure and baggage. The King of Persia had a second great victory against the Tartars of the Green Cape. From England came word of more executions. Thomas More and old Bishop Fisher of Rochester lost their lives for refusing to accept the King as spiritual lord. The Emperor made plans to attack Tunis. The Jewish corsair beat Canaletto, captain of the galleys, in a great sea battle off Corfu. At home the cook died, throwing even more responsibility on Sandro. To make things worse, the French ambassador moved in at the same time.

Sandro, down in the kitchen late at night, made terrible declarations. He had been serving Pole for years: who were these newcomers and nobodies?

'We now keep an open house,' he said. 'Contarini and M. Matteo are here every night after dinner. Bonamico, Lampridio, Bembo and Priuli come and go as if it they own the place. Priuli stopped a whole month – but then he's obviously in love with my master: at the last place, he came and stayed and wouldn't leave until he lured him to Padua. And then we all had to follow. Mind you, I myself haven't set foot out of this kitchen for a month. You'll see: some great ill will come of it, especially to us poor servants.'

'Yes, Sandro, it is terrible, we are all in grave danger,' we said, winking at one another. By then the winter was setting in, and Pole at last had set to work writing his book for the King. Days, indeed weeks, passed and there was no sight of him; he scarcely emerged from his chamber. Food was sent up to him and at night we gathered in Sandro's kitchen so as not to disturb him.

'What a work it will be!' said Harvel, pointing upwards to indicate Pole's whereabouts and genius. 'Nothing like it will have been seen in our time.'

'He has given himself up to *meteorologezei*: all the highest things in heaven and earth,' said Friar.

'The King himself is afire with impatience to read it,' said Lily.

'Yet only a short book was asked for,' said Harvel. 'I know that from Starkey, who writes from England to find out why it is taking such a time.'

'It has to be long,' said Friar. 'It is written for the English. We are not Athenians. We do not like to be convinced only by what is relevant.'

'Long or short, it will be a glory to England and posterity,' said Lily.

'A *monumentum aeternum* to his genius,' said Harvel.

'He is certainly one of the most learned men alive, and a very great friend of mine,' said Morison, who by then had come to live with us. 'My God!' he added. 'What would have happened to me this winter if Polonus had not taken me in? Look at me, in another man's breeches and with all my books, good as they were, a prey to the cruel Jews, and for very little, truly. No man could ask for a better friend. Let me tell you' – here he struck the table and tears started from his eyes – 'there is no punishment good enough for a man who says "Oh yes, so and so used to be my friend, but is no longer". Such an insult deserves to be wiped out in blood. Whoever has been a friend of mine is one still, and ever will be.'

Outside, an icy fog made halos around the lanterns of the few boats that were on the water. I was glad that Morison was with us in the warm kitchen and not in some attic with bare tiles over his head. On clear nights it was so cold that if you could have reached the stars and tapped them with a hammer the sky would have rung like an iron bell.

The new year came in, bringing more astounding news. The old queen, Katherine of Aragon, had died. And then, not long after that, we heard that the new queen, Anne, was also sentenced to die. The King revealed he had been under a bewitchment when he married her, the marriage was annulled and she was executed for many grave crimes.

Then we heard that Princess Mary was restored to favour. For two years she had been locked up without even pen and paper. She was now a young woman of eighteen, and, so it seemed, very beautiful. A poem about her arrived from England:

In each of her two eyes
There smiles a naked boy
It would you all suffice
To see those lamps of joy

If all the world were sought full far
Who could find such a wight?
Her beauty twinkleth like a star
Within the frosty night.

Everyone rejoiced at this rehabilitation: beauty and virtue rescued from disgrace and bastardy . . .

'Our country suddenly brings forth such events, such comedies and tragedies,' said Lily, 'there is no place to compare with it. I am quite homesick, I can hardly bear to stay here another day.'

'You may not have to,' said Harvel. 'We may all be going home soon.'

By this time, Pole had completed his book. Everyone had been eagerly looking forward to this moment. With Katherine and Anne both dead, and Pole back home, in favour and in high office, everyone hoped to be swept along with him.

Morison left first for England. He had been asked to join Cromwell's staff. Starkey, who was by then the King's chaplain, had had a hand in this. Morison's excitement was wonderful to behold.

'My joy and thanks cannot contain themselves,' he wrote to Starkey. 'They burst the banks, flood the fields of my friends, the more witnesses I have of my felicity the more it grows. To be praised by Cromwell! Who will not love the man whom you praise so in your letters to me, to Harvel and to the accomplished Pole.'

But for a long time Pole still hesitated to send his book. Things were changing so fast, it seemed, that whatever he had written was already out of date. The delay went on for months. In fact, it might have lasted indefinitely, but then there was an unfortunate turn of events. Early one morning, Pole appeared in my room at the top of the house. He had never been up there before and he came in, stooping under the low beams and looking all around, and then went to gaze out the window as if assistance could be found there. Finally he turned and faced me. His agitation was clear. The trouble was as follows: certain quires of his manuscript he had written for the King had vanished. The thief had chosen them carefully: they were the critical part of the argument, and the most personal and sensitive.

There was one suspect: a Frenchman, one of the ambassador's servants, who had just left the house.

'Those roosters!' I said. 'I never trusted them. I don't know why you have them in the house.'

He held up his hand to silence me, and then came to the point. At that very moment, he believed, the missing pages were on their way to Paris for the amusement and delectation of the King of France. It was essential that the King receive the book before any word of it reached him from that mischievous quarter, the French court. I had to hurry to London with the full text.

'I had planned all along to ask you to take it,' he said, 'if I ever sent it, that is. As everything is moving so fast, I have had some doubt whether my opinion is needed at all. But this calamity changes everything. Now the book must go. I have watched you for a year and I know you are discreet. I was right to trust you. And I know you ride fast. But there is one thing—'

'What is it?'

'There may be some danger involved in this task,' he said. 'The King perhaps will dislike what I have written. You should know that I have used some stern and bitter words. I had no choice. Flattery has been the cause of all the problems. The King is so used to hearing only hymns of praise, it is probable that he will hate me, like a patient who hates the surgeon approaching with the knife. You should know this – and yet there is danger in that as well. The best thing I think would be to take the middle path: you know a little about what I have written, but care for nothing in the world but hunting and hawking and riding across borders.'

I agreed to this and accepted the commission. In fact there was some truth in this disguise I adopted. People may wear masks which resemble their own faces. The very next day I set off with the greatest delight. It was early June, 1536. I was on my way home after more than four years away. In a few hours I reached the foot of the mountains and raced up into the pine forests; everyone I passed on the way seemed to be plodding along like beasts treading the straw as I flew by. And yet there was also some little dread in my heart. What did I have in my saddlebag? A book of stern reproaches which might cause the King to hate the writer. And I was the only one of the household who knew this. All the others had seen me off with great cheerfulness. Lily, Harvel and Friar came to the ferry and promised to see me soon in England.

'It is time for us all to go,' said Harvel. 'Cromwell has sent me a most benevolent message. You can tell Starkey I will soon visit him at court and that he must not be ashamed of me because I am a merchant.'

Lily and Friar said they were going straight home to pack their books. I waved to them from the deck as I set off, with no sign that I had any disquiet. But I did not believe we would soon all meet in England.

It was a long time before I ever read Pole's book, but my instincts were right. This, for instance, is what he wrote about the death of Reynolds, and the other three, the first, I think, to lose their lives under the new laws in England.

> Thieves die on the gallows, others by fire or by the axe, but these men were tormented in so many ways that they suffered the pangs of death three times over. Oh, faith of men and of God! Where in the world are we? What crime was alleged? Were they charged at all? Yes they were – their crime was that they would not agree to a new proposition contrary to their belief. You want to be Vicar of Christ, to take the place here on earth of the Son of God, and you plunge a sword into anyone who does not agree. How many men, in the name of God, have you slain? The whole world is amazed. I do not exaggerate when I say that not only in the barber-shops but

in every gathering of men, of station high and low, your name is mentioned with horror. When the news first came to me I thought I was dreaming, and those who wrote seemed to be narrating their own terrible dreams… The axe by which you thought to snatch these men's lives away in fact brought your own spiritual death.

7

THE MOST CURIOUS THING about all of this was that the quires had not been stolen at all. They were not on the way to Paris nor to Fontainebleau in its forest full of wolves but were just where Pole had left them, safely in his own library in a volume of Aristotle. Selecting the most vehement passages of his writing, those pages he least wished anyone else to see, he had put them there for safekeeping. And then he forgot. He forgot not only where he had hidden them but that he had hidden them at all.

You see how odd this is. In one sense the quires were in fact stolen – Pole stole them from himself. Perhaps – who knows? – there are many selves in a man: the bold spirit, for instance, who wrote the book for the King, fully intending the King to read it. Then a second, more cautious Mr Pole delayed and prevaricated until it looked as if what had been written would never see the light of day. The bold spirit then crept up on the cautious subject, put a blindfold over his memory, and proceeded to alarm him thoroughly with the imagined sound of laughter in the court of the King of France.

Thus the book was sent off and reached its intended reader.

The quires were discovered about a month or two later by Priuli, browsing through Pole's library. By then it was far too late for Pole to change his mind. I had long since crossed the mountains and reached England and the book was in the hands of the King. And here is a little more, for the inquisitive reader, of what appeared in

Mr Pole's
Book
written
at the command
of the King

From my childhood you chose me alone, out of all the nobility of England, as the one on whom to bestow your special care and attention. If I now was to repay you with lies, the name of 'traitor' would scarcely be enough to describe such atrocious behaviour. So I beg you to believe me when I say I mean you nothing but good.

And yet I must oppose your opinions. If you listen patiently, my Prince, I promise you that this work, this book, is in accordance with your best interests and your deepest wishes. I may seem to be your enemy. In fact I give you my hand to save your life.

How did you come to this opinion of yourself – that you, the only king in history to claim the title, were Vicar of Christ? There is only one conclusion possible: you have the most shameless flatterers of any king in history. They have corrupted your judgement so completely that one gives up any hope of good from you. Indeed good people now fear every evil. You have abandoned yourself to these pestilential advisors as if you were clinging to mud. You jeer at the men you have killed, whom I myself have heard you once describe as the greatest scholars in the world and the honour of your realm. You have slain those who wanted to save you from your real enemies, these obnoxious flatterers. You want to be honoured as Vicar of God but in fact you are more like the prince of pride, the man of lawlessness, of whom it was prophesied: '*I will exalt my throne above the stars of God*' . . .

To justify your new title you cling to the argument '*Honour the King*' like a starving lion clinging to its prey. Yet it is so futile, so lacking in erudition and eloquence, so contrary to law, custom, example or reason, it is like an obelisk which casts doubt on all that has been said. It is, in itself, a sign that you have been persuaded to seize this title, which not even Constantine aspired to, for another reason, a secret reason, which makes you hate anyone who opposes you. But why? What is the reason you hate them? Why does it not dare show itself?

Here is the real reason which, above all, you wished to hide: you, a man of a certain age and experience, were burning miserably with love for a girl who was eager only to outdo her sister, by keeping you as her lover. She knew very well from her sister how quickly you get tired of your concubines. *She* required something more: the firm bond of marriage.

You could think of no better plan than to say that divine law required you to give up your first wife – indeed, that it was a sin to keep her for an instant longer. The papal authority disagreed with this reading of the law, so it became necessary to replace the Pope with yourself. This is the origin of the narrative.

Your flatterers then lifted their voices in support. You sent to all the universities in the world to buy false witness from doctors of law and divinity. The shameful things recounted about Julius Caesar by his licentious soldiers – that he was a bald-headed fornicator – were not enough for you. *Your* army of supporters was ordered to state that you had lived in abominable incest for nearly twenty years. Then you displayed their letters like the news of great victories from an army sent to conquer Asia.

But how did those who truly loved you hear such news? I can hardly write for my tears. In your youth you were the object of so many hopes. All those who cared for England looked forward to a golden age when you reached the throne. In your first years as Prince what rays of excellence shone forth? A certain piety and, added to this, justice, mercy, generosity and wisdom, plus an innate modesty as if added by nature to guard your other virtues.

But then you became entangled in the nets of love. Satan himself trapped you there, knowing what a pleasing spectacle you would soon become for him. You did not think about how to escape the net, but only of ways of becoming more entangled. Then at last you succeeded. You got what you wanted – and had scarcely embraced your mistress when suddenly, as if some poison struck the marrow of your bones, you burst forth with great daring and not only rescinded your previous deeds but overthrew the laws of the kingdom, of all your royal predecessors, and of Christ himself. Now nothing in human law, or divine, was held to be certain. Everything was referred to your own will, or rather to your passions and desires wherever they should carry you . . .

All this misfortune, O England, comes from one fact: your King, although he had good advisers, listened instead to evil advisers, who whispered in his ear, 'All things belong to the King.' If only he had ignored these flatterers and listened instead to those who said, 'All things belong to the Commonwealth.'

Now, through slaughter, you have acquired the title 'Head of the Church'. You put your faith in torture and death for anyone who resists your lies. And thus you have entered into a league with death. But remember what Isaiah said to those like you: 'Your league of death shall be abolished . . . and shall not stand.' The men you killed have, by their deaths, already written the truth about you in their blood. Unless you turn back, what deeds of renown might be inscribed upon your tomb? Perhaps this:

'Like a raging animal, he tore to pieces the best men in his kingdom.'

Or what about this:

'*He poured out immense sums to get the title 'incestuous' conferred upon him by the universities.*'

King Sardanaplus chose as his epitaph these words: '*I have satisfied all my physical desires*'. Aristotle said that would have been better on the tomb of a cow than of a king. You, however, should hurry to claim it for your own, in case much worse things are written there . . .

This was only a small sample of what Pole wrote. I have selected it from the *précis* I made many years later when I finally read the book. And when I did, I nearly fell off my chair. *This* was what I, on bended knee, proffered to His Majesty? I should have been delighted when Starkey plucked it from my hands. He wanted the credit for it, you see, and in a way he got it. He was blamed, quite unfairly, for everything that was written, and for some time he was in danger of losing his life. I never saw such a change in a man.

And yet Pole had only done what was commanded. The King had said he would rather Pole fall down dead than hide his true opinions. And thus, Pole revealed them frankly.

He ended the book by apologising for the bitterness of the medicine and begging the King to seek forgiveness for his crimes. But I doubt if anyone read that far. The first twenty pages were enough. By then, the subject of the writing, the King, found his appetite 'marvellously whetted' to see his own subject, the bold writer, standing before him.

'No, indeed,' I told Pole when I got back to Italy, 'you'd better not go back. Not if you want to live. You'll be' – I had to search my mind for the phrase – ' "a morsel amongst the choppers".'

8

THIS CONVERSATION TOOK PLACE in Venice, where Pole went to seek the advice of friends.

We were back at M. Donato's house; the city was sweltering, all the doors and windows were open, the room was filled with sound of traffic and voices on the water. M. Priuli was there – his brother is now the Doge – who by then had attached himself to *il Signor*. Pole sometimes used to roll his eyes to heaven, as if to ask that knowledgeable source why he had been sent such a relentless shadow, but he was fond of him all the same: Priuli was well meaning and high-minded, scholarly and accident-prone; in short, he was unfit for the world, and a thousand absurd things happened to him every day. I'm sure he is the only person ever to have his horse stolen while he was actually riding it. But, as he explained, he was immersed in a book at the time.

Contarini was also there, the most able and brilliant man in Venice, a diplomat and great soother of storms. He took the view that many of mankind's differences are smaller than they seem, and may be solved with a little goodwill and patience and, if necessary, evasive action.

The question under consideration that afternoon was this: did a loyal subject, such as Pole, have the right ever to disobey his sovereign who orders him to come home and stand before him? At length,

Contarini related this fable: 'A great number of beasts visited a sick lion, but the fox alone avoided going to see him. The lion wrote him a kind letter, telling him earnestly that he longed to see him, that a visit from him would surely revive his heart. He assured the fox there could be no danger in his coming, since he neither would hurt him if he could, nor could if he would.

'The fox sent word that he would pray and supplicate the gods for the lion's recovery, but humbly begged to be excused the visit.

'In fact he insisted on it, he said, for this reason: he had seen the footprints of many animals going into the royal den, but could see no tracks going out.'

And that was the answer I took back to England. It was framed slightly differently. Pole wrote to the King:

> As I learn from Your Grace's letter, and more from Mr Secretary's stirring me vehemently, but most of all from the bearer [that was me] the most fervent of all, I should repair at once to your presence. There is nothing I would rather do . . . I would rise from a sickbed, I would run though fire and water. But there is an obstacle in the way, which you have put there yourself. It is a new law we never had in England before. Since you cast your love and affection on her who never bore any love and affection to you, everyone is a traitor who will not agree to make you Head of the Church. Yet that is the whole argument of my book. If I came, this law would make me a traitor to my own life, which I am bound to keep at the Lord's pleasure and not cast temerariously away . . . And yet here is all the difficulty for a prince. Who will tell him when he is at fault? And who has more need to hear it, with a thousand more occasions to fall?

This letter I took back to London in August. Pole showed it to me before I left. I was rather taken with '*temerariously*' – a very fine word, I thought. There was not, however, a syllable about sick lions and foxes.

What then induced me to bring them up I will never know.

There were four persons present: myself and Cromwell, behind me Morison, and, still looking somewhat abject but pleased not to be beheaded, Dr Starkey. Cromwell read over Pole's letter to himself, then read it once aloud, then laid it down and looked at me.

'So he is not coming?' he said. It was a strange question, I thought, considering the clarity of Pole's language. And Cromwell looked angrily at me, as though it was *my* fault he was not coming back – which I suppose it was, now that I think about it, but at the time I felt aggrieved at the imputation.

'Well,' I said, 'there was once this fox, you know, which . . .' and off I went. As soon as I embarked on the tale, I realised it was a mistake. I heard a faint hiss behind me. It was Morison, drawing in breath through his teeth.

He meant me to hear this as a warning, but it was too late: I had set forth with the lion and the fox and could see no way to stop until the matter was concluded. There was deathly silence when I came to the end of the narration. By that time, you must remember, it was forbidden by law to make any criticism of the King or the new laws. Only ardent praise of Henry was deemed acceptable, and indeed was all that was heard. 'We are the grass, you are the sun which makes us grow'; 'You have the wisdom of Solomon, the beauty of Absalom', that was the sort of thing which was required. And there was I, babbling about a cave, and footprints going in and none coming out . . .

'And what,' asked Cromwell, 'do *you* think, Michael, of this interesting fable?' He enunciated his words very evenly, like a lawyer.

'I?' I said as if astounded that my opinion should matter, or that I should have one at all.

I then gave the matter some thought. 'Well,' I said simply, '*I*'m here.'

Then, to my amazement, Cromwell laughed. It was not a full laugh, more a sort of brief bark, yet his teeth showed. As he himself had framed the new laws, perhaps he could observe them with more latitude than anyone else. It seemed I escaped the danger. After all, I was still useful. Nothing would be gained by chopping off my head, at least for the meantime. I was still his best connection to Pole.

I again heard a little sound behind me. This time it was not a hiss but a puff. Morison faintly blew air out over his lips like a horse in a stall.

After that, the mood of the meeting changed. They all became reflective: what was to be done? I was dismissed and told to return in two days. I begged for longer. I had urgent business, I said, in Gloucester.

Why did I say that? It was to Coughton in Warwickshire that I had to go. Yet all the way back from Italy to England, I was thinking 'Gloucester, Gloucester' – for some reason the name of Judith's home always had a strong effect on me, just those two syllables made some hidden wheel in my heart give a turn. By then I had decided the time had come to set all the wheels turning. In other words, I had ridden all the way back to England thinking of Judith, and marriage and no doubt the marriage bed.

'You are not to leave London,' said Cromwell.

'I must,' I said. 'I have a most urgent business to attend to.'

'What business?'

'I mean to take a wife.'

'No,' said the Lord Privy Seal flatly. 'You're not going to disappear on me a second time. You may be needed at a moment's notice. In any case, there's no hurry for that business you mention. No married man ever thinks he stayed single too long.'

He meant this as a pleasantry, but at the same time shot me such a sparkle of malignity that I was shocked. It was not, I think, even intended for me personally. I always had the impression that Cromwell liked me. That sudden glare was the expression of power that will brook no opposition. I saw then why he frightened people.

I bowed and went away, and later raged at this prohibition.

'Why do I have to obey him?' I said. 'He is not my master as far as I know. I am in service to Pole.'

'And to the King,' said Morison. 'We are all in service to the King. And Cromwell is the voice of the King. Be sensible. Don't fly against the wind. Wait till things settle down. Who's the lucky girl? If it was up to me, of course, I would let you go, but this is a high matter, a matter of State.'

Morison was deputed to keep watch over me. This was no great hardship for we were good friends. Several times we went over to Lewisham to hunt partridges – there were still partridges there in those days though they seem to have all flown away today. So off we rode together, side by side. It was almost like old times, although of course we were not in Venice but crossing English fields, I had a gun and dog at heel and Morsion was very well dressed.

He had been changed, I noticed, by his three months' proximity to power. He now pursed his lips and looked up at the sky with a frown when he stepped out of doors in his fur-lined cloak. But he spoke very candidly about the situation: quite apart from the fury that Pole's book occasioned, he said, there was great dread that he would publish it. Pole's reputation was so high both in England and abroad that this thought haunted the King.

'You don't think he will publish, do you?' said Morison. 'I know you scarcely know him – you were the baby of the house, he was barely aware of your existence – but you have seen him more recently than any of us.'

'I don't think he will,' I said. 'He made it plain that I was to hand it only to the King.'

'Then what's all this "O, England" and "O, my native land!" in there for?'

As I had not read a word of it I kept silent. Morison was really only speaking his thoughts out loud as we went over the fields.

'It's a worry, a great worry,' he said. 'And, frankly, no one has any idea what to do.'

9

AS SOON AS I saw I was trapped in London I wrote to Coughton, suggesting that my sisters come to town to see me and perhaps bring along – if she chose – our Gloucester cousin as well.

A message came back to say they would arrive on a certain morning a few days later. I was very excited by this. Until then I had never spent a full minute in front of a looking glass, but now – this was in the old family house in town – I presented myself there and inspected the wayward figure I saw. He was hard to make out: I suppose we are always in the dark on some matters – how we are seen by others, for instance – and I'm not sure how much a mirror helps us, but off I went and had my hair cropped and even bought a cap of red ormesia, thinking that such no doubt were what lovers wore, and in fact that the human race could scarcely have multiplied without them.

The party from Warwickshire was to arrive the next day.

That same night a message arrived from Cromwell: I was to depart for Italy the following morning. I must leave instantly and without thought of delay, as soon as several urgent letters for Mr Pole were brought to me.

At that I was almost in despair. Everything depended on who arrived first – the party from Warwickshire or a messenger from Whitehall. I slept badly. All night I imagined something being beaten out as thin as gold wire, I could hear the hammering in my sleep. Perhaps it was my own heart I overheard. Before dawn I was up and dressed and at the window watching the street.

Morison arrived first. At about ten o'clock he came sliding past below me as if on a wooden horse on a rail. With him were two archers. All three were to accompany me to Dover.

I prepared to depart. I said nothing about my private disappointment. The State, even in the shape of a man who used to wear your green breeches, has no interest in such matters. So we set out. There was no sign of the other party. For half a mile I kept willing them to appear, and then, just as we turned towards the bridge, I caught sight of them far away down Cheapside, browsing along looking left and right at the shops and the hanging signs as if there was all the time in the world. Behind them Tom Rutter's big red face rose like the harvest moon.

Instantly I turned and dashed towards them. Morison came rushing after me, complaining and declaiming in my wake. The archers followed, looking nonplussed. They were there only for grandeur and had no notion about what was going on.

I whirled around: '*One* minute!' I said to Morison, holding up my forefinger with such an absolute air that for a moment he was quelled.

And so I stole a little time from the King and Privy Seal and donated it to the affairs of my own heart.

I told the women I had only a few moments with them, being required by Cromwell to leave on urgent business abroad. My sisters cried out that it was a shame, they hoped that Lord Cromwell was ashamed of himself, taking away a brother so precipitately, especially since no one ever knew how long you might wait at Dover for a fair wind.

But I could see they were impressed by the archers, and the importance of the events I was involved in.

'I thought them two was going to nab you,' said Rutter, who had come along as servant and protector of the family honour, and who was watching the archers with narrowed eyes.

My cousin said nothing. She looked flushed. She sat in the saddle very erect and tense, alert to events, as if at that moment she had realised for the very first time that exterior forces have as great a say in our lives as our own wishes. I went to her side and took her hand and said very solemnly that I would be back to see her soon to discuss the great matter I had mentioned once before. She looked straight into my eyes and this time I knew she understood, but then (for Morison was wincing and furrowing his brow as if in horrible pain) I was whirled away again and off we went to Dover.

On the way I asked him what on earth had happened, and why I was being sent to Italy so suddenly, but Morison could no more slow down to explain our journey than a cannonball delay its passage through the air.

'On, on!' he cried, 'I'll explain as you go aboard.'

And so we reached Dover, where – as anyone's sister might have told you – there was no wind and no ships sailed until the following day, and so there we rolled to a stop. Morison then felt he was at liberty to describe the terrible event which had put us into motion in the first place.

It seemed that, only three days earlier, a letter had come from Pole to inform the King, as if it was the most ordinary thing in the world, that he had been summoned to Rome.

'Is he mad?' said Morison. 'He refuses to obey the order of his lawful sovereign to return home, and now proposes to go and kneel before the King's mortal enemy, the Bishop of Rome.'

'But what am I supposed to do about it?' I said.

We had walked out of the town, leaving the archers behind.

'Nothing, yourself,' said Morison. 'But I have certain letters for Mr Pole which will bring him to his senses. You must take them to him at once.'

It was by then late in the day. The air below the cliffs was breathless, the sea almost motionless. I could not go *at once*, I said. I must wait until a wind arrived.

'Yes yes yes,' said Morison, meaning this was no time for jokes. He embarked on a further long discourse, telling me far more than I could remember – that Pole was called to Rome to help prepare the way for a great council of the Church, and that the Pope had always been against such a council but now was for it, and the King of England had always been for it but was now against it, and so on and so on until my head began to spin.

'But that's only the start,' Morison said as we walked along, our feet sinking in deep pebbles. 'The reports we have say that if Pole goes to Rome he is to be made a cardinal, and then, everyone agrees, he will certainly be the next Pope. And just to spite the King, the present Pope is sure to die very soon . . .'

By now the sun was setting and the choughs and other birds were making their way into their homes on the cliffs, high above the range of any steeplejack.

'And think what a disaster that would be!' said Morison. 'Here in England everyone has completely forgotten all about the Pope and Rome. But if one of our own nation, and he of the blood royal, were to sit on that throne, imagine the confusions that would ensue, and which would admit no ordering.'

That was the prospect which had sent me rushing towards the coast and from there over sea and land back to Italy.

I found Pole once again in Verona and gave him the letters I was carrying. The first was from Cromwell himself:

> Master Pole . . . if you mark my nature, my deeds, my duty, you may perchance partly feel how your bloody book pricketh me and how sorry I was to see him, whose honour I am bound to tender much more than my life, so unreverently handled . . . The Bishop of Rome may bear you a fair face, finding you a useful instrument, but will never love you. Leave fantasies . . . you must leave Rome if you love England . . . The King is one who forgives and forgets

displeasures at once . . . Show yourself an obedient subject and I will be your friend.

I watched Pole as he read this. Not a feature of his face moved, and when he finished the page, he put it down calmly like someone laying aside a tailor's bill.

Then he went on to the next one. This was from his older brother, Lord Montagu, whom he loved very dearly.

> The King declared a great part of your book to me at length . . . which made my poor heart so lament that if I had lost mother, wife and children, it could no more have done so . . . You have been so unnatural to so noble a prince from whom you cannot deny you have received all things. And for our family which was clean trodden under foot, he set up nobly, which showeth his charity, his clemency, and his mercy. I grieve to see the day that you should set forth the contrary, or trust your wit above the rest of the country. If there is any grace in you, now you will turn to the right way. It is incredible to me that by reason of a brief sent to you by the Bishop of Rome you should be resident with him this winter. If you should take that way, then farewell all my hope. Learning you may well have, but no prudence, nor pity but show yourself to run from one mischief to another. And then, gentle Reginald, farewell all bonds of nature . . .

I saw that Pole, reading this, turned pale. Then he came to the third letter, which was from his mother.

> Son Reginald,
> I send you God's blessing and mine, though my trust to have comfort in you is turned to sorrow. Alas that I, for your folly, should receive from my sovereign lord such a message as I have by your brother. To see you in His Grace's indignation – trust me,

> Reginald, there went never the death of thy father nor of any child so nigh my heart. Upon my blessing I charge thee – take another way, unless thou wilt be the confusion of thy mother.

Pole now had the look of a man who receives a violent blow out of thin air. The page stayed between his fingers, and he looked around at all of us:

'I cannot go to Rome,' he said.

10

AT THAT, THE OTHERS in the room cried out, as with one voice. They were the two bishops, Giberti and Carafa, both very learned men, who had also been summoned to Rome to prepare for the council.

When they realised that Pole was determined not to go with them, they set out to change his mind with many arguments. But Pole was insistent: 'I have already lost the love of the King. Not even the Pope would ask me to lose my family as well, and cast off all the bonds of nature . . .'

The two bishops finally seemed to give way. 'Very well, perhaps you are right,' they said. 'You must write to the Pope and ask for a remission. But at least ride with us some of the way, so we can discuss all these things. Your King would not object to that.'

So we all set off together, with Carafa, Giberti and Pole leading the way, and a long train of friends and servants following behind. Apart from both being very learned, those two bishops were as unlike as night and day. Giberti short, stout, pallid – his stubby fingers grasped the bridle as if his life depended on it – had a down-turned mouth from which all his words departed reluctantly and had a kind of added force on account of their rarity. Carafa, on the other hand, was tall, fiery, voluble – he rode almost standing on his stir-rups, straining ahead to spy out any foe. He was a true son of Naples, fond of that black wine they make there, and given to sudden eruptions of rage or joy.

I rode just behind them alongside Marc'Antonio Flamminio, the poet. It was on that journey, I think, that our great friendship began. Flamminio nudged me as we rode along and pointed ahead: 'Look at them,' he said. 'Carafa rides forward like Mars, and Giberti brings up the rear like Saturn. And poor Signor Reynaldo' – as he called Pole – 'moves between them sadly like Mercury. He doesn't stand a chance.'

It was soon clear that the two had not given up their campaign to win Pole back.

Giberti was mild and thoughtful in his manner. He said nothing for a long time as we rode across the plains, and then he made one speech: 'It may be unwise of you to come to Rome,' he said. 'You must make up your own mind. Yet I keep wondering to myself how you will now live. You can hardly expect your King to keep paying your allowance. I know him well, we are very good friends and I have often noticed (for I have the same fault) that he is always eager to cut costs. Now that you two have fallen out, he will say to himself: "Well, at least that saves me a hundred pounds a year." And so you will be penniless. Nor will you be very safe, even in an attic in Venice. After all, Thomas More was killed for remaining silent, whereas you, as far as I know, have stated your opinions all too frankly. Do you really think that you will now be left in peace?'

Carafa then took up the assault. He was all for fire and courage. 'It is now many years since I was made a bishop,' he declared at one point, when we had stopped to eat by a stream, 'and I first went to visit a town which had urgent need of pastoral care. But my presence was insupportable to a petty tyrant of the place. He came to see me and in almost threatening form ordered me to have respect for certain ancient and devilish customs of the place. At that, I instantly departed and, outside the gate, following the holy precept of the gospel, shook the dust from my sandals, praying to God to provide for the inhabitants. When I was only two days distant, the people, unable to bear his tyranny any longer, rose up in a body against him, and the tyrant, having sought shelter in an oven, was found there and they tore him quite to pieces. Thus are evil-doers punished!' At this recollection Carafa evinced the greatest satisfaction, shaking a fist, so to speak, at all tyrants.

Further along the road, he addressed Pole again, saying that indeed it would be sad for him to lose the love of his family.

'It would be a great loss,' he said. 'Yet some have given up more. In fact, they have given up their lives for what is right. Of course, not everyone can be expected to follow the path of the martyrs. And yet did not Christ himself say: "He who will not give up his mother or his father or his brother for my sake is not worthy of me"?'

And then he spurred his horse on and galloped on ahead, forcing the whole party and the train of servants behind to pick up speed and follow.

After two days of this, Pole looked not merely woebegone but puzzled, as if he could not tell how he had got himself into this position or how to get out of it. The wind had turned cold and that day, the third of our journey, I saw the sky filled with veins of birds flying south. The summer was over. When we reached Bologna, Pole announced he had changed his mind again: he would go on to Rome after all. He then wrote a letter to the King, saying that he would not give in to his or Cromwell's threats, and he wrote to his family, begging their forgiveness, but saying he must follow his destiny. He handed me the packet, and I prepared to turn around and begin my fifth journey across Europe that year.

Before I left, I mentioned the rumours that when he reached Rome he would be made a cardinal. I begged him not to accept this promotion while I was still in England, as nothing would infuriate the King more.

Pole promised he would refuse as long as I was away, and so we set off in different directions, I turning back north while they went south into the hills towards the abbey of Vallombrosa. It was suddenly autumn; all the way across the plain the wind was blowing hard and leaves were streaming from the long lines of poplars. I should have taken more note of this, but I was young and full of confidence. I had ridden to England and back twice in the last three months, and I was so sure of myself I now decided I could afford a slight detour. I had it in my head to take back a gift for Judith. There was a bolt of blue silk cloth I had seen in a shop in Padua, faintly sprigged, as far as I could remember, with roses. What possible harm could there be in taking a few hours to go and buy a length of silk sprigged with roses? And what might not the effect of that be at Coughton, in Warwickshire!

I arrived at the shop late in the afternoon. This was in one of those dark, vaulted arcades in Padua where you can go dry-shod even in the worst weather. There was a very pretty girl serving there whom I had noticed before, and during our conversation two things happened. First she let me know her master was away for the night, and secondly, by mistake, she laid her hand on mine as we bent our heads together over the unrolled bolt of silk. The silk was in fact green rather than blue, and the flowers were not roses after all, but some other bloom, in a shade deeper than pink.

One thing led to another. It was dusk – she closed the shop and shuttered it – and led the way upstairs and, to cut a long story short, in climbing the stairs I fell, so to speak, and did not leave Padua until early the next day. Now this was very strange, because even when young I was not unusually given to licence, and yet on that occasion, on my first shopping errand for one I loved, what did I do but sleep with another girl?

We are strange beings, is all I can say, and even the most loving heart is unsearchable. And yet it is subject to harsh corrections. Almost as soon as I left Padua, these began.

I took the road through Grisony and no sooner was I among those mountains than the air thickened and the first snow of the season, which I would have completely missed a day earlier, began to fall, and then set to work falling in such volumes, without a breath of wind, that when I stopped and went into the inn at Lachen and looked at the window the whole room seemed to be rising slowly up through the air. At the same time a great hush had fallen over the world. In short, within two hours, every trace of a road in the land of the Grisons had vanished. I spent four days trapped in the inn at Lachen, where the stove smelt as strongly of rancid butter as any of those in Germany, and then finally both skies and the roads reappeared, and I rushed away and in fact soon began to make up lost time. I reached Paris, I flew through that city, and then came to Montreuil near the coast.

There, however, the donkey of a captain who keeps the castle took it into his head that I was an imperialist spy. (The Emperor and King of France were once more at war.) I was arrested and pushed into a cell. After an hour or so, Captain Donkey came to see me. The reason I was arrested, he told me, was that I had been heard speaking Italian.

'I was speaking,' I said, 'to my horse.'

'An honest man,' cried the captain, 'talks to his horse in his own language.'

'I talk to mine in Italian, as he is an Italian horse.'

'Your papers!'

Ten days passed before I was released. I do not know whether it was the effect of fatigue, but I slept better there in the castle at Montreuil than I ever have in my life before or since. There was nothing to do but wait. The straw was clean, the food was no worse than in some other places, my horse was stabled, my possessions were intact.

The captain had examined them in front of me. He glanced at the silk and dismissed it. He then came to the packet of letters.

At that point I held up my forefinger – always an earnest parable – and said:

'That packet contains letters for the King of England. If you so much as lay a finger on it' – and here I waved my own very slowly under his nose – 'then the King will come to know of it, and I assure you that he will feel most bitter resentment, not merely towards France but towards you, personally, Captain of Montreuil.'

At that, the captain, looking blackly at me, nevertheless shrank back a little. He was one of those miserable men of about twenty-eight, which is a very bad age to be in authority, too old to be generous and too young to be wise. I could see that he began to think he had made a mistake and would like to let me go, but he did not know how to go about it without losing his dignity.

Thus, for ten nights in a row, and during the day as well, for there was nothing else to do, I lay down and reliably went off into the deepest regions of repose that I ever discovered. I did not realise my good fortune at the time. Nowadays, I suffer from insomnia; I seem to have forgotten the way to that desirable kingdom.

Meanwhile, although I had no idea of it, the whole world was searching for me. In London, Brussels and Paris the embassies plied one another with enquiries. By that time everyone knew of the story of Pole and the King, and was eager to see what would happen next. But what had become of Pole's servant? I had been seen leaving Italy, was seen flying through Paris, and then nothing.

How exactly my whereabouts in Montreuil were discovered I was never told, but as I was ushered from my cell, I had the pleasure of catching sight of Captain Donkey looking thoroughly chastened in his own castle courtyard. He had a sulky air – he refused to meet my eye as I crossed the yard – and had clearly been reprimanded, and quite rightly, too: he had committed a grave offence. He had interfered with a tale which, that year, everyone was following – even God Himself, if the saying is true that God made man because He loves stories. In any case, I rode on happily to Calais in the winter sunlight. But my punishments were not over. There in Calais I fell violently ill. First there came a slight headache, then a fever, then a foul sweat, and then I became delirious, and for a week I lay in an inn not knowing if it was night or day. The episode gave me a kind of dread which has never quite gone away. There beside the northern sea I made my first acquaintance with mortality, or rather, I realised that one day even I would certainly die. In my delirium, a parade of creatures came to visit me – some, like the landlady who brought soup, relatively substantial, others ghosts and goblins or the images of my own dear departed. One night – which seemed to last a whole season – I was plagued by a little monkey watching me attentively from among the upper folds of the curtain.

This, it turned out, was one of the substantial visitors. It was the pet of an English merchant who was lodging in the inn at the same time, and who in due course came in search of it and then befriended me. He sat by my bed for long hours, telling me many incomprehensible details about his love life and his business affairs: he had been given the monkey by a married woman in Guisnes who was fond of him, and whose husband, a roofer, never the less proposed going into business with him, selling iron nails. As he talked, he held my hand to assure me I was not about to die. And all the time I was trying to count the days and nights I had been delayed on my journey, but the total kept changing and I grew more and more alarmed at the thought of the letters to Cromwell and the King. Then – this was on about the seventh night of Christmas – I begged the merchant to carry my letters to London and deliver them to the palace. He agreed, rather doubtfully, and sailed away.

Another week passed before my strength began to return and I was well enough to cross to Dover. But just as I rose from my bed and prepared to leave, I was arrested, for treason, and I sailed to England as a prisoner.

I was led to London and then taken to the Tower.

After a day or two Cromwell came to see me. There were none of those glints of friendship that I used to see in him. His anger was simple, bleak and official.

'Describe your journey,' he said.

I pleaded the weather, the winter, the snows, the ways impassable, imprisonment at Montreuil and illness in Calais.

Cromwell remained unmoved. There was the matter of the courier I had selected as my replacement – the merchant with the monkey from Guisnes.

'He is a true Englishman, a loyal subject of the King – the monkey surely is immaterial,' I cried.

'He is a pedlar who has been whipped for theft before now,' said Cromwell coldly.

Halfway across the Channel, I had discovered that the piece of silk I bought in Padua was no longer in my bag. I thought then I must have left it in Calais. But now I also remembered the disappearance of my father's ring which somehow had gone from my finger while I was lying delirious in Calais.

I hung my head.

'And to this – *fellow*,' said Cromwell, 'you entrusted documents of the greatest importance, which the King himself was asking for every day.'

Cromwell rose and went away, ordering me to write an account of my journey. I did so, and then nothing happened. Days passed and no one came to speak to me. I understood my offence: I was unlucky; I was in disgrace with the stars. All the setbacks I suffered on the road led to suspicions against my character and, under the new laws in England, to be suspected was itself a crime.

Finally one afternoon Cromwell reappeared. This time he had an even grimmer countenance. He had just received news, he said, that Pole had been made a cardinal in Rome.

I stared at him in disbelief, and then I flew into a rage. The thought of the peril in which Pole had left me, there at the mercy of the King and Cromwell, quite infuriated me. I snatched my hat off my head and dashed it on the floor and trampled on it and damned Pole as a villain and a beast.

Now this had a most wonderful effect on the Lord Privy Seal. His expression softened. He even tried to soothe my rage, and began patting my shoulder.

'Now, Michael,' he said, 'your master – or former master – has taken a very foolish step. We must remain calm, and consider how to proceed from here.'

In short, I was freed of all suspicion and soon was on my way back to Italy, but this time in the employment of Cromwell. He had decided to send me back to keep a close watch on all Pole's doings, to listen to everything that was said and to report back to him and Morison whenever I heard anything of importance.

I agreed to this.

'But of course I will have to tell him,' I said.

Cromwell looked at me as if I was mad.

'I am not skilled in deception,' I said. 'It would be far better to tell him that you have engaged my services and have it over and done with,' I said.

'You mean you will tell him, and yet continue working for me?'

'Yes.'

'And be my eyes and ears?

'Yes, my lord.'

'And he meanwhile thinks you are even more loyal to him than before?'

'Yes.'

'Well, Michael, I have some difficulty with you at times. I cannot decide whether you are too simple or rather too cunning for your own good, or at least for my service. But either way – why, I have decided to trust you!'

I was furnished with new letters to Pole, I will not describe them. They were in the same vein as before, accusing Pole of incredible ingratitude and wickedness and so forth. I was sent off at once. I did not even think of asking to go to Coughton, and rode to Dover very pensively. I was heading for a great unknown city, in service to two men, who were enemies, and I was in love with a girl I could never manage to see. Almost without noticing, I had journeyed far into the labyrinth, just as my brother George described it, and I had no idea where the exit lay.

Thus, in the first dark days of February I rode down the Italian peninsula towards Rome and one day, late in the afternoon, I arrived under the great Aurelian walls, which I had never seen before.

II

ON THE WAY TO Rome, in the town of Certaldo, I fell in with four Frenchmen, or rather three and half of them – a barber, a comb-maker, a cutler and his boy – and we rode on together and got on well enough, although, being French, they were naturally suspicious and looked down their noses at everything they saw in Italy, from the pastry upwards. Still, it is always better to travel in a group, especially when among those devils in Certaldo who will happily rob you of your last penny, and we agreed to go to Rome together, and so we finally came in sight of those famous walls which were just then beginning to kindle and turn red in the light of the setting sun. Then a great squall of rain came in and hid the city. At the same time, a ray of sunlight lit up the foreground and in the distance I saw a group of ten or fifteen horsemen, half on one side of the road behind a barn, and the rest sheltering at the side of a church on the other.

'Oho!' I said to my companions, 'I believe there is a welcoming committee waiting for us ahead.'

I pointed out the brigands, but at that moment the rain closed in and they were hidden from sight again.

'We must be wary,' I said. 'Remember: Rome was founded by infants suckled by a wolf, and the inhabitants have never rid themselves of their great-great-grandmama's cruel nature. I am as brave as any of you, and better able to defend myself, but there are more than a dozen men up there. I suggest we avoid them entirely. The walls of this city are in the shape of a ring. If we go a little further round the circumference we may get inside that gate without having our throats cut.'

Now the French hate to be led by any other nation, especially the English, and the barber and the comb-maker, who were extremely stupid men, rubbed their chins and contemptuously rejected my advice. The cutler, however, was shrewd and fat, and said that he had made many hundreds of knives but had no intention of being sliced up by one, and he therefore chose to come with me, bringing the boy along.

At this the barber and comb-maker shouted an insult or two and went off laughing at us and were never seen again (by me, at least – I admit they may have arrived in perfect safety) while we went in another direction. And then – how it happened exactly I don't know – we lost our way. What with turning into by-ways and crossing cow byres and pig-sties and dung heaps guarded by baying dogs, we travelled halfway round the circumference of the walls before finally, just as the sun went down – at which point the gates are shut – we came through the portal of St Sebastian. I suppose I must be the only man in history who, coming directly from England, has entered Rome on the most famous road in the world, the Appian Way, which stretches away to the south and east, and which, lined with ancient tombs, even broad daylight seems to lead down into the distant past.

Once through the gate, I looked all around in amazement. There within those famous walls was the last thing I had expected: ahead and on either side was nothing but wilderness.

The road led down through a dark wood. At the bottom of the hill we came out on an open moor. On one side, beyond thickets of brambles, rose some mighty ruins of brick. On the other side, an owl called from a wooded slope. Ahead, here and there among ruins, I saw the flicker of campfires, which I chose to avoid, for this was the hour when not only Minerva's bird comes forth and sees all things but so do the robbers and madmen and no doubt the demoniacs who live among the tombs. So we went on cautiously, staying in the middle of the road, and looking all around in wonder. The snow had begun to sift down again. Nearing the Capitol, I looked up and saw, carved on a marble frieze high above my head:

a skull   a ewer   a trowel   an axe   a spoon   a plate

This was a temple of Jupiter, built by some emperor who long ago escaped a lightning bolt. I did not know that then: all I thought was that that frieze, picked out with snow, on a building half thrown down by age and almost sunk into the earth, seemed higher than all the steeples of Haseley and Honiley, and any other church for twenty miles round Coughton, added up together.

On we went, wandering, as it seemed, in circles, and still without a sign of human life until, coming down a steep lane, and round another corner, I heard a murmur in the distance: a light or two shone, and then, quite suddenly, we found ourselves in the 'theatre of the world'. One moment a dark lane – and then: such a swarm of mankind – coxcombs, wenches, pettifoggers, whores, infants, pork-butchers, sergeants, dotards, glove-makers, grandmas, ticket-peddlers, swaggerers, mincers, chambermaids, buggers, carters, scribes, tatterdemalions, salt-merchants, matchmakers, pharmacists, pot-boys, monks, varnishers, lunatics, lamp-lighters, drummers, fiddlers, priests and lackeys – all hurrying this way and that, and arguing, embracing, expostulating, demanding and rejecting; such a swarm, as far as the eye could see (this was on the Corso), that we reined in our horses and stood there like statues for half an hour. It was not that I had not seen representatives of these noble callings before, nor that they were in greater numbers in Rome than elsewhere, but they had appeared so suddenly they were like a theatre troupe that is kept hidden until a signal is given, at which they all swarm out together and fill the dell. As I was gazing, I felt a tap on my arm. It was the cutler. He gave me a nod and then abruptly turned and went away. That was his farewell. It struck me as odd to end five days' companionship so sharply, but then I reflected that he was right: we had done our duty to each other as strangers on the road, and in the end all companionship comes to that, and now we should part. And so we did, he off into the world of cutlery and I to the sacred palace of St Peter, which was quite easy to find in the darkness as the stream of pilgrims was still running strongly to and away from it. In due course, though not entirely without difficulty (the coat I was wearing was sheepskin and still reeked of its first mortal owner; unshaven and smelling strongly of ram I myself must have looked like a brigand to the haughty doormen and porters I met) I arrived, deep within the palace, at the door of the apartment of *il Signor d'Inghilterra.*

I knocked. A servant appeared, lights were brought, I was ushered into a room of some splendour, and there, looking somewhat sheepish himself in the robes of a cardinal, was my master.

'I beg your pardon,' I said. 'I was looking for a Mr Pole who was to wait for me, but I see that no such person is here.'

12

THE NEXT DAY I wrote to Morison and Cromwell:

> Arrived here at noon yesterday – and found my master in a foul array and very strange apparel. I was sorry to see it, but where there is no remedy 'tis folly to be sorry. He will have great trouble with his red hat . . . He means well, but as for these people here they shall never persuade me that they do anything except for their own profit, cloak it as craftily as they do. I wish he had some of my own jealous and suspicious nature in him. I am grateful to my lord, and to you, for so loving a stomach in such a strange and dangerous time. I rejoice, Master Morison, I once showed you a little kindness. Follow the loving instinct of your nature – where other men get money, you get men's hearts.

Pole, I added, intended to travel north again soon, in order to be near England; I asked what I should do, seeking Cromwell's excellent counsel.

I did not mention the fact that I had forgiven Pole for breaking his promise to me. As soon as he saw me the night before, he had come forward and seized my hand.

'You think I have done you a great wrong,' he said, 'and perhaps

I have. But I assure you, it was not intentional. I accepted all this' – he gestured at his red robe – 'only when I was sure you had left England.'

'It is quite true,' his secretary told me later. 'I was there throughout. For weeks he refused the promotion, which has probably not happened in this city in a thousand years. And His Holiness appeared to give way. But then one night, very late, there was a great hammering at the door – that very door, there – and I went and opened it, and there was the secret chamberlain, with a message commanding that he submit. And behind the chamberlain stood the barber. I think it was that that did it. There's nothing more absolute than a barber at your door, at midnight, with his scissors. And so *il Signor* received the tonsure, but he submitted without joy, like the sheep before the shearer.'

'But why did the Pope change his mind?' I asked.

'No one is sure,' said the secretary. 'They say many messages came from England imploring his help. Others say the Emperor was behind it. He fears that one day Princess Mary will come to the throne of England and marry Pole, but he wants her for one of his own family. What better place to keep Pole out of the way – on the shelf, as it were – than the college of cardinals? But if that is the case, then Pole out-foxed him: he accepted the red hat, but refused to take holy orders. He is as free to marry as you are. Perhaps one day he will indeed marry Mary and be King of England. In any case, let me assure you, *nostro Michele*' – 'our Michael' as they all called me in those days – 'if he had known you were still in England he would never have agreed to his elevation, barber or no barber.'

Of all the aspects of this story, I confess that this one pleased me most: that I should have played a minor part in these high-altitude calculations, that and the way Pole came forward and seized my hand when we met again. Until then he had always seemed far above me. Now, having risen even higher, he seemed to look at me almost as a friend. Upon his promotion, I think, he felt a certain cold wind beat about him: congratulations had poured in from every quarter of the world, except one: his native land. That fact alone, I think, gave me more value in his eyes.

I told him I had been taken into Cromwell's employment. Pole immediately wrote angrily to the Lord Privy Seal, accusing him of *suborning* his servant. Thus both my masters, each believing I was loyal to him alone, were happy, which I always think is the best policy. Only I myself remained baffled as to where all this was leading; with every step, in fact, I felt myself moving even deeper into the labyrinth.

We remained in Rome a few more days while Pole completed a report on all the woes of the Church. These he blamed on the papacy itself. His argument, I see now, was similar to what he wrote to the King.

> Some popes, your predecessors, having itchy ears, gathered around them teachers who were not there to teach but to find ways for them to do whatever they liked . . . As the shadow follows the body, so flattery follows greatness, and Truth can hardly reach the ears of princes . . . These false jurists taught popes that all benefits belonged to them, that they could sell everything for their own gain, and, in short, they were above the law. From this single source, as from the Trojan horse, such mortal diseases have broken forth in the Church of God that they have reduced her desperation. Benefices are bought and sold. Everywhere the most uneducated youths of vile parentage and evil manners are ushered into the priesthood as the best place to serve Mammon. From this follow innumerable scandals. The clergy are held in contempt. Benefices in Spain and Britain are given to Italians. The flock go hungry for the shepherds are far away.
>
> As for Rome itself – this city, the mother of the Church and mistress of other churches, is the worst of all. Strangers are scandalised when they go to St Peter's and see slovenly ignorant priests so habited they could not appear cleanly in a nasty house. Nay, in

> this city, whores walk about as if they were goodly matrons and ride on mules and at midday are followed up and down by clergymen and men of the best account in the households of cardinals. We see no such degeneracy in any city but Rome, and here as well malice and hatred reign among private citizens. To bring men to good understanding and make them friends is the chief part of a bishop. You are Bishop of Rome . . . If you do not listen, the indignation of God, which now hangs over our heads, will fall upon us . . .

While this was being prepared for publication, I sallied forth to inspect the terrible city which now, on my first morning, lay stretched out under a blue sky as if darkness and confusion had never laid a hand on her. My friend Marc'Antonio Flamminio led me around, over the bridge and through great arches or low doorways which I would have never noticed on my own. In one passage, near Campo Fiori, I thought I felt the presence of an angel. But which angel? Not, surely, Flamminio with his long black beard and his bony wrists? It must have been some angel of the area.

Having said that, I noticed that Flaminio addressed every woman we met, whether a great lady in a mansion or the daughter of the octopus-seller at the stall near Trajan's column, so gallantly that he might well have seemed like an angel to them. I watched him closely. His whole manner with these ladies seemed to say: 'I take you at your true worth, which is inestimable.'

After a day or two I realised that the real sights of Rome were to be seen in Pole's own apartments, which were crowded with visitors all day long. All the luminaries of the city came to visit him – artists, cardinals, nobles, writers. M. Donato was often there, and del Piombo, the painter, and Farnese, secretary of state ('not a mouse stirs in Asia or Europe without Farnese knowing'). One afternoon in came the Marchioness of Pescara, Vittoria Colonna, the most famous woman in Italy, who arrived with M. Michelangelo.

The marchioness, who was of the most noble blood in Rome, was still fair and handsome, and had a kindly blue gaze.

'Yet she leads men in chains,' Flamminio whispered to me, 'through the force of her mind.'

He and I stood at the back of the crowd observing the scene.

'Well, she seems to dote on my master,' I said.

'That's true,' he said. 'Until a few months ago she used to wear rags and starve herself in order to save her soul, but *il Signor* laughed her out of it. "There are better ways to get to heaven," he said. "And your soul won't thank you for battering down its only earthly home." So she has given all that up and now eats well and dresses as you see, and is much happier. Indeed she is enchanted with her new *son*, as she calls him.'

In her wake trod M. Michelangelo. He was so famous that when he entered the room one felt that something else accompanied the man, something not quite human – his own fame, in short, enveloped him like a cloud wrapped around a mountain, or a monument, or a season of the year. Yet he was also just an aged man in drab, black garb, who came in with an air of uncertainty and looked around the room with a sharp, suspicious eye. For a moment I thought of a certain jackdaw, a fierce bird that once lived in a cage behind the stables at Coughton and whose gaze used to frighten us as children.

But I saw the artist had a noble, weary look as well, as if marvellous exertions, which no one else had ever achieved, had gone on behind that high, lined brow.

I also noted that his gaze followed the Marchioness around the room wherever she went.

We remained there for much of the afternoon, Flamminio and I, watching the comings and goings.

'These people all seem to hold my master in high regard,' I said.

'They do,' said Flamminio. 'They know what he has said both to the Pope and to his own king. But quite apart from that, everyone is delighted with his manner. What comparisons, what expressions – *bei motti* – flourish on his lips! No one can remember anyone like him.'

He added something about honey and bees but I forget what it was.

For a day or two, from the side window of Pole's apartment, I kept seeing a little gilt ball high in the air, just visible over the old basilica, which was then half dismantled. One afternoon I went to find out what it was. Flamminio came with me and we stood at the base of a great stone pillar and gazed upward. This was the obelisk of Nero, who brought it to Rome many centuries before. It was almost the only one still standing of a great number which had once been scattered as thickly through the city as hedgehog prickles; the others had long ago been thrown down by earthquake or the insane rage of the barbarians or the jealousy of the Christians. This one was spared, said Flamminio, because St Peter had been put to death just where we stood: it was the last thing he had beheld with mortal eyes.

Inside the gilded ball on the top of the obelisk, he said, were the ashes of Julius Caesar. He read out the words inscribed below:

O Caesar, who once the whole globe held,
See what a little globe now holds thee!

13

WE LEFT ROME A few days later and rode through snow as far as Lyons. Our hopes were high. In England, everything had suddenly changed. There had been an insurrection in the north; forty thousand men were under arms, demanding the retention of the monasteries, which were then falling, and the dismissal of Cromwell. Henry dared not call out the musters for fear the whole country would go over to the rebels. The King, it seemed, had been checkmated by his subjects.

He met the leaders of the revolt, gave them a royal pardon and offered to hold a parliament in York to hear their demands.

It was on this meeting that Pole set his hopes. He planned to loiter nearby in Flanders or Scotland until summoned to the negotiations.

'You see – it may all end with my marrying Mary after all,' he said.

There were about twenty in our party. Giberti, who was an old acquaintance of the King, was with us, and Priuli, and Lombardo the philosopher, three secretaries, four archers, five grooms. At first, Pole wanted to travel slowly as he felt unwell; Giberti declared this illness imaginary but he was then thrown by his horse which made him more sympathetic. Priuli fell off his horse at least once a day. Often I galloped ahead to see if the way was clear, and for the joy of it. The whole world seemed fast asleep: for mile after mile nothing moved in the whiteness but a few ravens which flew away cawing as we approached. Pole had only five hundred gold pieces to pay our expenses, but what did that matter? In a few weeks everything would be happily resolved, and I would be on my way to Coughton.

But then we came to Lyons, and this dream came to an end. The news from England was dreadful. The rebels had accepted the royal pardon, laid down their arms and gone home. Then a royal army was sent after them and a great slaughter commenced; in every town and village across the north men were hung in chains until no more chains could be found and then they were hung with ropes. Before execution some of the captives produced their pardons showing the Royal Seal. The King expressed wonderment that anyone should think those of any worth. His enemies had put themselves in his power. What did they expect? There was to be no parliament at York. The living were not permitted to bury the dead.

These further details reached us on the road between Lyons and Paris. Why we didn't turn back to Rome then, I don't know. Pole was a legate *ex latere*, which means 'from the Pope's side' – the highest grade of ambassador – and I suppose these grand cognisances have their own momentum. He thought he should at least go to Paris and speak to the King of France. So on we went.

On the outskirts of Paris we were met with all the pomp due to the highest grade of envoy. Cannons were fired, bells were rung and the Archbishop of Paris, the Constable of France and other great personages led us into the city. But then word came that King Francis would not receive the legate.

This was unheard of. Giberti hurried off to see the King and came back shaking his head. Things were worse than he had feared. The English ambassadors had got to court before him and besieged Francis with demands. It was not sufficient that Pole be expelled from France. He must be 'trussed up' and handed over, to be conveyed to England alive.

'The worst of it,' said Giberti, 'is this: Francis is considering their request. I saw the thought slide across his eyes. He tried to hide it by becoming imperturbable. Imagine – the witty King of France turned stolid before my eyes. It is all the fault of this war with the Emperor. The French are anxious not to exasperate Henry. The English ambassador, Gardiner, knows this very well. What a creature he is – more like a devil than a human being! Even his secretary seemed ashamed of him and took me aside and spoke gently about you – '*il povero signore*' he called you. You have many friends in England, he said, but you are in grave danger. What an age we live in!'

We departed from Paris with no ceremony, apart from riding very slowly to make it look as if it was not fear that sent Pole away. Before we left, some gentlemen of the court came to warn him that the danger was growing every minute. Henry, afraid the French might not hand Pole over, had made further plans. Assassins were crossing the sea to kill him. Some had already arrived, armed with hand guns and swords. We took the road north to the city of Cambrai, which was neutral in the war.

This was mid-April. On the outskirts of the wood of Héraumont we were met by the Bishop of Cambrai and other dignitaries. The whole wood was already in leaf and birds were singing joyously. Here and there on the horizon rose pillars of smoke; both their majesties, Francis and the Emperor, Charles, were busy burning villages and farms. And meanwhile from north, west and south assassins were making their way towards us.

We stayed in Cambrai more than a month. The fact of the matter was we could go neither forward nor back. France was closed to us. The Imperialists shut their borders as well, for the same reason: fear of exasperating the King of England.

In the end, the Regent in Brussels – sweating, it was said, with terror, she was so frightened of her brother, the Emperor – came to a decision. She would allow Pole into the imperial dominions but only in transit.

We left Cambrai and went to Bousshyn, then to Bavey, then to Anno, and finally we reached Liège. There we stopped again. Paris to Liège should take about three days. It had taken us forty.

On the way we stayed two nights at the monastery at Anno. This was the most dangerous part of the journey. Our Cambrai entourage had left us; the place was impossible to defend; a row of pumpkins could have managed matters better than those monks at Anno. On the first morning there I came from the garden – I have always taken a keen interest in a kitchen garden – into the barnyard where I saw an Englishman peering through the gate. Then he came in and began browsing all around, examining the lodgings of the pigs and hens as calmly as if he was at a market.

I knew he was English from the cloth he wore. It shows what a fine state of affairs we had reached, that the sight of English worsted filled me with alarm.

'What do you want?' I said.

'Ah, well now,' he said cheerfully, 'I have a message for Master Pole.'

He had light blue eyes and a thatch of hair cut to country standards. I took him for a poor country gentleman with perhaps a little learning.

'From the King?' I said.

'No, his own people.'

'His mother?'

'No.'

'His brother?'

'Yes.'

'Lord Montagu?'

'No, the other one. Geoffrey.'

That was Pole's younger brother. The messenger, whose name was Hugh Holland, said he was Sir Geoffrey's servant and had come across the sea for the wheat trade, but that he also had a message for my lord. I went to Pole, and then brought the stranger into the cool of the church where they could talk together, while I stayed close by.

'Your brother commends himself to you,' said Holland, 'and wishes to come here to join you. The world in England, he says, has waxed all crooked, God's law is turned upside down, abbeys and churches overthrown, you yourself are proclaimed the worst traitor ever known, Lord Cromwell announces your immediate destruction and Peter Mewtas has been sent to kill you with a hand gun.'

'I know all that well enough,' said Pole. 'I am sorry my Lord Privy Seal would like to kill me and I trust it's not in his power to do so. But what more do you have to tell me?'

'Nothing more,' said Holland.

Pole then shook his head sorrowfully at the thought of his brother Geoffrey – who was always somewhat light-headed – sending a messenger so far for no reason.

'Commend me to Geoffrey,' said Pole, 'and tell him to meddle in nothing and leave all things alone. If you see my brother Montagu, commend me to him by this token: "In the Lord I confide". And if you see my lady, my mother, by this token: That once she and I, looking on a wall together, read a motto there: "My hope is in God". And ask her blessing for me. Perhaps she will be glad of mine. And yet, if they are of the same opinion as the King – even though she is my mother and he my brother – why, then I *tread them underfoot.*'

And then he got up, very agitated, and went away.

I took Holland to the kitchen for a meal, and then I went with him down the road a few miles, talking of this and that, the harvest in England and so on. All the way I kept wondering to myself whether through him to send a message of my own to Coughton. At that time it was almost impossible to get letters into England or out. This seemed a good opportunity. But in the end something about Hugh Holland decided me against: namely, his cheerful and guileless expression. The world was a more dangerous place than Master Holland seemed to understand. So I said nothing. A great deal hung on that decision, though I had no idea of it for a long time.

14

AT LIÈGE, THERE WAS a period of respite, although in many ways our prospects grew darker than ever. Henry sent letters to all other kings outlining the incredible ingratitude of Pole, a wicked traitor whom he had nourished from the cradle and brought up in learning and who now wandered the world slandering his prince, against all equity, humanity and reason. The town soon began to fill with suspicious strangers. Everyone knew the old palace where Pole and his household were lodged. The people of Liège themselves well-nigh adored my master, and kept a watch on the strangers. Even in the depths of the night one sensed that many minds were turned in our direction.

And yet for all that, there was this atmosphere of ease, or peace, of *otium* as Pole called it, in the old palace. In the mornings, most of the household remained in their rooms, reading and writing, until about ten thirty. Then they heard mass sung by Giberti, then came lunch, conversation, walking in the garden, boating on the river late in the day. Painters and writers began to appear, from nowhere, like fish and frog spawn which arrive by magic in a new pond. Surrounded by spies and artists, Pole soon set up a little court. He had *la belle manière* and knew how to talk to every man.

From time to time I rode to Antwerp to talk to merchants and sailors and hear news from England. Nothing could have been simpler for me than to have slipped away and sailed to England myself. Officially I was still in Cromwell's employment, and could certainly make my peace there. It was on Coughton that my thoughts were set. More than once – and once after too much to drink – I stood on the bank and watched a ship with men I knew aboard swing out into the river and sail downstream with her lanterns lit in the dusk, and with my head full of wild thoughts – what could be sweeter than to arrive late one night at Coughton and tap lightly at Judith's window? Or, no – to accost her, as if by chance, one fine morning by the meadow on the road into the six-furlong wood: 'Why, my sweet cousin Judith!'

I often dwelled on these surprising encounters.

But then a counter-argument came to me. I thought of the King's rival favourites, Francis Bryan and Peter Mewtas, who were both abroad hunting for Pole. I knew both those fighting cocks by reputation and, being somewhat rivalrous myself, I could not allow either to succeed. How would I feel, back at Coughton, if the news came in that Pole had been shot dead in Liège, or, trussed up, had been brought to England alive? At that thought, terror seized me. I raced back to Liège.

After six weeks or so in that town, Pole came one day in search of me. By that time I had turned into a peasant and was in the kitchen garden tending a new crop of spinach, which in Flanders is called the 'captain of herbs'. Pole watched me hoeing as if he had never seen it done before, and when I stopped to talk to him he commanded me at least to finish my row. I did so and then, standing among the ranks of seedlings, I listened as he outlined his dilemma.

'The time has come to leave Liège,' he said. 'I did not want to go before, as it would only increase the King's vanity, and dishearten those in England who look to us for help. But I can do nothing for them now. Meanwhile the danger has not lessened. If anything it increases every day. Henry is now offering the Emperor not only money but ten thousand infantry for a year if he will hand me over. Philip of Macedon used to say he could take any castle into which he could secretly send an ass laden with gold. I'm afraid there are many asses laden against me. In the meantime, the Pope has summoned me to a council in Mantua in the autumn. As well as all that, it is beneath the dignity of a Roman legate to hide in a corner for ever. So what is to be done? We can't stay here. We can't go back to France. And we can't go through Germany, where the roads are watched, and plans are being laid.'

I stood thinking it over. The garden was very quiet. Most of the household were out on the river.

'I ask you,' said Pole, 'as we are in the same situation. The others may go where they please. You and I can never go home, even with a pardon, as *his* pardons no longer have a meaning. We are in the same boat . . .'

I could not think of an answer. Pole had no idea I was still in Cromwell's employment. I was still, in fact, completely lost in the labyrinth, and I was there all alone. Pole took my silence for despair.

'Never mind,' he said standing up and patting my back. 'All will be well. I see us back in Italy very clearly. It's just a matter of getting there.'

He picked up my hoe and held it for a moment. 'Oh, a hoe,' he said, as if to himself.

That night I had made my decision. I wrote to Cromwell and told him Pole was about to fly the coop. And once he was back in Rome, I said, he would publish the book he had written for the King, if only to defend himself against the charges that he was the worst traitor in the world.

> Yet this [I said] he does not wish to do. Apart from the difference of opinion concerning the unity of the Church, there is no one who more favours the king's true honour and wealth. I am astonished at the diligent procurement of this man's ruin which daily

comes to his knowledge, and yet he remains in the same love and constant mind towards His Majesty.

You, my lord, must consider what is best to be done. I suppose it is hopeless to think that you yourself might come here, or rather to some place in neutral territory nearby, to speak with him. I cannot think of anyone else who would help . . . Perhaps Maastricht would be suitable? These matters require greater prudence and a more pregnant wit than mine. I leave it all therefore to your wisdom.

Cromwell wrote back at once:

From Mortlake, at night

Though the King counts as nothing all that the malice of the Bishop of Rome can do, yet to save this man Poole whom he hath from his cradle nourished and brought up in learning, he will send two learned men, Dr Wilson and Mr Heath, to Maastricht there to entreat all matters with him. So write the certainty before his departure if he will answer to His Grace's clemency and affection and go to Maastricht and tarry there till Dr Wilson and Mr Heath thither repair.

I sent a message to the English embassy in Brussels, agreeing to this plan. Wilson and Heath, as I later learnt, were then summoned by Cromwell and given their instructions:

On your arrival you shall frankly declare to the said Pole his miserable condition, and on the other hand the great clemency of the Prince in suffering you to resort there for his reconciliation, and the great probability the King shall yet take him to mercy if he will return home, acknowledge his fault and desire forgiveness. You shall urge him to weigh what may be the end if he persist in his madness. In your conversation you must by no means call him by any other name than *Mr* Pole, nor in gesture give him any pre-eminence, but rather show by your bearing you hold him in less estimation for his vain title.

So everything was arranged. On the second to last day of August, in the blaze of noon, the people of Liège turned out to farewell Pole and we set forth from the gates with all the ceremonies due a legate and with a great entourage of local lords and gentlemen to accompany us.

All eyes now turned to Maastricht. I was aware that a number of our watchers and spies had already hurried there ahead of us. Who could say what reception was being planned for us? Indeed I felt rather anxious just to see Pole out on the open road again. But the whole world seemed to be at peace. The war had not come roiling in this direction. In the heat of the day even the birds had stopped singing, and the harvesters had laid down their scythes and were sleeping in the shade.

A few miles along the road we came to a wood, near Visé, and rode into its shadows for a mile or so. Then, at a place I had found a few days earlier with the help of some woodmen, the party divided. Most went on to Maastricht; the rest of us – Pole, Giberti, Priuli and I, and one or two Flemish painters who had conceived a desire to see Rome – turned softly aside and rode for many miles through the woods until we had passed clean out of the territory of the Bishop of Utrecht, and reached the river, and even then did not stop but went on by water as far as Speyer, taking no rest until we came in sight of the Alps.

15

CROMWELL'S NEXT LETTER TO me was very terrible:

Michael – you have bleared mine eye once, you shall not deceive me a second time. Your duty was to obey the King's commands, not your own fancies, but now you stick to a traitor . . . So he will declare to the world why the King takes him for a traitor? All princes already know it. Nay, some of them have told the King of the enterprises of this silly cardinal.

If those who have made him mad can persuade him print his detestable book, he will be as much bound to them as his family are like to be to him.

Pity 'tis that the folly of one brainsick Poole, or to say better, one witless fool, should be the ruin of so great a family.

If his lewd work go forth, will he not have reason to fear that every honest man shall offer to revenge this unkindness? The King can make him scarce sure of his life even though he goes tied to his master's girdle. Ways enough can be found in Italy to rid a traitorous subject.

Michael, if you were either natural towards your country or your family, you would not thus shame all your kin. The least suspicion will now be enough to undo the greatest of them.

Cromwell was as good as his word. Within a few weeks, my brother Sir George was in the Tower. He was accused of treason, yet as he had been hidden away in the country for so long, nothing could be maintained against him, except the accusation that he once made: that the King had slept with both the other Boleyn ladies, sister and mother alike.

This was not something that could be decently aired in court. Instead, therefore, he was accused of being in communication with me.

'Him?' he cried. 'My unnatural and unthrifty brother! I have not seen or heard from him for months or years. I was at dinner at St John's at midsummer, and there I met a man called Fermour who said he had seen him at mass in Antwerp and that he was in good health. "Good health!" I said. "Why, it would be better if he'd never been born!" To tell the truth, I never wish to lay eyes on him again – unless – if the King wills it, I were to track him down, yea, him and his master both, even to the gates of Rome, and there fall on them both, even if I die in that quarrel.'

All this he wrote out in a long tear-stained letter to Cromwell, which, by a very strange turn of events I will later describe, I was one day to sit down and read in perfect ease and security. At the time, of course, I knew nothing about it. But even if I had, I would certainly have forgiven him. If your own brother can't wish that you'd never been born, in order to save his skin, I don't know who can. All I knew then, however, was that he had been taken away and his wife was in a dreadful state, like a drowned mouse for tears. But she was the aunt of a lady at court, Mrs Parr, who had some influence with the King, and I was reasonably sure that George would survive his journey to London, which, after all, he had looked forward to for so long, and that he would come back safe and sound to Coughton quite soon. Which indeed he did. His arrest was only a rehearsal of the real sorrows, which commenced the following summer.

Riding down to Luftington in Sussex one day, Pole's younger brother, Sir Geoffrey, saw a strange sight on the road ahead. Coming towards him was his servant Hugh Holland, surrounded by archers, with his hands tied behind his back and his legs tied under the horse's belly.

'Why, Hugh,' he said riding up and saluting him, 'where are you *bound* to go?'

'Have no fear, Sir Geoffrey,' said Hugh, 'wherever I am going, you are *bound to follow.*'

And that was the beginning of the great tragedy, which took away so many lives and ruined many others.

In point of fact, it had begun a little earlier, almost unnoticed and, as a play should, it commenced with music. There was a certain harper of Havant, named Laurence, who had heard gossip that Hugh Holland had gone overseas to see Pole. This harper, who was much in demand at weddings, roamed all over Hampshire and further afield, and wherever he went he spread gossip in the form of his songs. Thus the tale of Holland's visit to the monastery of Anno gained currency. Finally it came to the ear of the authorities. Holland was then arrested.

Sir Geoffrey, as promised, soon followed. He was swiftly interrogated. He may have been tortured – at least he was shown the instruments – and at that dreadful sight, he lost his head and for a week he babbled everything he could think of to please his interrogators.

Then there followed a great wave of arrests. Pole's elder brother Montagu, his cousin, the Marquis of Exeter, their wives and children, their friends, servants, all the households.

Finally they came for Pole's mother, the Lady of Sarum.

She too was interrogated for many days, first in her own house at Warblington, then at the Lord Admiral's house at Cowdrey. Admiral Fitzwilliam and the Bishop of Ely carried out the interrogations, which were brutal enough, in accordance with Cromwell's wishes. But the Lady of Sarum came from a long line of kings and queens; she was not to be browbeaten by such nobodies.

'She would confess nothing,' they wrote to Cromwell. 'We entreated her with both sorts, sometimes with dulcet and mild words, now roughly and asperly, traitoring her and her sons to the ninth degree, yet will she nothing utter but make herself clear . . .'

> *Item.* She said that when she spoke to the King, he showed her how her son Reynold had written against him. And upon this, when her son Montagu came home to her, she said to him 'What hath the King shown me of my son? Alas, what a child I have in him!' Then Lord Montagu counselled her to declare him a traitor to her servants. And so she called her servants and declared she took her said son for a traitor, and for no son, and she would never take him for otherwise.
>
> *Item.* Asked whether Sir Geoffrey ever told her the King went about to cause Sir Reynold Poole's death, she said he did, and that she prayed God heartily to change the King's mind.
>
> *Item.* Asked if she knew Peter Mewtas had gone over the sea for the killing of her son, and that both her other sons would go over to the Cardinal, she denies utterly she ever heard Mewtas should so and prays God she may be torn in pieces if ever she heard such a thing of her sons.
>
> *Item.* Examined who told her the Cardinal had escaped the danger, she said her sons did and for motherly pity she could not but rejoice.

None of this could be used to convict the lady in a court. Her interrogators became almost piteous.

'We assure Your Lordship' – they wrote to Cromwell – 'we have dealt with such a one as men have not dealt withal to fore us; we may call her rather a strong and constant man than a woman. She has been so earnest, vehement and precise, we thought it a waste of time to press her further.'

In the end nothing of any use in court could be found against her. But she was not set free. Her goods, land and houses were seized, and, along with her grandchild, a boy of about ten, she was thrust into a dungeon, wearing the same clothes she had been arrested in months before. Then for a long time only vague rumours were heard about her, and no one was sure whether she was alive or dead.

16

AT THE NEWS OF the arrests my blood ran cold to think how close I had come to destroying Judith and perhaps everyone at Coughton. It was clear that the least word sent to England by anyone in Pole's household meant imprisonment and death to the recipient. I thanked my lucky stars – no, I thanked God Himself for giving Hugh Holland such a friendly and merry and trusting countenance, which had put me on my guard. Yet I was very sad as well. My sweet cousin had been saved because Hugh Holland was a fool. My brother had been saved because, I think, he himself was something of a fool. Whereas I, Michael, who outwitted everyone, had now lost everything. That, it seemed, was the exit from the labyrinth. I could not even tell Judith how close she had come to disaster. I could not write, or send a word.

I would never see her again.

What was I to do?

I must put her out of my thoughts.

'What nonsense,' said the Marchioness, Lady Vittoria, in whom I confided when I was back in Rome. 'Your King may be a brute, but he can't live for ever. You are young. How old is this girl?

'Eighteen.'

'There you are,' she said, 'morning has scarcely begun.'

'But I never spoke to her plainly. I definitely never kissed her. Why should she wait for me? You see – I've lost her.'

'Oh, *Michele nostro*!' she said. 'What do you know about these things? If she loves you, she will wait, precisely because the whole world is against you both. Women are very stubborn on this matter, which steels their hearts and they become far braver than men.'

The Marchioness was then, I think, about fifty-three. She was a widow. Her husband had died of wounds received in the battle at Pavia. By a strange coincidence my brother Anthony, whom I could hardly remember, had also died fighting at Pavia, and this fact gave us a kind of consanguinity.

The Marchioness dispensed much maternal advice. 'How many people do you meet in a lifetime?' she asked. 'Ten thousand? Ten times that? And yet how often does one catch your heart with love, as with a silver hook, and cause you a pain you cannot bear to give up. Once? Twice? What do you think, Michael? Is God so cruel that this silver hook has no meaning? Of course not. You must bide your time and see the good that will come of it.'

The Marchioness spoke with a high, proud look as if remarking on a subject that was now remote from her own life. I listened dutifully, but I knew quite well that she was by then in love with my master.

Unfortunately, the Cardinal was not very combustible material in this respect. He was not yet forty, many years her junior; it was true that he was not in holy orders and was free to marry, but everyone expected that if he did marry it would be at some far-off time, and to the King's daughter, Mary, far away in England.

No one spoke openly about Lady Vittoria's bad luck in this matter. She bore herself upright, and carried on her life and business and friendship with fortitude. Only occasionally her feelings led her too far, even as far as verses, which she wrote to Pole, and which I once glanced at.

Though your first, real mother in prison lies
Her limpid spirit is not lost or bound,
Yet I, your second mother, while free as air,
Find her heart trapped in narrow ground.

But if Pole was too young to be her lover, he was also too old to be her son. In short, he was made uneasy by her devotion. Happily for all of us, here I could step in. I was the right age: there was no embarrassment between the lady and me. I often rode around Rome as her bodyguard, and listened to her advice, which changed quite frequently.

'You must put this girl completely from your mind,' she said to me a few days after our first talk about Judith. 'I am convinced that thoughts can be overheard, as it were, by one's enemy. Therefore do not think about her any more, but keep her *here*' – she touched her heart – 'which is a much safer place. And, after all, I don't think you will have to wait long. From what I hear, your king is grossly overweight and has a terrible bad leg and flies into frequent rages, which are the best things imaginable to shorten a man's life.'

Out of love for Pole, the Marchioness had made herself a great expert on English affairs. She talked about the King endlessly. It was Henry, after all, who had sent Pole into her life. Secretly, I think, she was grateful to him for that and, in order to disguise such a shameful feeling, she never ceased to find new terms in which to condemn him.

'How is it,' I heard her ask Pole one day, 'that a young man so full of promise became the most strange and cruel ruler in all the world? Even here in Italy he was the object of so many hopes. Remember how he was described in *The Courtier*, written by our M. Baldassare. "The Lord Henry, Prince of Wales, grows under his noble father in all kinds of virtue, like a tender imp under the shadow of an excellent tree, to renew him in beauty and plenty when the time comes." And what do we see now? Why, he is a byword for savagery, and – and this is very rare – he is especially cruel to those who most loved him, and indeed to those whom he most loved. There is Katherine, his wife of twenty years who, when she was dying, begged to be allowed to see her daughter for the last time, and give her blessing, as is customary for a mother on her deathbed. Yet Henry refused.

And when the Princess asked the same thing, which not even the cruellest enemy would deny, he withheld his permission. And then there was the other girl whom he first married and then slaughtered, and his dearest friend, More, and that old bishop whom he most revered . . . Those he loves most he then murders! How can such a thing happen? What can take place within a personality to make it so ferocious? Was it the attack of a frenzy, or was he stricken by melancholia and then lost his mind?'

'As it happens,' said Pole, 'I know exactly what happened to him, and when and how, and who was behind it. But this would take time to explain and I'm afraid I would vex you with matters that are so complicated and remote.'

'On the contrary,' said the Marchioness. 'I think that you, who are close to the subject, do not realise the interest it holds to those who are far away from it. I know that M. Michelangelo is as curious as I am about these things and would be pleased to hear a clear account of it.'

This conversation took place outside Rome one afternoon about a year after we got back from Flanders. On this occasion Pole and the marchioness and one or two others, including Michelangelo, had ridden out of the city to the Quo Vadis to look at the site where my master planned to build a little chapel, hardly much more than a beehive or a dovecote as it turned out, for he had no money – after he escaped the assassins sent by the King. On the way back that afternoon we stopped in the garden of another church, the basilica of Nereus and Achilleus, very ancient, and somewhat ruinous in appearance, and built in the Syrian style. This was the church where Pole had been enthroned as a cardinal.

Strangely enough, it was the very place where the cutler and I had first stopped and peered about us and heard the owl call on the first night I ever came to Rome.

On this occasion, their Excellencies dismounted and sat down on some stone benches in the sun and had begun to speak on different matters, when the Marchioness put her question.

'Very well,' said Pole. 'I will tell you. But now we are here we should make some provision for ourselves,' and he asked me to send to the neighbouring house for a few refreshments. While this was being done I also took the chance to send out the attendants, including two archers who now accompanied Pole wherever he went, to keep a watch over the open ground so no one could approach us unseen. By then I had got to know that area quite well and often went out there to fly my two little hawks over the waste ground and the brambles that surround the towering ruins. I almost wished I had brought them with me to fly that afternoon while the others were talking. On the other hand, I was anxious to hear what Pole had to say, for he was naturally so taciturn that if it had not been for the Marchioness he might never have spoken on this subject. She had a way of inspiring candour in the most silent spirits. So I took up a position leaning on the pillar of the gate where I could look out on the road and at the same time listen to what was said within.

'I believe I know exactly what happened to our Prince,' said Pole again. 'He had been thinking of divorce, as you know, for several years, but there came a time when he told his closest advisors that he had decided to take it no further, seeing the obstacles were greater than he had expected. This he said with a deep sigh, but everyone around him was overjoyed as they could see only calamities ahead. But then a certain counsellor approached him, and made a long address, blaming his other ministers for failing to find ways to satisfy his wishes. They were too timid, he told him, and applied the same standards to kings as to ordinary people. They did not understand that, since good and evil are different in every place, they must be decided by men, and change according to human wishes. In that case, who had a better right to change the laws than the Prince? If Rome agreed to the divorce, well and good, he said, but if not, why, then Henry should free himself from subjection to popes, which was really a bondage imposed on princes, and declare himself Head of the Church. And then, taking Henry, so to speak, to the pinnacle of the Temple, he showed him all the monasteries, the bishoprics, the schools and hospitals and chantries, and said to him: "All these shall be thine. Only call yourself what you are – the Head of the Church." Any opposition, he said, would be treason. And what death did they not deserve who opposed his wishes?'

'Who was this counsellor?' asked the Marchioness.

'His name is Cromwell,' said Pole. 'He was once the companion of the common soldiery here in Italy and then a bookkeeper's clerk in Venice – I knew the merchant who employed him – but he then tired of this wandering life and went back to England, studied law and soon made a name for himself for a certain ruthless spirit. But there were still some human aspects to his personality; I went back to England ten years ago and had not been there long before he came up to me one day in the palace and engaged me in conversation. "What," he asked, "did I think were the chief attributes of a good counsellor to a prince?"

'"Well," I said, "he must above all be able to tell his prince the truth, for, of all men, princes are those who need to hear it most, and yet often are the last to do so."

'At this he laughed very merrily, saying that such ideas might sound very good in school, or when emitted from a pulpit, but they were of little use in the secret councils of princes. What, then, I asked, was his own view? The chief quality in an advisor, he said, was to know how to study the ruler's secret inclinations and find a way to satisfy them. This was harder than it seemed, because even the most powerful leader wishes to appear good and virtuous, while his desires often lead him in another direction. The best counsellor therefore was one who found a way to get the ruler what he wanted, without an open breach with law, religion and virtue.

'I was astounded at this,' said Pole. 'I should have said that if he had been an advisor when the murder of Nero's mother was under consideration, he would have been at no loss to justify matricide. But my wits were too slow, and I said nothing. He could tell from my expression what my feelings were and he laughed again. "Your trouble," he said, "is that all your learning comes from books; five minutes in the real world teaches a man more than fifty volumes of your philosophers. Yet if you must have books," he went on, "at least read those which value experience over speculation."

'He then offered to lend me one, written, he said, by a very acute modern, who did not, like Plato, publish his own dreams but laid down maxims based on real experience. I thanked him and we parted. He must have changed his mind because he never sent me any writing. But then, as I watched him rise in the King's esteem, I became alarmed and took the trouble of finding out from others what his favourite reading was. In fact, I took as many pains as a general does to intercept the dispatches of the enemy. And when I found the book he had referred to, I discovered that truly it was written by the enemy of the human race. In fact, I had hardly begun to read it when I recognised the hand of Satan – for if we say that books which inspire mankind to love and justice are of divine origin, then those which set men at each other's throats may be called satanic. Yet this one had the name of a man on the title page, and was written in a plausibly human style. Not to keep you in suspense any longer, the book was inscribed with the name of Machiavelli, from Florence, though he is entirely unworthy to have been born in that noble city, which I know, Master Angelo, is your own birthplace. But we know that the sons of God and sons of Satan are bound to mingle in life and will do so until the last day when he "whose hand holds the winnowing fan shall thoroughly clean the threshing floor".'

'I know the man you mean,' said M. Angelo, 'but I never heard this harsh judgement on him before. On the contrary, several people have described his work as well written, eloquent and containing excellent advice.'

'I dispute that,' said Pole. 'Among his works, for instance, he has composed something called *The Prince* – such a performance that if

Satan himself were to come to earth and reign in the flesh, and then bequeath the sovereignty to his son, he would need to leave him no other instructions than those found there. Listen, for instance, to what he says about religion, and justice and mercy, and all the virtues praised by the philosophers. Machiavelli tells his prince that nothing is more important for a ruler than a reputation for goodness, as no one can deceive the people better than a man about whose piety they have conceived some measure of hope. And yet, says Machiavelli, nothing is worse for a ruler than truly to be merciful, just and generous, as that will gravely limit his power.

'"And so," he says, "what should be done?" Why, one should follow the middle way – appear devoted to religion, mention God frequently, pray in public from time to time – but make sure you secretly ignore the precepts of the gospels, or follow them only when it suits you.

'You see what has happened here? Guile and deceit have become the basis of your rule. Machiavelli, in fact, is quite explicit about it: he urges the Prince to act in the manner of the fox and the lion. To those two beasts he transfers the *arcana imperii*, the secret power of state. To the lion he assigns first place, but when brute force is less effective, one should imitate the way that a fox enters burrows . . .'

Now at this point I dared to speak up. Usually I was as silent as a statue during conversations among these great personages, but I also had practical matters to consider. By then I was, in effect, Pole's chief bodyguard, and I saw that the shadows were creeping across the ground, and the great brick ruins nearby were beginning to redden like embers, for the sun was sinking. The threat to Pole was by no means over simply because he had left Flanders. On the contrary, Rome, I thought, was a much better place to have someone killed than, say Liège, where everyone knew who was coming and going and strangers could be closely watched. In Rome, a thousand travellers arrive every day. I had been badly frightened once or twice already by certain English birds of passage. So I spoke up tentatively and said that, considering the time of the day, perhaps we should think of making for home.

'What!' said Michelangelo, who hated being made to stay or to go unless he himself had made the decision. He wagged a finger at me. 'There's plenty of time yet. The Cardinal of England has not finished what he is saying, which is of the greatest interest. We might have hoped that you, especially at your age, would show a little more courage.'

I accepted the rebuke meekly. As a matter of fact I was completely in the dark about the risks we faced from one hour to the next, or rather, to be more precise, I had lost faith in my own instincts. A year before I had made a laughing stock of myself, being convinced that a great danger was approaching. In fact, many years later, it came about that I was quite right but I had been looking in the wrong direction. The peril was right there under our noses. But I did not know it then, and I was not forgiven for my mistake. Indeed I had not forgiven myself. So I fell silent and gave way.

After a pause, Pole went on. 'And this is the whole doctrine of Machiavelli,' he said. 'This is the poison which Cromwell poured into the King's ear: that under the pretext of virtue you may pander to your worst desires and ambitions. It was only seven years ago and look what has happened in England – the laws overturned, our ancient liberties, the customs of our ancestors, the ornaments of the land, the monuments of the nobility, the shrines of the saints, splendid libraries – everything of worth extinguished, violated, scattered, torn out by the root. A hundred hospitals emptied and sold. The old, the sick, the blind, the lame – thrust out to die in the street. Surely he was born with an aptitude for destruction, this bookkeeper's clerk! If a single legion of devils drove the Gadarene swine into the sea, how many legions must there be in Cromwell who has sent so many men down into the sea of death? No doubt he speaks in public of the Gospel and his desire to purify it and save it from priestcraft, but in private he uses very different language. And what of the King, who has followed his advice?

He is certainly richer and more powerful than ever, but is he safer, or happier? Once he was adored by the people, in fact our whole nation was stupefied with love for him. Now he sees deceit everywhere, and sheds blood without pity. Divine law is decided at drinking bouts in the palace; he has made religion a trap to catch his minions as if they were mice to be tortured. He has betrayed all the kingly oaths he took as a young man, and he accuses everyone else of betrayal. All this as the result of following the precepts of Cromwell. If a man's sole aim was to drag a prince down to his destruction, he could devise no speedier method than that by which Cromwell has led the King into the dark, namely the doctrine of Machiavelli. But apart from the wickedness of the writer, observe his stupidity! He warns a prince above all never to be caught feigning virtue, as nothing infuriates the people more than to realise they have been deceived. Yet that, most foolish of men, is precisely what human beings cannot control. It is in the hands of God. Nature herself says that nothing feigned can last. And it is especially true of a ruler, whose every action is scrutinised, and his words, and his sighs, his smirks, even his gait – all the bodily gestures which so often express what is in the soul.'

Here I began to despair, for it really was getting quite dark – it was late in the year – and I could see that Pole had no intention of concluding his speech. Just then there was a happy intervention. Nearby, so that no one could fail to hear it, came the prolonged cry of an owl.

'Ah, well,' I said. 'Did you hear her? It is a pity. Night has come. I can protect anyone in daylight, but after dark a single man armed with a dagger can slip in close and never be seen until it is too late. I can do nothing to stop him . . .'

At this, the Marchioness hastily intervened, saying that I was quite right, and that we should go at once, but meet again soon in order to continue the discussion.

'After all,' she said, it is not Michael's fault that night is falling. It is a rather frequent occurrence.'

I was very pleased with this, and with the bird which had come to my rescue.

'Perhaps,' I thought, 'it is the very same creature I heard here three years ago, and which now seems to be in alliance with me. How things can change . . .'

But just then I saw one of the youngest grooms, a cheeky youth named Girolamo, emerge from the darkness in the direction from which the owl had called. It occurred to me that here was the real source of the signal. I knew he could imitate an owl well because I had once taught him to do so. He looked very pleased with himself and glanced at me as if expecting thanks. I could not of course condone such deceit, especially when employed against their Excellencies, and I refused to look at him. All the same, I could only be happy with the outcome. Even Michelangelo was making his way to the horses, though he was still grumbling.

'Night?' he said. 'Night? It is not night which is to blame for the wickedness of the world.'

Then he stopped and recited a verse.

> Poor night, she is so dark, lonely and lost,
> The birth of one firefly can make war on her.

This recitation seemed to please him, and so he got up on his little chestnut colt, and we all made our way back to town.

17

DESPITE THE MARCHIONESS'S WISHES, we did not meet again for a long time as soon afterwards Pole set off to see the Emperor and the King of France. By then a ten-year truce was in place between them, although no one expected it to last. The talks, which were held at Nice, had been more like the circling of wrestlers before they clash. Even as the royal fleets had approached the port they fired on each other from sheer force of habit, and then, no sooner had the Emperor's suite come on shore than certain courtiers noticed a man raising and lowering a black flag at the base of a tower further along the coast.

This was taken as a sure sign that the Turkish fleet had gathered on the horizon, summoned there by the King of France so that the Turks could fall on the Emperor and destroy him.

The black flag was seen to rise and fall a hundred times, signifying that the Turkish strength was a hundred galleys. At that, imperial trumpets sounded in all directions, and the Imperialists made ready to dash out to sea to escape the trap. But then a brigantine which had been sent to reconnoiter came back and the captain declared no Turkish fleet was on the horizon and in fact there were no Turks there at all.

As to the signals from the base of the watchtower it was discovered that a farmer who had a large quantity of beans in shell was winnowing them in the breeze. Each time he threw them in the air it looked, from a distance, as if he was raising and lowering a black flag.

That was the degree of mistrust that prevailed between the parties: one man winnowing his beans nearly consigned the world to ten more years of war.

Nevertheless, after many delays and absurdities and displays of pride, a truce was agreed. I forget all the precise terms – what was to happen to Milan, for instance, or to the Duke of Savoy, who had nowhere to live – but one thing that the monarchs agreed on was the King of England. By then Henry had managed to outrage everyone. Not only had he attacked the living, now he turned his lightning against the dead. The holy martyr Thomas à Becket who had been in his grave three hundred years was accused of treason and summoned to hear the charges against him. Failing to appear, he was sentenced to stern punishment. His bones were dug up and burnt. His shrine was stripped and demolished. Two great chests full of treasure, deposited there by pilgrims over the generations, were taken to London by the King.

Becket's was only one of many shrines that fell that year, amid a great destruction of images, painted and carved, which were broken up or burned in bonfires, with, on occasion, a monk hung in chains above the flames so that his fat, dripping down, might accelerate the combustion.

The destruction of Becket's tomb, however, caused outrage in every country. The King of France was particularly incensed. Over many years his ancestors had sent jewels of peculiar splendour to the shrine. Now it came to his notice that King Henry was wearing them as buttons. At the conference of Nice, therefore, the princes had agreed to take action. But a year or more had passed and nothing was done.

Pole set out to try and arrange a trade embargo against England in the hope of causing another rebellion. This was his second legation. If anything, it was more disastrous than the first.

We left Rome at Christmas and had gone only a hundred miles or so when word came that the state trials had been held in England: Lord Montagu, Pole's elder brother, was already executed, along with his cousin the Marquess of Exeter, his uncle Edward Neville, Hugh Holland and others.

The charges and evidence alleged against Montagu were of this sort:

> *Item*: At Bockmar one day, Montagu woke and said to his brother: 'I dreamt just now the King was dead.'
>
> *Item*: Later he said: 'He is not dead but he will one day die suddenly and then we shall have jolly stirrings. Though he glories in the title of Supreme Head, he has a sore leg no poor man would be glad of.'
>
> *Item*: He also said: 'The King, to be revenged on Reginald, will kill us all.' 'Marry!' said Geoffrey, 'if you fear such jeopardy, let us be walking hence quickly.'
>
> *Item*: He said: 'The King will be out of his wits one day, for when he comes to his chamber he looks round angrily and then falls to fighting.'
>
> *Item*: He said he had never loved the King from childhood, and that the King's father had no affection or fancy unto him either.

There was no plot, there was no treason. There was nothing but a few words spoken between brothers, a dream, a reminiscence . . . But under the laws framed by Cromwell that was enough to end your life. I think we were at Piacenza when we heard this news. The effect on Pole was strange. He did not seem to be stricken with grief, although I knew he loved Montagu dearly. Suddenly he spurred on his horse. His blood was up. We rushed through Italy and Provence and into Spain. At Barcelona he and I left the others of the party and rode on ahead to reach the Emperor in Toledo as soon as possible.

But there disappointment waited for us. The English ambassador, Tom Wyatt, had got there first. 'Pole's words may be fair and pleasant,' he told the Emperor, 'but however the head is coloured the tail is always black and full of poison. Traitors like him must be odious to all princes.'

Henry then wrote to the Emperor in a similar vein:

> Most high, most excellent, and most puissant Prince, our very dear and beloved brother, and perpetual ally,
>
> We hear that Cardinal Pole has taken the road towards you. We know his nature to be so ungrateful that no good can come of it. While weeping crocodile tears, he will shed if he can the venom of his viper's nature . . . You must know that ever since he received his red hat, and before that too, he conspired to destroy our own person, that of our son, Prince Edward, and the lady Mary, and the lady Elizabeth . . .

These arrows found their marks. Pole was received coldly by the Emperor. The courtiers drew aside from us, as from infected men. 'Traitors must be odious to all princes' was the sentence to be read on those faces. One or two who knew Pole from the past, and perhaps felt sorry at the line which they must follow, came to see him in private and explained the situation. The Emperor had no intention of acting against England. Germany was in an uproar, the Turks were threatening on land and sea. This was no time to pick a quarrel elsewhere. In short, Pole had been thoroughly outplayed by both the King and circumstance.

The only good thing, in fact, that came from the whole journey was that in Toledo we met Robert Brancetor. He was a Londoner who, years before, when I was still in Venice, was one of the most famous men in the world, his name on everyone's lips. The reason for his fame was as follows: while still a young man he made a fortune as a merchant and then set off to visit the Holy Land. In the course of this journey – no one was quite sure how or why – he crossed the dominions of the Turk in disguise, and came to the court of the Persian King, the Sophy. This was at a time when the Turkish danger hung over Italy like a dark wave – their fleets could be seen on the horizon, their army was encamped in Illyrica. Now Brancetor inspired the Persian King to attack the Turks from the east. Tremendous battles ensued, and all the Turkish forces in the west were summoned home. Italy, and perhaps the whole of Christendom, was saved.

As Brancetor's fellow-countrymen, we in Pole's household at that time were filled with pride – I myself almost wept with envy – at the thought of his glory. It was said that he had led a wing of the Sophy's army into battle, and that he must surely be made no less than a duke. But then nothing more was heard of him for years, and he slipped completely from my mind. And there he would have stayed, in oblivion, except for the fact that one day, while we were in Toledo, he came up to me and, without any introduction, offered to assist Pole to get back to Barcelona.

I had no idea who he was. I could tell, of course, that he was English. That made me uneasy as spies for the King had previously tried to enter Pole's service.

'We need no help,' I said.

'You are wrong,' said Brancetor calmly.

I looked at him more carefully. I could see he was my superior in age and experience and certainly in strength: he was very strongly built, and still young, though his hair was white like sheep's wool or rather it was like the poll of a steer between the horns.

'I may tell you that you need all the help you can get,' he went on.

'Why do you say that?' I asked.

'I had the honour of being informed by the English ambassador himself, Sir Thomas. You are to be ambushed on the road from Toledo to Gerona, and then killed. Possibly Sir Thomas will kill you himself, as there is a large reward.'

'Who are you?' I said. 'Why have you come to warn us?'

And then he told me his name.

It is strange thing to meet an unrecognised hero, but even stranger to meet one whom for the meantime you have forgotten. When I heard the name Brancetor, I was nonplussed. It was as if I had to refer the matter to an earlier, now departed, self, to see what he would have thought; in my confusion I blushed like a girl, which infuriated me, and made me glare at the stranger. He remained unperturbed, as if he was used to waiting for others to order their thoughts.

'Why does Sir Thomas confide in you?' I asked.

'To impress me,' he said. 'He has been threatening me, in certain forms, for the last ten days, but he knows I am not afraid of him. I don't think that he is in a position to harm me. *You*, however, are another matter . . .'

Then he explained his situation. He did not tell me why he was there in Spain and not a duke in Persia, nor how he had managed to get home, indicating with a certain look that that was none of my business. He did say, however, that having arrived in Europe, he made his way to the Emperor, in expectation of a reward. This was duly promised but so far had not been forthcoming. In the meantime he had lived very quietly at court, and not without honour, although – he allowed me to understand – his famous exploit had earned him the hatred of some other courtiers. Those people did not perturb him. But then his presence at that court had been noted in England. This was a different matter. Almost at once he was commanded by Cromwell to return home. The English envoys – and there was always a stream of messengers of one grade or another to the imperial court – were perfectly affable but their persistence put him on his guard.

These envoys were also evasive.

Why was it so important that he go and stand before the King? he had asked them.

They smiled, they looked out the window.

It suddenly occurred to Brancetor that his splendid feat in Persia might not be seen as such in England. He had, after all, helped save

Italy; he had strengthened the hand of the Emperor. *Treason*! And just as he came to this surmise, Wyatt arrived and began to make veiled threats. Did he think the King's patience was limitless? Did he not know how powerful he was, and jealous of his rights? At that, Brancetor made a firm decision. The last place he intended to visit in the forseeable future was the city of his birth.

'I did not say so in as many words,' he told me. 'On the contrary, I often say how much I long to see the Thames again. Nothing is as sweet as the sight of your native land! But I point out that it would be absurd and ridiculous to leave this court empty-handed, having been promised my reward. Despite himself, Wyatt finds he has to agree with that. Now I do not know the terms of your dispute with him, but as he was magnifying the King's power to me, he mentioned certain plans being made against you. I do not approve. I would be happy, in fact, to help you defeat them.'

When I reported all this to Pole, he was incredulous.

'It is unthinkable,' he said. 'Ambassadors do not ambush one another on the highway. No – these are just the boasts of furious, impetuous youth.'

'Youth?' I said. 'Wyatt is two years your junior. In any case, it will not be possible to ask him if he wants to kill you. He has already left court.'

We ourselves were departing in two days.

'Perhaps he has gone ahead to wait for us,' I said.

'What should we do?' said Pole.

I explained that Brancetor not only knew the language of Spain but the country as well. He had advised us to take back roads and byways. He offered to guide us himself. Pole must ask the Emperor if he could borrow him.

This was what was done. We set off from Toledo, we slipped away without any fanfare, and taking bridle paths and goat tracks we crossed the moors of Aragon just as the gorse and broom were coming into flower in the cold winds of spring. We reached Barcelona safely, then Gerona, and finally found a haven in the town of Carpentras in Provence, where Pole's old friend Sadoleto, a famous scholar, was bishop. And there we stayed. And there, like a man who remains firm in the heat of battle but afterwards begins to tremble, Pole lost his nerve. The slaying of his brother, the danger which his mother and others of the family were still facing, the charges of treachery, the cold faces in Toledo – all these now seemed to overwhelm him. He could not face the world. He was ordered to return to Rome and he begged to be excused.

> If a man loses a parent, a wife or child, [he wrote] they are granted some leave. Should not I, who almost in the same instant, have lost all those dearest to me, have the same exemption? . . . Perhaps you have heard that my mother has been sentenced to death, or rather to eternal life – for unless I understand it in that way, my own life would be insupportable to me. Yet even with that firm persuasion, I cannot bear the light. I must hide in the cavern while the glory of the Lord passes by.

18

IN CARPENTRAS, POLE BEGAN a great work, another long letter or book, this one written to the Emperor. One might have thought that his first book had got him into so much trouble he might be advised never to pick up a pen again, but he did so to clear his name of the charge, now broadcast in every country, that he was the worst traitor in history. In England itself that year, in London and other towns, great musters were held at dawn and in the evenings in the hundreds of every shire all the young men, dressed in white, marched and swore oaths by torchlight against 'the spotted serpent, the Pope' and 'the arch-traitor, Pole'. At the same time a little book was published and sent by the King to every court in Europe to justify the recent state trials and executions. A copy soon arrived in Carpentras. The writer aimed his blows first at Pole's brother, Montagu:

> Might not this fond or rather detestable traitor have talked and dreamed of other things than the King's death? Might not he have been content with this world and the state he was in, leaving his lewd prophecies of the time that should make him merry, if he still tarried in it?

But his main target was Pole himself:

> To come at last to the arch-traitor, and to speak somewhat of him, whom God hateth, nature refuseth, all men detest, yea and all beasts too would abhor, if they could conceive how much viler he is than the worst of them . . .
>
> O Poole, full of poison, that would have drowned thy country in blood, thou thought to have overflowed thy prince and sovereign lord, thou thoughtest with thy traitorous streams to have over run all together. God be thanked, thou art now a pool of little water and that at a wonderful low ebb . . .
>
> I plainly protest, I am thine enemy . . . I wish thee to live for ever, never out of shame, never out of infamy.

And so it ran, for forty or fifty pages.

The writer was none other than my old friend Morison, who used to pound his fist on the table in Sandro's kitchen and, with tears in his eyes, swear fidelity to anyone who was ever his friend.

Pole affected to be scornful of this performance. It showed only the 'miserable servitude', he said, of Morison's mind. But he was stung, all the same, and composed several replies: 'You came to live under my roof as a brother, now you omit no form of curse . . . I have to say I smiled when you declared your enmity – a curse from a man such as you is like Balaam's curse, a kind of blessing . . .'

In the end he sent no answer to Morison. He wasn't worth the trouble, he said. I think that in fact there was a further difficulty: the charge he made against Morison – of base ingratitude – was exactly that made by the King against him. He laid down his pen for several weeks, as if he needed to think, and when he took it up again he wrote instead to the Emperor, telling the whole story of his relations with Henry and the murder of those learned men, Reynolds and others, in whose blood, he said, he saw God's finger, writing a terrible judgement on the King . . .

Meanwhile, Brancetor and I roamed about the countryside, filling in time. To tell the truth we were at a loose end. Pole and the household had left Carpentras and retired to a little monastery where he was perfectly safe. We had nothing to do. It is strange to say but when I look back at all the scenes of my life, that first half of the summer in Carpentras seems the worst – not the most tragic or cruel or puzzling, but the dreariest. The sun beat down. There was famine and drought in the countryside. Carpentras was papal territory and therefore home to many Jews who fled there over the years to escape the cruel French. But now there was famine, a war broke out between the peasants, who had eaten all the seed grain, and the Jews to whom they owed money. Cries of rage were heard in the town; the villages were silent and hungry.

Brancetor rode up and down looking as from a great distance at this quarrel over bread and money. We had no part in it.

'Don't intervene,' said Brancetor, as I turned one day without thinking towards the sound of shouting. 'What do you know about these troubles? Why should you join in the yapping?'

He was a strange man, at times full of human sympathy, otherwise cut off from all concerns but his own. I never knew what was being considered within that great head with its poll of white wool. How he passed through the midst of several million Turks unquestioned I never understood. Perhaps it was simple: he did not see danger. He did in fact have poor eyesight, but I mean something other than that: he did not consider that trouble had any claims on him. And so we rode on, and climbed up to the ridges and looked down on the villages where pinched faces watched us from black doorways.

After a while we began to travel further afield, staying away for a few nights, sleeping in inns or barns. On one occasion we came to that mountain near Aix where there is a cavern of incredible height, spacious and echoing, and where, it is said, Mary Magdalene ended her days. Beyond the cave, a path leads up through the juniper and aromatic bushes to the top of the mountain. I was feeling gloomier than usual that day. The latest news from England was as delightful as the last. We learnt that we had been formally declared traitors and condemned to death by act of parliament. It was the strangest legislation ever passed: the dead and the living were all mixed up together in the bill, as if Montagu and Exeter and the others had been or could be brought back from the next world in order to be sent there again, along with Pole, his mother, Brancetor and me and various others.

This was Cromwell's doing. It was a new form of law he had invented. There was no longer any need for judge or jury or evidence or any chance for the accused to hear and answer the charges. All that was needed was a list. The names of bad people, the worst of the worst, were collected and sent to parliament, which obediently declared their lives forfeit. I don't know why this new burden oppressed me so much. Perhaps it was the thought of Cromwell's power: not only were men's lives now easily destroyed, but so were their laws. No worse calamity, Pole used to say, can befall a country than to be ruled by a 'circle of the scornful'. I said nothing about this as we took the path to the summit, but perhaps Brancetor guessed what was troubling me. At any event, he began to talk.

Until then, he had told me nothing about his famous journey to Persia, but as we took the path upwards in the heat and then, sitting among the lichen-covered rocks on the summit of Mt Pilon, he told me the whole story, how he had been on a pilgrimage to Mt Sinai and from there, using a false passport, had travelled all the way to Babylon. He described the deserts of burning sands which he crossed alone, the language of the inhabitants which is close to the original tongue of mankind before Babel. Then he came to the Persian camp and was led to their king. He described the marvellous courtesy of the Persians, who live among their rose gardens and guard the tomb of the prophet Daniel, and the infinite condescension of their king, the Sophy, who with his own hand shaved ice into Brancetor's cup of wine. Then he described how, when the time came to leave Persia and he could not go back through Turkish territory, he set off for home by the new route, sailing with the Portuguese around a very distant cape where the men can outrun deer and at night a cross is seen among the stars.

As he talked, I could just see the sea like a blue porch away to the south, and for the first time I realised how small my own travels had been, what a tiny portion of the globe I had seen, and how slight, by comparison, were the dangers I had faced so far. And it was there on the summit of Pilon, above the cliffs where the falcons were breeding, that I felt my courage come back to me.

Perhaps in turn I transmitted some of this to Pole. When we came to leave Provence and go back to Rome, I persuaded him, at any rate, to turn off the road and visit the cavern, which is called St Beaumes.

I waited outside among the globe flowers and white rocks while he was in the cave.

When he came out I saw at once that he was changed. His step was firmer, his eye clear. We rode on a few miles before he cared to tell me what had happened. There is a little altar at the far end of the cave, and on going towards it he felt his despondency with renewed force. All his sorrows resolved into one image – that of the King as a young man, his cousin whom he had always loved, who had committed so many savage acts without remorse. Tears pricked his eyes. At that moment, from somewhere far away – either from within him or beyond him, it was not clear – it seemed that he heard a voice, a somewhat peremptory voice, saying: *Why do you waste tears over one I have cast aside?*

No answer was required. At that moment, it seems, Pole came to himself. He had in the last few weeks been stumbling with his letter to the Emperor. But now, after leaving St Beaumes, he completed it in a few days and gave it to Brancetor to deliver to the Emperor, who was then on his way to visit the King of France. Then we said our farewells. Pole and I and the others departed for northern Italy, while Brancetor rode off alone to Paris.

BOOK II

I

I WAS ALWAYS PLEASED to be back in Padua, and even when Pole stayed in Verona or Treviso or with Bembo at Noniano I would jump at the opportunity to go there 'on business' – to look at a horse or buy linen or whatever it might be, but really to wander the streets for a few hours among the students who were my own age. This gave me a strange sensation, as if I was walking back into my own past, into the life which I had left suddenly and without warning, and which I pretended to myself I might resume just as abruptly one day, rejoining those students, whom I partly envied and partly pitied. What did they know about the world? Who else in that throng in the streets of Padua had had an act of parliament passed against their very existence? The English students I avoided, however, partly because, when they realised who I was, they would draw back in alarm, and who could blame them? And I too drew back. Which of them could I trust?

I did have one or two English friends, though, in Padua, the closest being Tom Theobald. We became friends, it seemed, by chance, or destiny. Our paths crossed just at the moment I stood in need of ordinary companionship. I knew Thomas slightly already, and liked him; he had an open, cheerful, yet always somewhat rueful expression, which amused me; he was sandy, thin as a whippet, a good horseman, a poor fencer. He was thoughtful: he studied theology and law and knew bawdy verses in several languages. One afternoon, I saw him approaching and gave him a nod and walked on by, having determined not to have any more contact with my countrymen. This was up on the walls of the city where I liked to go to look out over the plains, especially when the crops were green and flowing in the wind like a river. Now on this occasion I happened to turn back and see Tom gazing after me with a certain fixity of expression. He then came after me and asked me to stop and then, with great simplicity, pointed out that there was no need for us to be enemies.

'I have known you now for a year or two,' he said. 'Here we are, from the same country and far from home. We should be able to be friends. I know the problems that arise with the others, but here's what I propose. If neither you or I ever mention any of *those matters*' – by which he meant politics, Pole, the King and so on – 'then we are on safe ground.'

I saw at once what was being proposed under these rules: if he was ever questioned by the English authorities about me, he could swear in all truth that he knew nothing of importance. For my part, I could be confident he was not gathering information which could be handed on. In my heart I immediately assented. I was moved by this proof of a clear and thoughtful nature. From that moment on, we became friends. Once or twice I tested him: I invited him to come to Nonianao or Treviso and meet Pole. Any agent of Cromwell would have leapt at the chance, but Theobald laughed at me.

'What would I say to him? No, let's stay here in Padua where there's a bit of life.' He would ask me to join him at dinners with his friends, sometimes including young ladies, or we would go to his lodging and have ham and pea soup and drink that black wine called— well, whatever it is called, I never can remember. Once, with Pole safely installed at Trevsio, I went off with Theobald to Ferrara and Forli where he had some business and then we came back along the coast, and raced each other through the pine forest with its red-carpeted floor. For me such moments were more rare and delightful than entry to a royal palace. No one knew where I was. I had no dangerous duties. I almost forgot the death threat always hanging over my head, the painful loss of Judith, and family, and country. With Tom Theobald as company, I had a glimpse of that magnificent thing, despised by many young men: an ordinary life.

But the time soon came when Pole had to return to Rome. I farewelled my carefree friend in Padua and took up my duties again as bodyguard, chief minister and master of horse for Mr Pole. It was early summer when we got back to the city. We had been away more than a year. And we were not back there long before astounding news came from England. Cromwell had fallen from power!

He was charged, as far as could be seen, with imaginary offences. My brother George, by then long since out of the Tower and back at home, was called on to provide some evidence against him.

'Why, yes,' said George, pleased to assist. 'He once said to me: "*I am sure of the King.*" '

This was a most detestable crime – a man as low-born as Cromwell, whose father made a living fulling cloth at Putney, to say he was 'sure of' his sovereign.

From his prison cell Cromwell wrote plaintive letters to the King:

> If it were in my power to make your Majesty live for ever young, God knows I would, and so rich and powerful that all the world would be forced to obey you, Christ he knows I would . . .
>
> God forgive my accusers. I never spoke to Throckmorton, your Grace knows what sort of man he is . . .
>
> Written with the quaking hand and most sorrowful heart of your most sorrowful subject . . .
>
> Most gracious Prince, I cry for mercy, mercy, mercy.

But there was to be no mercy. There was to be no hearing. Cromwell never met his accusers. No lawyers, judge or jury were called upon.

He was convicted by attainder, by act of parliament, the process which he had himself devised; indeed I think he was the very first to go to his eternal home, wherever that might be, by this new route.

Cromwell's fall caused a sensation in Rome, as in every other city, and occasioned much debate and speculation. What did it mean? What did it portend? The Marchioness was convinced that it signalled a change of heart in the King.

'Surely,' she said, 'now that the teacher is gone, the pupil will mend his ways.'

'Perhaps the teacher is gone because he is no longer needed,' said Pole. 'Perhaps by killing him, the pupil shows him how well he has grasped the teacher's doctrine.'

'But surely your King would like to regain the good opinion of others,' said the Marchioness. 'I know that the King of France has already written to congratulate him on being rid of that unhappy instrument, whose *malversation* turned him against the best of his subjects.'

Pole did not answer at once, as if he was unwilling to dispute the point.

'I would like to agree with you,' he said finally. 'And after all nothing is impossible. But I don't see how such a change can come about. It is too late. Even if Henry wished to change, I don't see how he could. He has convinced himself that his subjects secretly hate him, and he is wise to think so – his avarice, his blasphemies, his cruelty mean that they must regard him as an enemy. "Tyranny is a fine place," the Greeks used to say, "but there's no way down." It's an old story.'

We were sitting that afternoon in the garden of Faenza's house on the Quirinale. Faenza was away from Rome at the time but he was a great friend of Pole's and gave him the use of the garden whenever he wanted to escape the heat of the city below. It was the first time, I think, that Pole had met his circle of friends since the fall of Cromwell. The Marchioness was there, with her two attendants;

M. Michelangelo came, with his faithful Urbino, the colour-grinder; Flamminio was present, and M. Donato, and Bembo arrived – by this time he had been made a cardinal. With him, I remember, was a shock-headed youth named Ulisse, whose father was a friend of Bembo's and had sent the son to Rome for some reason or other, and who, from the moment he arrived in the garden, managed to irritate and upset me with his peering everywhere and roaming about and lifting things and snatching at lizards on the wall. I had a sense that he was going to cause me some great trouble that day, which indeed he did, although not of a kind I imagined.

At Faenza's house we were reasonably secure – there was a strong wall around the garden, and the archers and other servants watched the gate. A single elm cast its shade near the house, and two or three rows of vines led to a grove of pines which stirred every now and then in the breeze, like musicians preparing to play the fiddle, and beyond that a little menagerie – ducks and drakes, chickens, a peacock – were going about their affairs. Faenza had also planted more rows of vines on neighbouring land he had just bought.

'They're not much to look at now,' said M. Donato. 'Come back in twenty years and then you'll see something.'

'I cannot accept the invitation,' said Pole. 'Do you really hate me so much to think I will still be here, in exile, in twenty years?'

It was then that the Marchioness intervened to ask about Cromwell's fall and what it might mean.

'The fact of the matter,' said Pole, 'is that with Henry we have a tyranny of a kind not seen for many centuries. I used to think that the King had equalled Nero in his impiety and cruelty, but I was wrong. He has out-Nero'd Nero. Planning his persecution of the saints, perhaps on this very hillside where he watched Rome burn, Nero can still be counted among those for whom Christ prayed when he said "Father forgive them, they know not what they do." Nero did not know that those he killed were beloved by God. Indeed, he believed the opposite: he saw that their teaching was so opposed to the old religion that it was bound to destroy it. But what can be said of the King? That he did not know that those he loved were loved by God? But he killed them for that very reason – he knew they were good and learned and saintly. He knew that only such men would be brave enough to oppose him, and he removed them for that reason, and to strike terror into the rest of his subjects. On the last day, when Nero's victims appear as witnesses against him, their testimony will be less terrible than that given by the men Henry attacked and slaughtered.'

Pole paused here and seemed to be weighing up his words.

'I can tell you this,' he said. 'When I heard of the first murders – it was our Michael here who came to me with the news – I was stunned. I was almost speechless for a month. You will remember, my lord,' he said to Bembo. 'I talked to you at the time. I did not know what to think! It was as if everything was written in a language I did not know, in characters I could not read. Then quite suddenly I found I could read this strange script.'

'Which script?' said the Marchioness.

'When I thought of those men, Reynolds and others, torn apart as if by wild beasts, it seemed to me that I saw God's finger writing in their blood.'

'I could understand you better,' said Bembo, 'if you said it was the King who wrote in their blood.'

'No,' said Pole, 'it once pleased God to explain His will for us in the blood of his own Son, but Christ was not the last. His teaching was also written in the blood of the martyrs who followed. They were living books, *living letters*, by which both the learned and the ignorant might read the will and the judgement of God. In the limbs of those men I knew, torn apart in my own city, and nailed up in different places, I read the full truth about the King and knew what I should do.'

Michelangelo, who apparently had been sunk in thought, now spoke up, saying that this was a strange idea, one he had not thought of before, that men and women themselves might be seen as letters.

'I sometimes think that people are always at work painting and inscribing on the world,' he said, 'whether by building towers or ploughing fields or crossing the sea or, for that matter, having children or making war. But you say something more: that men's bodies themselves may actually form an alphabet. And yet, why not? Perhaps the letters of our own alphabet are derived from the shapes of men and beasts, just as they are in the writing of the Egyptians, which no one can read today but which we still see on obelisks and other fragments scattered around this city.'

'Yes, but they are very rare, the letters I refer to,' said Pole. 'The origin of our religion was written down in the blood of these martyrs. They were the original books in which the finger of God appeared. They are to be preferred to all others, written with ink on paper. And God has never ceased writing in such a way, in the blood of the martyrs, to show His will in the storms that divide mankind. No greater honour has ever befallen my country, in fact, than to have provided the world with such living letters now, in our own time, in our own streets . . .'

The others sat pondering this. By then, late in the afternoon, bronze-coloured clouds were towering up inland – a thunderstorm was on the way. The group began to stir in the way people do just before departure. Bembo however began to speak, saying he certainly remembered Pole coming to him years ago to discuss the matter, and then he said that it was a strange fact that the book in which Machiavelli's doctrine appeared was dedicated to the very same man, Duke Lorenzo, who was also the subject of a statue by Michelangelo on a tomb in Florence.

'It is a little thing, a mere coincidence of the kind that that appeals to an ordinary mind like mine,' he said. 'But it pleases me to think that this Lorenzo, who in a sense inspired this dangerous doctrine, also inspired a statue, which provided the antidote.'

He then mentioned that Pole, many years before, had caught a glimpse of the statue of Lorenzo along with the *Dusk* and the *Dawn*, which had helped him understand how to respond to the King.

Master Michelangelo at that point began to look anxious and puzzled. 'You saw this statue many years ago?' he asked

'Oh yes, before I ever went back to England,' said Pole.

'Ah, well, your Excellency must be mistaken,' said Michelangelo. 'The statues were not finished then, and in any case, the chapel was never open. You must have seen it more recently or perhaps dreamed the whole thing.'

'Oh, no, I assure you . . .' said Pole, but just at that moment, Ulisse, the wretched youth I mentioned before, reappeared, stalking along between the vines behind one of the birds of the garden, a fine cock with black and golden plumes intermixed and a comb as red as bacon. As he came near, Ulisse began to call out:

' "Oh yes – he is keenly aware of his renown as the guardian of the night! He has been given the task of arousing men to their labours and ending their slumber. Anyone who kills a rooster like him without need is just as guilty as a man who chokes his poor old father to death. In Greek he is called *alektor*, after the sun which also makes men leave their beds; and so this noble cock surely should be praised for his courage, his brilliance, his love for his own race and for the way he fights manfully for his dear little wives." '

At this everyone laughed and applauded loudly, which astounded me, for I assumed he had gone mad and should be confined at once in the cellar. But it seemed he was quoting a passage by an author of great renown, Pliny, or maybe it was Cicero, I forget which. And I was the only one present who did not recognise it.

This had a very great effect on me. In secret, and for the first time in my life, I was thoroughly ashamed of my ignorance. I truly regretted not devoting myself more to my studies, and I began to wonder how to make amends.

This incident made everyone forget the previous conversation, and just then the wind sprang up and the pines began to sough and everyone prepared to leave. The tower of cloud still looked to be half an hour away but as we rode down the hill it grew taller and taller above us and the storm broke just as we reached the marble statues of the horse-tamers where, amid thunder, we went our separate ways.

2

IF THE MARCHIONESS LOVED any man more than Pole, or her 'unique friend', as she called Michelangelo, then it was her brother, Lord Ascanio, the head of the family, a wildly imprudent head at that, who over the following months distracted her from all other affairs, brought war raging up to the gates of Rome and managed to lose all his family's Roman estates gathered, enriched and adorned over so many centuries.

The cause of these catastrophes was what? The price of salt. The Pope, in short, raised the tax. It is true that salt is a necessity of life, and the papal salt was now the most expensive on earth, but unlike everyone else, who groaned and bore the burden for a few years until it went away, Ascanio, the most powerful of the Roman barons, contested the point. He bought his salt elsewhere. The Pope then ordered him to appear before him. He declined. Some of his vassals were arrested and thrown into jail.

At this, Ascanio was roused to fury, which was always easy in his case. His wife had long since left him, taking their six children and accusing him of violence and homosexuality and also of alchemy. Now he went on the offensive, driving off long-horned cattle, trampling the harvest and ranging right up to the walls of Rome.

The gates were shut, sentries manned the ramparts, and young and old flocked to the walls to look down at the war, just as people in England go to the coast to look at the sea in a storm.

The Marchioness tried to make peace, hurrying back and forward between the Pope and her brother, but it was no use. Secretly both men wanted a trial of arms, Ascanio in order to put popes in their place, the Pope to rid Rome of the encirclement of Colonna castles.

'So much war over thirty cows!' said the Marchioness in despair, but since her own vassals were naturally fighting for the Colonnas she was forced to leave the city. The time came when Pole decided to leave as well. Rome was filled with mercenaries – Gascons, German Lutherans, foreigners of all kinds, including Englishmen, roamed the streets, paid by the Pope to defend the city. At this point, remembering one of Wyatt's threats in Toledo – that Rome was the best place in the world to kill a cardinal – we decided to follow the Marchioness's example and find a retreat in the hills. A place called Capranica – 'the place of goats' – was found. We were lodged in a house in the centre of the little town, from where you could look out in all directions.

'Petrarch came here and said it was a fearful place,' said Pole, coming out onto the terrace on our first day there. 'All day he heard nothing but voices crying "To arms!" and at night dreadful howling beyond the walls. And yet now look: it is the image of the golden age!'

We could see far and wide, beyond the walls and the chasm below the town. The woods were already in full leaf, the fields were already ploughed as if a great draughtsman had been at work. In the distance the cuckoo could be heard calling, just as in England, or perhaps a little faster, as if heated up more by the sun. The golden age had returned! And everywhere, in fact, that spring there were signs that the world was on the mend. A great conference was then being held at Ratisbon between Catholics and Protestants to settle their differences. Even Henry the Eighth sent a delegation, with Gardiner and young Knyvett at the head of a hundred horsemen arrayed in grey velvet with gold chains round their necks riding through the German woods to Ratisbon. The King had also taken a new wife who was said to have a kind heart and to moderate his rages.

One day Pole showed me a document which had just arrived. I should explain that little scraps of information often came from England, sent out by ambassadors and then transmitted to Pole by his friends in foreign courts.

This was a copy of a tailor's bill. It had been sent from the Queen's tailor, John Scut, to the Privy Council.

I doubt if any tailor's bill in the history of the world has produced such feelings in another country a thousand miles away as this one on my master Pole. He came looking for me and found me by the main door leading onto the street and there, with the door open – we felt such security in Capranica – he displayed it to me as if it reported a great victory or the birth of a son.

Re Garments for Countess of Salisbury, namely:

One night gown, furred

One kirtle, worsted

One petticoat, furred

One nightgown lined with satin of Cyprus

One bonnet

Four pair hose

Four pair shoes

One pair slippers

Total: £11.16.4

'A *furred nightgown*,' he said. 'An excellent garment, that, a very good garment!' He looked back at the paper. 'And a kirtle, worsted – that's a fine thing too, you know, against the cold.'

I hardly liked to look at his face, for happiness and fear showed there equally. The unspoken dread was that for the last two years his mother had been in the dungeon with only the clothes she had been arrested in. But we could not dwell on that. The main thing was that Master Scut's bill proved not only that the Lady of Sarum was still alive, but that the King intended that she should continue to live. One thing was certain: he was not a man to spend £11.16.4 on an old woman he intended should die. And if she was not to die, why should she not soon be freed? The departure of Cromwell and the presence of the new queen at Henry's side made anything seem possible.

This was in late spring in 1541.

From my point of view, the best thing about Capranica was its size. It was so small that no stranger could arrive and take up a post there – as assassin, for instance – without at once being known. As well as that, all the roads into the place were easily watched. The whole hilltop town was its own watchtower, and I was the sentinel. Even when I went out early in the morning into the country to fly my hawk I could, from several places, look up and down the length of the road and see whoever was coming.

One such morning, on one of the hills above the hanging woods, I noticed in the distance two figures riding towards the town from the south. For some reason, I thought of Brancetor, but I dismissed the idea. He had joined us in Rome the previous month but remained there when we left. He was planning to get a commission to fight the Turks who were then battering the gates of Budapest and, having a great interest in war, he had decided to stay and watch Lord Ascanio's argument with the Pope. But when I got back to the house an hour later I found Brancetor installed in the kitchen, eating eggs and bread, and surrounded by servants, who wore grave expressions.

'Robert!' I said, 'What brings you here?'

'Pity,' he said.

'Pity?'

Brancetor often spoke tersely, but you always got there in the end for he was not a man of mystery.

'With news more worthy of compassion than anything else,' he said.

This was true. The Lady of Sarum was dead.

The news came in the usual form, a copy of an ambassador's letter sent from London:

> I must now report the strange and lamentable execution of the Countess of Salisbury who was beheaded yesterday at seven in the morning. When she was told that she was about to die, she could not believe it; she knew of no crime of which she was accused, nor how a sentence had been passed. But at last, seeing there was no remedy, she went out of the dungeon where she had been held for so long and walked to the middle of the space where there was no scaffold, nothing but a small block.
>
> She commended her soul to her creator and prayed for the King and Queen and the Princess and the Prince. The ordinary executioner was absent. In his place a wretched and blundering youth was given the job, who hacked her head and shoulders to pieces in a most pitiable fashion.

There was nothing to say. We all gazed at one another, Brancetor and I and the servants. *Il Signor* had been given the news, they told me, and had taken it very calmly. He had retired to the oratory by his chamber and when he came out after half an hour or so his face was devoid of grief. And so, strangely, were the faces around me in the kitchen.

To someone waiting in his room – I think it was his secretary, Beccatelli – Pole said that a far greater honour than noble birth had come to him: he could now say he was the son of a martyr. But he also said that he must understand it that way, being otherwise beyond all human consolation.

For our part, in the kitchen below, we had no words. For years we had stood like this, in rooms in different houses and countries, and looked at one another in amazement at the latest deed of the King. We had become used to it: it was the part given us to play. But then there always followed some emotion – anger or sorrow – and speculation as to his next move. This time it was different. The murder of a woman closely allied to him by blood, aged and growing feeble, renowned for her virtue, not only innocent but without any charge against her, ended all thought of Henry as a man living among fellow men. From him there was now nothing to expect or hope for.

I went away and set my hawk down in her cage, spreading out her tawny wing through my fingers, and then went to see my master.

3

'HEAVEN IS HIGH, THE earth is deep, but a king's heart is unsearchable', which I'm sure is true, and I only wish I knew who said it, in order to commend him to you. And yet even unsearchable hearts have their reasons. Kings look at the clock and the calendar like everyone else and then make their calculations. In this case, we would never understand why the Lady of Sarum had been killed just then and not earlier and not later. I have always been puzzled, for instance, by the tailor's bill. Over the next few days, Brancetor and I talked this over several times, out on the roof of the house or walking over the fields. He gave me one explanation for the old lady's death, and here it is, for what it is worth.

You will remember that after we left Provence, Brancetor went to Paris to deliver Pole's long letter to the Emperor. His arrival there was immediately noticed. Wyatt, who had reappeared as ambassador to the Emperor's court and was then in Paris, sent a message commanding him to come to his house. This Brancetor ignored.

Wyatt then went to the French authorities to complain that a sort of beggarly renegade was in town, an English traitor, a man of low degree, a merchant's clerk who had once robbed his master. He demanded that he be handed over in accordance with the treaties. The French saw no reason to refuse. Orders were given to the provost to make the arrest.

This was on the seventh day of Christmas. That night, as evening fell, Brancetor came back to his lodgings and had just lit a candle and blown the fire aflame in the hearth when the door burst open and an unknown figure rushed into the room, fell over a stool and then, with a groan, called out from the floor.

'Since you would not visit me, I have come to visit you.'

Naturally Brancetor at first assumed this was a demon from hell, but then he recognised the English ambassador. Instantly he threw some papers he was reading onto the fire. Wyatt, although half dead with pain – he had hurt himself badly falling over the stool – scrambled across the floor and snatched the papers out of the flames, singeing his fingertips as he did so.

The two men then began to grapple and dance madly to and fro, snatching the document from each other's hands.

Meanwhile several other men came into the room, one of whom cried out: 'Gentlemen, gentlemen, be good to each other, I beg you!'

This was the French provost who had been sent to assist in the arrest. The two Englishmen both turned on him and began to shout.

'Here is the traitor – pinion his arms,' cried Wyatt.

'I am a servant of the Emperor, and in his train,' shouted Brancetor. 'He will defend my right.'

And taking more papers from a cerecloth he kept in his bosom, he thrust them into the provost's hands.

'Those are the property of the King of England,' said Wyatt, snatching them from the provost.

'Remember the honour of the Emperor, a guest in your city,' said Brancetor.

Astounded at the onset of these great personages in the quarrel, the provost stood gaping. Then he separated the two men, put Brancetor under guard, and taking all the papers with him, went to the chancellor for advice.

Wyatt and Brancetor remained there, puffing and glaring at each other like game-cocks. But the provost was away for a long time and after a while they began to talk.

'Come back to your King,' said Wyatt. 'He is altogether loving and merciful. He will forgive you.'

'He cannot forgive me as I have done him no wrong.'

'You have helped his enemy, and thus became one yourself. And yet your offences are not too great to pardon.'

'This king pardons people, then hangs them in chains. I believe I will stick to the Emperor.'

'You will not be pardoned for that. Remember, the King has a long arm.'

'In Toledo you once said to me: "Kings have long arms, but God has longer." '

'The King's arm, and God's,' said Wyatt, 'are joined together – what length does that make?'

'It is an ill figure – a horrid figure – for a poet,' said Brancetor.

Wyatt, who was known to write verses, frowned and then they both fell silent, gazing at the floor. After some time the provost returned and, with many apologies, told Wyatt that he could not have Brancetor or the papers, and told Brancetor that he must lose his liberty for the meantime. He and his documents were to be held by the French, pending further enquiries.

The next morning Wyatt hurried to see the imperial prime minister, Granvelle, and demanded an audience with the Emperor. But it was not until Twelfth Night that Wyatt was admitted to the imperial presence. He knew the Emperor well and did not beat about the bush.

'A rebel of my King seems to hang about your court,' he said, 'a low man, much disliked by your ministers.'

'Who is this nasty person?' asked the Emperor.

'His name is Brancetor.'

'Ah,' quoth the Emperor, 'Robert.'

'The same.'

'I shall tell you, Monsieur l'Ambassadeur,' said the Emperor, 'it is he who was in Persia.'

'So he says.'

'No, Monsieur l'Ambassadeur, it is true. I know it by good tokens. I sent a knight of Rhodes with a message to the King of the Persians, and on the way, on Mt Sinai, he fell ill, and Robert, knowing the great love that exists between your king and myself, looked after him, and when the knight, whose name was Balbi, saw that he was going to die he opened his heart to Robert and told him what a great service he would do to me and to all Christendom if he would undertake the mission. And so Robert went to Persia in his place, and it is certain that he did so, for the Sophy soon after invaded the Turkish dominions, and afterwards Robert came home by the new route, by the sailing of the Portingales from the gates of Hormuz, and brought me sure tokens given him by M. Balbi.

'Now this,' the Emperor went on, 'was no small service he did. And I have had him follow me for years in all my voyages in Africa, in Provence, in Italy. And in all that time, I do not see how he can have offended the King of England, unless it be by going with Cardinal Pole, who asked for him because he spoke the language in Spain.'

'He's a rebel and that's all there is to it,' said Wyatt. 'To ask more is to sickle-scythe another man's corn. His long absence from England and his service to your Majesty do not excuse treason. He has been condemned by parliament.'

'Well, we shall look into it,' said the Emperor. 'And yet I hear that you have already tried to seize him here in Paris, at which I marvel, for you knew he was a follower of my court. I promise you, Monsieur l'Ambassadeur, that was evilly done. In fact, I am not disposed to give him up, on that account alone.'

'It is not you who has to give him up, but the King of France,' said Wyatt. 'We ask nothing of you.'

'What?' cried the Emperor. 'You would have me stand aside and allow such discourtesy to a man who follows me and whom I have not yet rewarded? I assure you that if I go to the Levant, I may want to take him with me. No, Monsieur l'Ambassadeur, I tell you now plainly: I will speak for his freedom, both to the King of France and to the Constable, and I trust they will not do me such dishonour as to allow one of mine to suffer damage. Let me be frank: even if your master had me in his Tower, I would not change my honour and conscience. I will stop at nothing to set Robert at liberty.'

'Have you no gratitude?' said Wyatt.

'Stop!' said the Emperor, flying into a fury. 'Whom do you charge with ingratitude?'

'Both your Majesties, I fear,' said Wyatt, 'your own and that of France.'

'Impossible!' said the Emperor. 'No doubt the king of France can answer for himself, but as for ourselves, we owe your master nothing. In any case, the term "ingratitude" cannot be used of a superior by an inferior.'

'That is absurd,' said Wyatt. 'A greater may be ungrateful to a lesser.'

'I think I know the meaning of the word,' said the Emperor coldly. 'I cannot believe your master, the King of England, would use it here.'

'It is exactly what he would use,' said Wyatt. 'He is of that opinion at this very moment.'

'I am not convinced that all your master's opinions are good ones.'

'They are all wonderfully good,' said Wyatt, 'and most profitable to himself and his State.'

'*Your* opinion on that is perhaps not the best,' retorted the Emperor. 'Do you really think it reasonable for me to deliver up Brancetor to the hangman, without knowing why?'

'Do you call my master a hangman?' said Wyatt, going pale.

'Well,' said the Emperor, 'I am not so ill bred as not to know that princes are not spoken of in such a way. Yet I do know that the *process* against Brancetor is complete, the sentence has been decided, and nothing remains but to chop off his head. Perhaps I do not say "hangman" – but how can I avoid the term "cruel prince"?'

At that, Wyatt stared and then put his finger to his forehead and tapped it, indicating that the Emperor was fantastical. Upon which he was dismissed and, hobbling from the room, he well-nigh fell in a heap outside the door, for the Emperor had never invited him to sit down, in spite of his injury.

The next morning Brancetor was set free and returned to his lodgings. Soon the news of Wyatt's audacity – tapping his forehead in front of the Emperor – was all over Paris, spread by the Emperor himself who was amazed, as he had never seen this gesture before, or at least not directed at himself.

Now the English envoys turned their attention to the French. The ambassador to the court of France, Bishop Bonner, hurried through the woods to see the King in the castle at La Fère to complain that Brancetor had been released.

'It is infamous, unjust, and contrary to the treaties,' he told the King. 'In this you act against reason, against God and against your duty.'

At that, Francis started up from his seat, going white with rage, and ordered Bonner to leave his sight.

Later that day, when the King went hunting with the Queen and her ladies, and again when he came back again at night, he refused even to look up at Bonner's window or acknowledge his many eager salutes.

'You would think he might look more cheerful in public,' Bonner reported to London. 'He was wearing a crimson cloak but was deathly pale – whatever can be troubling him?'

Now this whole affair had profound effects. Henry was enraged. He had been called 'cruel prince'. Two of his ambassadors had been repelled, one of them, Bonner, sent home in disgrace. Henry's attempts to drive a wedge between France and the Emperor had failed. He had not a single friend on the stage except certain German princes and dukes. And just at that time he found himself married to the sister of one them, an innocent maid whom, unfortunately, he could not bear to embrace. This was blamed on Cromwell. Shortly afterwards, Cromwell lost his life.

The story did not end there. It seems that the French, who had eagerly read Brancetor's papers, informed Henry that among them was a letter from one of his ambassadors, Richard Pate. Pate had a reputation as one of Henry's most loyal servants, and was most vehement against the Pope. But Henry's suspicions were easily roused and Pate was ordered home.

On the way, he stopped at Cologne to go and see the cathedral, and there, waking in the middle of the night and taking his coffer and one manservant, he stole away from his entourage and fled to Rome to join Pole.

At this point the French, charmed with their success, may have played a further game with the King and told him that Pate was not alone – his other envoys were suspect as well. In any case, all English diplomats abroad were ordered home and thrust into prison. Wyatt himself was marched into the Tower, his wrists pinioned, surrounded by twenty-four archers. Everyone accused everyone else of secretly supporting Pole.

'Never have I seen these people so crestfallen,' wrote the French ambassador happily. 'They do not know whom to trust, and the King, having offended so many people, mistrusts everyone . . . And in his irresolution and despondency, he goes on dipping his hands in blood wherever he conceives the least suspicion.'

That winter, out of sympathy for the trials of his brother-sovereign, the King of France sent Henry six great venison pasties. Henry was delighted and sent a message to say he had tasted them all and found them all marvellously good.

'We rejoice that you liked our pasties,' replied Francis, 'especially since we and our sister, Queen of Navarre, were present at the seasoning and tasting thereof.'

At the French court, many jokes were then heard: 'Poor man – he lost his *Pate*, so we sent him six *pâtés* of ours. One could do no less.'

That above all was something Henry could never bear: the sound of laughter from across the Channel.

He realised he had been outsmarted. He had been made a fool of. He had arrested his own diplomatic corps. His equals, the Emperor and the King of France, held him in low esteem. It was then, said Brancetor, that Henry's mind turned to Pole. Pole was the source of his mortifications. It was Pole whom Brancetor preferred. It was to Pole that Pate fled. And at the same time, all that winter and early spring, the King was in agony with his ulcerated leg. Even that affliction seemed to be connected to Pole. The ulcer had opened at the same time that Pole, his own flesh and blood, first came towards his kingdom with the title of Roman legate. There was even a joke about that. 'An ulcer ate his leg, but a legate his soul.'

Now the King, brooding over his setbacks, wanted vengeance. Pole was far away in Italy and all plans to kill him had so far failed. There remained one sure way to punish him.

And so, said Brancetor, the King had the Lady of Sarum led from her cell and across the grass, where a youth was waiting with an axe.

This was Brancetor's view of that event, and he put himself in the centre of the story, as people will, yet there may be something in it.

As to Pole's nephew, Montagu's son, a child who had shared his grandmother's dungeon and who from time to time had been allowed out to run around the castle, he now disappeared from view. On the same day that she died he was taken to another cell – much worse, it seemed, than the first one.

This was not intended to be kept a secret.

'He is but poorly and strictly kept, and not desired to know anything,' one of the ambassadors reported from London. In other words, it seemed that he was put into solitary confinement, and left there cold and hungry and in the dark. But no one ever knew, for he was never seen or heard of again.

4

WHEN POLE'S FAMILY WAS first arrested, the Pope refused to grant him an audience, saying he could not look him in the face. This time he did not turn away. On the news of the death of his mother, Pole was summoned to Rome, and there he was appointed governor in Viterbo.

This was the capital of the Patrimony, the oldest and most beautiful of the papal dominions, the land of ancient Etruria, bounded to the north by Umbria, by Tuscany to the west, by the Tiber to the east, and to the south by the rolling waves of the Tyrrhenian Sea.

In effect, Pole became the ruler of his own princely state. And the fact, which may sound heartless, is this: then began a period of happiness for many of us in Pole's household. When all is said and done, the world is a very strange place: the cruel murder of an old lady in one country opened a door into a kind of delightful and princely garden for about twenty people far away in another.

I do not include Pole among them. His mother's imprisonment and murder, as a result of his own actions, at the very time of life when most men are planning to take care of their parents in their old age, had a profound effect on him. But by 'profound' I also mean well-hidden. The subject was hardly ever mentioned. But I knew him well and I saw a change in him – beneath concealed grief there was now a certain motionlessness to him, an immobility of soul, as if some part of his inner being stood rooted to the spot in horror, and he would never move free of care through the world again.

Yet for me, I have to confess – the first year or two at Viterbo was the best time of my life up until that point. I was still at an age when sorrow can't get a good grip on you. My duties, as chief body-guard, were less alarming than before. Without doubt he was safer there in the hills, with his own government, small as it was, than in Rome where the world's currents surged in and out every week. And his high office distracted him, I suppose, from his grief. There was some irony in this: Pole had never sought the magistracy of state.

'I have never wanted that office,' he used to say. 'I never wanted – as so many do – to tell one man to go here and another one there and a third to stand on the spot and await further orders.'

The world being what it is, this is what he got. And for several years we lived in Viterbo and he governed there, carrying out the office perfectly well. It seems there is much less to the business than our rulers like us to think: their demands for grandeur and splendid rewards would have to be reduced if it was known that all that is required is the application of some reason, moderate foresight and a mild interpretation of the laws. But perhaps I'm wrong: perhaps Viterbo was a special case. Only fifty years earlier the city had been infamous for bloody feuds. Then one day a group of youths dressed in white began going around the town saying: '*Pace, pace, si con noi*': 'Peace, peace be upon us. The Madonna commands it.'

The streets fell silent. People put down their weapons to consider the idea. The Governor and the Bishop came out of their fortresses to give their approval. And '*pace, pace*' has reverberated in the air ever since above Viterbo. There was hardly any crime to speak of in our years in the governorate. It's true there was a cat-burglar who plagued us for a while but, one night, seeing the local policeman approach, he jumped back *into* the palace and was collared by Priuli, whereupon he burst into tears and then confessed all. Now this was a clear miracle since the officer in question was, as usual, at home and fast asleep in bed at the time. In short, a phantasm had been sent to aid us.

Only the shepherds outside the walls never rid themselves of the habit of sliding a dagger between one another's ribs, but they lived widely scattered and did not meet every day. In general, the administration of justice in Viterbo was completed by noon or, at the most, by two in the afternoon. After that, the members of the household devoted their time to conversation, books, painting, riding out and so on. The Marchioness came to live nearby, and as Viterbo was just over the horizon from Rome, beyond Mt Soracte, which in winter could be seen shining with snow from certain high windows in the city, many visitors came out: Carnesecchi, Piombo, Michelangelo, Farnese, the secretary of state ('not a mouse stirs in Europe or Asia but Farnese hears it'), Bembo, Gianotti, Lily and Pate.

It was there that Marc'Antonio Flamminio and I became close friends. By then he was about forty-five, an old man in my eyes, with a tawny beard, but there still seemed to be a cheerful boy behind that mask of age, still looking for adventures. He used to come out hunting with me early in the mornings – hunting was banned in the Patrimony but who would enforce such a law? – and we would slip out of the gates before the sun came up, Flamminio the strangest hunter you ever saw, stalking along through the vines wearing a Turkoman's padded jacket embroidered with roses or a conical hat that he had picked up on the wharves in Venice. In his youth he had been famous for his amorous verses, on the 'sweet thefts of love in the woods' or a certain flute which his girlfriend liked to fondle. Now he had become ambitious for salvation and was busy translating the Psalms. Even so, on cold winter mornings, when he saw the hillside turning russet from the summit down, or glimpsed two hares dancing on frosty ground at the end of the vines, he would stand and gaze, and declaim a verse or two addressing some nymph or dryad or sylph or Nature herself.

'Who is this *Nature* of yours?' I would say. 'She seems a cold-hearted minx to me – at least she has very cold fingers. You'd be better off back in bed with a nice, warm, real girl – that's my opinion.'

'Ah yes, but you are a rude barbarian from beyond the Alps, which God put up as a fence for our beloved Italy, and which he paints with snow every year as a sign to keep you out. And yet here you all are. Whatever are we to do with you?'

I never got used to his quips and sallies and strange fancies, which were what I liked most about him. He always had in his pocket, for instance, a little ball, a *balla de mondo*, with the lands and seas of the world painted on it.

'What *is* that?' I asked him one day.

'This? Why, I have carried this ever since the Spaniards, having sailed away in one direction, one day came back in the other, thus proving the world was a sphere. Of course we knew that already, but theory and fact are very different things. Did you not observe at the time that the world then seemed to float more lightly and that the forests and mountains to echo more than before?'

'No,' I said. 'I did not.'

'Good heavens, I noticed it distinctly,' he said. 'After all it is a splendid thing to live on a sphere aloft among stars, *thus*' – and he tossed the ball into the air and caught it again. Then he looked at it and said: 'Is that really you, O little ball, divided by fire and sword among so many nations?'

And then, with an earnest expression, he said to me: 'Yet think how large and fair she would be if love reigned among us.'

In summer, Marco and I used to climb into the hills, high above the shepherds' grassy kingdoms, and fish for trout in the pools below waterfalls. When they leapt through the air – the trout, I mean – he called them 'low meteors'; and on the way back down we would stop and drink a little wine and eat ewes' milk cheese with the murderous shepherds. You see what a delightful life it was.

Of course the idyll could not last. After a year or two, people began to drift away from Pole's court and the shadows crept towards us. Two great friends of Pole and the marchioness fled to join Calvin in Geneva and then went on to England. Their flight created a great stir. By then the peace conference between Catholics and Protestants had failed and the schism was worse than ever. The office of the inquisition was then set up in Rome. This was done by the ever-zealous Carafa who persuaded the Pope of its necessity. There could be no more conferences with Protestants, he said, no more compromises. Germany was lost. In Italy, heresies must be detected and rooted out. He was so eager to begin the process that he paid to fit out his own house as a court for the hearings.

At this news, a cold breeze and shadow went through the air in Viterbo.

'The inquisition was invented by Satan to destroy the Church,' said Pole. And Flamminio recited some verses he had once written:

When harsh zealots light the fires
And poor Hieronymo writhes in pain,
'Cruel men, desist,' Religion cries,
'Tis not error, but I who am slain.'

At the same time, the fact that Pole now ruled in his own princely state seemed to infuriate the King of England more than ever. Henry sent more assassins, at first in ones or twos. For a while they failed to disturb our little paradise. An angel with a sword must have been guarding the gate. Later, the King's plan of action against Pole became much more ambitious. But that was still some time off.

5

SOME PEOPLE PLAY MANY different roles in their lives, like actors who take on new parts with zest, while others play only one or two and refuse to extend their range. I myself have had only a modest number – student, courier, prisoner, bodyguard – but in Viterbo one came along which I had never expected and did not relish: that of gaoler.

This was assigned to me when the first of our assassins were caught. It was my task to convey them to Rome for investigation.

Marc'Antonio came along for the ride only, he said, to see such a sight: the greatest ruffian in the world playing the part of a *screw*.

I told him to be quiet. I was upset as it was. I felt most uncomfortable mustering my prisoners with their hands tied behind their backs and their legs tied under the mules' bellies, and leading them out of the castle and through the streets and out into the countryside where the sun was shining and the birds were singing sweetly. But what was I to do? In my charge was a Bolognese villain named Alessandro with a buff jerkin and a black beard growing the length of two fingers beneath his chin, and with him two English youths who had come to Viterbo disguised as his Flemish servants. They were terrible assassins – their boots were English, they spoke not a word of the Flemish language, they scarcely knew what country they were in.

That was always Henry's downfall when it came to killing Pole – he just would not spend the money. He would only promise vast sums when the job was done. This, however, was soon to change.

In the present case Pole himself questioned the youths and announced that he was going to let them go, that he found no harm in them, they were more dupes than anything else.

At that, there was an outcry from his secretaries and chancellor. Leniency was one thing, licence to murder another. A most evil enterprise had been discovered – a plan to slay a high officer of state, the Governor of Viterbo. What the Governor himself thought was neither here nor there. At this Pole gave in, and sent them to be examined again by the Governor of Rome. So we set off – four archers, three prisoners, Marc'Antonio and I.

Flamminio was interested as well in the expression on the English faces. It was one, he said, that was new to him. They hardly seemed to acknowledge or to care about the straits they were in. 'At most, they look slightly discontented, like a man who opens his breakfast egg and finds it's off.'

I told him that he did not know how to read English faces. I could tell, from a certain pink colouration on these ones, that dismay and alarm were working away within. To cheer up the prisoners as we rode along, I told them that, whatever happened, they weren't going to die. Pole had to send them to Rome for further investigation, but he alone would decide their punishment. As Governor of Viterbo, where the crime was to take place, this was his right.

After this, the treacherous pink – no Englishman likes to admit his fear – subsided from their cheeks. They became quite cheerful and on the way down to Rome we began to talk as if we had all just met on the road to market. One of them, who was from Maidenhead, told me news about Bisham, which was the ancient seat of Pole's family. After the murder of Montagu and his mother, it seemed that the King had taken Bisham for himself and used it as a pleasure-house where he dallied and feasted with various women. Astounding quantities of eggs and cream were ordered in. They were supplied locally. This fact remained prominent in the young man's mind.

'I know some of the farmers. Why, I've even been to the farms,' he said carelessly, as if personally acquainted with the cows and ducks that had been pressed into royal service. Even tied on the back of a mule on his way to prison, you see, a man does not lose sight of his distinction. This information, about Bisham, I decided not to tell Pole.

By then I had become protective not only of his body but of his morale. Yet I found it of great interest myself, and we rode down to Rome talking about farm prices, the horse-market in England and so forth, and when the time came to deliver my prisoners into the city gaol, I was sorry to lose them. In fact I felt rather despondent. Those ordinary voices from home had struck me deeply. I saw more clearly than usual my own situation. While those two might one day soon be on their way back to England, I remained in exile, and would perhaps never see my home again. It was one of the times when I disobeyed the Marchioness's instruction not to let my mind dwell on my Judith. I could not help myself. She kept appearing and disappearing among my thoughts, and each time my heart was struck, as with the hammer in the forge, causing a new pain. On that visit to Rome I was very unhappy.

We did not go back to Viterbo at once. Pole had told me to stay until the investigation was over and then report back to him. Thus Flamminio and I had a week in the city together, and it was then that I first saw the fresco of the *Last Judgement* which had been finished about a year before and which the whole world had flocked to see and talked of endlessly, to the exclusion of all other matters.

We went to the sacred palace early one morning, Marc'Antonio and I, along with Pate, the ambassador who had run away from the King and who was then resident in Rome. At that hour the palace was nearly empty. It was one of those dark summer mornings that seem to ignore their proper season. I felt a certain gloom as we went through the halls. This, I'm afraid, is in my character: whenever I approach some famous scene or person I expect to be disappointed. In this case I was sure I would appreciate the painting less than people of true discernment, like Flamminio and Pate, for example, who were hurrying forward eagerly as if to a sumptuous breakfast.

What did I, Michael, in my exile, care about a fresco?

In any case, I thought, I am always more pleased with things which are not famous, and which speak to you, as it were, in private. That was my state of mind as we reached the antechamber of the chapel. Then I saw ahead of me a high, dark cave like the one I once visited France, but, even in the poor light of that dark morning, I could see was faintly inscribed with the figures of men and gods, and at that moment it seemed to me I was at the threshold of a grand cavern made not by men but by an angel. Marc'Antonio led us in and we marched boldly to the end of the chapel. There my heart sank again. It was just as I feared. Before us on the wall rose a vast blue field, a swirl of bodies, naked and clothed. In short, I could not make head or tail of it.

Flamminio had no such problem. He stood before the painting as confident as a captain inspecting his troopers.

'Lord, what fools these Romans are,' he said. 'I must have heard reams of nonsense about this painting of Judgement Day already. The "harsh and terrible Christ", "his face like thunder", "all nature in terror" and so on. But look at him – he is merely lifting his right hand. It is "he who holds the winnowing fan". Do you see?'

'No,' I said, 'I don't see.'

'Well, then, I will show you,' said Flamminio, and, like one of the pilots who lead ships through the shoals of the lagoon at Venice, he proceeded to show me the way through the blue field, pointing out how on the left all mankind – the dead sitting up and brushing the earth from their eyes – began to rise together into the sky, and then, on the right, some remained above, and others blew away to the horizon and tumbled into the fire.

'It is the great winnowing of mankind,' said Flamminio. 'And here the wind is light – the light, that is, of self-knowledge. The wheat and the chaff know their own weight. Some of the damned whom you can see falling there will perhaps try and fight their way back up, but how can they get past those fierce angels, or that row of martyrs, holding out the instruments of their torture?'

Flamminio then fell silent and with his feet crossed and his thumbnail pressed against his lip he stood looking at the fresco for a long time. Then he spoke again.

'Ah, I have it,' he said. 'M. Angelo is rightly called *il Terribile*, but he is not above following the inspiration of others. I see he has listened carefully to our friend, your master, Pole.'

He pointed out three martyrs – Catherine with the wheel on which her body was broken, Blaise holding the iron hackles that tore off his flesh, Sebastian holding out the arrows that killed him . . .

'Do you see it?' he asked. 'Can you read what these figures say?'

I should tell you that Flamminio had a great fondness for puzzles, anagrams, cryptic mottoes and so on; and now he began to jot down various signs and ciphers on a tablet he had with him and then held it out to show us:

ζωή

'But what is it?' I said.

'An alphabet that only Master Michelangelo would have dared to form, from the bodies of men and women tortured to death. Catherine is ζ, Blaise ω, and Sebastian, down on one knee, looks to me like ή.'

'But what does it mean?' I asked.

'Why, it is a pun,' said Flamminio. "They are indeed the living letters of which Pole speaks. Along with the instruments of their death, their bodies form a word in Greek.'

'What word?' I said.

'They are martyrs,' said Flamminio, 'and they are letters, and the word the letters spell is – “living”. Their tormenters and murderers now shrink at the sight of them. How can they argue against such evidence? While their victims stood for life, they themselves, the tyrants, the cruel, the unjust, they made a league with death. Do you see them now, falling down below, lost for ever?’

We stood gazing at the figures of the damned, who were crowding the banks of the river which flows into the underworld.

‘When the Holy Father came in and saw these folk for the first time,’ Flamminio said, ‘why, he fell on his knees in terror and begged forgiveness for his sins. Yet he is not actually represented among them – unlike poor M. Biagio, whom you can see over there . . .’

Then Flamminio pointed to a devil standing in the midst of the condemned, who had exactly the features of a certain high official in the Vatican, namely the master of ceremonies in the palace, M. Biagio, who before the fresco was finished had gone about defaming it, saying it was full of shameful nudity and while it might be suitable for the walls of public baths it had no place in a Christian temple.

‘You see how Biagio has been punished?’ said Flamminio. ‘Michelangelo has put him there at the very entrance to hell, stark naked as you see, with a snake biting his sexual organ. A reasonable reward, I suppose, for seeing evil where there is none . . . After all, truth and nakedness have a long relationship. Now M. Biagio will have to spend many centuries here on the wall with that very painful snake attached.’

By this time everyone knew this story, and the conclusion to it – how M. Biagio had gone to the Pope and complained even more bitterly about this figure, his own portrait, than any of the others.

‘Alas, I can do nothing for you,’ His Holiness replied. ‘I have some authority here on earth, and in heaven, but none whatever in hell.’

‘And who else do we see down there on the banks of the river?’ Flamminio went on. ‘Zealots, misers, wicked popes and robbers of the poor . . . That demon with the boot-hook, he looks familiar. Surely that is Machiavelli? I recognise him from the cold little smile and the heavy temples. But who is the younger man he is pulling towards him with a boat hook – though there is really no need, as he is already stepping lightly down into the sea of death? And there, behind him . . . who is *that*? What a figure he makes! Like a great bird, his arms outstretched, but unable to fly upward. He comes forward blindly, knowing there is no hope. Yet he retains his dignity, he is every inch a king.'

By his look I saw plainly that Flamminio was suggesting this was an image of the King of England.

'Our King looks nothing like that,' I said. (Even in exile we did not like Italians to be too forward in interpreting our troubles.)

'Perhaps not,' said Flamminio. 'The painter of this fresco never saw your King. For that very reason, he sees his soul more clearly than those who are paid to make his portrait.'

6

THREE DAYS LATER I went back to Viterbo to tell Pole that things were looking very black for our three assassins. The authorities in Rome had examined them diligently and found no mitigating circumstances. The Italian, Alessandro, admitted he was in the service of the King of England. For several years he had been in his pay as *cavalariccio* – a courier. As to why he had gone to Viterbo, he would say nothing. The Englishmen had nothing to say on any subject, except that they were his servants. The authorities then made their judgement. These miscreants had entered papal territory with the fixed intention to murder one of its leading officers, an ambition tantamount to the violation of the security and honour of the Holy See, of which they – the authorities – took the most jealous care, and that therefore it was impossible for them to be pardoned. Even taking into account the Cardinal of England's admirable and beautiful inclination towards mercy, it would be necessary for the three to lose their lives. Or at least to spend the rest of them in the galleys.

When I returned to Viterbo with this message, Pole, in turn, became more jealous of his office than I had seen before.

'How dare these people encroach on my right?' he cried. 'Am I or am I not Governor of this State? I will decide the sentence in this case. They are *my* killers, after all.'

He got his way, and the three were sent to row in the papal galleys for a month and a day.

When the term was up, Pole sent me down to the port of Civitavecchia to make sure the prisoners were set free. It seemed the master of galleys was often strangely negligent in this regard. I presented myself at the port and had the irons struck off three sets of ankles and led my men ashore.

Alessandro made off like a scalded cat, unable to believe his luck. The English pair stood there looking uncertain.

'Well, there you are,' I said. 'You are free. You can go.'

They nodded solemnly.

'Where?' said one, after taking thought.

'Where what?' said I.

'Where, sir, do you think should we go?'

'Why, you can go home to England,' I cried.

They looked at each other and nodded again, but they stood there still. I saw the problem. The fact was they had no idea where they were or where England was or how to find it, they had no money, and in short neither of them knew in what direction to take the very next step. As well as that, they were rather pallid and lean after the galley diet, and covered with sores.

On the other hand, they had good boots, they were young, and they had escaped a terrifying fate. They should have been in high spirits. I, for example, could not march off happily towards England that morning. There was a limit to my sympathy, but I had a little in stock. I took them to one of the nearby tables, fed them red fish soup, gave them some money to start the journey and wrote down the names of all the towns they must go through on the way to Calais. And so they set forth, to walk home, to England. Which is a very long way. But it was a fine, still autumn day, they were free, and justice had not been impugned.

And that was the end of the policy of mercy towards assassins sent by Henry. The dangers were to become much more serious. But it was not for about eighteen months that anyone began to grasp the scale of the operation by which the King planned to rid himself once and for all of his hated cousin, the only one of his subjects who had dared to stand up to him and who was still alive to tell the tale.

In the meantime we continued our peaceful life in Viterbo, sometimes, in foul weather, never setting foot out of the fortress for days on end. Flamminio for a while devoted himself to my renewed education, and a very harsh taskmaster he was, piling my table with books, and then coming back to question me on their meaning. When I complained, he replied that I myself was a far more cruel taskmaster, especially in summer time, making him rush up hills and fall over cliffs in pursuit of me as I went in pursuit of fish and fowl.

On my table he piled great mountains of his own: Vitruvius on architecture, Vegetius on war, Aristotle on the soul, George of Trebizond against Plato, Bessarion against George of Trebizond, Aristobulus against the Jews, Luther against the Pope, Panornitamus and Chrysostom, the Hexaemeron of Basil and the Aphorisms of Hippocrates. Even the Bible he lent me was a new translation, and began at the end of the book, in the Jewish manner.

At times I rebelled and was not seen at my desk all day. Flamminio read me a lecture. 'What is a book but the flying word held captive?' he said. 'Books are full of the voices of the wise, and full of lessons of antiquity, full of moral and legal wisdom, full of religion. Books live, they speak directly to us, they show us things far remote from the times we are in, and, as it were, place them before our eyes as if they were present today. So great is the power of books, so great their dignity, their grandeur, that without them we should have almost no memory of the past, no examples to follow, no knowledge of human or divine affairs. Were it not for books, the tombs that consume men's bodies would bury their names in oblivion.'

So I went back to my studies. I was determined never again to be ashamed of my ignorance. All the same, habit is a strong force. I was always glad when business compelled me to ride off somewhere, north or south, always watching with a keen eye for danger, which, for us, had suddenly magnified.

When the King's new plans against Pole became plain, they were at first hard to credit. It was no longer a case of sending off a few spies or assassins in the hope of crossing Pole's path. Instead, Henry went about to establish a fortress in the heart of Italy, a base from which he might strike his enemies, make alliances, threaten the Pope and, in short, behave in Italy like the other great kings.

Luckily the whole operation from the beginning was managed from Venice, by our old friend Harvel – Siggy, as we used to call him – who was now the English ambassador there.

For a year or two after Pole wrote his detested book and sent it to London, Siggy had kept up a friendship with my master. But the time came when he had to decide whose side he was on. He was a practical man, a man of the world: he chose the King. Thus he had come to hate Pole *ex officio*, which is just as bad as the other kind. He was now put in charge of the plan to destroy him.

But again fortunately for us, Venice is, of all cities, a place of whispers, keyholes, listening walls. On a map, in fact, it resembles nothing so much as a great ear with its grand canal. Soon all the important facts of Harvel's operation were known to us. We had the names of all the captains he had hired, led by a bravo named Ludovico da l'Armi. I still remember the list. Even when I fell asleep those names seemed to rise before my eyes like the phalanxes of warriors who spring up where dragons' teeth are sown. The captains were divided into three companies. The first, under Ludovico da l'Armi, were: Ippolito Palavicino of Piacenza, Capt. Bartolomeo Moreni of Modena, Cavalier Lunardo of Ravenna, Capt. Gramegna of Bologna, Capt. Andrea of Forli, Capt. Ludovico de Monte of Verona, Capt. Borbino di Carpi of Ferrara, Capt. Giustiniano of Faenza.

The second, under Count Bernardo di San Bonifacio: Count Antonio Benilacqua of Verona, Capt. Battista Oliva of Mantua, Count Bonifatio Tresino of Vicenza, Capt. Lunardo Zanelleto of

Reggio, Count Orlando di San Bonifatio, Capt. Giulio Bottoni of Reggio, Capt. Pietro Maria Belloni of Reggio, and Capt. Bernadino Corso.

The third was led by Fillipo Pini of Lucca, commanding Capt. Ventura and Capt. Lorenzo Carli of Lucca, Capt. Ceccho Franzone of Pistoia, Capt. Bissabocto of Castello, Capt. Camillo Dazi of Urbino and Alessandro of Castelnuovo.

A first payment of a thousand pounds had been sent from London to Venice to be distributed among these men.

The Pope called in the Venetian ambassador.

'We see this villain da l'Armi near at hand,' he said. 'He is our rebel and on any account deserves a thousand deaths. We see that the King of England has no other enmity than ours in Italy and is plotting who knows what mischief. We know his agent in Venice supplies these fellows with vast sums of money. Angels, which are a kind of English coin, are circulating all over the place. Everything threatens mischief. It would be a great satisfaction to me if Venice would take precautions, at least by sending da l'Armi away. We have these evil conjectures about him, we take care to have him watched. There is the question of Cardinal Pole, whom these ruffians have been ordered to entrap. Venice should show us some goodwill. By tolerating such an outrage, out of respect for the King of England, it does not follow that he will give you anything good in return; he will only boast of his own industry.'

The Venetians, however, would do nothing. The lords of the council, the Signory, had no desire to annoy Henry. There were the shoe factories to consider; Italians have a sort of weakness in the head when it comes to shoes, and the best leather comes from England. The import trade must not be imperilled. These are the calculations men of the world must make.

'We think day and night only of new ways to please Your Holiness,' the Venetian ambassador said, 'yet we must also have some consideration for the serene King of England.'

If Pole had remained in Viterbo, I could have defended him even if all twenty-five captains, each with twenty men behind him, arrived at the gates. But the time came when Pole had to make a long journey from his capital. After many years of debate and confusion, finally the great Council of the Church was to be held, in the town of Trento – in my view, the very worst place in the world for such a gathering, a little town surrounded by mountains on the road to Germany, near the French border, impossible to defend. And even reaching Trent was problematic. I was forced to invent a new shift or stratagem to outwit the enemy. This, however, is the kind of problem I like. It was known that hundreds of men in Harvel's pay were watching the roads in north Italy. And everyone in Trent was at the same time waiting for Pole to arrive, as he had been given the honour of making the opening address to the council. This is what I devised. I first made public the date when he would leave Viterbo and by what route he would travel. But then, four days before that, the Cardinal of England suddenly and very openly left town and, with only two companions, raced across the country by a second route. He made sure that as many people as possible saw him coming – and going – at high speed. Church bells only just began to ring for the distinguished visitor but the sound was already fading in his ears. Thus the famous Pole reached Trent in record time and perfect safety.

But then, when da l'Armi's men were still in disarray and gazing after him, a second Cardinal Pole left Viterbo very quietly, with a good entourage, and took a third route entirely, and after several day-long marches, also arrived in Trent safely.

The second Pole was the real cardinal. The first was none other than a Mr Michael Throckmorton, gentleman, of London and Warwickshire. And I must say I thoroughly enjoyed this experience. The speed of travel, the pleasure of outwitting death (they would not have spared me if I had fallen into their hands), all of that I found most exhilarating. I was dressed in the usual travelling habit of a prince of the Church. I saw some pretty girls on the way and I suppose they were surprised when I blew them a kiss. I do not agree with Flamminio that books are alive – they are quite dead, and one should not spend too much of one's life exclusively in their company. Yet although dead, they make life itself more alive. My favourite reading that year had been on medical matters, the passage of blood through the body and so on, and I also read some authors on the care and management of horses. And as I raced across Italy I saw myself in quite a new light: a creature filled with blood riding on the back of another also filled with blood, as if the sunlight now made us a little transparent.

7

OUR TROUBLES WERE NOT over once we were in Trento. Where exactly was Ludovico da l'Armi? Every evening I would stand under the great firs in the garden of the palace and look up at the hillsides where a dozen campfires were beginning to twinkle. Who was up there? Mercenaries, renegade soldiers, tinkers, brigands, Lutheran bands, shepherds? I developed a dread of those little fires which appeared every night just as the stars came out and shone down evenly upon us all. Ludovico had already been seen once in Trent, in disguise, and then again galloping wildly through the town heading north. No one knew his whereabouts from hour to hour. Luckily, there was another circumstance greatly in our favour: Ludovico was a fool. No one had quite realised this before. Both his friends, like King Henry, who thought the world of him (he twice visited England during these years) and his enemies at the English Court (of whom there were many, on account of his handsome figure and the crimson cloak and cap he wore to make everyone stare at him) agreed that he had a very *vengeable wit* and was *disposed to work mysteries*. But as soon as he set to work with Harvel, his pride and insolence overwhelmed him. No one could describe the follies and outrages committed by Ludo and his men over the next two years. Even in Venice itself he could not restrain himself. One night the captain of boats, on patrol through the city, encountered Ludo and eight or ten of his bravos, including the cook, who was quite as mad as any of them.

It was a night of thick fog.

'Halt!' said the guard. 'Identify yourselves!'

'To arms!' cried Ludo, and then they all fought in the dark with their swords until Ludo's men ran away, leaving the pavement bloody.

Now this finally was too much for the lords of the Council, and a warrant was sworn for the arrest of Ludovico and his household.

A day later he was seen galloping through the main street of Trent, going north as if the demons of hell were after him. The Cardinal of Trent himself, who was an old schoolfriend of Ludo's and still loved him dearly, looked out of his window by chance and saw him go past.

In six weeks or so he was back in Italy with a letter from the King of England, asking the Venetian authorities to forgive his agent, who, he said, had acted only in self-defence. The Venetians complied.

'We must have consideration for the most serene King of England.'

Soon after that, da l'Armi was discovered to be fortifying Castel Goffreddo in the duchy of Mantua, in the middle of the Italian plain. With a base there, Henry would truly have arrived in our midst.

The King made a great effort to persuade the rulers of Mantua to agree to his presence. Ludovico undertook the negotiations:

> King Enrico of England [he wrote] desires the utmost welfare of the illustrious family of Gonzaga, and wishes me to visit and to offer you his favour, authority and all his forces. It should be remembered the power of the King of England is not inferior to that of any other king. His immense wealth is much greater than that of many princes, and the valour and dignity of his well-proportioned frame may vie with any other sovereign. In Italy he already has more than mediocre allies, through whom in future he will have much more power and opportunity for obliging his friends and injuring his enemies.

The other powers – Venice, Rome and France – argued the opposite case with the Gonzagas. The Regent of Mantua, Ercole Gonzaga, was a friend of Pole's but he was also a *statesman* which is a very different animal from a mere *man*. They think differently. They have a certain heartlessness: the weak must accept the decisions of the strong. The mouse must be sacrificed to the cat. If great and powerful Venice was swayed by Henry's wishes, how could little Mantua resist?

The question hung in the balance for a month. Then the Mantuans replied. The Duchess and her son, the Duke, who was still a minor, sent a letter to the King of England thanking him for his recollection of the devotion which the Gonzaga family had always borne towards him; and for his offers of alliance, which could not be more dear to them and which they accepted heartily with the intention of availing themselves of them in full accordance with opportunity.

> Unfortunately an ancient law has just been remembered, which forbids the recruiting of men or the building of bases on Mantuan soil by any foreign power.

Pole was so pleased at this that he sent a gift to the Regent – a drawing by Michelangelo, which had been commissioned by the Marchioness, who then gave it to Pole, and which showed the dead Christ lying across the knees of his mother, who raises her arms to heaven.

Above her on the vertical beam of the cross, Michelangelo had put the words: 'men little think how much blood it cost'.

I was sent to Mantua carrying this valuable and envied gift in a special leather quiver with a round cap. You have to realise at that time, just as they do today, every prince and king, not to mention mere dukes and cardinals, desired above all to own a work by Michelangelo, even a sketch, and they were almost always disappointed.

'Tell the Regent,' Pole said, 'that it is no loss to me; I can easily get another.'

The Regent was delighted. That was the first time I saw the city of Mantua with her strong walls and shining lake – 'the brilliant eye of Italy', Flamminio used to call it – and her handsome shuttered houses, which always remind me of a crowd of people closing their eyes against the rays of the sun.

This gift of Pole's had several consequences. The Regent gained a Michelangelo. Ludovico was sent packing and went back to Venice where he continued to cause uproar. And I discovered the city where I now live. But there was another result, sad, lamentable, which Pole had not foreseen. The Marchioness was cut to the quick on hearing he had given away the drawing. I may even say it was a mortal wound, for at the news she fell ill and never recovered. I was in Rome at the time – but why say that? It was I, unfortunately, who delivered the blow.

After leaving Mantua, I went on to Rome to open up a house for Pole, who intended to take up residence in the city again. After a day or two I sought out the Marchioness simply to pay my respects. I went first to her lodgings with the sisters at S. Caterina. There I was told she could be found at the Lateran palace where she had had some business. And there I saw her crossing the piazza, just a few minutes after I set myself in the shadow of the pillar to wait for her, as if we had made a rendezvous.

She had aged a little – two years had passed – but was still as pretty as ever, with her noble and placid air, kindly, well disposed, complacent. No matter how evilly some people might act, her blue eyes seemed to say, one should take no notice; the world was more richly determined by what *she* deemed right.

At the sight of me walking over the wide stones to accost her, her eyes shone. Then I realised what a mistake I had made.

'You have brought a letter from your master?' she said eagerly.

But I had not.

'A message?'

I had nothing. I had come empty-handed. For a moment I thought of at least attempting a standard salutation – 'His lordship sends you his most cordial greetings, etc.,' – but I could not find the formula and she knew it.

At that moment I was as uninteresting to her, I saw, as the stones we were standing on. She attempted to pass this off and began to talk gaily enough on various matters, but always returning to Pole – asking when he would return, where he was to live, and shaking her head over him, as he had failed to write to her for six months. I saw how hurt she was.

To cover my confusion I talked on, I described my trip to Mantua and the excellence of the Regent, Lord Ercole, and then I mentioned the drawing I had taken to him.

In my naivety, and ignorance of women, I expected she would be pleased with this fact, that her gift to Pole had played a noble part in the great rebuke to the enemy. She looked at me with a peculiar expression, I felt as if I had caught her staring at me through a keyhole.

'My drawing?' she said. 'The *pieta*?'

I nodded dismally, aware I had embarked on a second blunder.

'Oh,' she said, 'oh!' – and then, speaking to herself, she said, 'He gave it away!'

And she began to laugh, a strange, careless laugh, rather deep, quite unlike any I had ever heard uttered by that noble lady, Marchioness of Pescara, princess of the Colonna race. And then, as if remembering another engagement, she called her secretary, who was standing discreetly nearby, and she went away, telling me to call on her, but without any lustre in her voice.

A few weeks later, having fallen ill, she went to the lengths of sending a message to Pole to upbraid him for his cruelty, his hardness of heart, his pride, his vanity, his carelessness and so on and so forth.

This was not written down. She sent someone to sling these reproaches in his face, poor John Lily, one of the household who had remained in Viterbo with the Marchioness, when we had all gone north to Trent and who, during our absence, had fallen under her command.

I was at first not only surprised but amazed at the whole episode, but later I understood it better. For her, the *pieta* was more than a drawing. It had been a declaration of love. She loved Pole – he was still a handsome young man – but it was not a carnal love. The separate pinnacles they stood on, their different ages, hardly permitted thought of intercourse. But ingeniously, with her woman's heart, the Marchioness devised ways to be in his story. She even wished, I think, to suffer alongside him, to share his pain. That was what the drawing meant. It was not really a picture of Christ and the Madonna at all, but of the Cardinal of England and his *second mother.*

Pole, at a loss how to respond to the many proofs of her affection, gravely accepted the gift.

And then he carelessly gave it away.

I do not think she ever recovered from the blow. When Pole came back to Rome there was a reconciliation of some kind. I was not present, Flamminio was the chief negotiator, he bent all his thoughts to the matter, finding as ingenious a way out of the trouble as she had found into it. It was something to do with the new theology, in which he followed Luther – that just as God's love is too great to be repaid, payments should not be demanded between human lovers. Perhaps the Marchioness accepted this. In any event, their friendship was restored, although, like a piece of earthenware that has been broken and then repaired, it was perhaps less valuable than before. But it was her earthly frame that gave real cause for concern. The Marchioness's illness had struck deep. By Christmas no one expected her to live. All her friends were aghast. Pole, Flamminio, Michelangelo gathered at her sickbed.

I stayed at a distance. Strangely enough, although she forgave Pole for the hurt he had given her, she never forgave me for providing the information. That is one of the hazards of being the messenger. But I was rueful all the same, in fact I felt very hurt myself. I had not gone to the Lateran that day as a courier but as the humble friend, almost the son, of a great lady who had been kind to him, and who then, that day, looked at him as if he did not exist.

She died in the new year of 1547. Everyone was stricken with grief – the Marchioness of our hearts had gone! From a distance, I thought how strange it was as well. Her prayers had in fact been granted: she had entered Pole's story, and suffered greatly, as she wished. But it was not the King who tortured and then killed her, it was her own loving heart.

During all this time, the threat from the King had not gone away. Ludovico da l'Armi continued his outrages. Towards the end of the year, as the Marchioness lay dying, he surpassed himself and sent his men to murder a certain Venetian agent – or spy, or traitor – named Maffei, in the pine forest near Ravenna. Don't ask me to explain it – I doubt if anyone understood the whole story – but what was clear was this: Maffei was stabbed many times and all his secrets bled away into the earth under the pines. In this, Ludovico gravely affronted the state of Venice which considered itself the owner of those secrets. As usual, however, nothing was done.

'We must have some consideration for the serene King of England.'

Then one day in early spring in the year 1548 there came surprising news. Ludovico had been arrested, in Milan, and then, surrounded at first by forty, then a hundred, then one hundred and sixty men, all heavily armed, he was taken by road and ferry to Venice to be tried for many crimes.

I myself was in Forli at the time, looking for new horses for the household, when I first heard of his arrest and transportation and I had difficulty making sense of it. But the next day, while I was walking across a field with a gentleman who had just arrived from Padua, he mentioned the da l'Armi business, and then he uttered a sentence which explained everything, and also made me stop as if thunderstruck.

'In Venice, of course they have now reached an end of consideration for the serene King of England, as he is dead.'

8

THAT WAS HOW THE news reached me – Henry VIII was dead! For the first time in my life I was no longer his subject. I had never drawn a breath but he was my sovereign lord – although he sought my life for the last ten years of it – and now . . . he was gone.

And I was still here, in a green field, near Forli. I looked all around. I saw the water-trough half-mantled with green, the gateway mud was thronged with hoofprints, in the next field was a big bay stallion with his yard hanging down. All these things I saw very clearly as if the world itself, and not just a gentleman from Padua with tan boots, was the messenger: *Henry is dead.*

I did not feel joyful but rather sombre, like an orphan who now must face the world alone. The mares and foals were watching us uneasily as we came over the paddock towards them, and then suddenly I lost all interest in the business I had come for, I apologised to the others and left at once, taking the road for Rome.

Several times on the road the same fact kept striking me anew. *He's gone!* But even then if I wanted to stand in the stirrups and shout or wave my hat or embrace a passer-by, that other sombre self forbade it.

My thoughts led me straight to Coughton, though it was very strange – I had not permitted them to fly there for so many years, they seemed halting, as if unsure of the way. 'Why,' I thought, 'it's . . .

possible . . . that I will see Judith again. No. Surely not. Who knows what has happened to her? And yet . . . there must be someone there still. Perhaps I will see them all alive again, after all. Perhaps very soon. Yes! That's true! I may see Judith within a month. In a month, I might be standing in front of her and then take her by the hand.

'Impossible!' I thought a minute later. 'In any case, they will have forgotten me. Why do I feed on these fantasies? And yet I have not forgotten them. Perhaps someone there remembers me still.'

In short, I did not know what to think or to hope for.

Over the next few weeks everything remained uncertain. Edward, son of the third Queen, Jane, was now the King. But he was a child, ruled by his upstart uncles, and no one knew where they would lead him.

Then certain signs of change began to appear in the world. From a prison cell in Venice, Ludovico da l'Armi had been sending frantic messages to England for help.

The new government in England at length replied to the Signory: 'We have no knowledge of such a person.'

That was the end of poor Ludovico. I admit I felt some pity for him – the thought of any man on the road surrounded by one hundred and sixty others all bent on his death – that displeases me. But his fate was sealed. Sentence was passed: 'Ludovico da l'Armi shall be taken on Saturday next to a high scaffold between the two columns where his head is to be severed from his shoulders so that he dies.'

So it was there, between the two columns by the sea, in the heart of Venice, that the many years of English policy – to kill 'Traitor Pole' – came to an end.

A few months later it was announced in England that 'the enemies of the old King' were pardoned.

There were two exceptions: Pole, and his cousin Exeter's son, who was still in the Tower, remained under sentence of death for treason. There was no mention of the other child, Montagu's son.

I decided to go to England at once. Pole was enthusiastic. After Henry's death, he had written to the new boy King. Pole was his nearest kinsman on the royal side. But his letter had been returned unopened by the maternal uncles who ruled England.

Pole nevertheless decided to send another Englishman with me, one who could discuss the great questions of State and Church on his behalf. Dr Hilliard and I were on the very point of departure – my foot was in the stirrup – when Pole and others of the household came hurrying into the stable.

'The trip is off,' he said.

'Off?'

'It seems the Emperor Charles will be offended. I have just seen his ambassador. The Emperor does not wish anyone to handle these gentry' – he meant the government of England – 'except himself. Of course, he is very suspicious and grasping in all matters, but one must not exasperate Caesar.'

'Caesar may do as he pleases, including going to hell,' I said, and mounted my horse. Some of those present looked shocked at my words, but I thought them quite pious and reasonable in the circumstances. 'The King of England banished me for ten years,' I said, looking down at them all. 'I will not be kept out of my own country by some other prince, even for a day. It's not his realm. I'm not his subject.'

'Things are not so simple,' said Pole. 'You will be thought to represent me, and through me, the Pope, and therefore—'

'I don't care about that,' I said. 'As soon as I heard of this pardon, I told myself *I'm going home*! I may even get married there. I may take a wife, if she will still have me, and the Emperor has nothing to do with it.'

'Ah!' said Beccatelli, one of Pole's secretaries, 'you see: his decision is made for love. And off the cuff – *alla ventura*! No one can stop him, and why should they?'

'Exactly,' I said, and nodded to Beccatelli to show he was right.

He was usually right, Beccatelli, he was short and fat, and short of breath, and of sight as well, but he knew the heart. All the same, I then dismounted. It was clear what was going to happen: Hilliard would stay, and I would go. New arrangements were therefore needed. Two days later I departed alone, just as I used to long ago, setting off to ride from Italy to England. But this time I was carrying a message for no one but myself.

I did, however, promise to speak on Pole's behalf, and try and open communication between him and the rulers of England, if I could find the right ear to whisper in.

In the days before I left, I became known as the venturer.

'*Alla ventura!*' people said to me on the stairs.

'But you must also beware,' said Flamminio. 'The dangers created by your terrible King Enrico are not over. There is thunder and lightning to come. Why do you think so many people have gone off to the next world recently?'

There had in fact been a heavy harvest of late. It was not just King Henry and the Marchioness who had died – the King of France soon hurried after Henry, no doubt to continue their quarrels in the underworld. Bembo had gone, Contarini, Giberti, Sadoleto all departed, even Tom Wyatt had made off into eternity . . .

'I have no idea,' I said.

'Summonsed!' said Flamminio. 'To attend a trial in heaven. When a great tyrant is alive, everyone is punished. When he dies, many are subpoena'd. I have often noticed the phenomenon. There will be more deaths to come.'

I pretended to pay careful attention to this. But I was more concerned about Flamminio himself. He was looking very poorly. I thought then that he too might not be long for this world and I began to dread his absence.

When I reached Calais I stayed there for several days, watching the ships sail for England. This was a delicate manoeuvre I was engaged in; it required thought and luck, and some stagecraft, as in the masques of love seen at court.

I posted a letter to Coughton to say that I would be in London on such and such a day, and that I hoped to see any of my relatives – including nieces, nephews and cousins – who might care to lay eyes on me once more. We forget how strange things were at that time. Nothing like it had ever happened before: for ten years even a word from me could have cost my family their lives. We had been made strangers and enemies, by force of law. Who knew what the effects of that might be? What did they think of me, the 'unnatural and unthrifty' brother? What did *Judith* think of me? I had made her a kind of promise, then vanished for a decade. Was she still at Coughton? Was she married? Was she even alive?

In Calais, I counted the days until I was sure my message must have been delivered, and then, my mind dwelling on all those questions, I set off across the Channel. At Dover I lost patience with my doubts and my questions, and ran through the town like a hunting spaniel, looking for horses for myself and for a young Savoyard who had attached himself to me in Calais and who was eager to see London and all the faraway towns in the world, just for the pleasure of it – an ambition I once had myself, but have now lost. I wonder where it went.

We rode out of Dover at ten in the morning. At noon we stopped for an hour to shelter under my Lord Cobham's hedges.

'I see there is no shortage in your country of wind, rain, thunder and lightning,' said my Savoyard. He was pleased with all he saw. And I was pleased with his 'your country'. I felt at home, although in a strange way, as if I was not fully visible to those who had never left.

It was almost midsummer, I remembered, and then I thought to myself: 'Twelve years ago I was riding along this very road, planning to seek Judith out and ask her to marry me. And here I am, older and more foolish, and wet through, under another man's hedge, and still hoping to do the same. Is my life really as pitiable as it looks?'

Everything, you see, depends on description. I've known men hang themselves from the branch of a tree because they would insist on describing their own lives in dismal terms. As if any of us know much about the matter.

In a few hours I had an answer. I reached my grandparents' house in London. (By then, they were both dead.) Two servants I had never seen before let me into the house. They told me that certain members of my family were about to arrive. The servants did not know their names. They had been written to and told to open the house for the owners. These servants cared nothing about any of us, in the way of Londoners who watch strangers come and go, and quarrel and marry and rule from their city, while they, the real owners, carry on with their ordinary lives.

I waited in the house with my Savoyard, who had nothing else to do but follow me about, and who was pleased with all he saw.

By this time I had lost all my moods: hope, fear, gloom. I became as hard-headed as a lawyer. Everything contracted down to questions of fact. Would Judith come? And if she did, who was she to me, and I to her? Was there, in this contracting, a contract between us at all? I looked around and noted these facts: the floor was swept but there was dust on the wainscot. Strawberries used to grow in a bed in the narrow back garden but now there were none. There was a cranefly, which the children call father-long-legs, on the window; for the first time I saw how fine were the panes of his wings.

And at that moment the door opened and my sisters were staring at me together, Ursula and Elizabeth. They came in and at once began weeping a great deal, quite as much as on previous occasions. Behind them came my nephew George, a brave youth who had fought at the gates of Boulogne and was not likely to weep. And then, lastly, I saw out of the corner of my eye my Gloucester cousin enter the room.

It was very strained and curious. I saw she was a greater stranger to me than the others. She did not look me fully in the eye. Her head was turned away a little; she seemed downcast.

'Cousin Judith,' I said. I took her hand, it was very soft and light. And away blew all my doubts. 'It came true!' I thought. 'Here I am, just as I thought I would be!' A glimpse of her grey-green eyes, her upper lip, rewrote on my heart what she had written there long before.

'Why,' I thought, 'here she is, as near to me as the ball of my eye, and if she was married she would not be here or at least not downcast but triumphant as young married women often are—' and a great many other thoughts went through my mind, very confusedly, but I said nothing to her. And I did not dare kiss her, kisses being far too light for such a serious moment.

In the room there was still a great deal of hubbub. My sisters had dried their eyes and found themselves pleased with my Savoyard and engaged with him on many subjects, the state of roads, the puddings and drinks in Paris and so on, and then George took up with him the question of the siege of Budapest, and my sisters disclosed the fact that no subject was ever more fascinating to them. During all this, no one took any notice of Judith and me. I led her towards the window looking over the little narrow garden; for a minute or two I had the impression we were completely alone as if out on an open moor.

'You know you gave me something once,' I said.

'I?' she said.

'I gave you nothing back, although once I tried to – but never mind about that. Yet I always kept your gift to me.'

I took out of my pocket a cord of red silk, tied in a loop.

She looked at it with puzzlement. 'What is it?' she said.

'One night you showed me a cat's cradle on this. A difficult one, too, which I have mastered, although I can do no others, even the very simplest.'

She took the ribbon. In her hand I saw that over the years it had become frayed and faded almost to pink. She turned it over her fingers.

'But why ever did you keep it?' she asked.

For a moment I thought of the last ten years of my life, hunting up and down the roads of the world, alone or in a crowd, and I could think of nothing to say. Yet I could see she was pleased. She knew the answer. And only then did I understand that the question in my mind had in fact been decided many years ago – ten, eleven, twelve? – one cold summer night in front of a fire at Coughton when she last held that cord looped on her fingers.

We were married three days later – early one morning before anyone was about – in the church by a priest who knew his way round the banns. I was desirous to leave England at once. My nephew George made discreet enquiries as to my legal status. Another nephew, Nicholas, was well placed inside the government; he was a friend of Mr Secretary Cecil and even, to my wonder, of Morison, by then a wealthy and important man in the government. It turned out that I was not nearly as safe as I had imagined. I was perhaps no longer an attainted traitor, but I was still a creature of the detested Pole. My presence in London was known, but not officially. Eyes, however, would not be averted for ever.

I was given to understand as well, by George, that there was a tremendous commotion in the West Country. It had something to do with Pole – he would say no more – and for that reason my presence was especially inconvenient

We rode to Dover immediately after the marriage. As it happened, there was a Venetian ship in port belonging to a certain Lorenzo Bembo, a cousin of my old friend, if I could call him that, he being so high above me in the world, but on the basis of that friendship, the captain, an excellent man, agreed to give us passage to Antwerp. He was waiting for the right wind.

When he heard it was my wedding day, he declared, on behalf of Lord Lorenzo, and of the late Lord Pietro Bembo, and all the

Bembos who had ever lived, that as newly-weds we would have the use of the best cabin.

'It is very good luck for a ship,' he said, inventing this superstition, I think, *alla ventura*, off the cuff. And that was where I entered the married state. The walls were hung with a certain amount of green damask. We had the impression of being in a casket made for precious objects. Before the candle was blown out, Judith remembered something.

'The cat's cradle I showed you *was* very complicated,' she said. 'I think it makes two knots, one a man and one a woman. In the end, the man catches the woman. I doubt that you remember it at all. You will have to show me.'

I proved to her that I did. Then I showed her again in real life. In the night the wind came up and the ship set sail, amid much shouting from above; an hour before daybreak I went on deck and there, under the finery of the stars, with the silk cord back in my pocket, I saw how well we were dashing along over black abyssal seas.

9

JUDITH WAS SLIGHT, DARK-HAIRED, fierce; she had her own distinct kind of beauty and every day I felt I was seeing it clearly for the first time. She coloured easily, and stamped her foot. She had been well named – she, Judith, would chop off the head of a tyrant as quick as look at him. Even before we had set foot on dry land, she let me know that she was coming to Rome out of love for me, but she would have no *Works*, and as to *Merit* and *Satisfaction* – why, she set them at nothing.

These were exactly the terms of the great theological debate I used to hear in our household in Viterbo.

I soothed her, saying that her views – which were those of Master Luther regarding salvation – had been held by many of my friends, especially Flamminio and the Marchioness, and perhaps even Pole himself. At that she seemed very surprised and as we rode along, stopping here and there on the way, she questioned me about all my friends, especially the Marchioness, and I described her truthfully – as she was for most the time, that is – as a kind of second mother to me, at which Judith looked very sad and said she wished she had met her.

'It was the Marchioness,' I said, 'who taught me how to keep our love safe. She told me not to keep you *here*' – I tapped my forehead – 'but hidden *here*.'

I put my hand on my wife's breast. My *wife*. It was at that moment I began to realise what a wife was: another being, a stranger infinitely familiar, a deep reflection of the self – and someone else I could never quite catch sight of.

Later we came to the wood near Visé where I reined up and showed her the entrance to the forest path which Pole and I and the others had taken many years before instead of going to Maastricht to meet Mr Wilson and Mr Heath.

Judith peered down the dim green lane which was now much overgrown.

'And so *that*'s where you vanished off to,' she said.

A bird was calling somewhere nearby but other than that it was very quiet in the wood.

'I knew you had gone,' she said. 'And I stopped thinking about you too. It was, in fact, too dangerous; the Marchioness was right. No one at Coughton ever mentioned your name. But all the time I kept you *here*.'

And then she put her hand on *my* heart. So we lay down there, deep in the wood at Visé, before noon, and later fell asleep for a little while.

Later that day we galloped on fast as if we had to make up lost time, but of course we did not. We were as free as the day was long.

There was not a soul to be seen in the fields; the harvest was not ready. We seemed to be alone in the world. I was very happy to be in that company. When I first saw Judith come into the room in London I could see that she had aged. After that day, she never seemed to age by a day.

She was not, however, one to let sleeping dogs lie. She soon came back to the question of Master Luther and justification by faith or by works and all the terrible questions that have set everything ablaze.

'But what,' she demanded one night in bed in the inn at Lachen, 'do *you* think?'

'Well,' I said, 'sometimes, on Mondays and Wednesdays, as it were, I would take the Protestant view, that man is saved by faith alone, that grace pours down free, like sunlight, and cannot be ordered or paid for by good deeds. And at other times – on Tuesdays and Thursdays – I believed the Catholics, that a man must participate in his own salvation, and is transformed by his own actions. And then it sometimes seemed to me that they were both right – in turn, one after the other, as the soul grows up. But how can they both be right, I thought, when so many people much cleverer than I am want to kill the others for being wrong?

'So finally,' I said, 'I came to another conclusion. I dared to say to myself: *I do not know*. Strangely enough the sky did not fall in. And from that day on, that has been my secret doctrine. On any question, to my mind, that is the first truth: *I do not know*. It is that admission which strips the mind naked, as it were, and lets it roam about in the light, and see further than before.

'And my second doctrine,' I went on 'is this: at any time, be ready to say to yourself: *I was wrong*.'

Then I told her the story of the youth Ulisse whom I saw stalking through Faenza's vines, addressing a chicken, and whom I took to be mad, but who was in fact far better informed than I.

That afternoon on the Quirinal under the towering clouds had changed me for ever, I said. Judith listened carefully, looking at me from under bent brows. I was pleased I did not have a wife who agreed or disagreed on principle, or one who was not interested in these matters at all.

A few months afterwards, when we were living in Rome, she came to me and said she had thought long and hard about the tenets of my secret religion – 'All this "*I do not know*" and "*I was wrong*",' she called it – and had come to the conclusion that it was not for her.

'You must forgive me,' she said. 'I find it very uncomfortable. Knowing and being right are far more agreeable to me, and profitable. I'm sure that I'm right about this.'

'And I am happy for the meantime not to be sure that I am,' I said. 'On that basis we can have a pact of mutual toleration.'

To this she agreed and we sealed the arrangement in the way lovers choose, with a kiss. My marriage to Judith was in fact the time of my deepest happiness. I see that now, as it is the saddest to look back on. It was not to last long. It was quite different, as well, from the happiness I knew in Viterbo. There I lived a simple life, roaming about *in Arcadia.* The happiness of marriage is very different, much deeper, and in the depths there are more fears and cares. In a word, I soon became a father as well as a husband.

When my son Francis was born within a year of our marriage, I thought back to that wood at Visé. He is now a sprightly child of seven with a hard head, and sly, amused eyes as if he is watching you through wood-shadow. I have certainly never thought of him as made at sea.

10

ONCE BACK IN ROME I found my duties in Pole's household much reduced. He had given up the government of Viterbo. All the archers who protected him had been sent away. There was no sign that those ruling England sought his death. Nor, however, did they want any communication with him. The Protector sent him a letter full of comic abuse of popes, superstition and error. Pole sent a letter back which was very fierce. What did it say? I almost forget:

> It is the custom, nowadays, among those who delight in showing off their wit to treat the affairs of Rome with ridicule . . . No greater scourge can befall a kingdom than to have such men as rulers, who sit 'in the seat of the scornful' and for whom a great downfall soon comes.

Brancetor, who had come back from the wars, took over my role and delivered this to the English ambassador in Paris. Meanwhile Judith and I were setting up house. We had an apartment by the palazzo Spada, near where the big statue of Pompey was found under a wall the next year. For weeks we went out together shopping for furniture and fittings. Until then I had not realised how many items are indispensable to a household. I knew them all by sight, as it were, but had never listed them and gone out to acquire the lot. Judith wanted everything of the best quality. She was used to living in a dainty manner. Every day I was reminded of yet another essential object. And of course she was right. How could one live without, say, scissors? Or a grater? Or a candle-snuffer? Or a salt vat? A meat board, a cheeseboard, a mustard pot, a tin butter dish, a ledger, a coal shovel, a waffle iron? A tablecloth press? It was out of the question. These things took almost all my attention.

The daily events in Pole's household, which was always busy, and even the bloody unpheavals in England became somewhat remote to me. When I was in London, as I said, there was some great commotion in the West Country, but the full scale of it was only slowly becoming known. It had begun when the ruling council abolished the mass: thousands rose demanding they keep their ancient form of worship, and also that Pole come back to England and take a place on the Royal Council.

Soothing promises were made, but then an army was sent in. The priests were hanged from their steeples and thousands of prisoners were taken. The prisoners were tied up and put to the knife – nine hundred, it was said, in one afternoon, seven thousand in a fortnight. I knew of course that all these things were grave and fearful, yet to me, sitting with my son on my knee, they seemed oddly remote. My life now took place within the four walls of my own house. And then, as if to prove the point, disaster arrived right there in our midst. In the second year of our marriage, another child was born and then – behold! – another appeared, hot on her heels. I had fathered twins. But they died on the day they were born. God sent them in the morning, as the saying goes, and took them back in the evening. It is a common event to lose a child, I know, and yet we suffered more from the loss of those two little ones, whom we had scarcely met, than at the departure of very old friends.

When it was plain they were not to live long we christened them 'Michael' and 'Judith'.

That is almost all I remember of that year. More than ever we closed the door on the world. Judith, Francis and I formed our own little circle and lived away from everyone else for several months. This was in the year 1549.

Then one night, in the autumn, someone came and hammered at the door. It was John Lily, who had been sent by Pole. The Pope, he said, was dying. All those in Pole's household, of which I was still a chief member, were asked to go and wait on *il Signor*.

For years, many people had prophesied that when the Pope died, he would be replaced by the Cardinal of England, the illustrious Reynaldo Polo. I suppose that my master is the only person in history of whom it was ever said, 'He's sure to be the next pope – or perhaps the King of England.' Now the time had come to see if there was anything in these prophecies.

Paul III had been ill for some time, of an apoplexy brought on by the evil behaviour of his grandsons, and so his death was not wholly unexpected. That day he had fallen into a deep sleep from which it was thought he would never awaken. I went to Pole's house and waited as the news came in. For a while it seemed that the Pope might recover after all: his infant great-grandson had been brought in and he suddenly opened his eyes, and blessed him, then blessed him again, which so exhilarated him that he asked for a boiled egg and half a glass of wine. Then he ordered the return of some property of the Jews, to whom he was always very partial, and the remission of the grist tax, but then fell back into unconsciousness. He died about noon the next day.

That night the whole city stood by to watch his coffin go from the Quirinale to the palace of St Peter. I was among those of Pole's household who waited on Monte Cavallo, by the marble statues of the horse-farmers, and then we moved off with the procession. In the darkness all that could be heard were the horses' hooves and the sound of weeping. This is by no means the conclusion to all pontificates.

On my way home I saw that in the bankers' shops all the wagers were for England, the only cry was 'England! England!' and no one else was even mentioned.

11

ON THE DAY THE conclave began, I found myself back in the Sistine to help install Pole and his baggage into his temporary lodgings. It was the first time I had been there since going with Flamminio to see the new fresco, and I cast a glance at that great blue field of sky to see if I could see it in the same light again, but that was impossible – the crowds of servants, conclavists, baggage handlers, pot-boys, butlers, footmen, candle-men, sightseers from every country, even England – Master Hoby was present, a great Lutheran who by then was the owner of Pole's family seat at Bisham – German barons and baronesses, bankers' spies, carpenters hammering away as they finished the cabins, each of which was hung with silk curtains – green for cardinals made by the last pope, purple for the rest, or was it the other way around? – and then the cardinals themselves, sweeping past among their attendants – it was hard even to keep a footing in that throng, much less stand there and consider the final meeting of heaven and earth, as imagined by M. Michelangelo. Then at about four in the afternoon a loud voice rose above the tumult – '*Depart, who must depart*!'

At that, everyone except the cardinals, each with two conclavists and a few servants to assist them, went away, and the great outer door swung closed.

Half an hour later, it swung open again and certain interlopers who had been found there, as expected, under beds and behind curtains – two madmen, three spies from the bankers' shops, four gentlemen merely curious to see the election of a pope – came forth and bowed to the crowd who greeted them with many jeers and whistles.

Then everyone stood outside and watched as the highest windows and the lesser doors were mured up, and finally the bricklayers came to the main outer door itself, and set to work. Only one small opening, called the wicket, was left.

It was at the wicket that I spent the next three days and nights, along with a crowd of prelates, ambassadors, Roman barons and officials.

The prelates guarding the door were negligent. Servants of the cardinals came in and out as they pleased, their boots stuffed so full of letters that they went over at the ankles and could scarcely totter along at all. In short, everything taking place inside the conclave in great secrecy was known across Rome within an hour.

At the first scrutiny, Pole won twenty-one votes, six short of the two-thirds majority. At the second, he won twenty-four. At the third, twenty-five. If he found one more supporter, and chose to vote for himself, then my master, Mr Pole, of Staffordshire birth, aged forty-eight, and with a death sentence still on his head, would become the Roman pontiff.

That night at midnight (this was on the third day of the conclave) not a single cardinal, except for Pole, remained in his cabin. From the wicket, you could hear a distant din and buzzing as from a beehive.

Then, at one in the morning, we learned that Farnese had gone with another cardinal to Pole's cabin. The two men knelt before him.

The extra votes had been found, said Farnese. The matter was therefore concluded.

All the other cardinals had assembled in the Pauline chapel and were waiting there to elect my master by acclamation.

From that point on, at the wicket, it was impossible to follow exactly what was happening. First we heard that Pole had set forth from his cabin to be made Pope. Then that he had retired again. Then he stepped out once more and set off on his way to the Pauline. And finally, it seemed, he had turned back again, saying: 'If God wants me to be Pope, he will still want it in the morning.'

The vote, therefore, was to be held the next day.

By morning, this was known across the city and the *campagna* beyond. By four in the afternoon a great crowd had assembled in front of St Peter's, along with the papal troops and city militia, all with flags flying. From within, you could now hear the sound of splintering and cracking. The cabins were being demolished; the servants were packing up their masters' belongings and sitting on the baggage in readiness for the Roman mob, which always honours a new pope by bursting in and looting the electors. Everyone was filled with speculation as to the future of the world with this English pope: he would ban the inquisition, he would reach out to the Protestants, the schism in which new hatreds flourished like weeds would come to an end.

This was early December and dusk was already falling. A great rain-cloud hung over the city.

Then the announcement came: '*Their lordships have ordered supper.*'

A groan went up from the crowd. The scrutiny had failed. And then the rain began to fall, and did not cease for many days and weeks until the Tiber began to give cause for alarm.

The only people who were pleased were those of the French faction who were at the wicket.

'It is just as well,' said the French ambassador, M. D'Urfé, the corners of his mouth turning down eloquently. 'My king could scarcely bear an English pope, but one of the English blood royal – it is unthinkable!'

'You are always absurd,' cried the imperialist ambassador, Don Diego Mendoza. 'Do you imagine that your master's wishes have anything to do with the election of God's vicar on earth?'

'Oh! – and yet *your* master sends you bustling along here every hour of the day and night, causing tumults and smuggling in his orders. It is well known why he wants Pole elected – to prevent him marrying the princess Mary, should she ever come to the throne. What a way to use the chair of Peter, which is after all the seat of Moses, to put a marriage rival on the shelf!'

'Gentlemen, gentlemen!' said several voices in the tone that is heard just before a brawl breaks out in the tavern.

'All I will say is this,' said M. D'Urfé. 'My king cannot, in any case, accept a result reached before the cardinals of France have entered the conclave.'

'Oh, yes, and where are they now?' said Mendoza, laughing, 'I suppose we shall see them come down in the rain in the next half hour.'

M. D'Urfé, over the course of the previous two days, had announced the miraculous progress of the French party, from Marseilles to Corsica, to Genoa, and then almost within sight of the Roman port of Ostia.

Over the next days we found out what had happened in the scrutiny which had failed.

On that morning, when all the cardinals gathered in the Sistine to vote, a tall figure, his eyes burning, stood up and demanded the right to speak before it was too late. His conscience, he said, required it. It was impossible for Cardinal Pole to be pope, he said, for a simple reason: he was a heretic. He could not therefore be Head of the Church, for the head must be a part of the body, and a heretic was not a member of the body. In a word, Pole was not a Catholic.

The charges he made were these: first, Pole was a Lutheran: he endorsed Luther's doctrine on justification by faith alone. His views on prayer and the mass were suspect. His friends were suspect as well: some had fled to Geneva and England. Under his government, Viterbo was a sink of liberty and licence. No one was ever prosecuted for heresy. The civil administration was lax. The hangman and the axe-man languished and fell into despair: their services were so little in demand they had quite forgotten their skills, greatly adding to the demoralisation of the people.

As well as that, Pole's personal life was scandalous. His household was full of whoring and sodomy; his own affair with a certain woman (he meant the Marchioness) was well known. He also had a love-child, a daughter, now hidden in a convent in Rome. He, the speaker, could name the house.

The speaker was Pole's old friend, Carafa, who, years before, riding forward like Mars, had urged Pole to give up his family and go to Rome.

All this took place beneath the *Last Judgement*, which Carafa had already denounced as 'a furnace of naked bodies' and at which he now glanced from time to time, as if to confirm that a thousand heresies were creeping towards the chair of Peter . . .

During this speech Pole defended himself stoutly, now laughing, now quoting holy writ and in general, it was said, treating his attacker *como un loco* – like a madman. He rebutted the charges: if Luther was heretical in some respects, that did not mean he was a heretic in all. His own friendship with the Marchioness had always been – to the fury of the malicious – entirely above reproach. The girl in the convent was an orphan whom Pole took care of when her parents died penniless. If the hangman in Viterbo had forgotten his trade, surely that was a cause for congratulation: the people there chose to live good lives. In any case, he added, it was not part of the clergy to rule the flock with grim authority, but to try and win them with love and gentleness.

All the same, it was reported, during this speech my master had gone very pale. In all the years he had known Carafa, he had never suspected this burning hatred.

When Carafa finished speaking there was a long silence. Many of the cardinals then began to wag their heads and abuse him, calling out that they would all ostracise him from now on.

Nevertheless, one of his listeners had been shaken by what he heard. When the votes were cast, Pole's total had dropped back to twenty-six. And there it was to remain week after week, month after month, as the rain fell outside.

The missing French cardinals did not appear for another ten days. Bourbon arrived first, bespattering the whole world, as mud had become the universal element. More Frenchmen followed, and then the deadlock became intractable. Conditions in the conclave grew worse; the stench and smoke from a thousand charcoal braziers at which their Lordships warmed their fingers was intolerable. In the dim light, servants no longer doffed their bonnets even to the most eminent lords.

The physician-general of Rome, Dr Norsia, was sent in to tell the cardinals they would all be brought out dead if they carried on much longer. No one took any notice.

'Very good,' said Norsia. 'One by one you will succumb to the falling sickness, which commences with a little giddiness. It will then proceed to sweep these rooms clean.'

'All well,' said the imperialist cardinals. 'But we will die with Pole's name on our lips.'

'For our part, we are happy to stay for a thousand years,' said the French. 'In fact, compared to conditions in the French court, we consider ourselves to be in a sort of paradise here.'

Some days later several cardinals came to the wicket to discuss the problem.

'You must reduce our meals to a single course,' one said.

'To bread and water,' said another.

'Bread and water, certainly,' quavered Cardinal Pacheco, putting his head almost through the wicket. 'But perhaps a little drop of wine.'

'*No!*' cried several voices behind him. 'No wine!'

Pacheco vanished abruptly, and Farnese appeared in his place.

'Bread and water will not do the trick here,' he said. 'You'd better send in swords and daggers. Nothing else can settle this.'

Disputes rose between the prelates guarding the door and the barons of Rome who wanted to stop the messages getting in and out. And daily the populace stormed before the palace, demanding a pontiff.

One day, after two or three months of this, I met the Venetian ambassador in the street. He was very downcast.

'It is quite hopeless,' he said. He explained that the balance of power in the world was so exact and complex that a fiend could not have contrived it better. And this state of affairs was reflected precisely within the conclave.

'All the same,' he said, 'your master will win in the end. You may depend on it. His vote never wavers. And it is still "England!" in the betting shops, where they know far more than anyone else, except the Holy Ghost.'

That same night, when I was at home having supper with Judith, I heard a great clamour outside. There was the sound of shouting and running feet. I looked out. Everyone had armed and was hurrying towards the Vatican.

I went out after them and there in the street I heard the news: a Pope had been elected. He was a compromise candidate who had the great advantage that each faction knew the other did not want him.

12

THE NEW POPE, DEL MONTE, had every disqualification for high office in a crisis. He had a great dislike of bad news, which upset his stomach, so he could not be told any. He loved music, theatre and architecture. He also owned a pet ape, an animal of such savage temper that no one dared approach it.

With the ape came a youth from the gutters named Innocenzo. Innocenzo was the only person who could manage the beast, which he did by leaping on it and beating it into submission.

Before he was elected, del Monte was told by the other cardinals that if they chose him he would have to give up the ape and Innocenzo. This he refused to do. As there was no other way out of their prison, the cardinals relented and elected him.

The Imperialists outside the conclave were furious at the outcome. Del Monte had not been on the Emperor's list of acceptable candidates. The ambassador went to see him at once and found him still robing.

'Here am I – Don Diego Mendoza,' he said.

'Do not look so dismayed, Don Diego,' said the Pope.

Don Diego offered to kiss the pontiff's foot.

'No need for that, it is neither the time nor place,' said the Pope. He made him rise and then embraced him.

On leaving the chamber, Don Diego said with a laugh: 'It is possible I may not care to kiss him again.'

It was then remembered that the new Pope had a passion for onions. Soon cartloads of them were to be seen on their way to the palace.

Before long it was announced that the Pope intended to raise Innocenzo to the cardinalate. Everyone was amazed. Pole went to see him and argued with him until the third hour of night, but he would not change his mind.

'Popes have always promoted their nephews. I do not happen to have one, so my brother has adopted this fellow. And he is a youth of great spirit – just what's needed in the hour of danger!'

Pole came away shaking his head. At the same time as this, Flamminio was dying. I went to see him constantly, but it was a sad, irksome duty. My Marc'Antonio, the best friend I ever made among the Italians, had already departed. It was a replacement, it seemed to me, who was doing the dying, a man I hardly knew. On almost the last day of his life I went up the stairs to his room – he had taken shelter in Pole's house – and found a haggard figure lying there, his beard springing round sternly compressed lips, expressive of great authority and impatience.

There was no conspiracy between us to pretend he would be up and about any day now.

I asked him whether he was afraid of what lay ahead.

'Afraid?' he said. 'Of course I am not afraid. Haven't you seen the frieze of little demons, carved on the tombs of the ancients, laughing at mankind's fear of death? And quite right too. Nothing could be more improper, and especially for a poet.'

'Why a poet?'

'Why a poet! What else is poetry, and indeed any art, but a rehearsal of that moment? That is why artists are always forgiven their misdeeds. Mnemosymne, the god of memory, is the mother of the muses, but she is also the chamberlain at the hour of death when a man sees his whole life for the first time as clearly as if it were a painting or a poem. That is why people come to watch us form so many things in front of them – in his heart every man knows at the end he too will compose the shape of his life.'

'I never heard this before,' said I.

'Of course not – what do you know about anything?' said Flamminio rudely. 'That's why I'm taking the great trouble to tell you. If art is splendid, that is because life is, and therefore so is death. After all, remember: "*Why fear death, which comes from the hand of the same master who made life?*" '

He was quoting M. Michelangelo, I think, and I wanted to ask him more, but he shut his eyes and waved me away. He was very sick by then. It was always his stomach with Flamminio, or his liver. And so I went away, promising to return, but in fact I never saw him again. He was dead two days later. In his final hours, two men slipped into his room, one concealing himself in a wardrobe while the other bent over him and urgently plied him with questions. The subject was theology or specifically Flamminio's doctrinal beliefs.

At length the questioner was satisfied. The second man then came out of his place of hiding and began chatting easily to the dying man on other matters. It was Carafa, the arch-inquisitor. He had come to make sure that Flamminio, celebrated poet and friend of Pole, was not escaping to the next world in possession of heretical opinions.

That, in a way, marked the end of our life in Rome. Everywhere there were new men and new ways of doing things. Pole was no longer a member of the inner circle. It was about this time that he began to make his plans to depart from Rome. He intended to go to some retired place and resume his studies – always his favourite occupation in any case.

On hearing this, many people began to blame him bitterly and accuse him of desertion. The Pope, for instance, to show his high regard for Pole, had appointed him as a member of the court of the Inquisition. By taking himself off to some lonely hill town or monastery, he would abandon the field to the zealots, Carafa and others.

At the same time as this, the true extent of the disaster or tragicomedy of the conclave was becoming clear. The new Pope threw himself wholeheartedly into the design and construction of a beautiful pavilion on the banks of the Tiber, leaving the gravest matters of state to underlings. Innocenzo was not only made a cardinal but appointed Secretary of State, replacing Farnese. Universally known as Cardinal Monkey, he at once began to disgrace himself and his order, climbing over roofs, rioting and getting the girls pregnant.

All of this would have been averted, people said, if another pope had been elected. People began to think back, looking for the missed turning on the road. It was then remembered that in the conclave Pole refused to canvas any votes, showed no ambition, declared himself to desire no magistracy or high office. In short, as one cardinal said, 'one might as well have been voting for a log of wood'.

Pole's star began to wane. He was accused of lassitude, passivity, pusillanimity, cowardice, indolence, selfishness, indifference to the common good. He had too great a love of quiet, of gardens, of the library. In short he was said to be another Lord Bembo, who also had too much love for his *otium*, his ease.

People's minds then turned back to the midnight hour when Pole had actually been chosen as Pope, and the electors had sent for him and begged him to come to receive the acclamation, but he had refused. He had been offered the chance to save the Church and perhaps all of Christendom (for even the Lutherans had some faith in him) but he flinched and turned away.

As these charges were being aired, a strange tale circulated in the household. I heard it first from Beccatelli, in whom Pole himself confided, and then I heard it again from Priuli and Pace.

It seemed that on the night in question, when the two cardinals came to Pole and offered him the pontificate, his very first thought was of the ass's colt which two men came to fetch so that the Lord might ride it into Jerusalem the next day.

For that reason, he listened to the ministers and agreed to go with them.

Then, when they left him to report back to the others, it struck him how dark it was and how late the hour, and he thought that if he was elected by acclamation at midnight, that might well lead to endless accusations of electoral fraud, of 'coming in through the window instead of the door'. So he changed his mind and sent a message after Farnese saying he should wait until daylight.

Two more cardinals were then sent to assure him that an election at that hour and in that manner was entirely legitimate, just, canonical and in accordance with ancient precedent. So he agreed again and sent them ahead to prepare for the ceremony.

But then, alone in the chapel for a few minutes, something strange happened to him. He thought again of the ass left at his master's door and now it seemed to him that he actually began to take on the character of that animal. First he felt a complete indifference to earthly honours. Then he saw the pontificate in a new light, as it really was or should be, divested of all worldly wealth and honour, and well-nigh naked. And then, as in the ancient fable of Apuleius, he felt he was actually turning *into* an ass, with its hairy pelt and long ears and reedy voice.

All that could actually be seen in the dim light of the chapel at that hour were those figures of the tyrants and wicked souls painted by Michelangelo on the wall. A kind of terror seized him. He called his conclavist and hastily sent him after the cardinals to say that the election must be deferred until dawn.

Thus the vote was held the next day, but it came only after Carafa's attack on his character and doctrine, which cost him one vote.

So it seemed that my master lost the pontificate because, for a minute or two, some strange power turned him into an ass's colt that was frightened of the dark.

Whether this was the work of providence, or of the evil spirit which saps a man's courage, I leave you to decide.

13

FOR A LONG TIME, before I even began roaming the world as a courier in the service of Pole, I had devoted myself to the study of horse-breeding, but from a distance, in secrecy, as it were. Having no money or opportunity to put my thoughts into practice, I kept them to myself for fear of looking absurd, rather like those gentlemen who talk expertly on war but have never been seen on a battlefield or who, by the droop of an eyelid, imply that no woman is safe from them when in fact they live very modestly in that regard. But when the time came that Pole decided to leave Rome for good and go and live quietly in a monastery, I saw that my service to him was coming to an end. It was time for me to choose a new occupation.

My thoughts turned naturally towards bloodstock. I had some capital, Judith had more, and an income from a parcel of land in Gloucestershire – I've always said it was an excellent county, Gloucestershire – and so we made our plans accordingly.

I chose this city of Mantua to start our new life. I liked Mantua from the start; I liked the lie of the land, and the Regent was always amiable to any friend of Pole's, especially one who once brought him a drawing by M. Michelangelo. And so, leaving my family in Rome, I came north to visit the place again and to survey the neighbouring countryside.

I found a very good little farm a few miles out of town at Cerese, with serviceable stables and five paddocks for grazing. Then I went to Forli and bought a stallion, a handsome beast named Prince Aeneas, a black – the true jet black, not the rusty – which I had been watching quietly for several years, and I took him back to Cerese to cover the mares I already owned.

Then I went to Rome to collect my family, which by then had grown in size – we had had two more sons – and brought them all back with me and we settled into a new life in Mantua.

And here this story might have been expected to reach its end. It certainly seemed that I had come to the end of my adventures in service to the illustrious Pole. In short, I looked forward to a tranquil life, although I must now question if there is any such thing. In the end a great storm always comes. In my case, even the periods of calm have never lasted long. In fact, just then, the worst disaster of my life was approaching from a direction I had never dreamt of.

Judith was as pleased as I was with Mantua, a rich city with its shops and silk factories, and innumerable Jews, who, in Mantua, consider themselves to be in a kind of paradise: there is no ghetto, there are as many printing presses as in Venice, they write comedies and they practice medicine and, furthermore, the Regent, Cardinal Ercole, loves them and protects their interests. When, for instance, a little later on, the order came from the Inquisition to burn all copies of the Talmud (this was after the great quarrel among the Jewish publishers) he called in certain Jews before taking any action, and spoke quietly to them so that they might know what to do. It was through the Regent that I eventually met Portaleone, a doctor, a writer of comedies, and now my literary advisor. But that was still some time in the future.

In the meantime we settled in. I took this house not far from the palace and the water, a high, narrow house in which I installed my little brood all as content as doves in a cote. By then, as I said, we had more children, and another adult had also joined the family.

When Judith had found she was pregnant again, she wept and said she would not go through childbirth without a woman of her own country at her side. Then she spoke fiercely. She seemed to blame me for something – that her mother was dead, that I had led her far from her English sisters. So of course I took the blame, and went hunting about for a companion for her. This was how I found Agnes Hide. She was the daughter of a Southampton merchant who had set up in Venice, trading in English stuff, woollen clothes and hides.

Agnes was the exact opposite of Judith. She was tall, fair, blond, sleepy, peaceable. She spoke good Italian; Judith's was lamentable. Being quite different, they were nevertheless very pleased with each other.

From this house we ventured forth to see where we were. After inspecting the ducal palace, the great church of S. Pietro, the palace of the Te, and the shores of the lake, which was as flat as millpond whenever you looked at it, but which still rose up and drowned people without warning from time to time, we ranged over the Mantuan countryside. For some reason this is never threatening or gloomy as the *campagna* around Rome can be in a certain light. We saw the little brick house where Virgil once lived and kept his beasts as a shepherd, and the big river – 'slow-treading Mincio' as Flamminio called it – moving among its robes of reeds.

Five miles beyond the town we came to the beautiful pleasure-house called Marmerol, where the Duke keeps his orange trees in great tubs, which he moves from one place to another according to his ducal whim.

We were happy with everything that we found.

There was no inkling of what was to come: beautiful Mantua was to be Judith's last home on earth. A tragedy was in preparation. Yet everything appeared prosperous. All the mares had conceived. Judith found she was pregnant again. And about the same time, my nephew George came to live with us. More than ever I liked his brave and gentle nature. He had come to Italy to learn the language and gain experience of the world. On the way he had stayed in the German cities, in Switzerland and Venice, and he brought with him the latest books on science, astronomy and the techniques of husbandry. Late into the evening he would sit up and, translating as he went, would read aloud to me:

> To make a trial of your stallion and see whether he is fit for procreation, you should press the genital members with two fingers and with locks of wool draw out his seed. If it cleaves together, he is a good stallion, but if it hangs together like bird lime or milk and whey, you should not let him cover your mares.
>
> Your mares should be well compacted, fair and beautiful, with large belly and loins, and aged between three and ten.
>
> The appetite of the female for the male, which is called the *horsing*, lasts sixty days and is easily recognised by these signs: first they leave their usual company and prefer running towards north and south rather than east and west. They will let no one near them until they are tired or have met a male. If they meet a female in the same state as themselves they rejoice in her society, lifting their tail, changing their voice and sending forth from their secrets a certain thin humour like the seed of the male.
>
> Among all females in the world there is none, apart from women, more greedy for procreation, which carries them over mountains and rivers. In Spain, on Mount Tegro by the ocean, the mares rage so far in their lust that they conceive by the south-west wind, just as hens lay eggs without being trodden by the cock. The foals of these unions, however, do not live long.
>
> The best time for joining the horse and mare is from the vernal equinox to the summer solstice, so that the foals have warm weather and green grass from their birth.
>
> Good foals will rise quickly when stirred from their rest, and run away fast: they should be cheerful, wanton, contend with their equals and race against them, not be terrified by any strange sight, and should leap over a ditch, and appear meek when provoked.

> They should be long-bodied, full of muscle and sharp, with a little head, black eyes, open and wide nostrils, sharp pitched ears, a soft and broad neck, a thick mane falling to the right side, a broad and full breast, large shoulders and shoulder bones, round ribs, a little belly and double backbone, loins pressed downwards broad and well set, a long tail with curled hair and high, straight and equal legs, round knees, round buttocks, brawny and fleshy thighs, high, hard and hollow hoofs, and the veins should be conspicuous and apparent all over the body.

By this time I had four yearlings which, more or less, I thought, matched this description, and now the mares were in foal again. I don't know which is the source of greater contentment – hearing words that conform to reality, or seeing reality confirm the authority of the written word.

Soon our numbers increased again. We were joined by Elizeus Heywood, a wild, wayward young man whose father had sent him abroad to keep out of trouble. He made a beeline for Pole. Pole, immersed in his books, sent him on to us. Finally there arrived another nephew, John Throckmorton, Long John, as we called him, for he was so tall he towered over all of us and indeed over every head in the Mantuan street. The young men brought a lively spirit to the household. Judith already knew my nephews well; she found herself queen of a little court which had sprung up around her. We spent most of the summer in the country, at Cerese, where the air was sweeter than in town.

I told the boys they must not stop with us old folk out in the sticks but hurry off and see the world.

'Oh no, dear Uncle,' said Long John. 'We're staying. We know which side our bread is buttered on.'

Being a married lady, and pregnant again as well, Judith ruled them all easily. It was to Agnes Hide they made love. She, in turn, at the age of twenty-six, laughed at them. George was the oldest and he was only twenty-one or twenty-two.

'She would love me if I had more money,' said Long John at supper one evening. Every night we had supper at the long table under the apricot trees.

'You know nothing about these matters,' said Elizeus. 'Lovers live on love as larks live on leeks.'

'Ah – but there's more to marriage than four bare legs in a bed,' said John.

'That's enough,' said Judith, who would not permit any hint of indelicacy at her court.

Agnes, tall and fair, sat there smiling but with her eyes lowered as if she had a secret.

Late one night a white bow was seen across the fields. It was a night rainbow – a thing never dreamt of in a lifetime but when you see one you know at once what it is.

Sometimes I had to blink at what had happened to me. There I was, with a wife and children, possessions, horses, and English visitors coming and going without any danger. It was hard to believe my old life spent half on horseback, with nothing to my name but a few books and clothes, and the forces of a dangerous enemy, my own king, always threatening on the horizon.

In the autumn the time came for Judith's lying-in. John and Elizeus had gone off to Florence. I remember that week very clearly. George was always with me in the parlour; he read aloud to entertain me and keep my mind from wandering upstairs. Above our heads there was a great campaign under way: I could hear the drumming footsteps and orders, as to the commissariat, for linen, hot water, lidded basins, a winestoop, a warming pan, pictures of St Margaret . . . Men are kept at a distance from this campaign, and in fact know no more about its progress than people on dry land who hear the sounds of a battle out at sea. George by then was reading aloud the history of all the four-footed beasts – I remember that night we met the sphinx, which belongs to the ape family and stores its food in its cheeks, and the hedgehog whose ribs, dried and powdered, are a cure for colic, and two types of the vulgar little mouse, the rustic and the urban: 'They can discern their enemies: not fearing the ox, they run from a cat. Thus it is clear they have sound judgement and make good choices.'

Seeing that I could hardly concentrate, George turned his attention back to the horse, the most noble of the animals:

> The eyes of a horse are great or glassy; it is reported of Emperor Augustus that his eyes were much brighter than other men's, and resembled those of horses; their eyes also see perfectly in the dark . . . Homer affirms that there are in horses divine qualities, for, being tied to their manger, they mourned the death of Patroclus, and foreshadowed what would happen to Achilles . . . They lament their lost masters with tears and they foreknow battles . . . They love wet places, and baths, and also music – the whole host of the army of the Sybarites taught their horses to dance to the sound of a pipe.

I could not listen any longer. I begged George to put his book aside. Above us the footsteps were thudding back and forth very furiously. There came the sound a husband dreads – most pitiful cries. After a time there was a silence, and then came another sound which I could not fail to recognise. It was the newcomer, who, lifting her voice, made herself known through the whole house. This was my sixth child.

The neighbours came in and gave me boxes of pickled pumpkin, which is the reward for new fathers in Italy. In Italy, as well, the newborn is washed in warm white wine. In half an hour my little daughter was brought down to me smelling sweet and, frankly, rather bibulous. The maid-servants allowed me to hold her. I kept her in my arms, and went straight upstairs, but at the door of the bedchamber I met Agnes.

She looked pale and she tried to keep me out.

'Not yet,' she said.

But I went past her and went in and saw Judith, who was the colour of snow. I saw at once that although body and soul were still together, life itself was marching away. I instantly ran down and called for a doctor. This was Portaleone, whom I knew by then but only slightly. Sometimes Jews could or would treat gentiles, sometimes not – I never made out the rules too clearly. In this instance, Portaleone came at once and then there commenced a great battle to order back the force that was retreating before our eyes.

How long the engagement went on I scarcely knew. Portaleone was the commanding general, I was a messenger and foot-soldier. Judith herself seemed oblivious to the danger. She took the baby for a moment, and smiled at me.

'She has a little cap of black hair like me,' she said, 'but she has a resemblance to you, which makes me love her.'

Then she slid back on the pillow. I became truly fearful. There was a great deal of blood being lost. Basin after basin was taken away. Later, Portaleone said that I began to act like a madman: at one point I left the room and came back with a songbird in a cage. That was true, but it was not wholly a deranged act. The bird was Judith's pet, which she greatly loved. I had the idea that if she heard it sing that might alert her to how far she was journeying from us.

The bird in fact did sing a little, and hopped back and forward in the candlelight. What did it know about our human tales? But I thought that Judith's eyes moved under their lids. I was not mad, but as watchful as I have ever been in my life. In time, I saw that Portaleone had given up the engagement, though he said nothing and kept applying compresses and poultices and elixir of sage.

Finally he turned to me and opened his hands. I sent for the priests. I realised then it was morning. The boys were brought in to see their mother, but she did not open her eyes. Francis was then five years old. The priests began to chant the prayer for the dying. The bird chirped too, now and then, but no one dared put it out because of my glance. But I was not mad. It was only much later, when I realised what I had lost, that despair and self-pity seized me. When I went down the stairs early that afternoon I was a widower with four living children, but I still hadn't taken in that description of myself.

14

THE BABY WAS CHRISTENED Judith. A wet nurse had been found immediately, but she soon dried up, and so did the next one, and then a third. Looking back now, I see that that baby flew round Mantua like a sample of new silk, but then I was hardly aware of the fact. Agnes Hide took care of all those matters; I was abstracted and in despair. No, it was more than that: I was in a rage with God. Why, after so many years apart, and such a little time together, was she been taken away from me, my love, the true companion of my life?

Why do you do this to us?, I demanded. Why do you search for new ways to break people's hearts?

There was no answer at the time.

The worst thing was this: I discovered that my thoughts almost always took the form of an imagined conversation with Judith. How long this had been going on I had no idea; I only noticed it when she had gone. Perhaps everyone has a conversation running in their mind with someone or other – wife or husband or God, or their children, or their men or dogs and horses. This idea filled me with alarm, for mine was only with Judith, who would never actually hear me or answer again. Yet so strong was the habit I could not stop doing it, which was painful and absurd. But for whom else was I to form my thoughts? My children were infants, I had no fellow-countrymen nearby – George had suddenly been called home – and I'd had enough of talking to dogs and horses.

The long and short of it is this: three months later I married Agnes Hide.

One day she came to me and said she had decided to go home to her father in Venice. Everything was settled now, she said. The children had their nurse; little Judith had a wet nurse who stayed wet. And, she said, since she had come as a companion to my wife, who was no longer there, it was time she went away.

I stared at her aghast.

'To *Venice*?' I cried, and I leapt to my feet and embraced her.

I see now that that is what she hoped for. And why not? The fact is that I have been extremely lucky. I have had one great love of my life, but two good wives. The children loved Agnes already, and she them, as far as I could tell.

Then there was the question of propriety. It is unseemly for a man and a young woman to live under the same roof without the arrangement being regulated in one way or the other, after – let's say – three months.

I had few doubts on the brink of the marriage and none afterwards. One night a few months later, speaking tentatively as though admitting a grave fault, she declared that she had long ago fallen in love with me, and had therefore decided that she would never marry anyone.

'This was my secret,' she said. 'I did not hope for my own happiness. How could I? You were married to Judith. She was my dearest friend.'

Agnes Hide is as unlike Judith as anyone could be. She is tall, fair, peaceable and always anxious to be just. Judith was not so scrupulous. Life for her was to be lived with passionate feeling. Agnes, even on the wedding night, always reminded me of the woman in the zodiac carrying the scales.

This marriage also turned out to be fortuitous for practical reasons, although I had never dreamt of what was going to happen next.

15

A FEW MONTHS AFTER Agnes Hide and I were wed, a message came from the palace commanding me to appear before the Regent. I promised the herald – a skinny youth who came huffing and puffing out to the farm at Cerese – that I would do so at once. However, I did not increase my pace. To tell the truth, the Regent Cardinal Ercole summoned me to the palace rather more than was strictly necessary. He was very interested in horse breeding; he was considering sending one of his mares to my *rozzone* – my brute – of which he had heard good reports – although, he warned me with an upheld forefinger – 'one should beware of a handsome horse, as of a handsome man. Despite appearances, there may be no good in him at all.'

Lord Ercole was also interested in England and indeed the whole island of Britain. Sometimes he called me in and read aloud reports that he had received from the Mantuan ambassador there or from other sources, stopping from time to time to stare at me as if it was *my* doing that no vines grew in England, or olives, or that the tide rises the height of a house twice a day, or that the English affirm that torture is a great evil, which injures not only the bodies of the innocent but the soul of a commonwealth.

As for Scotland, that country, being still more remote to his imagination, pleased him even more.

'Scotland is marvellously mountainous, sterile, rugged and marshy, and therein is its safety. As half the country is without trees, they burn stones' – here the Regent stopped and looked hard at me – 'and peat, of which there is plenty. They have wool and gold and silver mines, but do not know how to work them. The plenty and the variety of fish in Scotland, as also the size of the whales and sea-monsters, are incredible.'

The fact of the matter was that Cardinal Ercole was somewhat bored. Mantua is of course a splendid place but it is not Rome or Venice. It is what you might call a handkerchief state. I sometimes felt depressed at the narrow horizons myself. That very morning, in fact, when the skinny herald came out to the stables looking for me, I was in that frame of mind. It had been raining all week; there was a kind of mould on the apricot trees. I had lost my dearest companion in life. So far I had spent all that morning examining horses' hooves. My own life, it seemed, had shrunk to that, in a mildewed corner of the world.

So I dismissed the herald and after checking that all the mangers were sweet and clean, and then going home to bathe and dress, I presented myself in the ducal palace.

When I arrived, the Regent, most uncharacteristically, was in a rage.

'What have you been doing?' he cried. 'Didn't my messenger tell you the case was urgent?'

Then, without waiting for an answer, he spoke further, saying something which I could not at first catch. I heard the words '*Madama*' and '*Maria*' and perhaps '*regnante*', and, to tell the truth, I got it into my head that he was telling me that one of his mares was pregnant. My mind was running on horses and pregnancy a lot at the time. I dare say I gaped at him: if what he said was true, it had nothing to do with me. My 'brute' had not yet been near his mares.

Then, with exasperation at my dullness written on his features, the Regent spoke very plainly and clearly: 'Madame Maria now reigns in England.'

That was how I heard that the young King of England, Edward, was dead. His elder sister, Mary, the daughter of Katherine of Aragon, was now Queen.

'It is beyond all doubt,' said the Regent. 'I have it from separate sources although they have arrived together. Here is a letter from London:

> At the proclamation such demonstrations erupted that not only you who were not there but even I who was present can hardly find it credible . . . Men ran hither and thither, bonnets flew in the air, shouts rose higher than the stars, fires were lit on all sides and from a distance the earth must have looked like Mt Etna. The people were mad for joy and the streets crowded all night long.

'And here also,' the Regent continued, 'is a brief letter from your illustrious lord, Cardinal Reginald, begging me to send you to him at once, this instant. You should have left two hours ago. I cannot understand your tortoise steps. There is no time to tell you more. I will send my secretary with you and two guards in case you fall by the wayside. Now – begone!'

So I hurried home and farewelled my wife and children and was away from Mantua within two hours.

On the road I could not help observing that if Judith had been alive I would never have left, for she would not have let me go; and if Agnes was not my wife, I would not have gone either, as I would not have left my children alone like orphans.

And, as I also observed a few miles further down the road, it had never occurred to me to ask Agnes's advice, much less her permission.

A young man from the palace rode along with me: he was one of the Capilupo clan who serve the state of Mantua as secretaries and envoys and, with their sharp eyes and ears, do it very well. As we travelled he told me all he knew. The mood in England was not one of unalloyed joy. There were fears that Mary might ruin all and marry a foreigner, or bring back the Pope, which was dreaded equally by all the Lutherans and many of the Catholics, who now owned abbey land and did not want to give it back. Yet, by and large, the people were happy to see the end of the last rulers, the lords who had poisoned him – this was quite certain, said Capilupo; the boy had lost all his hair and his stomach was hard as a cannon-ball – and who had then put a trembling girl on the throne so they could rule without interference.

On seeing this, he said, the whole country rose in support of Mary, who had fled to Framlingham, or from Framlingham. The details were sketchy; Capilpuo had no idea what or where Framlingham was, but being an ambitious youth he liked to appear knowledgeable about the world, and so he spoke airily of that lofty seat.

Then Mary, at the head of a huge number of men and horses, rode to London, and all the conspirators fled.

When we reached the monastery near Lake Garda where Pole had taken up residence, I saw he was in a state of extreme agitation. He had a hectic spot of red in the middle of each cheek. I took them to be badges of vexation and anxiety.

He asked me to go to England immediately and take a message to the new Queen, seeking his admission to the kingdom.

The great threat hanging over her, he said, was that the Emperor, who had never lifted a finger to help Mary in all her troubles, would now gobble her up and take England for himself, in order to complete the encirclement of France.

Pole showed me a letter that had already come from the imperialist ambassador in Venice, warning him to stay out of English affairs.

> His Majesty is the chosen instrument of God in all that has happened here and should continue to be so. He knows best, with his great zeal and prudence, what roads the negotiations should follow and when they should be undertaken . . . Nothing can be usefully undertaken without his direction . . . He is the paranymph here.

'What's this *paranymph*?' I asked.

'What indeed?' said Pole. 'It means the best man at a wedding. Perhaps the word slipped out inadvertently. But it is clear they are planning to carry her off by marriage – either the Emperor will wed her himself, or marry her to his son, Philip. She must be warned of the danger.'

I could not see why Pole did not immediately go to England himself

'I intend to,' he said. 'I would go and beg my bread from door to door if that would help her to see that she is being tricked. But I must wait here for my letters-patent from Rome. I am to go to England as a legate. There have been some delays . . .'

For that reason, he said, I was to hurry on ahead and seek his admission into England.

'On no account say anything about marriage,' Pole warned me. 'She may have already taken it into to her head to marry Philip, and, if she is like other women, any hint of opposition will only make her stubborn. I will have to see her myself, and wean her away from the idea.'

I raced away, crossed Germany and reached Flanders without any impediments. But there, in Brussels, my journey was interrupted. I was arrested. No explanation was given. Why should they bother? It was a simple exercise of power. All was done politely, even smilingly. My letters were not taken. My horse was not taken. The more angry I became, the more benign their expressions.

'You will be in England soon,' was all that was said. 'Of course you will – no, you *must* go! After all it is your native land. And what can be sweeter than the sight of one's native land? For the moment, however, your onward journey is . . . *inopportune*.'

No real attempts, however, were made to conceal the reason. Everyone in Brussels knew what was taking place. Great powers are able to conceal shameful secrets for a short time; those which please them are known almost at once. I was shocked to find out, as soon as

I arrived, how far the project had advanced – namely, the captivation of the Queen. For this, half a dozen great imperialist officials had assembled in London before the news of the Queen's accession had even reached Mantua. They were led by several lords, including that same Don Diego I used to see at the wicket in Rome.

The master spirit, however, the chief wooer, the Cupid who fired the arrows into the Queen's heart, was a certain Simon Renard, Lieutenant d'Amont.

Renard, a Burgundian with a forked red beard, was the first man to awaken thoughts of love in Mary, a spinster aged thirty-eight who had never known a day's real affection since her mother was lost to her.

All the details of this wooing, on behalf of the Emperor and his son, were gossiped about openly in the imperial court. From the balcony of Flanders I was able to follow the play, scene by scene. Almost every evening at dusk Renard slipped through the gardens of the palace, at Richmond or in London, to talk to the Queen alone. For a month, he circled round the subject.

'When I mentioned marriage to her, she began to laugh, not once but several times, giving me a look which plainly said how agreeable the subject was to her . . .

'I know her to be good, easily influenced, inexpert in worldly affairs, in fact a novice all round . . . And her counsellors are so grasping that if one cares to try them with gifts and promises, one may do what one likes with them.'

That love-bulletin had been written while I was still on a farm outside Mantua, looking at my horses' hooves.

The proposed husband, the Emperor's son Philip, who was in Spain at the time, was wholly amenable to the project.

'I am rejoiced to hear that my aunt has come to the throne,' he wrote to his father, 'not only out of natural feelings, but because of the advantages to us where France is concerned. If she suggested marriage between herself and your Majesty, it would be the best thing possible. But if you wish to arrange the match for me, you know that I am so obedient a son that I have no other will than yours . . .'

I took great pains to find out all these things and every night copied down everything I had heard, especially from the Mantuan envoy, another Capilupo, M. Giulio, and sent them to Pole, so he should know what steps to take.

16

POLE, MEANWHILE, WAS STILL in Italy, waiting for his letters-patent. It turned out that Innocenzo – Cardinal Monkey, who was hardly ever seen in his office – had on that occasion personally issued the documents for Pole's legation to England. Naturally he made a fearful mess of it, the seals were not affixed properly or something of the kind. You might not credit that such a trivial thing should matter, but from that omission a great deal hangs.

If not for that, Pole may well have reached England, where he alone had enough authority over the Queen, whom he had known since childhood, in time to prevent her marriage.

It was not until mid-October, however, that he crossed the Alps.

By then the Imperialists had mustered against him. In Germany, just north of the mountains, he was stopped on the road by the Emperor's most senior ambassador, Don Juan Mendoza, who barred the way with a great array of secretaries and archers.

'His Majesty has heard of your legation to England,' said Mendoza, 'and can only praise the zeal of His Holiness and the choice of person. Yet he deems the execution untimely. He has sent a courier to Rome, explaining why you should on no account go any further. And therefore, my lord, I exhort you to stop and wait until we see what the Pope replies.'

'Any suggestion from the Emperor must always be held in the

highest regard,' said Pole. 'If it were up to me I would be happy to stand here in the road all day long, if that would gratify His Majesty. But I must have respect for my duty. I have an express commission from His Holiness to go forward. Unless there is some new and extraordinary reason with which I could justify myself for disobeying him, I do not see how I can halt.'

'The fact of the matter is this,' said Mendoza. 'The English loathe the papal authority so much that your appearance in their midst will create confusion that will admit of no ordering. It would be far better to go about things the other way around – perhaps the Queen should marry someone first and secure her throne. And one other thing is certain: if she marries an Englishman, she will open Pandora's box and every discontent will erupt among the nobility.'

'From what you have just said,' said Pole, 'the real reason behind your presence becomes clear. The Emperor wishes the Queen to marry his son. Until he has accomplished that, he will stop at nothing to prevent my going to England. He cannot convince himself that I will help him to place my country in the hands of a foreigner.'

For a long time they argued this back and forth, standing there in the middle of the road, at a place called Dillingen.

And on that very day, according to M. Capilupo, Renard, like a fox that has inspected the entrance to the burrow several times, finally made his move in London. At six in the evening he came up the water stairs from the river and slipped into Westminster palace and, having being led to the Queen, told her flatly that the Emperor thought the time had come for her to marry.

'But how can I marry?' she replied. 'I have never felt love, nor harboured thoughts of voluptuousness. Marriage is against all my inclinations. It is true the women around me talk of nothing else, but I could never mention the subject to my council. How could I keep a straight face? Besides, who is there in England to marry?'

'His Majesty has given the matter a great deal of thought,' said Renard. 'He wants you to choose someone agreeable to you, he bears you such affection that he hopes that person will be adorned with every virtue, and be of an age and character you desire. If an Englishman were chosen, however, he fears that he would try and claim more authority than is his due. When a man gets power or riches greater than might have been expected, it always turns his head and makes him insolent. There is young Edward Courtenay, for instance, Exeter's son, but he has spent his life in prison, which is not a suitable education for a king. Cardinal Pole, on the other hand, is in a prison of a different kind: he is in holy orders, he has no desire to marry. And in any case, given his very great age of fifty-three, he would not be suitable.'

'I will never marry Courtenay,' said the Queen with some violence. 'Why should I marry a man just because my chancellor has taken a fancy to him?'

'Then, as no Englishman is suitable,' said Renard. 'we must cast our eyes further afield. His Majesty knows you would never give your hand to a foreigner unless it was acceptable to your people. Yet he thinks you should certainly marry and bear children. Therefore he would like nothing more than to marry you himself. But given his age and poor health he believes he would be doing but little for you in offering you his own person. And so he wishes me to say that he can think of no one better than his son, the Prince of Spain.'

'Never can I thank His Majesty enough,' said the Queen. 'Such an offer – far greater than I ever dreamt of! But I do not know how the people of England will take it, for, as you know, they are of a certain character . . .'

'They are certainly of a changeable and contradictory temper,' said Renard, 'restless, turbulent, seekers after innovation; surrounded by the sea, they share its character since it is their natural element. As well as that, being a thoughtless race, and vindictive to boot, they hate foreigners, even foreign artisans who come to live among them for their own benefit. Despite these failings, however, they are not fools: they would never bear ill-will towards a prince who brought them peace, prosperity, liberty, safety for Your Majesty and increase for the Crown of England, whose enemies never cease their wicked designs. If, for instance, England were united with the many countries which will one day be governed by His Highness, that would be a good means of keeping the French in check and making them hear reason. The Crown of England might even recover France, which is its own property, and also reduce the Scots to proper obedience.'

'If His Highness has as many realms and provinces as you say,' said the Queen, 'I doubt that he will be willing to leave them and come and live in England. Do you really wish me to marry a man I will never see?'

'It would be much better to choose a king with many realms than an ordinary king with only one or two,' said Renard. 'In any case, His Highness would have no dearer wish than to stay with you day and night. And besides, his kingdoms are so near one another and so close to England that when he is in one he could hardly be said to be away from the others.'

'That is all very good,' said the Queen, 'but I know nothing at all about him. I may have heard that he seems younger than his years and not as wise as his father. And I hope you will not tell me that he is disposed to be amorous, for that is not at all to my inclination.'

'As to His Highness's character,' cried Renard, 'you have been informed by very doubtful characters, fond of slander, with vile motives and without any regard for the truth. He in fact is so admirable, virtuous, prudent and modest that he may well seem too wonderful to be human, and although Your Majesty may think I am speaking the language of a servant, in reality I minimise his qualities.'

'I am as free as the day I was born,' said the Queen reflectively, 'and have never taken a fancy to anyone in my life. Yet how can I make up my mind? How can I confer with my council? When they once brought up the subject of matrimony, I rebuffed them so severely they have never dared mention it again.'

'If your council sincerely desire the greatness of England, I do not believe they will oppose you,' said Renard. 'Besides, when you have made your desires known, it is their duty to find a way to bring them about.'

'I have heard,' said the Queen, 'that when the King of Bohemia went to Spain he gained great renown for the way he conducted himself and his affairs, and in comparison the Prince of Spain is not highly thought of in this regard. O Lieutenant d'Amont, I conjure you: tell me truthfully what his character is.'

'Such a prince,' said Renard, 'so noble, so mild and so puissant that no one in the world could suggest a better match for you. And remember – you have many enemies, none of whom will ever cease to cause you trouble if they can: the French, the Scots, the heretics, and the lady Elizabeth, who is to be feared for she has the power of enchantment. With such a husband at your side, you will be safe. You may think he is is too young, yet in fact he is in his twenty-eighth year, with a son aged eight. In fact, he is of such a stable and settled character that no one could possibly call him young. And besides, a man who is nearly thirty is nowadays considered as old as men used to be at forty.'

There was another pause. Then the Queen took Renard's hand.

'Are you speaking the truth?' she said. 'Or are these the views of a servant or subject influenced by love or fear?'

'I beg you to take my honour and my life as hostages,' said Renard, 'if you should not find that what I have said is the truth. His Highness has qualities as virtuous as any prince that breathes.'

At this, the Queen pressed his hand and breathed the words: '*That is well*' and then she asked him to leave her.

'By which I understood,' reported Renard, 'that she was so moved she could not say more.'

17

THERE ALWAYS ARE AND always will be, Flamminio used to say, wonderful new follies making an appearance among mankind. Yet few can be as wonderful as this: a government that puts its foreign policy in the hands of men who are devoted to the interests of another state. That is what happened to the Roman See.

The Pope left all the decisions about England to several cardinals working more or less openly in the imperialist interest. When the Emperor's letter, seeking to stop Pole, arrived in Rome, they seized their opportunity. An order was sent commanding him to stay in Dillingen until further notice.

That was the moment, in my view, when he should have resigned his red hat and gone straight to England, travelling through France if necessary. After all, what could have happened to him? Would his cousin, who adored him in her youth, have cut off his head? And almost everyone else in England greatly desired his presence there, even the Protestants, for they dreaded the Spanish marriage more than anyone. But once again, as at midnight in the conclave a few years before, my master fell prey to that fearful indecision, that immobility of soul which finds reasons to delay and do nothing. And so he did what he was told, and stayed where he was.

In due course, a month later, the betrothal between Mary and the

Prince of Spain was announced, and the whole kingdom descended into uproar.

Pole contented himself by writing to the Emperor in these terms, saying the church of Rome might be unpopular in England, but 'it is not nearly so universally odious as this marriage to your son.' In any case, he added, the Queen, at her age, should content herself with the love of her people, and leave the succession to itself.

For this he was sorely punished. Renard immediately informed the Queen of her cousin's opinion. She then wrote him an icy letter, in Latin, as if to an unknown foreign official, to tell him that his appearance in England would be inconvenient.

Apart from the chance that sent Cardinal Monkey into his office one day, everything had been managed brilliantly by the Emperor himself. He gave up all other affairs to concentrate on the match alone. Ambassadors going to see him on other matters were kept waiting twenty or thirty days for an audience. This was told to me by the Mantuan ambassador in Brussels, M. Giulio.

'And if you do get in to see him,' he said, 'you get three minutes, as long as it takes to say the Credo, and you're out on your ear again. He is lying in the dark in any case – one scarcely knows in which direction to bow. He is crippled with gout in every member of his body, even to the back of his neck, and is so afflicted by catarrh he can speak only in a whisper. And as well as that, he suffers from haemorrhoids which have swelled up and which torment him so much he cannot turn over in bed without tears.'

'And there's our paranymph!' I said.

'That's him, indeed,' said M. Giulio. 'Night and day he dwells on this marriage. They say he spends long hours sunk in thought and then weeps like a child. But no one in his household has enough authority to dispel his dark imaginings. Even his sisters dare not say anything to him. The success of his whole life depends on this match, which now looks certain to go ahead. Already the French are so troubled and amazed, so terror-stricken and enfeebled at the thought of it, that they cannot conceal their melancholy.'

Thus the wooing and capture of the Queen was accomplished by her uncle, the most powerful man in the world (though he couldn't turn over in bed without tears) who ended his niece's brief moment of happiness, and in fact ruined her life.

As the French ambassador in London was to say a year or two later: 'I am truly sorry for this tragic queen, who tried to win a husband's love and the love of her people and who has lost both because she listened to evil counsel.'

In December I was allowed to leave Flanders. It was judged, I suppose, that I could no longer do any harm. The marriage plans had been announced. My letters from Pole, seeking admittance, were long out of date. As well as that, my plight had become known in England. I was now an embarrassment: if the Imperialists were already arresting Englishmen as they pleased, what would they be like once they had installed their own fellow on the English throne? One day I woke to find that my restraints – my guards, my smiling attendants – had all vanished. Nothing was ever said to me. I went to the coast unhindered, I sailed away, I reached London. And as soon I got there I made my way to the palace. I did in fact have a new message from Pole to the Queen, which the Imperialists knew nothing about. My nephew Inglefield was then on the council and was able to arrange admittance for me.

It was strange to be approaching the great brick gate again, seventeen years since the last time I came there. From the outside everything looked much the same. I could see the King's beasts – the wooden dogs and griffins on poles – above the garden wall. And, after all, what had really changed? There I was, once again with a message from Pole, going in to see the sovereign Prince of England who, like her father before her, insisted on marrying a young person who was not the least bit in love with her.

Of course there were some of the changes, of the ironic type, which

Time loves to ring: on my first visit, Pole was ordered to come to England, but he would not go. Now he wanted to be there but was ordered to stay away. And this time, as I was led into the Presence Chamber (inside the palace everything had changed around and I had lost all my bearings) there, instead of a great bearded man with a dagger slung on his hip, I saw a little pale woman, not unhandsome, in a plum-coloured riding costume of mannish cut, who, despite an attempt to seem imperious, was looking at me with somewhat frightened and even imploring eyes.

The atmosphere in London at that time was terrible. The Queen's ladies spent half the day weeping and trembling for their lives. The town rang with talk of revolt and rebellion. Even within the palace, obscene pamphlets showing the Queen giving suck to Spanish goblins had been found scattered about. A dog with its ears cropped had run shrieking into the Presence Chamber and out again. Cries of 'papist' and 'heretic' were heard at divine service. The Queen at times gave herself up to tears, and each day asked anxiously whether a letter or note had come from her beloved.

She was already, her ladies assured me, violently in love, although Philip had not yet bothered to write to her. All she had was a portrait by Titian, showing the Prince in white wolf-skins, and that was on loan from his aunt in Brussels and had to be returned.

When I took her hand, so thin, light and cold, to kiss it, I almost said aloud, 'Ah, you poor thing'. Red wine, beefsteak, an arm around her – that's what she needs, I thought, but of course this was not a proper sentiment for a subject kneeling before his sovereign. In any case, my sympathy would be out of place. For she also looked at me with some hostility: I came from the enemy, the man who opposed her happiness in love.

'My councillor tells me you have a message from a certain personage,' she said with an indifferent air.

'Only this, noble madam,' I said. 'The Cardinal wishes you to know that since he is not allowed to return to his own country, or even to come near it, or to serve you in any way, then he intends to retrace his steps and go back to Italy, where he will never molest you again.'

At this she looked somewhat appalled. The fact was that she did love her cousin, in the abstract at least, as the only kinsman who had never deserted her cause. It was just that she did not want him coming along and spoiling her marriage plans.

She said nothing. I rose and bowed and went away.

As I left the court I could not help noticing that, within, all the women were rather plain. Outside in the streets many beauties could be seen.

A little while after this, Pole received a message in Dillingen saying that he was now permitted to come a little nearer the imperial court, and even visit Brussels, but he must approach softly – *pian piano* – as the very thought of him would infuriate the English people.

And after a little further time in London, I was summoned to the chamberlain's office. In recognition for my signal services to the Queen, I was informed, I was to be rewarded with grants of land.

It was impossible to believe what I heard next.

'All lands at Ullenhall in Wottom, Warwickshire; lands called "Packers" in Shustock, Warwickshire; the messuage or farm of Wynerton in Wynterton, Warwickshire and all demesne lands and profits of the same; the manor of Honeley alias Honylie and Blackwell; lands in Alcetter, formerly belonging to St Sepulchre's priory; and all lands and profits in Ullenhall, Wynterton, Wynerton, Honylie, Blackwell and Wotton, belonging to the said manors, the manor of Haseley, late parcel of the lands of John, the Duke of Northumberland, attainted, and advowson of the rectory of the church of Haseley, the herbage, agistment and pannage of Haseley Park, the reversion of the said park, and the lodge, house and mansion in the same, with free warren and chace and liberties of park within the same.'

This was nothing less than the land of my childhood, and still occasionally of my dreams, that lay on the horizons of Coughton – hilly land, flat land, rich fields, shadowy woods, torrents and chases. Some of it was even property my brother rented from the owners. Now I was the owner. Of course, I had done nothing to deserve this. The grant was a signal from the Queen that she still bore affection to my master. All the same, I was glad that poor Sir George was no longer living – he had died the previous year – as the shock of it might well have killed him.

18

SINCE HE WAS UNABLE to get into England, Pole turned to the second part of his legation, to make peace between the Emperor and the new King of France, whose countries were back at war and fighting more bitterly than ever.

After many days wait, he was permitted to see the Emperor, who greeted him coolly but invited him to sit. The Emperor himself was sitting on two chairs, with his foot up on one because of the gout, which had nonetheless improved over the last month.

On the question of Pole's going to England, he would not budge. The hatred of Rome was so great there, he said, that no risks could be taken. Perhaps after the wedding . . . On the question of holding peace talks with the French, he did not completely close the door.

Pole then left for Paris.

He crossed the frontier in early spring. For twenty miles on either side of the border there was nothing but devastation. The very ground seemed to smoke, his secretary said, and yet, from out of the ruins great crowds appeared, from holes in the ground, as it were, weeping and strewing green branches in the legate's path and begging him to bring peace.

That night, further along the way, Pole sat down and composed an address to both rulers.

> Behold the evils for which you alone are responsible, and remember them well, because for these things you will be held to account by a most dread judge. Your trial will be different from that of ordinary people. They will be charged with their own failings. You, as rulers, will be held to account for much more – all the crimes, the torture and murders performed by the men you command and have sent to war. The very least of these offences is not found worthy of mercy in a human court. How then will you stand before that far more terrible tribunal?

On reading this, Henri, the King of France, smiled and said it was a most interesting oration. If only he had known Pole earlier, he added, he would certainly have wanted him to have been made Pope at the last conclave, thereby cutting short a drama which had perhaps gone on too long. As to peace with the Imperialists, Henri was sure it could be obtained with only one or two adjustments, such as the return of Milan, which everyone knew belonged to France.

The Emperor, by contrast, when Pole came back to Brussels, was furious.

'You have done nothing but make blunders,' he shouted as soon as Pole entered the room. 'This little trip of yours to France turns out to be very costly. It makes the world think *we* are against peace.'

'And yet nothing is more foreign to His Majesty's righteous mind,' said his chief minister, Granvelle, who was standing beside him.

'Now I suppose there has to be a conference, otherwise people will say we are the aggressors,' said the Emperor.

'And what good will a conference do?' said Granvelle.

'It might bring about a good peace,' said Pole.

'A good peace will be made only by a good war,' cried Granvelle.

'Having been down there,' said Pole, pointing towards the south, 'I may tell you there is no such thing.'

'Well, the French started this one,' said Granvelle, 'but they won't be the ones who finish it – at least not in a way they like. In a month or two, we shall have such an army that they will be very happy to scamper home – if they can get there. Why, his Majesty has so many realms, including Peru, that I would love to know what I'm supposed to think of the King of France, who has only one, and who has already started melting down the church chalices.'

'And yet your subjects want peace as much as his,' said Pole.

'Oh, he is a very learned and virtuous person,' said Granvelle, now speaking as if Pole was not present, 'but he knows nothing about the world.'

'In fact, he has performed more harm than good,' said the Emperor. 'The demands of the French are so impudent, he would have done better to have kept them to himself.'

'He would have done better to have gone to France and stayed there,' said Granvelle.

'He would have done better never to have left Italy in the first place,' said the Emperor. 'That young hothead' – he meant the King of France – 'has wronged me more in a year than his father managed in a lifetime.'

'And now he fetches in the Turks, the enemy of all Christians, to join the fight on his side.'

'And we are supposed to sit down at a table together, as if we were equally to blame.'

'There, you see?' said Granvelle, 'We are in an impossible position – and it is all his fault.'

Then they both turned to glare at Pole, and continued glaring as he was led to the door at the far end of the great chamber.

'In fact, short of using cudgels, they could not have been more violent towards me,' said Pole afterwards.

After that, there was no question of his going to England, even when the wedding was held, and the marriage of the Queen was an accomplished fact. Pole's punishment was to extend far beyond that date. Yet it was judged that he should be represented, for the people of England held him in high regard, and looked with grave misgivings on the whole proceeding.

For that reason, it fell to me to go to court a day or two after Philip married Mary, and to speak on behalf of the illustrious Cardinal.

I was rather nervous, I will admit, as I went into the great Presence Chamber. This was in the palace at Winchester. Outside, the rain poured down. Within was the greatest gathering of lords, nobles, prelates, dukes and duchesses ever seen in England.

I had to wait a long time, watching various ceremonies, before my turn came to speak. The Queen was just then receiving her new relatives from Spain. The last to enter was one of the most exalted, the Duchess of Alba, who came to pay her respects.

The Queen went to the door to greet her, took her by the hand and led her to a chair, and then, sitting on a cushion, begged her to be seated. The Duchess utterly refused, imploring the Queen to take the chair. The Queen declined. Two stools appeared – the Queen sat on one and invited the Duchess to have the other. At that, the Duchess sat on the floor. The Queen then sat beside her on a cushion. The Duchess begged her to rise; she relented; she was back on a stool again; she then *commanded* the Duchess to take the other.

At last, all honours completed, both ladies were seated side by side and could begin to discuss the weather. It seemed the Duchess had suffered badly from storms on the voyage from Spain.

During these proceedings I was standing in the midst of a group of insolent young lords from Spain and Italy who were watching the Queen and commenting on all they saw, imagining that no one nearby understood what they said:

'She's old,' said one, 'she is old and she is flabby. I'll tell you what – I hate to see our Prince with such an old bag.'

'But look how happy she is,' said a second. 'He treats her kindly and hides the fact that she's no good from the point of fleshly pleasure.'

'She should dress in our fashion,' said a third, 'which might improve her appearance.'

'She is short and has no eyebrows.'

'She is a perfect saint but dresses badly.'

'They all dress badly here. Their petticoats have no silk admixture in them at all as far as I can see, and the dresses themselves are badly cut.'

'Look at the expression on the Duchess's face – she won't be back here again in a hurry.'

'They show their leg to the knee, which is passably immodest even when seated, but when it comes to dancing . . .'

'Dancing? Do you call that dancing? I call it mere strutting and trotting about.'

'None of us is going to fall in love with any of them, nor they with us.'

'There's already been knife-work here in the palace, between their servants and ours.'

'They're afraid of us. They think we have come to manage everything and steal their wives.'

'They've been robbing us in broad daylight from the minute we landed.'

'They have the advantage over us – we steal by stealth and they by force.'

I was so intent on this that I did not notice a hush had fallen and that the chamberlains were gazing at me and making strange gestures with their eyebrows. It was time for me to make my address.

This was cast as a speech to Philip alone, on the occasion of his becoming King of England.

I made my way forward and began.

'*Serenissime Rex!*'

A great silence had fallen. I heard my own voice as if I was listening far away, though also much closer than I had ever heard it before. But I was no longer nervous. 'After all,' I said to myself, 'what's the worst that can happen? There may be dangers here, but none worse than the brown stallion at Forli that tried to kill me, or the robbers who live in the forest near Chambery,' and then I played a trick on myself, imagining that those savage beasts were also present, along with the hundreds of people staring in my direction. This fancy worked; my voice grew stronger.

'Cum maxime antea laetatus essem,' I declared, *'cognito ex fama ipsa et litteris meorum optatissimo majestatis tuae in angliam adventu et felicissimus nuptis quae cum Serenissima Regina nostro summo omnium gaudio et gratulatione celebratae sunt tunc hanc meam laetitiam— '*

And so on and so on . . .

I had the impression that my great audience of lords and ladies, stallions and robbers, was a little disappointed. Everyone knew who Pole was, and why he was not present, and his great reputation for telling the truth. Yet here was nothing to be heard but *gratulatione* and *felicissimus.*

That was the pinnacle of my career as a messenger. It could scarcely carry me higher. And yet, I thought to myself, as I heard my voice from far away, it was sad, as well, that there, on the pinnacle, I should for the first time hear myself telling many great lies in Pole's name.

But what else could I expect? After all, this was the celebration of a wedding, when it is far too late to go about telling the truth.

That was roughly the view that Pole himself took, when I reproached him later. He had not lied, he said. His words were quite sincere. After all, the marriage was a fact, and, as such, providence must have played some part in it. Therefore there was nothing to do but hope for the best, or at least hope that his worst fears were proven wrong.

BOOK III

I

DURING MY SPLENDID ORATION before the court at Winchester something quite unexpected happened: I realised that the time had come for me to leave England. In the very midst of the speech, an ardent picture of Mantua suddenly came to mind. I had a great desire to be there, to see all my children, my little centaurs as I called them. And it also became clear to me that it would be a long time before Pole would ever set foot in England. This I learnt from my nephew Inglefield. Everything in England, he told me, was now decided by Stephen Gardiner, the Lord Chancellor. This was the same Gardiner who once, years before, had gone on his knees to the King of France, begging him to hand Pole over so he might be *trussed up* and conveyed alive to England.

He still greatly hated Pole, said my nephew, so much that the very sound of his name induced in him such fits of jealousy that his secretaries and fellow councillors and even foreign ambassadors were obliged to soothe him.

Gardiner's great fear was that once the wedding was over, my master would be summoned to England, and then, basking in the Queen's favour, would replace him as the highest minister of state. This, at all costs, he intended to prevent.

I decided, therefore, that my task as Pole's agent in England had come to an end, and in fact I would have ridden off from Winchester there and then and not stopped until I came to the door of this very house in Mantua, but I found certain obstacles, strange and unfamiliar, in my way.

For the first time in my life I had property to detain me. Pole used to call wealth 'golden shackles'. Mine was more like a forest I could not get out of. My acres, my woods and houses and chimneys and windowpanes – they were fine, excellent in every way, but with them came bills, leases, rents, many tangled briars (lawsuits were pending), all of which had to be attended to.

This, however, is not something a man can decently complain about; I went to Coughton to attend to them and was there nearly three months. It was not a happy house. The family was not a happy one. I had never imagined I would miss George so much. Of course I dearly loved my brother up to a point, but never thought him very wise. Now I saw how well he had kept order under that roof. In his absence, there was endless arbitration about everything under the sun from the food bills to the weight of the horseshoes, but most of all it was religion that caused the perturbations. We had not, in Warwickshire, yet got to the stage of Essex and Suffolk, where rapiers were appearing in the churchyards, but that didn't seem far off. Dinner was a convocation of enemies. One hardly dared to speak, for discord rushed in. Nicholas was a great Lutheran. Long John held the mass an abomination worse than murder. George wanted things back as they were under King Henry. Robert preferred things as they were before the Divorce. My nephew Clement was a hot gospeller who wanted no more ceremonies of baptism. My aunt, who had been a nun until convents were torn down and who still kept a 'poor door' at the house to feed beggars who came wandering our way, sat at table with her lip trembling. I myself was now the owner of former monastic lands.

In short, we were all at sea over religion. And yet that itself rises from our deepest thoughts and it's no use saying we should do away with it. For my part, sitting at dinner at Coughton, I began to think that when I reached Mantua and found my family again I would not bring them back to live in England after all, despite my acres. Life in Mantua under the Regent seemed to take on a new and serene aspect. In the end, after weeks and months, I signed over the house and land at Haseley to Clement, who had a wife and child and was therefore most in need of them, and then, putting all the rest of the property in the stewardship of old Walker, I left Coughton and set off for London and Dover.

By then it was mid-November. I stayed in London a few days, and one morning I rose early to ride down to the sea. I had gone downstairs – this was in the old house in Throckmorton Street – and was standing in the dark with my hand raised to unlock the door, when, at the very same moment there came a very rapid knocking on the other side.

'Who's there?'

'A herald.'

'What herald?'

'Inglefield herald.'

'What does he want?'

'Open the door.'

I opened the door. I saw a very small man standing there, a Moor, very black of skin. His aspect in itself surprised me, though why I don't know – messengers may come in any shape or size they like, and why should you care?

'My master, Inglefield, sends to tell you that your master, Pole, is now on the sea,' he said.

I can still see the brass key in my hand, and the lock stile, and the dwarf who brought me the news at that moment just before the day had begun to light the street behind him. Mr Pole, *Traitor Pole*, the Cardinal of England, after many years of exile, of danger, long journeys, great fame and final mortification, was on his way home.

This astounded me. I could not understand how it had come about. From all I knew Gardiner had not changed his mind about

Pole, and the Queen, besotted with her new husband, gave little thought to her cousin in exile. But I could not stand there all day and debate the matter with myself. Nor was the messenger a likely source of insight – he was a saucy devil and cocked his hand on his hip as he looked up at me, as if to say he was well aware that *I* was someone of little importance.

Without going to the lengths of strangling him, I learnt that Pole would land at Dover, cross to Gravesend and come to London by water. Hearing that, of course I changed my plans and decided to take the barge downriver to Gravesend to meet him.

Everything then went wrong – the tide was flowing; I turned back and rode instead, and arrived at Gravesend after dark; there was no Pole. In the morning he was still not there. I set out on horse to Canterbury, puzzled as to how all this was to fall out – and then, suddenly, coming around a corner, I met my Lord Cardinal.

It was not, of course, a face-to-face encounter. On the opposite side of a valley somewhere near Ospringe I saw flowing down the hill a vast crowd of thousands and thousands, moving forward as the honeycomb flows, and as dark as the wintry woods on either side of the road. It seemed that the whole county had joined the Cardinal on his route to London, and even as I watched I could see more people on foot and horse hurrying across the fields to witness what was passing.

I was somewhat nonplussed. I had forgotten how I used to imagine Pole's eventual return to England but it was nothing like this. I rode forward and met the crowd. There was no chance in the world of speaking to Pole or even seeing him clearly in the crush of lords and bishops and ordinary folk, half of Kent, who rode ahead of him and behind him and on either side and who came on as far as Gravesend.

And this, I could see, was how things would be from now on. For ten years these folk would have lost their lives if they mentioned my master's name except with a curse; half of them, I suppose, would have handed him over to the hangman without a second thought.

But now he was back and approaching power, things were different. Ah well, I told myself, this is the slightly bitter taste of long loyalty. But then I became impatient and seized the nettle. By dint of speaking sharply in Italian to the English who swarmed around him, and sternly in English to the Italians who swarmed about him, I managed to get near my master and old friend – he gave me his hand briefly with a look as if to say 'Don't blame me if I scarcely recognise you, everything is changing before my eyes' – and he was whisked away again.

All the same, I got aboard the leading barge, where in my view I deserved to be, for this, the final scene of all his years of wandering. But I was well at the back, and I never saw his face.

As an attainted traitor, Pole had been forbidden from displaying any signs of office when he arrived in England, but at Gravesend an order had come from London relaxing this command. For the last part of his long journey, up the river Thames, the silver cross of a legate stood at the bow of the barge.

The Italians, who had never seen a tidal river before, declared a miracle as the current bore us inland. From Deptford on, the banks were black with people.

At one o'clock we shot the rapids under the bridge, and a few minutes later reached Whitehall. The new king, Philip, came to the water-stairs to meet the newcomer, and then Pole was lost to sight as he went into the palace.

'Well, that's the end of him,' I thought. And it seemed quite possible, since I was about to go to Italy, and he had vanished into the throng that surrounds power, that I might never see him again. But the next day he sent for me.

2

'I AM BESIEGED BY dozens of members of my family who have lost everything,' he said. 'I can do little for them. There are so many grave public matters to attend to. But one thing is preying on my mind. It is a private matter, a family matter, perhaps I should ignore it, but it won't leave me be.'

He asked me to make enquiries, as discreetly as possible, to try and find out what had happened to his young nephew, his brother's son, who was sent to prison as a child and of whom no word had been heard for years.

'I don't expect good news,' he said. 'But we should know something – when he died, where he is buried . . . At least we should not accept knowing nothing and forget all about him.'

This meant at least another month away from Italy, but I undertook the commission out of duty and curiosity and pity as well. I thought of my own two dead children, my newborn son and daughter who – I sometimes had the impression – came to me in dreams, bidding me not to forget them entirely either.

I set to work at once. Here was another new role, and one for which I was peculiarly unfit. I had no idea where to start, and had to ask Pole how I should go about it. Above all, he said, discretion was needed: if there were secrets to hide, those who hid them might well be in a position to prevent their discovery. On the other hand, some help would be required from strangers. So for the first time I set my foot inside the archives, going first to the King's paper room and later to the records of past lords Privy Seal and then to the books and logs of the lieutenant of the Tower.

On the first day, I admit my heart sank at the sight of the walls stacked with rolls and folios rising higher than a man's head, and going back, no doubt, for centuries. There were clerks there, who were neither helpful nor unhelpful. I showed them a letter from Pole, a kind of safe conduct through those dry mountains, but the clerks looked at this document with indifference. In their eyes, hunting for knowledge among their papers was great folly: the wise thing to do was to keep them undisturbed, as far from prying eyes as possible.

In the end, it was Tom Rutter of all people who came to my aid. He had come up with me when I left Coughton. I could not stop him doing so.

He came along just to see London again, and then, since I was staying on, he decided to stay on as well, as my servant and, as he saw it, my guardian.

He was now a tenant of mine and as my tenant – and a very bad tenant, at that – he regarded me as a most valuable property. He did not like to have me out of his sight.

'But how can you stay on, Tom?' I said. 'What about your wife and children?'

'Them? Right as roaches.'

When I first went to work in the paper room, Tom stayed well away, standing out in the street with a strange, innumerable acquaintance he had gathered, I don't know how, in a matter of hours. Then the cold winds drove him inside. He began to gaze over my shoulder. Until then I had no idea that he could read. As time went on, he became interested in my progress or, rather, continual failures. I soon noticed that he could deal with the clerks better than I. They were unsettled by his unblinking stare. They gave up their secrets to him. He also had the poacher's instinct for what lies hidden in the thicket. It was Tom who learnt of the existence of a trove of papers which had been taken from Cromwell's own house when he fell from power. The clerks perhaps would not have brought these to my notice. It was there that we found a few faint tracks of young Henry Pole. These came in the form of memoranda which Cromwell wrote – 'remembrances', as he called them – on matters that he meant to refer to the King's attention.

These separate notes were much thumbed and creased with black – they had been folded and kept inside the pocket of the Lord Privy Seal himself:

> 6 October 1539: *Remember the diets of young Courtenay and Poole and the Countess of Salisbury, and to know the King's pleasure therein.*
>
> 31 October: *What the King will have done with the Lady of Salisbury. For the diet of young Pole.*
>
> 10 November: *Remember the two children in the Tower.*

That was all I could find regarding the children. The 'remembrances' came to an end – as Cromwell himself came to an end. But by then we knew what to look for, and could follow the spoor elsewhere. In the spring of 1540 there had been a general amnesty for those accused of treason, but there were certain exceptions: '*Not to extend to the following: Thomas Cromwell; the Lady of Salisbury, Edward Courtenay, Henry Pole, son of Lord Montagu.*'

Cromwell was then put to death, but it was possible to follow the little doomed party for a few months more, this time through payments made to the lieutenant of the Tower:

> *King's monthly payments to E. Walsingham, for the diets of Margaret Poole, Edward Courtenay and Henry Poole:*
>
> 8 July 1540 – £13/6/8.
>
> 3 October 1540 – £40.

10 November 1540 – £64

2 December–2 February 1541 – £26/13/8

3 February–3 March – £26/13/4

31 March–25 May – £26/13/4.

Then the group dwindled again. Lady Salisbury was no longer mentioned. She was killed at the end of May. The expenses fell.

Payments to Sir Edward Walsingham for the diets of Edward Courtenay and Henry Pole, at £4 a month, each:

30 March–24 May – £16

May–July – £16

20 July–13 September – £16

There the trail ended. We looked on ahead for several more years. Young Courtenay was still mentioned, but there was no sign of Henry Pole. From the record, it appeared that he had died four or five months after the last words we ever heard reported about him: 'He is but poorly and strictly kept and not desired to know anything.'

At the Tower itself, no one knew anything. The old lieutenant had died, the new one could not help me. The guards, from the youngest to the very oldest, who had been there for years, found they too could not assist in my enquiries. When I stated the year in question – 1541 – their eyes bulged in wonder that such infinite distances should be compassed by the mind of man. I might have been asking about the Fall of Troy. But one day, on my second or third visit, two of the older warders relented and led us down into a dark cell with no light but that from a grate, and showed us some words written there on a wall, in what may (or may not) have been a childish hand.

Ubi lapsus
Quod feci

Which is to say: Where have I fallen? What have I done?

There was a sort of legend, the warders said – very vague and unreliable, they said – among the guards, that this had been written by one of the children held prisoner at that remote and long forgotten era.

There the search came to an end, without any conclusion. I reported my failure to Pole. It had all taken much longer than I expected and was a sad and painstaking business. Yet I have to admit that in a way I enjoyed it as well: it was strangely calm, and at times exciting, like tracking deer in a fog over a moor. And once I had stumbled on Cromwell's papers, I could not keep away from them. For there in the paper room, before my very eyes, was the story of my own life from twenty years ago.

The first thing I found with a kind of shock of recognition were letters in my own writing – a bold, youthful hand, carelessly committing to paper – the very pages were back in my own hand again! Many disgraceful lies:

> O my lord Cromwell, what shall I do now? I seek your excellent counsel, as no man has proved better the profit of true fidelity.

And:

> I rejoice I showed you once a little kindness, Master Morison, where other men get money you win men's hearts . . .

I found Cromwell's instructions to Wilson and Heath as they left for Maastricht: '*Declare to the said Pole his miserable condition . . . By no means call him by any other name than* Mr *Pole*'.

I found the records of the interrogations of the Lady of Sarum, both her sons, their servants, Hugh Holland. I found my own poor brother's tearstained page: '*Michael? It would be better if he had never been born!*'

And there also, while turning over the private papers of Cromwell just as I pleased – something neither he nor I could have dreamt of eighteen years before – I came across a letter which I had never dreamt of either. It was sent from Padua in the year 1538:

> My lord – Since writing last I have twice spoken with Michael Throckmorton since he was in Padua buying linen and household stuff . . . The first time he was merrily disposed and boasted how he deceived you, my lord, and Master Morison, when in England in message for his master, thinking that but for his crafty and subtle conveyance, you would have beheaded him – as if he was a person whose life mattered to either you or the King, or that you or the King would violate the security of a messenger! He is much simpler and less discreet than he thinks, and is more in credence and trust than authority with his master.
>
> The second time was the eighteenth day of August, rathe in the morning, when he came clothed in a coat of wolf skins and a cap of mail, as pale as ashes, blowing and puffing like unto a raging lion. He said he had not slept all night – the cause was one Harry Phillips who had arrived here in Padua from Flanders arrayed like a Swiss, or a ruffling man of war, with a pair of German boots.
>
> Throckmorton thinks he was sent by you, my lord, to destroy his master. How could anyone try such a deed alone and in a strange country, I asked. He said it could be very easily done. When Poole rode out as usual with five or six unarmed men, they could be attacked by three or four hardy fellows who could then escape to the mountains in four hours.
>
> Throckmorton then went about hunting for Phillips and beset the gates to know which way he went and with whom.

A few hours later he returned somewhat merrier, having done off his wolf skins and coat of mail, and remitting his fierce countenance and old fox's conditions and returned again to the nature of a young sheep. He had found Phillips was in poverty, with no friends and nowhere to go. But ever since, for a whole fortnight, Pole has been very much afraid. Yet it was nothing but a fantasy engendered by continual fear for his holy body and delicate flesh. I think these gentlemen have a very weak and slender faith and little hope in Christ and the life to come, seeing their mortal security does so move and torment them. Every wagging of a straw now makes them afraid . . .'

This was addressed to Cromwell. I had trouble at first deciphering the name at the bottom, then I made it out: *Thos. Theobald.*

I stared at this in wonder. My friend, Tom Theobald!

Never had it crossed my mind, even in the bleakest hours when anything can be imagined, that he was in fact my enemy.

'Great God!' I said to myself. 'Tom! Tom Theobald! Why, you—!'

But then I thought: 'Well, well, well – I tricked Cromwell and the King, which no one else in the world ever managed, but Tom Theobald hoodwinked me, so I suppose he must take the prize.'

Then strangely enough I began to feel sad, not at the loss of friendship or of youth but just at the thought of the summer morning long ago, which now came back to me in all its details, and I almost wished myself back there to see it all again. I marvelled how everything – those young men themselves, their fears and deceits and jokes – had vanished as completely as the sunlight of that distant morning.

Even my coat of wolf skins, I thought. There was a time when I would hardly let it out of my sight. Now I could not even remember where I had cast it aside.

Before finally giving up the searches and leaving the King's paper room for good, I came across one other important document.

This was a letter to Cromwell from the renowned divine and preacher Latimer. He wrote it just after the murder of Pole's family had commenced:

> Blessed be the God of England . . . whose minister ye be. I heard you once say after you had seen that furious invective of Cardinal Pole that you would make him eat his own heart, which you have now brought to pass, for he must needs eat his own heart, and be as heartless as he is graceless.

Why this struck me so forcibly at first I hardly knew. It was merely an opinion, common enough at the time, expressed to Cromwell by one of his friends. But then I understood. *It had come true.* The writer's prayer had been granted. It was just as I had thought over the years: from the death of his family on, Pole had indeed become *heartless*, that is to say, he had lost heart, he had lost his courage. I thought of the Pole who would not grasp the pontificate offered at midnight, the Pole who left Rome rather than stay and moderate the inquisition, the Pole who loitered on the road at Dillingen rather than go marching off to his native land.

In short, he had become afraid of the world. Which, after all, had shown itself more dreadful than he could have imagined. His aged mother led out to meet a boy of fourteen with an axe, another boy of ten or twelve dying alone in a cell, while his uncle feasted in the family house . . .

When I went to give Pole the result of my searches, I saw that he was surrounded by new troubles. Shadows were gathering around Mary's reign. Along with many others, Hugh Latimer himself – just to take an example – was in prison, waiting to go on trial for heresy. At times I have wondered whether, in his own cell, Latimer remembered what he wrote that day to Cromwell, and perhaps regretted that his hope had been so thoroughly fulfilled.

3

I DID NOT ATTEND any of the great ceremonies of reconciliation in the first week of Pole's return, when parliament revoked his death sentence and he in turn absolved the kingdom of the schism, and all that had happened was said to be *cast into a sea of forgetfulness.* I was no longer a member of his household – now at least a hundred strong – nor of the King's, nor the Queen's, nor of either house of parliament, nor of the convocation of clergy. I was merely a certain Mr Michael Throckmorton, Esq. of Warwickshire – a remarkable nonentity when it comes to drawing up a list of the guests of state.

At the end of that first week, however, I did go along to the public mass of thanksgiving held at St Paul's. The King had come from Whitehall with a vast retinue and four hundred guards, Pole came by barge from Lambeth, and they both then stood at a window of the cathedral to hear the sermon preached at Paul's Cross in the churchyard. It was there, in a crowd that stretched from the east door through the graveyard and beyond as far as Bread Street and towards the river, and indeed up into the sky, what with men leaning against chimney pots and boys in the bare branches of trees and women leaning out of windowsills, that I – along with Tom Rutter breathing down my neck – heard the famous sermon preached by the Lord Chancellor, Gardiner, to mark the reconciliation between England and Rome.

He took as his text 'Now is the time we wake from sleep'.

We who have slept, or rather dreamt, these last twenty years . . . First, as men intending to sleep, separate themselves from company and desire to be alone, so we have separated ourselves from the See Apostolic and have been alone, no other realm like us . . .

Then, as a man who wishes to sleep puts out the candle, so writers were condemned, libraries broken up, books torn up and burned, and a thousand images – which are the books of the poor – taken down or covered up in every corner of the land . . .

But now the Pope has sent this Reverend Cardinal, not to revenge injuries done by us against him, but to bless those who defamed and persecuted him. Rejoice in this day that such a noble man of birth has come – I mean my Lord Cardinal Pole, who speaks to us in our own language as brothers, not as strangers – a prophet, yea, a minister angelical—

It was then I heard a strange sound; a kind of sigh ran through the crowd, that immense crowd stretching as far as Bread Street and beyond.

'Yea, this minister angelical . . .' said Gardiner again, and there came that sigh once more, a rustle, like the wind in the shrouds.

At first I could not place it. After all it is rarely heard. But then I knew it: it was the sound of fifty thousand people trying not to laugh. For everyone there knew how much Gardiner always hated Pole.

'Hark, how he *claweth* the Cardinal!' said Rutter, and he kneaded my forearm like a cat to make the point. And it was at that moment I began to see why Pole had been allowed back into England. The laughter, suppressed, of fifty thousand is an infallible guide. Gardiner had not changed. He still hated Pole, and Rome, but he wanted him back for his own reasons.

> And as in sleep men dream of horrible things, sometimes of killing, sometimes of maiming, sometimes of drowning or burning, sometimes of beastliness as I dare not name but will spare your ears . . .

'Oho!' I said to myself, 'what sort of fellow has dreams of this kind to report?'

The answer then seemed as clear as day: *one who is planning a persecution.*

And for that Pole's presence was required in England. Gardiner still hated him, but he hated others more, namely Cranmer, Latimer, Ponet. Yet they had all been Henry's men. Henry made Gardiner Bishop of Winchester. At the coronation of Anne Boleyn, it was Gardiner who bore up the laps of her robes. He wrote a book, *De Vera Obedientia*, denouncing the Pope. But at the same time he had fallen out with the others over questions of theology. When the King died, Cranmer and Latimer struck. They degraded him, stripping him of crook and mitre, and sent him to prison. A new man, John Ponet, was installed as Bishop of Winchester.

Ponet was famous for running away with the wife of a butcher who sued for her return.

In the Tower, Gardiner remained intrepid.

Asked by a visitor if he thought he would ever be Bishop of Winchester again, he said: 'Why not? The butcher got his wife back.'

When Mary came to power, everything was reversed. Ponet fled from England, Cranmer and Latimer were locked up. Gardiner became chancellor and was determined to have his revenge. But here a problem arose. It was impossible to attack his enemies as heretics when the Queen herself considered her kingdom to be in schism. The position with Rome must therefore be regulated. And for that reason, Gardiner had changed his mind and wanted Pole back into the country.

It was that, I think, which caused the rustle of laughter, gentle as a breeze through a wood, that passed through the vast crowd outside

St Paul's. The Cardinal was back, but a great trap had been laid for him . . .

And that is just what happened. A few weeks later, a new parliament met. The laws for burning heretics were restored. No monastic lands were to be given back. The Church was penniless, but the stage was set for a persecution. Gardiner managed everything. Pole had no say in these matters. Before leaving Brussels he had been made to promise not to interfere in the administration of the laws. He had returned to England after many years, and sailed up the Thames in triumph, but in fact he was now *trussed up* by Gardiner better than Henry or Cromwell ever could have dreamt.

That was my view, and events proved me right. I tried to warn Pole when I next saw him, but he rebuked me, saying I had no faith in human nature.

'The Chancellor has a stern and harsh exterior,' he said, 'but even he is susceptible to the power of grace. Why, that sermon he preached at Paul's Cross was, I believe, the finest I ever heard in my life.'

That same week, just as the laws against heresy were going through parliament, Rutter came home to Throckmorton Street one night, his eyes starting out of his head. He had been over the river to see the sports and while he was there the great blind bear at Bankside burst his chain and ran through the crowd and caught a poor serving-man by the leg and bit out a great piece of his calf. The man's life was despaired of. In fact, he was to die three days later. I had to tell Rutter that even in London he could not expect to see that every day.

4

THE HERESY TRIALS BEGAN immediately across the river at Mary Overies, which was Gardiner's own church as Bishop of Winchester, in London.

After the first day's hearings, Pole summoned all the bishops, some of whom were judges in the trial, and ordered them to go back to their own dioceses, there to treat their flocks with gentleness and win them with love and mildness, not harshness and rigour.

This caused a great stir. It seemed that a battle of wills had commenced between Chancellor and Legate. For several days the trials were suspended. Then, on the Friday that week, they began again. Everyone was amazed. Pole was papal legate. How then could the Chancellor, in defiance of papal authority, try people for rejecting papal authority?

I left my searches in the paper room and went over the river to Southwark to watch the proceedings. When I arrived, the first defendant, who had been heard on the opening day, was on his feet again. John Rogers, a preacher, married with ten children, had been held in prison for many months, though under what law no one knew, after preaching a sermon at St Paul's in which he denounced popery, idolatry and all such superstition.

'If Henry VIII was alive now,' he cried, 'and if he called a parliament this day, and determined an act which, for example, made the present Queen a bastard and himself the Head of the Church again, then *you*,' he said, pointing to Gardiner, 'and you and you and you' – pointing to all the other judges – 'would say: "Oh, Amen to that!" and "Indeed, most excellent" and "*If it please your Grace.*" '

'Sit down, be silent,' cried Gardiner. 'You are here to be instructed by us, not us by you.'

'I will not sit,' said Rogers. 'I stand. Shall I not be allowed to speak for my life?'

'Shall we allow you to tell tales and prate?' said Gardiner, coming to his feet and shouting 'Silence!' whenever Rogers opened his mouth.

'Taunt on taunt, check on check – yet you will not make me afraid to speak,' said Rogers.

'See what a spirit the fellow has,' said Gardiner, 'finding fault with my earnest and hearty manner of talking!'

This was the first time I had seen Gardiner close up and I had time to gaze at him – his appearance was perhaps not as terrible as the picture painted by Ponet – '*eyes an inch within the head, wide nostrils like a horse ever snuffing the wind, sparrow mouth, talons on his feet two inches longer than the natural toes, so he cannot suffer them to touch the stair*'. Yet all the same his was one of those faces like a granite cliff against which men's hopes are dashed. He had a harsh expression, and a lock of hair standing up at the top of his forehead which he continually smote with the heel of his hand.

'I have a true spirit, obeying the word of God,' said Rogers. 'You have sent me to prison without any law and kept me there a year and a half and taken away my living – and I with a wife and ten children!'

'Did you not preach against the Queen?'

'That I did not,' he said. 'I can prove it, if I stand trial according to law.'

'I sit as Bishop of Winchester – here in my own diocese, by the way – in my own church, and I may do this and more, lawfully,' said Gardiner.

'But against the law you have kept me in prison and never

conferred with me until now, when you have got a whip to whip me with and a sword against my neck.'

'Well, then,' said Gardiner, 'let us confer. Is the Church false and anti-Christian?'

'Yea,' said Rogers.

'And the doctrine of the sacrament?'

'False,' cried Rogers, throwing up his hands. 'The Church of Rome is the Church of Antichrist, with its false doctrine and tyrannical laws, and their maintenance by cruel persecution used by its bishops.'

'Oh, did you hear that?' cried Gardiner, turning to the audience. Everyone agreed that they had.

'They agree only because they are your servants, they would agree to anything,' said Rogers.

'What?' said Gardiner. 'Did you not say just now the sacrament was false?'

'I did' said Rogers, 'and will say it again.'

'Ah, there is no reasoning with the fellow,' said Gardiner, and he hit his forelock with the heel of his hand, and then read out the sentence of condemnation and Rogers was led away.

There was a long pause before the next defendant was brought in. He was a young man named Bradford, tall and spare and somewhat sanguine in complexion, with a fair beard. He had been a soldier who had fought before the gates of Boulogne and then gave up war and fighting in order to preach. He had already been a year in prison where, it was said, he had dreamt that the chains for burning him had already been purchased.

'Six times in my life,' said Bradford, 'I have sworn that I shall never consent to the authority of the Bishop of Rome in England: three times at Cambridge, and three times after that. How can I do what you demand?'

'Tush, those were Herod's oaths which no one has to keep,' said Gardiner.

'Oh my lord, they were not Herod's oaths, not unlawful oaths, but oaths according to God's word, as you yourself affirmed in the book which you wrote in favour of the King and against the Pope, to which you gave a very good title, *De Vera Obedientia*: On True Obedience.'

At this, the Chancellor was silent.

'Never mind that, sirrah,' said another of the judges. 'Have you not seditiously written and exhorted the people?'

'I have written and spoken nothing seditiously, I have never had a seditious cogitation – I thank God for it – in my life, and trust I never shall,' said Bradford.

'But you have written letters from prison, calling Catholics antichrists, and mangy dogs, that should be shunned as Simeon shunned Ustazades, and not sons of God but bastards who live in the security of a Jezebel, by which you mean the Queen,' said the judge.

Now Bradford fell silent.

'Why don't you speak?' said Gardiner, 'Have you or have you not written as he says?'

'What I have written, I have written,' said Bradford.

'Lord God, what an arrogant and stubborn boy this is,' cried Gardiner, 'behaving stoutly and dallying before the Queen's council!'

'My lords,' said Bradford, 'the Lord God, who will judge us both, knows that I stand before you with reverence and I desire to behave myself accordingly and I shall suffer with all due obedience your sayings, and doings too, I hope.'

'These are gay glorious words of reverence,' said the Chancellor, 'but as in all other things here, you do nothing but lie.'

'I would God, the abhorrer of lies, pull my tongue out of my head if I have lied to you.'

'Why then do you not answer? Have you written these letters objected against you?'

'As I said: what I have written I have written. I stand before you and you may lay my letters to my charge, or you may not. If you lay anything to my charge which I have written, and I deny it – then I am a liar.'

'Lord help us, I see that we shall never have done with you,' said the Chancellor. 'Be short, be short – will you have mercy?'

'I pray God give me His mercy, and if you extend yours I will not refuse it, but otherwise I will not,' said Bradford.

At that moment the sheriff's men came in and whispered in Gardiner's ear and then everyone rose and went away for their dinner.

'You are a young man,' said Gardiner at the next session in the afternoon, 'and perhaps there is some good in you. We offer you the Queen's pardon in consideration of the fact that Her Highness is wonderful merciful.'

'My lords,' said Bradford, 'as you sit now in the seat of the Lord, who sits in the midst of judges judging, I beseech you to follow him in this session – that is, seek no guiltless blood.'

'There is a true sentence,' said Gardiner, 'although by your manner you show you are full of vainglory and stubbornness. For all that, it is a true sentence: I seek no innocent blood.'

'And I have taken my oaths,' said Bradford, 'and followed your teaching in your book, *De Vera Obedientia*. I shall never consent to the jurisdiction of the Bishop of Rome. I am not afraid of death, thank God. I have looked for nothing else from your hands for a long time. But I am afraid of having perjury against my conscience.'

'More gay and glorious words, full of hypocrisy and vainglory,' cried Gardiner.

'I have been now almost two years in your prison,' said Bradford, 'and all this time you never questioned me about these things, when I might have answered freely without peril. But now you have a law to hang up and put to death men who answer not to your liking. Ah, my lord, Christ used not this way to bring men to faith.'

Here the Chancellor looked somewhat shaken and was silent for a moment.

'This was not my doing,' he said in a low voice, 'though there are some who think it is the best way. For my part, I have often been challenged for being too gentle.'

'Far too gentle,' said Bishop Bonner, who was sitting beside him.

And there was a general nodding in the audience. 'Ever so gentle', 'none more so', 'gentleness itself', said voices around me.

'My lord, I pray you,' said Bradford, 'stretch out your gentleness so I may feel it. For up till now, never have I felt it.'

At that Gardiner looked uncertain. A silence fell over the court. Outside you could hear the voices of the gulls above the river.

Then Gardiner suddenly smiled and smote the lock of hair standing up on his forehead.

'With all my heart!' he said. 'And not only I, but the Queen's Highness will stretch out her gentle mercy to you, if you will only return to us.'

'Return!' said Bradford, with a look of horror. 'I did not mean that! God save me from that! The dog may return to the vomit, but I will not.'

So they fell to wrangling again, and Bradford was sent down, to await further hearing, and more defendants were brought up.

By the end of the day, the sentence of excommunication had been read several times, and those convicted were consigned to Newgate Prison on the other side of the river. When the evening came I crossed the bridge behind a procession of prisoners and archers and guards with their bills and hooks and halberds. As we set off, the sheriff sent men ahead to put out the candles of the costermongers so that people should not see the prisoners pass. And so all the way over you could see the darkness spreading out in front of us as the costermongers' candles winked out, one by one.

5

THE FOLLOWING MONDAY, AT eleven in the morning, Rogers was burnt at Smithfield. At the end of that week, on Saturday, another of those condemned was burnt at Gloucester. Those were the first to die for religion in Mary's reign. The next day, on Sunday, in the palace at Greenwich, there was a great sensation. In a sermon before the whole court, the King's chaplain denounced the fires.

'This was not the way that Christ won men to faith,' he said. 'The executioners did not learn this from Scripture. It is not through severity that men are brought into the fold, but by mildness and good example. Nor is it a bishop's business to seek the death of those who have strayed. Bishops are in effect fathers of the people, and parents do not kill their children, even if they err or run away . . .'

There was a deathly silence. Mass was then heard and afterwards, outside, consternation, somewhat delayed, broke out. Some courtiers said it was the King's doing, as he did not want to be blamed by the English people for the deaths.

Yet the King had been heard to say that, by and large, he approved of the 'corrections'.

Others said it was only the private opinion of the chaplain, who was a Spanish friar named de Castro. Yet he was also known to approve of penal fires – if other measures failed – and had written a book to say so.

In short, no one knew who was behind the sermon. I myself heard about this only from a distance. But de Castro I remembered: he was an old acquaintance of Pole's, and used to sit with him in the garden at Trent and argue about liberty and power and so on, while I stood on guard nearby, watching the campfires of unknown wayfarers twinkle on the hillsides above.

From my new and lowly vantage point – I was very far from the secret counsels of those in power – I guessed that this sermon was, in fact, the next shot fired by Pole in his contest with the Chancellor.

Whether that is true or not I never found out, but whatever its origin, it had some effect. There were no more *charbonnades* – or barbecues, as the French are good enough to call them – that week or the next or the next. A month went past, and it seemed that Pole had defeated the Chancellor and that his policy of mildness was in the ascendant.

Now the time really had come for me to return to Italy. Agnes Hide – as I still always think of my wife, mystery as that is to me – was infinitely patient and good but even in her letters a forlorn note could be detected. Was I *ever* coming home? I was. But there was one more slight delay. The Queen decided to send an embassy to Rome, the first from England for decades, and I was asked to go along with them, almost as if no one could remember the way after so long.

With Lord Thirlby, Lord Montagu and Sir Edward Carne, Mr White and others, I crossed the Channel and we made our way into Picardy in late March, just as the green of spring was beginning to creep over the ground and up the boles of the trees.

The moment we reached France I was in a fever to get home to Mantua: I looked back, I could not believe it – I must have fallen under an enchantment – nineteen months I had been away! So I rode forward and urged the party to hurry. But I had forgotten, if I had ever known, how slowly lords and wealthy gentlemen travel through the world when there is no danger behind them and none pending. They were ambassadors to Rome. Rome was eternal. What was the hurry? We moved south as slowly, I think, as the beautiful goddess of spring moves north. Three or four leagues a day satisfied the party. And in any case, they were eager to see the sights.

At Fontainebleau we were led into the presence of the King of France and received very genteelly. He had a grim countenance, but was gentle and meek in his manner, and their Lordships were very pleased with him.

At St Denis we saw a great crucifix of gold, the Christ lacking only an arm which had been melted down to pay for the war.

In the marketplace at Clermont were six gallows with a different portrait hanging from each. The six miscreants in question had run away, so their portraits had been commissioned and executed in their place. All parties, it seemed, were satisfied by this arrangement.

At length we came to the mountains, and ascended into winter again. We lost only one horse over an abyss – the bay belonging to Mr White, who fell a long way with it but then saved himself on a thorn bush. At places in those mountains the road between England and Rome is not twenty inches wide.

Further on we passed below to a waterfall with a throw of water as great as a mill which midway through the air turned to snow and fell continually in great heaps on the ground. Through this we trod and went on our way.

At last we came down to the plains of Italy, which, resigning myself to my destiny, I now must acknowledge as my home.

Flat, hazy, lined with poplars, and with no wild wood or forest for miles, that land is not entirely to my taste. My heart, I suppose, has always been in Warwickshire. But my wife and children, my ease and contentment and joy, were somewhere in the haze of the great plains stretching away like the sea, bush after bush, tree after tree, town after town, tower-girdled, as far as the horizon.

In every town we came to, the ambassadors were greeted with great demonstrations. Troops of handsome youths and beautiful maidens were assembled at the gates to lead us in, and on the street corners children were mustered, calling out '*Vive, vive l'Inghilterra!*' with all the Italian vivacity.

At Mantua, I accompanied their Lordships to the ducal palace where a banquet was held and the first green almonds of the season were placed before them. Mr White and Lord Thirlby had never had green almonds before. It was there that, as agreed, I resigned my commission and hurried through the streets to the door of this very house, where, after twenty months apart, I embraced my wife and kissed my children.

Little Judith was just two years old. She had no idea who in the world I was. At the sight of me she wept great tears – never have I seen such tears – shining, spherical, rolling slowly on her cheeks. After a few minutes, however, she became somewhat resigned to my existence and, with tears still brimming, she climbed on my knee to pat my beard with the flat of her hand.

6

LATER THAT SAME DAY we rode out to Cerese, where my eldest son Francis took me by the hand and led me gravely round the whole establishment – stable, mangers, kennels, hay barn, chaff house, orchard and dwelling houses – to show me in what very good order everything had been maintained. It is a golden occasion in life to return home after a long absence and find nothing has been neglected. I almost ran out of terms of praise. I knew Agnes was a good wife but had not realised she was such an excellent manager and breeder of horses. Four yearlings I had never seen before were in the far paddocks, and the new shaky-legged foals of that spring were nearby nuzzling their mamas. I am sorry to say I almost ran out of an inclination to praise. How well everything flourished! It seemed that they had no need for me there at all.

But this was unjust. On the way back to town, Francis rode in front of us, solemn and upright, like a page before a dignitary.

But as we passed some urchins of his acquaintance, he squeaked '*Mio padre!*' – and jerked his thumb over his shoulder at me, like one of the stable lads, to show me off. I realised that my long absence had in some way impugned his dignity, and there and then I resolved never to leave them alone again as long as I lived.

This resolution I kept for a good long time; in fact I would have said that from then on I turned my back on the world and gave it no more thought, except that it now came visiting me so often there was no chance of that. Now that I was no longer a 'dead man', an attainted traitor condemned to death, it seemed that every Englishman who set foot in Italy beat a path to my door, coming to me for advice, food and shelter, even new horses. I soon heard everything that happened at home, the good and the bad. A month or two after I had left, the burnings had resumed. The King then departed from England, pleading pressure of business in his other realms, and leaving the Queen desolate. It was reported that he had no intention of returning. The tempo of burnings increased. Pole, meanwhile, devoted himself to foreign affairs and presided at a peace conference between the French and Imperialists in a great wooden city, built specially for the occasion in a field near Calais.

The Archbishop of Canterbury, Cranmer, and Latimer were put to death. Cranmer recanted and confessed his errors, but was burnt anyway, against all customary usage.

His great enemy, Stephen Gardiner, then promptly followed him into the grave.

'*Mortuus et sepultus est,*' said my guests cheerfully: 'He's dead and buried and gone to hell, so we'll talk no more about him.'

But after Gardiner was gone, the penal fires continued. Bishop Bonner – the same who once demanded Brancetor's arrest in France – was now the leading light, if I can use the phrase, of the persecution.

'The great cockatrice is dead but his chicks live on,' said my visitors, now speaking more mournfully.

Many of the English in Italy were exiles, leaning towards Luther or Calvin or Zwingli, and, since I had left England as well, they assumed I was sympathetic and they spoke frankly to me. Among them was young Edward Courtenay. This was the Marquis of Exeter's son, Pole's cousin, who had spent his youth in the Tower. He was now a fine, handsome man of twenty-five or so. Unfortunately, what the Emperor once said of him – that being brought up in prison rendered him unfit to wear a crown – was true. In fact, he was hardly fit for life beyond the prison gates. On reaching Venice, he soon found himself in grave trouble and sent a message begging me for help.

I rode over at once and found him in a state of terror. Certain agents and courtiers of the King of England were seeking his life. Assassins had been hired to kill him.

This was not something Courtenay had imagined. Arrests had been made in Venice and confessions obtained.

'I am not safe anywhere,' he said, staring all round. 'I don't know what to do.'

'Calm down,' I said to him. 'This Republic will protect you. The Signory has a long arm, it takes hares by cartloads. These lords do not like to see their noble visitors murdered on the doorstep.'

'That's true,' he said, brightening. 'They have just sent me a present of the finest wine and jams. They understand my importance.' Then he began – as the phrase goes – to magnify himself. 'I will require you to purchase me some horses,' he said, 'noble animals, good for both *ménage* and beauty. A man in my position cannot be seen on one of the wretched beasts the Paduans try to sell me, and at three times their value.'

Courtenay was convinced that, one way or another, through French plotting or marriage to Elizabeth, he would one day sit on the English throne.

I sighed to myself. He was a moth to the flame. Yet I was fond of him; in fact, I loved him like a son – it was not his fault that he had been fatherless since he was a boy and had been brought up by prison guards instead. And, although unfit for the world, he was highly intelligent. In prison, while hardly more than a child, he had translated a book that had been written by Flamminio when we were living in Viterbo. Courtenay still knew the book by heart. His Italian had a strange theological ring to it: he couldn't ask you to pass the butter, but could discourse easily on the free gift of God's grace and the benefit of Christ's sacrifice.

How Flamminio's book had come into his hands in prison in England I do not know, but when I looked at him I thought of Marc'Antonio and me roaming high in the hills in the summer, the silver Tiber glinting far away below us. It made me think that we must all be bound together in some way, perhaps too close to see.

I tried to talk some sense into Courtenay.

'Take up the study of the law, here at Padua. Nothing can be more steadying. Look what it did for me. And at all costs stay away from Ferrara. It's swarming with French who would love to draw you into another plot against the Queen. And this time, England would go to war with France.'

I should explain that as soon as he had been freed from the Tower Courtenay had rushed from one folly to another. All the prettiest girls flocked around like butterflies and he quickly made up there for lost time. The Queen made him Earl of Devon, which only increased his vanity. She and he quarrelled over whether he might wear blue velvet at her Coronation. He enraged her by calling her 'Mother' or perhaps it was 'Aunt' – I forget exactly which term of abuse was employed. At the same time, he was said to have a liaison with the Princess Elizabeth. This he denied so vehemently there was probably something in it. He was then involved in a plot hatched by various young men to kill Mary and put Elizabeth on the throne. All the conspirators lost their heads as a result, except my own nephew, Nicholas, who was too clever to be caught, and Courtenay, protected by Gardiner, who had taken a great fancy to him when they were both in the Tower.

Nevertheless, he was sent back to prison again, where, like a tame bird that dreads the open cage door, he was probably happiest.

A year later he was sent abroad, first to Brussels and then here to Italy, ostensibly to keep him out of harm's way, but in fact to be rid of him. He might be safe, I thought, if he behaved wisely, but otherwise . . .

Of course he took no notice, and his story turned into a very sad one. But in the meantime I tried to look after him as best I could.

The following morning in Venice I took him across the lagoon to an island where I used to go to fly my hawk in solitude, when I too had been a young man trapped in that great city, with no idea of what the future held.

7

CROSSING THE LAGOON THAT morning, Courtenay was more sensible and more forthcoming than the night before. There were just the two of us, with our hawks, on a skiff steered by a black Venetian who never uttered a word all day long. Courtenay's pride dropped away. He began to talk openly. His mother was a lady of the Queen's bedchamber and Courtenay had all the inside information about the English Court. The state of affairs there was appalling. The Queen was hysterical with grief and rage. Her husband, who had gone to Brussels, kept promising to return but every day one or two more of his household slipped away to join him. She wrote to him every hour. He replied occasionally, mentioning the burdens of his work and his fragile health. But her own spies informed her of everything. Philip went out masked every night, even in the worst weather, and often returned at dawn.

'You know the sort of big, fat girls he likes,' said Courtenay. 'They cheer him up, he has these great debauches and eats bacon fat by the handful. The Queen knows all about it. My mother has seen her fly at his portrait and attack it with her nails. Then she falls weeping on the floor. Then, perhaps after an hour, the storm passes. She sits up again. She smiles: she remembers the dream of love. She calls for the musicians to play that song of Heywood's, who is always hanging around:

She said she did love me and would love me still
She swore above all men I had her good will.

'She listens, and remembers anew the sweet hours with her husband. He was always kind to her, you see. He hid the fact that he was dying to get away – every hour with her was like a thousand years for him. He was frightened of her as well, what with her terrible temper. She has no idea of his true feelings. So she smiles with grief, and with love. Her anger departs. But then a new frown appears. It is not her fault that he has left. It is her subjects who are to blame! They have rejected her prince of love. Some of them hate him because he is a Catholic. They, especially, must be punished. Thus she turns a *mauvais visage* on her people and prepares to fill the realm with smoke and blood. Truly, she is just like Dido who set her city on fire when her prince of love sailed away.'

Courtenay had grown agitated as he spoke. His face was red. For weeks he had had no one to talk to frankly about these things. It was late in the morning – the heat of the sun came through the black awning and the gusts of wind fanning the water did nothing to cool us.

'It is horrible,' said Courtenay, bursting out as if he could no longer contain himself. 'I don't think you realise what is happening, Michael. There is no one to protect the little people from the law – the weavers and tallow-chandlers and butchers and widows. And the blind! I don't know how many blind folk have been sent into the flames in the last year. I suppose they are the easiest to catch; officers of the law are always lazy, they prefer to hunt down the easiest prey.'

He proceeded to tell me ugly stories of burning limbs, of three, four, five people all consumed in one fire – 'to save on wood' – of the great crowds that flocked to see the *charbonnades* in market squares or in the gravel pits outside town where cherry-sellers sold cherries by the horse-load.

During this exordium I began to feel very uncomfortable. I

told myself it was the heat, but in fact it was Courtenay's voice drilling on and on. It is unpleasant to be lectured by a youth for whose powers of judgement you have felt only pity. I wished the voyage would end but we were not even halfway across – the red towers of the city and S. Giorgio Maggiore were clear and sharp behind us, and the island we were going to was still only a line on the horizon.

'There is nothing you are telling me that I don't know,' I said. 'In any case, what can be done? After all, Pole is there. Imagine how much worse things would be if he were not. Look at the Netherlands. How many have died there? Thousands. And in England? A handful. Fifty. Eighty.'

'*Pole!*' said Courtenay. 'No doubt Pole speaks to the Queen in private, urging moderation. But on this matter she does not listen to him. His leniency makes him suspect. So he gives up and says no more. Yet it is his responsibility. None of this could happen without him. He is the legate. If he was not there – if you had not worked so hard to get him there – how could these people be burnt?'

'Me?' I said in amazement. 'This is not what I foresaw. It was your patron, Gardiner, who led us down this path.'

'Well, perhaps Pole is not wholly to blame,' said Courtenay. 'It is a terrible thing to be in the favour of the great. The Queen clings to him – with the King gone, she won't let him out of her sight. She adores him, and takes no notice of him, which is something only a woman could do. Yet he allows her to get away with it. Here is the man famous for telling kings the truth, and now he devotes himself to church problems – finances and liturgy and so on. He is like a priest performing a wedding who refuses to see the Angel of Death is also in the aisle.'

'But what can he do?' I said. 'The laws are in place. He is forbidden from interfering. In any case, how can he save these people? They are not hunted down. They huddle together and then come forward to declare themselves openly. They go to the justices and proclaim their opinions. They walk into the fires joyfully. In fact, they choose their own deaths.'

When I heard myself say that, I was reminded of something I could not quite place, a voice from long ago which had once seemed terrible to me.

'They choose their own deaths!' said Courtenay, looking at me in amazement. Then he proceeded to tell me a long story about a tailor from Clerkenwell who had been denounced by his wife as a heretic as he would not go to mass. He was arrested and taken to the Lollards' Tower and held there a fortnight.

His son, a boy of eight, then went to Bishop Bonner's house to look for him. One of the Bishop's chaplains met him and asked what he wanted.

'I want to see my father,' he said.

'And who is your father?'

The boy pointed towards the Lollards' Tower across the river and said his father was in there.

'Why, your father is a heretic!' cried the priest.

'He is no heretic,' said the child. 'You are a heretic, for you have Balaam's mark.' Balaam was the false prophet who went to curse Israel and the way was barred by an angel. At that, the priest took the child by the hand and led him into the house where he was whipped until he was bloody. After he was whipped, the boy was taken by the summoner over the river to the Lollards' Tower.

Seeing the boy covered in blood, the father cried: 'Alas, Will, who has done this to you?'

'A priest with Balaam's mark,' said the boy. Then the summoner seized the boy and carried him back to the Bishop's house, where he was kept three days. Fearing that his servants had gone too far, Bonner let both father and son go, but the boy died a few days later.

'And did he *choose his own death*?' said Courtenay. 'And remember: the Lollards' Tower is at Lambeth. It is a part of Pole's own palace.

This cruelty took place almost under his own roof. I know he is hardly ever there for the Queen keeps him by her side, yet how can he avoid responsibility for such a crime? A child, whipped to death . . .'

This conversation made me most uncomfortable. I had that unpleasant sensation which everyone tries to avoid: a guilty conscience. The fact was, I had been hearing such stories for many months, but I had put them out of my mind or minimised the cruelty or justified them in one way or another. In short, I had become cold-hearted. I had lost my human sympathy.

And that, in my view, means one is something less than a man. My conscience could see this – I did not want to see it myself. And that was the state of affairs as we scudded into calm water and the prow touched sand.

The boatman set us down and immediately lay down to sleep under his awning. Courtenay and I went ashore. That island is really only a sand-bar between the lagoon and the sea – a few miles long, half a mile wide, a great solitude except for a few parched vineyards at one end. There is never much game; a few teal are sometimes seen on rainwater ponds in the centre, and here and there the footprints of a hare might be noticed. We went on inland and climbed to the highest point, a dune where a single tree grows, which they call a parasol pine, and we set up camp in its shade. The sun by then was high in the sky and you could hear the boom of the waves from the open sea.

We let the birds sit barefaced for a while, then went out and sent them up. Courtenay was singing the Heywood song he claimed he disliked: *All a green willow, a willow, a willow.* His hawk liked the boisterous weather – she was a well-mettled bird, but 'hard of hearing', as we say, and uneasy at being reclaimed. Mine were more loving but less venturous.

After a few flights I brought my birds in and went back to the shade of the pine. I ate some bread and cheese and drank a little wine, and began to feel sleepy, which was unusual for me in the middle of the day. I watched Courtenay's hawk hover and stoop and

I heard his cry 'Hey gar gar' becoming fainter and fainter. And then, just as I was falling asleep, I saw that only a few yards away there was a walled courtyard that I had not noticed before. Curious about this, I got up and walked to the entrance and looked in.

There I saw a seated figure with his back turned to me. I took a step into the court. At that the figure seemed to wake, he stood up, he came towards me and walked straight past. I had only a brief glimpse of the face of this stranger, yet it was a very remarkable one, as far as I was concerned. Although younger, and more resolute, and in fact more noble in appearance in every way, he was identical to myself.

He went off out into the world without a glance, while I took his place on the chair and fell asleep. Some time later I woke up, still – of course – lying under the shade of the pine.

8

CIRCULATING IN VENICE THAT summer was a remarkable letter, so absurd and painful at the same time that no one knew whether to laugh over it or cry. It had been sent from Poland to a Venetian gentleman with high connections, begging for his help. The sender was a certain Lewis Lippomano, who had been sent as papal legate to Vienna and Poland.

This Lippomano, seeing religious controversies erupt in those places, had advised the Emperor and his brother, the King of the Romans, who ruled in Vienna, and, then, similarly, the King of Poland, to seize the Lutheran leaders and chop off their heads:

> I, according to instructions, gave counsel to the Emperor and his most noble brother, the King of the Romans, that they should cause these men's heads to be openly cut off as the ringleaders and maintainers of heretics.
>
> For by this means, and with this terror, an end should have been made of all heresy in Germany. But their Majesties thought it best not to follow such counsel.
>
> And, having the like commission from our most Holy Father Pope Paul IV, I have often given counsel to this most noble King of Poland exhorting him that he would cause to be cut off the heads of the chief of those that go about to stir up the doctrine of the Lutherians.

Now such a matter of so great importance, which should have been kept a secret as ever any one was, lest it should have bred envy and hatred of the most holy vicars of Christ's church – such a matter, I say, I fear has been disclosed and opened abroad in every corner . . .

Consider how I stand . . . What think you they will do to me if I remain in their sight? I can look for no other than to be cursed, railed, cried out upon . . . And they will go about and spread horrible tales abroad against our Holy Father's Holiness, and they say that these be the counsels that His Holiness will make, and that is with chopping off of heads and other such like violence: yea, I understand they speak it already and wonderfully blow it abroad . . . All men are against me, none will hear me, all minds are alienated from me, and I cannot tell where to save my life, they speak such evil against me.

All over Venice, as I say, people were shaking their heads over this performance, firstly, because Lippomano was a Venetian and it was feared he might have damaged Polish–Venetian trade; and, secondly, for its manifest absurdity. Lippomano wept over the tales being told about him, having just stated they were true.

When a copy of the letter came into my hands I was already brooding over what Courtenay had told me about events in England. I could not get rid of the thought of Pole and the charges against him that Courtenay had made – namely, that he averted his eyes from great cruelty and bloodshed. I was very unhappy. There is nothing so captious, I suppose, as a newly wakened conscience. But I could see no course of action to take. I had no one even to talk to about these things. Agnes is a poor antagonist, she tends to agree with whatever I say. Portaleone has no interest in the disputes amongst those of our religion.

Having no one to talk to, I therefore found myself in want of solitude and for the first time since coming to live in Mantua I went in search of it. But this is difficult to find in the neighbourhood. The woods are not deep, the fields are flat, open and busy. Still, there is good hunting in the marshes, and I went out with my dog and an arquebus, taking a little boat into the deepest recesses of the reeds, with these thoughts in my mind.

A few days after reading the Lippomano letter, I went out hunting as usual and in the course of the afternoon I happened to emerge from the reeds near an old church, called Maria della Grazie, a few leagues from Mantua. I had heard of the place, and went in to look around. It was very curious within: ancient, august in atmosphere, with dark red walls, and cluttered with innumerable images, statues of stone, of tow, rags and paper, waxworks in niches, wooden hearts, breasts, babies, garlands and boils, votive offerings and crutches – objects of every size, shape and age, and yet strangely all of a piece, like things cast up by the sea.

Among them I noticed the tomb of Castiglione, the author of the famous book *Il Curtigiane*, or *The Courtier*. Lord Bembo had composed the tomb inscription.

Here lies a Mantuan adorned with all
the gifts of nature and of art.
In Latin, Greek and in Tuscan learned,
a poet known to all, in Toledo he died.

This summary, I knew, had been criticised as frigid and flat. Almost as soon as he wrote it, Bembo followed his subject into eternity. One should be more fulsome to the dead, people said, as you are bound to run into them shortly. For me the effect was different. Standing in front of that scroll of cold marble, I suddenly became resolute. For years I had heard Pole refer to *The Courtier*. '*Here is the great difficulty for princes . . . They lack above all what they need more than anyone else, namely, someone to tell them the truth.*'

And at that moment I saw that this applied to no one more urgently than to Pole himself. It is true that he was not exactly a prince – although the Venetian ambassador said that, with King Philip away, Pole was now more or less the King of England, being always at the Queen's side. In any case, whether he was a prince or not, he surely now had greater need of a courtier who would put the truth before his eyes than ever before in his life.

In short, standing at the tomb of Catstiglione I decided that that was my task, the duty clearly fell to me, who had for so many years served and protected Pole. And there and then I decided to translate Lippomano's absurd letter into English and publish it in my name, with the hope that this might make Pole see what was happening under his own eyes in England.

Leaving the church I noticed a group of young people who had gone there for what purpose I don't know – to meet, to whisper, flirt, make love. One of them, a young woman of exceptional beauty, slim and straight-backed as Minerva, was sitting slightly apart from the others. As I passed she lifted her head and looked at me with a full gaze. Her eyes were blue. For a moment it seemed that I too, there in Maria della Grazie, was lifted up by a wave of the sea.

I took this as a good sign for my project. It was remarkably easy to carry out. I had a copy of the letter. I translated it in half a day. Portaleone knew all about publishing, and could send it off to Germany in no time. The only thing that took some effort was the dedication.

There I was harsh and violent in my language. I remembered what Pole himself had said of Henry long ago. 'He must be made to *see* what he has done' and 'Flattery is the source of all the problems' and 'Lift up your voice like a trumpet!'

Well – my voice is no trumpet. Lippomano's letter in any case spoke for itself. But I tried my best: I spoke as bitterly as I could. I felt my rage rise as I thought of those churchmen, puffed up with pride, whose titles and robes themselves seem to have driven them mad and made them cruel. How was Pole any different, I asked, from such prelates? '*You will go on as you have begun, in chopping off the heads and hanging up for holidays the favourers of the gospel? . . . Your handling of the Pope's affairs has brought misery and dissension to the realm . . . Beware lest the visor of hypocrisy is plucked off and your bribery and blood-letting come to light . . .'*

I wrote all this – it was a page and a half – with Portaleone chafing at the door. Then I sent it off. The title page was as follows:

A copy of a very fine and
witty letter sent from the right
reverend Lewes Lippomane
translated out of the Italian lang
uage by Michael
Throckmorton.

And beneath my name, so that he might remember all the years I faithfully served him in exile, I signed myself:

Curtigiane, at Rome

9

A FEW DAYS AFTER this was sent off, a message came from the Regent asking me to come and see him at once. This alarmed me. I thought he must have somehow seen my manuscript or by some gift of second sight he knew the language I had used against prelates. Then it suddenly struck me how little I myself knew about the whole affair. Was that Lippomano letter itself real? How could I be sure that it was not a forgery or a satire published by the Pope's enemies? Even the stories which Courtenay had told me, the boy, for instance, whipped to death by cruel priests – what proof was there that that had really happened? In short, I was suddenly overwhelmed with uncertainty, and I made my way to the palace with profound misgivings. When I went in, I saw at once that the Regent was very agitated. He was sighing and walking up and down and as soon as he saw me he came up and began to speak in sorrowful and upbraiding tones.

'He is old,' he said, 'he is old, he is very, very old – and that's a blessing, yes, at least there's that to be said for it.'

Now the Regent is one of those people who often launches forth on a subject without any introduction, assuming by some miracle that you have been thinking about exactly the same thing, which is never the case in my experience. All the same, I felt vastly relieved at his words. Whatever he was talking about this time, it seemed to have nothing to do with me. In this I was right. The source of his unease was in Rome. I should have said that a year before a new Pope had been elected. Pole had not come from England for the conclave. In his absence, the terrible Carafa had been chosen and had ascended the throne of Peter at the great age of eighty or eight-one.

Almost at once, alarming events were reported from Rome. But it now appeared that something new and worse had happened.

'Yes, indeed,' said the Regent, still sighing and shaking his head, 'these mad pranks he plays are surely the result of extreme age. Truly he may be said to have now arrived at that stage of life called second childhood.'

And then, leading me to the window, and leaning in the marble frame, the Regent began to outline the lamentable events in Rome.

The latest policy, he declared, was so bizarre, so dangerous, there could be only one explanation: the Pope had lost his reason. To put it simply, he had decided to declare war on the Emperor.

He had taken into his head that the time was ripe to set Italy free of the imperialist yoke. In other words, with a few thousand troops at his disposal, mostly Lutherans and the mercenaries from Gascony – a rabble more like devils than human beings – the Pope planned to attack the greatest power on earth and chase its armies from Naples and other Italian cities which the Emperor ruled.

This had been brewing for a few months, but no one could quite bring themselves to believe it. But then – and this was why I had been summoned – the Pope had suddenly arrested the Emperor's ambassador and his postmaster in Rome, and also the Mantuan envoy there, who was another of the Capilupo clan, named Hippolito.

These prisoners, the Regent told me, were now in the Castle S. Angelo, and being subjected to the torture of the cords to force them to reveal the strength and secret plans of the Imperialist forces in Naples.

'That is the information I have,' said the Regent. 'The cords are being tightened every hour. It is beyond madness. It is that wretched little idiot Carlos who is behind this. For thirty years, Carafa would not let his nephew darken his door. He knew very well what sort of soldier he was – his arms were dyed red to the elbows. But now he has made him a cardinal and listens to no one else. You may depend on it, Carlos has dreamt up this war. He thinks that if he brings the whole house of Italy crashing to the ground, he will somehow emerge a duke. As if dukedoms grows up in one night, like mushrooms!'

Then, leaning out in the open air and looking across the lake, the Regent asked me to undertake a most delicate task. This was to go to Rome, to contact various cardinals and make sure Capilupo was not harmed, and find out what was happening on the military front. Mantua, being in alliance with the Emperor, could not send one of its own citizens without exposing him to great danger. I, by contrast, an English subject, should be quite safe.

'You know your way around Rome,' said the Regent. 'You know these people I want you to talk to. Is there some innocent reason you can think of that might take you there?'

Well, I said, there was a chest of books which I had left there five years before and always meant to collect.

'Excellent!' said the Regent. 'Your books should certainly be here in Mantua!'

I left almost at once. I did not hesitate to carry out the commission, partly out of love for that excellent Regent, and partly out of relief to know that I was not in trouble for my words against prelates in general, in the preface to the '*Fine and Witty Letter*'.

10

BY THE TIME I reached Rome, the papal army had already marched south towards Naples. The war had begun. I made careful enquiries about the prisoners. It was true what the Regent had told me: they were under torture. Only the postmaster of the embassy, however, was tied to the cords. The two ambassadors, out of deference to their rank, were merely fed salt meat and given nothing to drink. These measures, it was announced, were highly effective: detailed plans for an Imperialist invasion of Rome were now known. These were wholly fanciful, though it was true that Rome had been sacked by the Imperialists thirty years before. A furious programme to fortify the city was now underway. Houses and vineyards, even those belonging to the most illustrious citizens, were being demolished to improve lines of fire. The most beautiful trees in the city were being cut down to no military purpose, but it is well known that Mars, the god of war, hates the green groves and will use any excuse to destroy them.

In all my travels I had never seen a city in this mood before. War had already planted her standards, as it were, on every face: fear, surly resolve, and, here and there, irrational hilarity. The public prostitutes were required to donate one mattress each for the soldiery, the Jews were harnessed to the guns to drag them to the bastions, and the priests and monks had been put to work with picks and shovels, under pain of ten years in the galleys for truancy.

In Naples the imperial commander, the Duke of Alba, issued a statement: 'We are like a man who is attacked by an elderly parent with a naked weapon, and who reaches lovingly to take it from his hand.'

On 6 September 1556 two companies of imperial cornets crossed the frontier into papal territory. The news caused uproar in Rome. Drummers perambulated the streets shouting 'Who will take soldiers' pay?' Only women and children were allowed to leave the city.

The next night, all the bells began to ring madly. Shrieks were heard, women ran dishevelled through the streets with infants at breast, several miscarriages were recorded. The men, however, mustered bravely enough.

Later it was given out that this was a false alarm, ordered by the authorities to see what they might hope for.

Then there came a curious lull. I had little to do. I wandered around to inspect Rome in her new guise. The city in the heat suddenly became silent and forlorn. I felt as though I was roaming about during a siesta before a great ball. I went to visit M. Michelangelo but was told he had left Rome and gone to visit hermits in the woods, the only place, he said, where a remnant of wisdom might be found. I heard that he had become more withdrawn than ever. His beloved Urbino, the colour-grinder whom he expected to look after him in his old age, had gone and died before him. The Pope had threatened to whitewash over the *Last Judgement* or at least have breeches painted on the naked angels and martyrs.

M. Angelo was still, however, in charge of building the new St Peter's.

'I am at the twenty-fourth hour,' my friends quoted him as saying. 'I still serve God with my body, but my memory and judgement have left and gone ahead to wait for me. We will meet again at the hour when death and my soul contend for my final state.'

I went to see how the building of the cathedral had progressed in the last few years. All work had stopped. The workmen had gone away. Grass was growing in the nave. It was a windy day: high above my head, the cornice of the new drum was filled only with blue sky and flying clouds.

On the tenth, eleventh, and thirteenth of September, the papal fortresses south of Rome surrendered to Alba's army. On the sixteenth, the sound of distant cannons could be heard from the heights of the city.

That same day, the Emperor left Flanders and set sail for Spain. For a year he had been meaning to abdicate, but the crisis in Rome held him back. Once the decision to invade was taken, there was nothing to detain him. He left Brussels, turning back again and again and weeping bitter tears at his last sight of the walls of that city where he had lived so long and been so happy, and done so much mischief to mankind.

Reaching the coast he set sail for Spain alone with his thirty-six servants, his collection of twenty-eight clocks and a Fleming, named Manolo, to read aloud to him.

His son, Philip, was now in charge of all. His army drew closer to Rome. At dawn on 14 November, the boom of the cannon could be heard all over the city. It was strange to think that those thuds, growing louder, were the footsteps of the Catholic King of England, coming to pay a visit to His Holiness.

The port of Ostia fell the following day. And that same morning, seven hundred cavalry under the command of Marcantonio Colonna – he was the Marchioness's nephew – were seen on a hillside not a mile beyond the walls.

That evening I paid my first visit to Bernardo Navagero, the Venetian ambassador to Rome. Navagero had sent me a message to come and see him; he would be pleased to help me, he said, and tell me what he knew about the general situation on account of the great affection he had for Capilupo, the imprisoned Mantuan ambassador, 'than whom,' he said, 'no one is more beloved in this whole court'.

Now the Pope was anxious for Venice to join the war and therefore Navagero was welcomed into the inner counsels, and heard everything that was being said.

Navagero was a remarkable figure himself – tall, austere, with thoughtful, deepset eyes in which, however, an unexpected, additional spirit flickered. If he had not been an ambassador he could certainly have been an impresario or actor on the stage. Reporting the talk in the papal palace, he unwittingly took on the character of the speaker; with the flash of eye or movement of mouth or wrist, he became the Pope (whom he rather resembled) or one or other of the dignitaries around him, and yet he did so very gravely, like a man adding important information to serious matter.

Despite the military setbacks, the Pope remained obstinate and full of contempt for the enemy: 'We used to hold the Duke of Alba in some consideration,' he said, 'because his grandfather was a good man, but now I deem him the silliest person living – so ignorant and inconsiderate that we anticipate certain victory by reason of his stupidity. Why, if he advances another foot, or by so much as this' – here Navagero laid a toothpick on the table – 'we'll show him.'

'Who is this "we"?' asked Cardinal Farnese.

'The French are behaving well, they will come to our aid,' said the Pope. 'They are the sort of men who do whatever is wished for. Of course one must cultivate them, and every now and again make some small demonstration of love, and then they behave themselves. When they arrive, you will see how easily we will drive away all these Spanish ruffians. Perhaps we may allow a few to remain in Italy as stable boys or cooks – but as our masters? It is unthinkable. Their iniquities are such that we nauseate at the mere mention of them. How inscrutable are the ways of Providence! To set free the noble province of Italy from this race of men by making them unbearable in the first place! I knew the Emperor when he was a boy and even then detected in him certain flowers of evil – an insufferable pride, a rage for domination, a contempt for religion. Now you see he has been punished, for he is dead – yes, I regard him as dead, although he still exists in that filthy body of his, but God has certainly deprived him of his wits, just as he did his sister and the mother who were both quite mad. And now here is this accursed son of his, the King of England, who secretly supports the Lutherans and eats meat in public on Fridays. "Oh, but my stomach does not permit me to fast." Scoundrel! Eat in your chamber! What sort of men are these? And who are their forces? A mix of uncircumcised Jews, Moors and Lutherans. They did far worse to this city the last time they came a-calling than ever the Goths did. Is Rome one of their woods which they may come and fell every thirty years? Are we a meadow to mow whenever the grass grows high? At least when the French run over Italy in their fury, they afterwards go back where they came from. But when these demons grapple, they never let go – unless their knuckles are very smartly rapped.'

'In alliance with my king,' said du Bellay, one of the French cardinals who was present, 'you have nothing to fear.'

At that the Pope flew into a rage.

'Who needs your king? We have the Emperor right where we want him under these feet,' and he danced with rage on the marble floor.

'The King of France is your faithful servant, that's all I meant to say,' said du Bellay humbly, although by nature he was very proud and haughty.

'Very well,' said the Pope, somewhat mollified. 'We love your king. He is an obedient son and does what is required of him. But it is not your business to speak when we are speaking. In any case you are always tedious, and no one else ever gets a word in when you're around.'

'But Holy Father,' said Farnese, retuning to the point, 'there is no sign of the French.'

'Very well! The Turks will not fail us!'

'Holy Father!' said Cardinal Morone. 'I am sure your Holiness is of such goodness you will not have recourse to that infamous source of aid.'

'Sultan Suleiyman is very good. He will send galleys,' said the Pope. 'Given an enemy as devilish as these Spaniards, it is quite lawful and indeed praiseworthy to turn to anyone else for help. Jews, Moors, Turks – they will all be eager to give assistance.'

11

A FEW DAYS AFTER the fall of the port of Ostia, a truce was called for forty days. The Imperialists hoped to reach an accommodation with the Pope while he wanted to spare his forces until the French arrived.

I took the chance to leave the city and went home to Mantua. There the Regent asked me to go back again and be his eyes and ears in Rome.

'The game is not finished,' he said. 'I doubt that it will end as badly as we feared. But Capilupo is still in gaol, and I have no one as good as you at getting information out.'

I had devised a system of writing letters to my wife in English, which no one else understood, and posting them through Venice.

I accepted the commission and went back, not entirely reluctantly. In fact, I even considered taking young Francis with me. It was time, I thought, for him to get a measure of the world. Agnes Hide was horrified at the idea. She stood, her arms enfolding Francis, glaring at me as at a ravening monster. I retreated, laughing a little at myself and at her. But I was pleased in a way: it was the first time she had ever defied me and it was love for my own child that made her do it. In any case, I thought, perhaps she was right. No one knew how things would end in Rome.

There was very little happening when I got there. I took lodgings in the street of the bowmakers near Campo Fiori. During the day I went to work writing this book, which I had begun the year before in Mantua. On most evenings, at an hour after sunset, I went to Navagero's house. On my first night back in Rome he reported his latest interview with the Holy Father.

'Thank goodness you have come,' the Pope said to him, 'at least before that great ball has set' – here Navagero stood and pointed dramatically at the shutters – 'for now we no longer give audience after sunset and indeed have ordered our chamberlains not to dare to bring any message whatever, even if it were to report the resurrection of our own father. But we are always delighted to see you. We have often spoken to you of the wickedness of the Imperialists, and of their desire to destroy this state so that they can seize yours as well. Yet, like Cassandra, we have never been believed. Tomorrow, or perhaps the next day, we shall depart this life and you will remain behind, and amid the ruins will remember this poor old man and lament not having provided against his downfall. Indeed it is marvellous that you remain so calm. By God, when they have devoured us, Venice will be the salad! You will be next between the shears! But never mind – we recommend that you hang out a carpet and place a cushion on one of your balconies on the Grand Canal so you may sit at your ease and watch your destruction approach. Ah, well – whom God wishes to punish he first deprives of reason. Perhaps you think there is some ray of hope from the sea, like the frogs which jump into the water at the first sound of footsteps. And yet, after all, what is there to fear? This tyrant of an emperor is of no account. And what proof of himself has his wretched son, the King of England, ever given? This empire of theirs is like an old house – take one arch away and the whole thing falls. If we start by giving them a little cudgelling here in Italy, everything will go arse over kite.'

'The government of Venice,' said Navagero, seizing the chance to speak, 'is highly desirous of peace, and knowing Your Holiness's own great love of peace, believes that with some care a catastrophe can still be averted.'

'Yes, it is true,' said the Pope with a sigh, 'I have done far more for peace than is strictly becoming. But against such devils, nothing of that kind avails. The Emperor cannot bear either you or us. Our freedoms are the furies that drive him wild. In the devilish soul of Charles, in that filthy body, there remains an active malignity which has conceived universal monarchy. And as well as that, it is remarkable that this Holy See has maintained itself at all, seeing that our predecessors did everything they could think of to ruin it, especially that bloated Pope Leo. But nor, from the life he led, could anything else be expected . . .'

That same week the news came that the French had indeed broken off diplomatic relations with the Imperialists and were preparing for war. Suddenly the whole world was drawn into the conflict.

The Queen of England was delighted. At last her husband had need of her. She offered him ten thousand infantry and a thousand horses – but only if he came back to visit her. This he agreed to do.

In London, war – 'by fire, sword and bloodshed' – was proclaimed against France.

A herald was sent to Paris, but left in such a hurry that he neglected to observe the proper forms.

'Where is your safe-conduct?' asked the French king.

The herald, Norroy King-At-Arms, admitted he did not have one.

'Oh dear,' said the King, 'then the law requires you to be hanged, as a spy.'

Norroy King-at-Arms went pale.

'Now, now,' said the King, 'We didn't mean it. You are pardoned. Look, we have brought in all these gentlemen, the ambassadors, to show that we receive you.'

'Your Majesty is too good,' said the Constable of France. 'If you took my advice, you'd hang him on the spot.'

'Nonsense,' said the King, 'he's as white as a sheet. Give him your gold chain to *encourage* him.'

Then he read the patent, in which Mary declared that she defied the most illustrious Henri, most Christian King of France, to war.

'Consider how I stand,' said the King, laughing, 'when a woman sends to defy me to war. However, I expect God will assist me.'

Soon the Danes, the Scots and the Turks began to edge towards the conflict. German mercenaries were raised by both sides, and set off from home singing, arm-in-arm, like brothers, which in fact sometimes they were. But as they came up to the border where some must go to the French camp and some to the Imperialist, they began to exchange dark glances, then words, then blows, and then tried to trap and even to murder one another, without a single order to do so.

Thousands of German troops also marched through Venetian territory to join the imperial army approaching Rome.

Hearing of this, the Pope refused to see Navagero for several days and left him sitting on a stool outside the audience chamber. But then, feeling the tide of war was running in his favour, he called him in again.

'We hear from many channels that the very stones of Venice complain of your not being able to obtain audience of us,' he said. 'We have always given you preference over everyone else, and how were we rewarded? But never mind – once there was a decrepit old man who was supposed to sit in a corner bewailing his infirmities. Instead he showed himself valorous and chose to act against this mongrel race of Spaniards who take root like weeds wherever they attach themselves. Now we hear that that accursed silly boy, Philip – would to God he had never been born – has taken himself off to England to see the Queen. We are of the opinion that the people of that kingdom would gladly remain at peace. The English are not very easy to *coax*, you know. Nor do we believe they will remain under Spanish domination for long. We intend soon to publish such a tremendous sentence that it will darken the sun. We will deprive this hateful youth of all his realms, and release his subjects from their obedience to him. If the English were to rebel now, what might we expect! And, keep in mind, there is always Scotland. It is incredible how willingly the Scots pass into England under arms, but, being almost savage and having nothing, they go there joyfully in the hope of gain. Would to God that that little beast, Philip, understood the matter better. *Dubius eventus belli!* Now he has excited the great he-goats, which might bite him in earnest!'

12

DUBIUS EVENTUS BELLI. 'NOTHING is certain in war.' Never did the Pope speak more truthfully. After a few more months, during which time a French army arrived in Italy, it became clear that something unforeseen and mysterious was taking place: His Holiness was changing sides.

The first sign of this was not recognised for what it was. It took the form of the arrest of Morone, one of the most senior cardinals in Rome. But as he was known to be of the Imperialist party, his arrest was not inexplicable.

The Pope himself, however, set the matter straight. He summoned Navagero to the palace.

'My dear son,' he said, 'I am delighted to see that you have arrived, for it is getting late and as you see I am old and must look after myself and have regard for my life. Nevertheless, we still have a little time left now, in our life and even in what remains of the day. Now, as to this war: perhaps it is time to think of stepping back. We have always longed for peace and have done far more in pursuit of tranquillity than was seemly. But popes should not make war – it is fishing with a golden hook, by which I mean you risk much to get very little back. And remember: they are all barbarians, without exception, both the French and Spanish. These Frenchies, especially, give us cause for suspicion. They make many demands and now want to take possession of our seaports, if you please. But beyond all that, we now have a much more serious matter to consider.'

Then, drawing Navagero to the window, and swinging his foot back and forth, he continued; 'We shall now give you an account of the arrest of Cardinal Morone. It was not a case of treason that forced us to act. Alas, if only it had been we perhaps might have let it go. But it was something much worse. Imagine our sorrow to discover that among the cardinals are certain people tainted with heresy. To be honest, we ourselves saw this danger in past conclaves, but no one would listen. Now we have decided to act, to make sure the devil does not place in this Holy See one of his own children, who will induce everyone else to lead his sorry life. A heretic cannot be pope. One who is not a member cannot become the head. For this reason we have arrested Morone and ordered all other cardinals, especially the Cardinal of England, to return to Rome at once.'

I should have said that by this time Carafa and Pole had long since made peace, Carafa many years earlier had withdrawn his accusations of heresy and apologised to Pole for his speech in the conclave. Now it seemed that his suspicions had suddenly revived.

'We wish Venice to open the road to peace between us and Philip,' the Pope continued. 'You must write at once to your government, because certain calamities are at hand. In fact, they are so close they may be said to resemble the lightning that immediately follows the limbo.'

The road to peace was more difficult than the Pope had foreseen. The Imperialists made many demands, including the restoration of all the Colonna estates. They sent Marcantonio Colonna to Rome to announce their terms.

'Is it possible for us to be disbelieved?' the Pope exclaimed to Navagero. 'Is it blockishness or divine judgement that drives them to this madness? How often we have told you these Imperialists are traitors, that they preach peace for the sole purpose of making war more commodiously! This boy, Philip, declared his will for peace. And so we offered ourselves to him, we opened the bosom of commiseration, such being the duty of anyone seated on this throne. And how are we rewarded? The Duke of Alba sends a Colonna to us, a rebel of ours, an excommunicated convict, an accursed son of Satan, giving him enough soldiery to insult us face to face. Anyone who thinks a pontiff would accept conditions from such an abominable person deceives himself.'

Alba therefore continued slowly to approach Rome.

At length he arrived under the walls of the city. He drew up his soldiers and addressed them, promising them double pay if they would not sack the city. The Germans indignantly rejected this suggestion.

The scaling ladders were then brought forward. Terror filled Rome.

Faced with this new threat, the Pope gave in. He sent his envoys to meet Alba, who was waiting under a tree near Cavi. They accepted all his demands and the next day returned to Rome and, booted and spurred, hurried into the Pope's presence. Peace had arrived.

At that moment, the Tiber suddenly rose the height of a morris pike, drowning men, women and children in their houses, carrying off cattle, grain, oil, wine and mattresses towards the sea, and then, just as quickly, subsided.

This flood marked the end of the War of the Campagna, as it is now called.

Immediately the Pope turned his full attention to his new obsession: the question of Cardinal Pole.

When Pole had been ordered to return to Rome, there was outrage in London. The English ambassador went to the Pope to demand the decree be revoked.

'This excellent and most sainted cardinal must remain with us. He will not come to Rome, not for any occasion.'

'It is impossible for us to revoke our decree,' said the Pope. 'That would be derogatory to our dignity. But a solution has appeared. I have just remembered a certain old Englishman, a bare-footed friar named Peto, who was once the Queen's confessor. I have decided to make him a cardinal and given him the legation to England.'

'With regard to Peto personally,' said Carne, 'I am willing to accept your opinion that he is learned, and a good Christian, yet I do not think the appointment a good one, for he is also an old dotard who can bear no fatigue and who will remain in his cell reciting his orisons. Nor do I see how this is supposed to please the Queen. To take away from her a close relation whom she dearly loves and replace him with a decrepit old friar who was never, in fact, her confessor – he confessed her once when she was seven – no, it's out of the question. Nor will it please anyone else in England. As you know, the English esteem only those who are wealthy or powerful or of noble blood. Friar Peto is none of those things and will have no respect paid to him whatever.'

'We are unable to change our mind,' said the Pope. 'We choose to have our son Cardinal Pole here to assist us in certain very difficult enquiries. Together with the brief for the new cardinal, we command him to come to Rome at once.'

'You may do as you please,' said the ambassador, 'but you will have to send your own courier. I do not dare convey such a message to my sovereign.'

Many months passed and neither side would give in. The Pope refused to restore Pole's legation. The Queen forbade any messenger from Rome entry to the kingdom. The Pope had still not given any reason for Pole's recall. One day, Navagero went to see him to say that a certain bishopric in Venice was about to fall vacant, as the incumbent was dying.

'The Signory of Venice,' he said, 'ask me to remind you of the promise, called an *accesso*, that the bishopric will pass to Alvise Priuli, one of their own noblemen and brother to the present Doge.'

On hearing the name of Priuli, Pole's oldest friend, the Pope held up his hand to prevent further speech and stood for a moment muttering and swinging his right arm, and gazing at the ground like someone who is greatly oppressed by his thoughts.

'Magnifico Ambassador,' he said at length, 'say no more on the matter. We are ready to do whatever we can for the Signory, but now they must limit their appetites and not misuse the love we bear them.'

'The Signory seeks only something that is reasonable,' said Navagero.

'Were our considerations weighed against yours,' said the Pope, 'they would greatly over-balance them, ours being most exalted and firmly grounded, so much so that we cannot listen to you without nausea. What is the meaning of this word *accesso*? Never was there an invention more diabolical than this one, nor one that has more scandalised the whole world. It was never heard of by the ancient fathers. It deprives a pope of his liberty, and besides that it points a dagger at the throat of the living bishop. For that reason we have recently repealed all *accessi* granted by our predecessors.'

'If the term *accesso* displeases you,' said Navagero, 'perhaps you will find another way to satisfy my government.'

'You speak of a thing which is impossible,' said the Pope. 'Besides the *accessi* being diabolical inventions, we repealed them precisely on account of Priuli.'

Then putting his mouth close to Navagero's ear, he whispered: 'We must at any rate tell you – Priuli is a heretic.'

'Holy Father!' said Navagero, 'the whole of Venice consider him a Catholic who leads a good life. As he may have been slandered by someone, you should not deprive him of his right. That would be to condemn him before he knows the charges, which he might well refute.'

'We do not speak of something we do not know for a certainty,' said the Pope. 'It is a fact. There are many who know it, we have witnesses. Priuli is of the accursed school and the apostate household of Pole, the Cardinal of England. Why do you suppose we deprived

Pole of the legation? You will soon see what is coming: we mean to proceed. Pole was the master, and Morone, whom we have here in the castle, the disciple. Priuli is on a par with both of them, and as bad as Marc'Antonio Flamminio, whom we would certainly have to burn if he were not already dead, just as we had his brother burnt the other day in front of the church of the Minerva. Oh Magnifico Ambassador, let us not speak any further on the matter! If our own father was a heretic we would carry the faggots to burn him. Say no more, we beseech you – our cognisance of this case stinks in the nostrils.'

As to why his old suspicion of Pole had crept back into the Pope's mind, he gave no indication.

13

IN THE EARLY WEEKS of the war, at the same time as Alba's army could be heard approaching Rome, a procession of about thirty people was seen crossing the fields of eastern England. Anyone watching them long enough would have noticed something very strange. At the outskirts of all the towns they passed through, they stopped, and a single long rope was looped around the waists, hands and shoulders of most of the party so that they appeared to be under restraint.

Leaving town, they stopped again, the rope was removed and they went on their way through the fields of wheat.

The procession consisted of a sheriff and six or seven guards, and twenty-two men and women who had been arrested in Colchester on suspicion of heresy and who were being marched to London to be examined by Bishop Bonner. It was just before harvest and it would have been easy for prisoners to run away and be hidden in the wheat which was moving this way and that in the wind. This, however, they assured the sheriff they did not wish to do. On the contrary, they were eager to meet their judge, and they sang hymns as they went across the fields. The sheriff was so pleased with their behaviour he saw no need to tie them up, except in the towns, where he might otherwise get into trouble.

When they reached London, the rope came out again and this time was properly tied around wrists and shoulders. The captives attracted immense attention. By the time they reached Bonner's palace in Fulham, they were accompanied by several thousand people.

Bonner became alarmed. He wrote quickly to Pole, saying he had examined all the prisoners and found them all to be desperate heretics who should be despatched at once, but 'fearing your Lordship's wrath' – which he had recently incurred in a like case – he sought permission first.

A reply came back forbidding this action and ordering the captives to be sent to the Lollards' Tower at Lambeth Palace. There they languished for about a week. Then one day Pole himself appeared at the door of their cell. After talking to the prisoners for a while, he set them all free, on their swearing of an oath which he himself devised, of the lightest terms imaginable: 'that they promised to be good Christians and subjects to the Queen'.

The twenty-two then set off and walked home through Essex. Their release, which took place on 22 October, occasioned much comment. Nothing like it could be recalled. But the story did not end there. A few months later, in December or January, their parish priest, Sir Thomas Tye, wrote to Bonner and to Lord Darcy, Lieutenant of Essex, about some of the prisoners released by Pole.

> Since their coming home, they maliciously and seditiously have seduced many from coming to the church, mocking those that frequent the church, calling them church owls, and calling the blessed sacrament a blind god.
>
> In the town of Colchester, ministers of the church are hemmed at in the open streets, and called knaves, the blessed sacrament of the altar is blasphemed and railed upon in every ale house and tavern.

At this, new warrants were sworn and three of them were re-arrested, taken to the moot hall and then to Colchester Castle, where they were examined again. They answered very stoutly, saying the mass was an abominable idol, that the bread and wine were not changed by consecration into the body and blood of Christ – if anything they were rather the worse for it – and that all these things stank in the nostrils of God.

'So you will not be a member of us?' asked Doctor Chadsey, the judge.

'I am no member of yours,' said one, a girl named Rose Allen, 'for you are a member of Antichrist and will have the reward of Antichrist, unless you repent.'

'Then what do you say of the Holy See and the authority of the Pope?'

'I am none of his,' she said, 'and as for his sea – it is for crows, kites, owls and ravens such as you are to swim in and by the Grace of God I shall never swim in it as long as I live.'

All three were later taken out and burnt at the stake, calling out from amid the flames to beware of idolatry.

All of this was well known in England. My nephew Clement, for instance, who was eager for me to adopt his religious views, wrote and told me about it. But there is no reason to think the story would have ever reached Rome and come to the ears of the Pope except for one thing: Bonner informed him. The imperialist postmaster in Venice, who had a marvellous way with sealing-wax, had opened his letters and read them, and it was soon known all over Venice that a great English bishop had been sending 'evil reports' of Pole to Rome.

It was this tale of the twenty-two prisoners of Colchester which, I think, revived the Pope's ancient suspicions. He, in any case, saw heresy everywhere without the slightest evidence. What then would he think of this story – Pole, the arch-heretic; beautifully disguised in the red robe of a cardinal, appearing in the prison door to set free his agents and send them forth to seduce many more, to mock church owls, blind gods and the blessed sacrament of the altar?

The Pope knew also that he must be nearing the end of his own life. Another conclave would soon be held. His greatest dread returned: at any hour, a certain English heretic might ascend the chair of Peter and induce everyone to lead his sorry life.

That was the calamity at hand, 'as close as the lightning which follows the limbo'. For my part, I could not help noting that Pole had appeared at the door of the Lollards' Tower and set the prisoners free at about the same time as my little book, *The Fine and Witty Letter*, reached London.

14

ALTHOUGH THE WAR HAD come to an end in Italy, in the north it was still thundering on, bringing a rain of calamities.

First came the news that Calais had fallen. At a stroke, we lost our mastery of the Channel, the power to harass France at will, three hundred artillery pieces and a great quantity of wool and other booty.

The French were in seventh heaven. Even here in Mantua the French party ran through the streets in velvet slippers carrying roast dinners to one another's houses.

Next came the battle of Gravelines. This time the French army was attacked by Egmont with three thousand horses and all his German infantry. The French ran away and crossed the River Aa, thinking they would be safe, but the Imperialists kept them in sight, and eventually the two sides met.

The battle was fought on the seashore, in the presence of the English fleet, which, unable to assist in any other way, shot off its cannons from afar. The French cavalry were instantly routed; the infantry stood firm for an hour and were then utterly dispersed.

This news, reaching Paris, made everyone turn pale.

By that time, which was early this year, 1558, the Pope had completed his transit from the French to the Imperialist side. He now found himself delighted with Philip, the King of England.

'He is as great a prince as any that has ever reigned in Christendom,' he told Navagero, 'and is soon to be even greater. Negotiating with him is much more secure and solid than with certain other persons whom we might name . . .'

The war against the Emperor and Philip, he added, had been a great mistake, foisted on him by certain wicked persons.

'I should send their heads flying from their shoulders and it is greatly to my regret that I am too kind-hearted to do so,' he added, staring hard at the French cardinals who were present.

He had quite forgotten, said Navagero, that it was his nephew Carlos who was the master spirit of the war.

Carlos was now sent to Philip in Brussels to undertake certain vital negotiations, chief among them the extradition of Pole to Rome. He came with a glittering retinue and set about a great round of banquets, gambling and hunting. He was also armed with a summary of the charges against the Cardinal of England.

He saw no need for discretion. On the contrary, he was a model of candour. Soon the whole court, and then the world, knew the extent of the depravity of Reginald Pole and his household.

> Reginaldus Polus . . . an accomplice of heretics . . . a favourer of heretics . . . He approached people in conversation to find out their doctrine. He persuaded others to the heretical view . . . He broadcast it . . . He considered heretics his friends . . . He was commonly thought of by Catholics as a heretic . . . He defended Luther's doctrine of justification by faith alone . . . He condemned the theology of the schools . . . He said there was no harm in what he believed . . . He argued that the gospel should be declared pure and simple . . . He asserted that a vow of chastity should not be observed unless it was a gift from God . . . He was the father and spiritual teacher of false doctrine to the Marchioness . . . He was chosen by her alone . . . and adored by her with excessive reverence and affection . . . and extolled

> excessively by her . . . a lover of that man, as can be seen from many letters . . . whom she lavishly praised . . . and called her Elijah . . . and felt burning love for . . .

When I read this – for a copy soon reached Mantua – I almost laughed aloud. It sounded like nothing so much as the ancient complaints of a jealous lover. The Marchioness, I think, had once been a follower of Carafa. She devoted herself to mortification of the flesh, and wore rags and starved herself to an inch of her life – exactly the austerities that Carafa admired. But Pole laughed at all this, and she listened to him, and soon she moved to the centre of my master's circle. Had Carafa been brooding over this all these years? Was there really a woman at the bottom of it all?

In any case, I thought, no one could take seriously the charges which Carlos brandished in Brussels. But I was wrong. King Philip was enchanted to find himself in the Pope's good books and he meant to stay there. He was greatly tempted to assist him in this matter. In any case, he and his ministers were angry with Pole for their own reasons: they saw him as the chief obstacle to their power in England. It was Pole who stood against Philip's coronation, and against the English fighting Philip's wars, and against allowing Philip's troops into England.

In short, here was a moment of grave danger for my master. He was suddenly surrounded by enemies. The Pope sought his life. The King and his ministers would like to see the back of him. The English 'weathercocks' hated him – those ministers of fury such as Bonner and Lord Rich, who once backed Henry and now persecuted and burnt on behalf of Mary. The English Protestants, as well, had no love for a Roman cardinal. The French saw him as an imperialist. Even the Queen could not be relied on. If it came to a choice between him and her husband . . . well, Pole was only her cousin, and she still passionately loved her husband.

It was strange to consider that now my master, once again, stood under threat of being trussed up and sent over the sea to his doom, this time in the opposite direction. It was also strange, I thought, that the two older men whom Pole had most revered in his life – one of them King of England and the other now Pope in Rome – both turned on him and sought his destruction. Whatever else you may say about fate, once she chooses a theme for a man she does not idly let it drop.

One day in spring this year I received the following document. It was sent by my nephew Clement, who appended no comment:

Cardinalis Polis commissio ad procedend. Contra haereticos.
REGINALDUS, miseratione divina tituli sanctae Mariae in Cosmedin, sanctae Romanae ecclesia cardinalis Polus, dilectis nobis in Christo filiis, magistris Nicolao Harpsfeld legum doctori . . .

In short, this was a commission issued by Pole to proceed against certain heretics. You have to understand what this meant: apart from the first one against Rogers and Bradford, etc., which had been placed in his hands when he first arrived in England, and whose harsh proceedings he tried to mitigate, Pole had never himself issued such a commission to prosecute heresy. All those that had followed over the next three years had proceeded from the Queen or her council or certain bishops.

At the sight of this document, then, a terrible thought came to me: *Pole is in danger of the fire. So he has decided to push others in first, to save himself.*

Such an evil suspicion . . . Once you've had a thought like that, things are never the same. Even if Pole was innocent, I felt *I* had been changed for the worse. But I still hoped I was wrong, and I had good reasons for doing so. There was something very odd about the wording of this new document. Anyone found guilty, it stated, was to be punished only *si facti atrocitas* – 'if the atrocity of the case required it'. Here, perhaps, I thought, was a loophole invented by Pole himself.

For although he never utterly denied the right to punish heretics, he had always avoided doing so.

It occurred to me that he had been trapped or forced into making this commission. By then – earlier this year – it was becoming plain that our Queen does not have long to live. All her 'pregnancies' have proved false. They say she spends hours lying with her knees drawn up to ease the pain. Something is amiss with her, and it is getting worse. And when she dies, then there will be a great reckoning. Someone will be held to account for the *charbonnades*. If Pole could be proved to have blood on his hands, that would be most convenient for those below him, especially the 'weathercocks', who have led the persecution.

I thought that Pole might have found a way to escape the trap. In short, I had high hopes of *si facti atrocitas*.

But then one day this summer, a copy of a writ arrived, sent by my nephew Clement. It states that John Cornfoth of Wrotham, Christopher Brown of Maidstone, John Hurst of Ashford, Alice Snoth of Beddenden, and Katherine Knight of Thornham had been found guilty of heresy, and should be punished in the usual way by the secular arm. It is signed by Pole.

There is nothing more to be said. Disappointed hopes are not as savage as sudden blows. In any case, I appear to have reached the end of my service to the illustrious Pole. I have carried on with my life as usual. And I have continued to write this account of all my deeds. Why stop now? It is a kind of cure for insomnia – if I don't write everything down then I lie awake thinking about it, and sometimes I am even woken up, it seems to me, in order to think about it.

At some of these sessions, I have truly considered the possibility that my whole life in service to Pole has been wasted. Are the old charges against him – he is indifferent, too fond of ease, pusillanimous – true? Is he a coward? Was he, then, always a coward? Or did he just *lose heart*?

'. . . and now he must eat his own heart, and be heartless as he is graceless'.

On this question, I can only turn to my secret doctrine: 'I do not know'.

In September, two months ago, I went to Padua to stand at the grave of young Courtenay. I thought someone should perform that office. He died while I was still in Rome, and he went friendless into the tomb. Some people declare he died by misadventure. One day, they say, he went back to the island of Lio where I had once taken him to fly his hawk, and on the way home he got soaked in a storm, and then he did not change his clothes and then he slipped on the stair in his own house and then was shaken dreadfully in a coach on the road to Padua . . . These things together killed him. What a number of mishaps are needed to end a life nowadays! It amazes me anyone manages to die at all.

These many causes were listed for me by Peter Vannes, English ambassador in Venice, shaking his head very mournfully as he recited them. The state of Venice agrees and would shake its head mournfully too if that could be managed. Instead, it has seized Courtenay's chest and papers, which might have thrown light on the matter and which will now never be seen again.

I stood by his grave at the church of Eremitani, in Padua – he is soon to be moved – but nothing happened in my heart as I looked at the stone. This is the way of things at the moment. The world, to tell the truth, seems rather flat and bare lately. I sometimes think of Bembo, as he grew old, saying: 'Oh, that I were a shepherd, and could look down on Urbino again!'

At that, everyone would laugh merrily. Anyone less like a shepherd than the elegant Lord Bembo was impossible to imagine. But now I understand him better. Oh, that I were roaming over the hills behind Viterbo again . . . Sometimes in the summer Flamminio and I would stop on the heights and look at the headwaters of rivers far away and without names. But I don't suppose I will ever go back up there again.

This month, however, we – Agnes Hide and I – have decided to go to England next spring, Pole or no Pole. I have a great desire to be in Warwickshire in May once again and see the woods in all their heavy green robes. The other day, when the Regent read out one of his reports from England, I felt – even at my age and after living here so long – the pangs of the young traveller far from home.

> The largest city is built on the River Thames which here has the form of a bow, and therefore the town is shaped accordingly. At one extremity of it is a castle called the Tower, with a serraglio in which, from grandeur, they keep lions and tigers and cat-lions.
>
> At the other end of the bow, in the great church of St Peter's, there is a chapel much decorated with marble and gold, called the King's Chapel, in which are the tombs of late kings and queens . . .
>
> Of the women in England, this may be said: in general they are of ready wit, as shown by their prompt replies, and many of them are very learned in Latin and Greek. They have a handsome presence, fine complexions and great liberty of action, and no one enquires what they do, either at home or out, which causes them to be but slightly continent.
>
> Englishmen do not hold women's honour in account, and even if the lie is given, they cannot be induced to fight, but do so only from caprice. Then, after exchanging two or three stabs with a knife, they make peace at once, and go and drink together . . .
>
> They are naturally very obstinate, but are also fickle, and most inconsiderate in their actions. They are extremely courageous, the more so in proportion to the difficulty of the undertaking.
>
> They have often been seen going to the stake and gibbet laughing, and, as it were, ridiculing martyrdom; and many persons, members of whose families have been executed, are accustomed to boast of it.
>
> Lately, a foreigner, having asked an English captain if any of his family had been hanged and quartered, answered 'not that he

knew of'. Another Englishman whispered, 'Don't be surprised, for he is not a gentleman.'

As the Regent read this, he stopped and gazed at me several times with his usual expressions of amazement, which, for some reason, I always find most gratifying.

That was a month or two ago; it was the last time I was out of the house. Since then I have been unwell. Portaleone first diagnosed catarrh, then ague, followed by a general malaise, which he counters with egg whites and the ink of the squid. The ague is very severe this year. The Pope himself fell ill and the whole world held its breath, but then he came round.

Navagero was summoned to his bedside.

'Ah, my son, we did not expect to see you alive,' came a voice from the pillow. 'We were about to go to the Lord. We had our mouth closed and they had to force it open with a spoon. For a week we lived on jelly broth alone and ordered the college of cardinals to elect a good pope, and not a rogue, but now we have had a good night's rest and are brisker than ever!'

The Emperor, we have just heard, has also died, in a monastery in Spain where he retired to live alone with the monks, whom he greatly terrorised, and his twenty-eight clocks.

'What folly to try and make men agree on matters of religion,' he said in the end, 'when I cannot even make my clocks agree when to strike the hour.'

I must now tell you what happened to me last night. I was here in my room just after dusk. The house was very quiet as my wife and children have gone to the farm for the autumn bonfires. As I was dozing off by the fire, I heard a great rumbling in the street. I got up to see what it was. On the way across the room, however, I noticed a door in the room I had not seen before, and went through it and found myself in the courtyard of the palace of the Te.

Now this of course was absurd as the Te is a mile across town, but I did not know I was dreaming.

And there I saw the same figure I saw before, a captain on a stone chair with his back half turned to me.

Once again he rose as soon as I entered and came towards me, but this time he stopped. Again, I saw he was identical to me.

'But who are you?' I said.

'Oh,' he said and laughed: 'Don't you *remember*?'

Then I opened my eyes and found I was still sitting in front of the fire. And I thought 'It was my soul!' Outside the rumbling was getting louder. This time I really did get up and go to the window and looked out, but it was only the Duke's orange trees going past on heavy wagons on their way to the palace of Te.

Afterword

THE DATE OF 1 November 1558 is recorded for the death of Michael Throckmorton. If this was known in London three weeks later – the velocity of news in the sixteenth century was never much more than eighty miles a day – no one in the city, in any of the palaces, even in Pole's own household, would have taken much notice. By that time, far more momentous events had taken place. On 17 November Queen Mary died.

That date itself is now no longer inscribed on English memories, as it was for centuries. At about midday that day, Mary's sister, Elizabeth, sitting under an oak tree (perhaps) in a garden in Hertfordshire, saw several men crossing the grass towards her. They came to tell her that she was now Queen. Nine hundred years of Catholic England came to an end. Protestant England was reconstituted. Mary was soon to become 'Bloody Mary', as she remains.

Against that, what was the death, far away, of a certain Michael Throckmorton, courier, bodyguard, condemned traitor, country gentleman, who one summer morning rushed around Padua 'as pale as ashes' looking for an assassin, and who later was well known for his hospitality to English visitors to Italy? Even some members of his own family might have been excused if they took little notice of his death. His nephew Nicholas, for instance, was one of the messengers racing towards Elizabeth. He was carrying the black enamelled ring from Mary's finger as proof that she was dead.

Mary's husband, Philip, did not visit her on her deathbed or appear at her funeral.

'The Queen my wife is dead,' he wrote to his sister in Spain. 'I felt a reasonable regret for her death and will miss her accordingly.'

For that *reasonable regret* Mary had sacrificed a great deal – the love of her people, her happiness, perhaps her life. The cause of her death is generally given as cancer of the ovaries.

Almost to the end, she continued to issue writs. The last of her subjects to be burnt were John Cornforth of Wrotham, Christopher Brown of Maidstone, John Hurst of Ashford, Katherine Knight, or Tingley, of Thornham, and Alice Snoth, or South, of Beddenden, who died at Canterbury on 10 November.

In other words, the last in her reign to die for religion are the only ones whose deaths are definitively linked to Reginald Pole. He established the commission which tried and excommunicated them, and he signed the writ of *significavit* which called on the state to punish them.

The Queen died in her palace at Whitehall at about seven o'clock, as the sun rose. The news was rapidly conveyed over the river to Lambeth Palace, just visible on the opposite shore.

Cardinal Pole, however, was not informed. His 'familiars' judged that he was too ill and the shock might be fatal. But his household was very large, and had many Italians in it, and in the early afternoon one of them approached Pole's bed and mentioned the death of the Queen. Priuli wrote to his brother in Venice:

> On hearing this, he remained silent for a short while and then said . . . that in the course of the Queen's life and his own he had ever remarked a great conformity as she, like himself, had been harassed during so many years for one and the same cause; and afterwards, when it pleased God to raise her to the throne, he had greatly participated in all her other troubles entailed by that

elevation. He also alluded to their relationship, and the great similarity of their dispositions, and to the great confidence which Her Majesty demonstrated in him. Then he said that considering these facts, as also the immense mischief which might result from her death, he could not but feel deep grief thereat . . .

His most Reverend Lordship then kept quiet about quarter of an hour, but though his spirit was great, the stroke entered his flesh, and brought on the paroxysm earlier, accompanied by more intense cold than he had hitherto experienced, so that he said that he felt this would be his last. He then asked that there be kept near him the book containing the prayers that are said for the dying. This was about two hours before sunset . . .

And so he continued to the end, which he made so placidly that he seemed to sleep rather than to die, and if it had not been for a physician who observed the act, he would have died without anyone noticing . . .

So there they lie – two cousins, a Tudor and a Plantagenet, one on each side of the river, in palaces within sight of each other, one dying at dawn, the other at dusk.

Many years before, in Florence, we saw Pole step through a marble door into a half-built room now famous throughout the world and even then the subject of intense curiosity in Italy and beyond. And there, we heard Bembo later declare, he glimpsed his destiny in the shape of three statues – the *Dawn*, and the *Dusk*, and '*Lorenzo*', symbolising Thought.

In a way Bembo or rather 'Bembo', was right. The statues were a kind of manifest for Pole's life. But he was wrong as well. He picked the wrong statue. It was not *Il Pensoroso*, the Thinker, who most truly represented Pole's future but *Dusk* – the sad figure of a middle-aged man, looking back with regret at the remains of the day.

In a word, Pole died a failure. His life ambition – to restore the unity of Rome and England – was doomed. Elizabeth now reigned,

England was to become Protestant, and the great enmity with Rome, which Henry had sown, has flourished for centuries.

Pole was aware of this – it was the 'great mischief' he foresaw – and he could not blame himself for all of it. But there was a personal failure as well. There is no way around the fact. He was the man who told the truth to princes as he did to Henry, to two popes, to the Emperor and a King of France, but when it came to Mary, he fell short. Whatever he said or did to moderate her policy, it was not enough. More people perhaps were put to death for their religion in her father's reign and certainly in her brother's, but it is Mary who occupies a place of notoriety in the English mind. She is surely behind the Red Queen in Lewis Carroll's *Alice in Wonderland*, she has the cocktail named after her . . . The nature of her victims and the peculiar horror of their deaths – by fire, in public – ensure that. And Pole, who was by her side, is implicated to some degree. His successor, the next Archbishop of Canterbury, gave him the terrible title 'scourge and butcher of the English Church'. For centuries historians have joined in heaping execration on his name. Even today, in the great hallowed sanctuary of Canterbury Cathedral, he seems to be in disgrace. His tomb, covered in a kind of grey paint, bears the cold inscription *DEPOSITUM POLI* and nothing more.

If there are doubts about his responsibility for the vast majority of Protestant deaths under Mary (probably about four or five hundred) there are always those last five, burned at Canterbury, who appear as witnesses for the prosecution.

Yet there is something strange about those five deaths as well. First, they were delayed a long time. The five were found guilty in midsummer, and were still alive late in the year. Before execution for heresy, a second writ was needed – one issued by the sovereign, ordering the sheriff to light the fires. It appears that Pole never applied for this.

When it was issued, he himself was gravely ill. And there is evidence that someone else went to great trouble to ensure the sentence was carried out.

'Some there be that say' – wrote the martyrologist John Foxe – 'that the Archdeacon of Canterbury, being in London, and understanding the danger of the Queen, incontinently made all post-haste home to despatch these whom he had then in his cruel custody . . . In the which fact, the tyranny of this archdeacon seemeth to exceed that of Bonner . . .'

The Archdeacon Nicholas Harpsfield, along with his brother John ('Dr Sweetlips'), Dean of London, and Bishop Bonner, was one of England's most notorious zealots in hunting out heresy. And here another odd fact emerges. At the very time that Nicholas was making sure the prisoners in Canterbury died before the Queen did, John Harpsfield and Bishop Bonner were setting their own Protestant prisoners free, for precisely the same reason: the Queen's reign was nearly over.

Those who escaped death in this way later acquired a kind of celebrity. Foxe tells the story of a preacher named William Living and his wife, and a friend named Lithall, who were being watched by a 'promoter' – a police spy – named Cox. One day Cox searched Living's house in Shoe Lane and his eye fell on a book of astronomy, *De Sphaera Mundi*, with a gilt cover. He took it out into the street to examine in the daylight. Opening it, he found page after page of diagrams: circles, triangles, the sun, moon and stars.

'Aha,' he cried, 'I have found him out at last! It is no marvel the Queen is sick, seeing there are such conjurers in privy corners. I trust he shall conjure no more.'

Living, his wife and Lithall were led to the chancellery, interrogated, put in the coal house, robbed by the constable, put in the stocks, taken to Lollards' Tower, offered mercy and refused it, all the while denouncing the Pope and the mass in the usual terms. Lithall was led into the cathedral and was wrestled to the ground in a general scrum when he refused to kneel before the crucifix.

He and the Livings resisted – and were then released.

At the same time, Nicholas was racing to Canterbury to put to death those condemned by Pole's writ. There is only one way to explain the discrepancy: by setting their prisoners free, and making sure Pole's died, responsibility for the entire persecution could be laid at his door, as indeed has often happened.

Seen in this light, the Livings and Lithall appear in a new role – as witnesses for the defence of the Cardinal. It may be that five deaths for which he is personally blamed are the only ones of Mary's reign he never knew took place.

If that is the case, then Pole should be judged less harshly. He was, after all, in a situation of almost impossible difficulty, caught, trussed up, in a net of competing interests, including his own lenient heart. And if we grant that, then perhaps in his final hour, as the river between the two palaces grew dark, a certain likeness does come to him of the third great figure, the *Lorenzo*, which, of course, in no way resembled the real Lorenzo of whom the sculptor said: 'In five hundred years no one will give a damn what he looked like.'

Note on Sources

THIS I SUPPOSE MIGHT be called a 'documentary novel', by which I mean anything cited in it as a document – whether a letter, a treatise or tailor's bill – has been excerpted (often only approximately in Throckmorton's 'recollections') from documents which do exist and which may be consulted, easily enough for the most part, in the calendars of state papers, principally: *Letters and Papers, Foreign and Domestic, from the Reign of Henry VIII* (London 1862–1932); *Calendar of Letters, Despatches and State Papers Relating to the Negotiations between England and Spain* (London 1862–1954); *Calendar of State Papers Relating to English Affairs in the Archives and Collections of Venice and in Other Libraries of Northern Italy* (London 1864–98); *Calendar of State Papers, Domestic Series of the Reign Mary I.*

The same assurance is not given or, presumably, sought with regard to the conversations, though a good many of those are derived from the written record. Pole's speeches to Vittoria Colonna and Michelangelo about Machiavelli, Cromwell and Henry are for instance taken almost entirely from his book written for Henry VIII, known as *De Unitate*, and from the long letter he wrote to the Emperor, *Apologia ad Carolum Quintum Caesarem.*

An English translation of *De Unitate*, by Joseph Dwyer, was published in 1965 by Newman Press; the quote on pages 53–4 is taken from this.

Apologia ad Carolum Quintum appears in a collection of Pole's letters, *Epistolarum Reginaldi Poli* . . . [etc], ed. Angelo M. Quirini, 1744–57. A new collection of Pole's letters, edited by Thomas Mayer, has recently been published by Ashgate Press.

Other works written, rewritten or translated by people in this story are:

Richard Morison: *An Invective against the Great and Detestable Vice, Treason, Wherein the Secret Practises and Traiterous Proceedings of Theym That Suffrid of Late are Disclosed*, 1539

Michael Throckmorton: *A Copye of a Verye Fyne and Wytty Letter* . . . [etc], 1556

Castiglione: *The Book of the Courtier* (English translation, Thomas Hoby, 1561)

Pietro Bembo: *De Aetna*, 1495

Beccadelli: *Life of Cardinal Reginald Pole. Translated into English with Notes Critical and Historical*, 1766

Marco Antonio Flaminio: *Il Beneficio di Cristo*, 1543

Edward Courtenay: *The Benefit of Christ's Death*, 1548

ACKNOWLEDGEMENTS

I owe particular thanks to the late Dr Ian Roberston, and to Will Hobson, for their translations. I want to express my deep gratitude to all those people who gave advice, encouragement, technical enlightenment, hospitality, long lunches, and the use of houses in Italy, France, England and New Zealand; especially Dan Witters, Sam Russell, John and Nan Fogarty, Jane Campion, Jenny Todd, Roland Gift, Louise Meldrum, Malcolm McSporran, Jonathan Lamb, Sarah Herriot, Justine Hancock, Sophie and Tony Torney, Susan Hancock, Louis Baum, Kathy Walker, Leah Seresin, Mary Kisler, Glynis Hall, Tim Gorton, Alice Duckworth, Rebecca Kamm, William Henderson, Mel Humphreys, Barry Fraser, Penelope Bieder, Sarah Lucas, Gretchen Albrecht, Jamie Ross and Andrew Marshall.

I am very grateful to my editors, Liz Calder and Bill Swainson, for their insight and long forbearance, to David Godwin for his constant support, to the staff at the Rare Books Room and Manuscripts Room of the British Library, and to fellow readers there, who become your colleagues in passing.

And I am especially indebted to Margot and Fergus Henderson, and to Sue Smith, who, in Covent Garden and on the coast of Coromandel respectively, were the first to listen to this story as it took shape and who seemed to think it was worth hearing.

A NOTE ON THE AUTHOR

Peter Walker is a New Zealander who has lived in London since 1986. He worked for seven years on the *Independent* and spent three years at the *Independent on Sunday*, where he was Foreign Editor. He has also written for the *Financial Times* and *Granta*. His first book, *The Fox Boy*, was published in 2001.

NOTE ON THE TYPE

The text of this book is set in Baskerville, and is named after John Baskerville of Birmingham (1706–1775). The original punches cut by him still survive. His widow sold them to Beaumarchais, from where they passed through several French foundries to Deberney & Peignot in Paris, before finding their way to Cambridge University Press.

Baskerville was the first of the 'transitional romans' between the softer and rounder calligraphic Old Face and the 'Modern' sharp tooled Bodoni. It does not look very different from the Old Faces, but the thick and thin strokes are more crisply defined, and the serifs on lower case letters are closer to the horizontal with the stress nearer the vertical. The R in some sizes has the eighteenth-century curled tail, the lower case w has no middle serif, and the lower case g has an open tail and a curled ear.